THE FALLEN MAN

by

Bethany Maines

Blue Zephyr Press
2661 N. Pearl, #360
Tacoma WA 98407

Cover art by **LILTdesign.com**.

ISBN-13: 979-8-9867745-0-3

CONTENTS

THE FALLEN MAN

Jackson

J.P. GRANGER

Jackson Zane had been a Deveraux for nearly seven years, but he still hadn't gotten over having his own plane. Winging from New York to San Francisco was easy when all he had to do was pick up the phone. That kind of luxury was a world away from his childhood in Chicago. And the gulf between his life now and the life that had gotten him sentenced to five-to-seven for armed robbery was even more immense.

He looked down at the knuckles of his left hand, where faded blue prison ink could barely be seen. He suspected that he was the only one who remembered that something had once been there. It had been at least ten years since that tattoo and seven since prison. Seven years of being rich, but if he was honest, he still didn't feel like a real Deveraux.

Jackson watched as the runway of the private airstrip grew ever closer. It was a bright streak of light in a field of black. He could see a smear of San Francisco lights in the distance, and he knew that's where he was really heading. It seemed close and yet too far at the same time. His leg bounced up and down, trying to distribute excess energy. It wasn't working. He could feel the knot of tension between his shoulder blades. His fingers flipped open the file on J.P. Granger for the hundredth time. At this point, he knew what was on every page without actually reading them.

Four years earlier, J.P. Granger, former CEO for Absolex Pharmaceuticals, had falsified research results on a depression medication and then sold the resulting drug Zanilex to the V.A. for treatment. Veteran suicides had increased, and Congress had called for special hearings to investigate why. Which was when J.P. Granger had called in a hit squad of mercenaries to intimidate Senator Eleanor Deveraux into canceling the hearings. Something that put the Deveraux family squarely in his crosshairs.

Something that Jackson found unacceptable. Fortunately, his cousins—Evan, Aiden, and Dominique—were more resilient than any batch of spoiled rich kids had any right to be.

Jackson looked at Granger's Aboslex headshot and compared the sleek, smug man in that picture to his sullen mug shot, with his quickly fading hair dye, sallow skin, and bloodshot eyes indicating that Granger's various addictions weren't being properly handled. Even after Granger's arrest, he'd still managed to take another swing at the Deverauxes. Jackson's older cousin Evan had nearly paid the cost on that one, but the Deverauxes had surprised everyone once again.

The moment Jackson met his grandmother Eleanor Deveraux in an interview room in Joliet was a bookmark in his life. There was before and after. And after included private jets, parties, and all the things that wealthy people had. Jackson liked those things. They were enjoyable. But they weren't what had convinced him to leave his life—and last name—behind to join the Deverauxes. After all, never being acknowledged by his father hadn't exactly been a stellar endorsement for the family. But Eleanor had something that Jackson wanted: cousins. His before life had been one long sputtering train wreck of loneliness and desertion – from his mother's death to her family's refusal to accept him, no one ever stuck around. And then came a fairy grandmother with three cousins who might pass for his siblings and the promise of a family that wouldn't ever leave him again. Jackson had done enough prison therapy to know that he was probably latching onto his cousins to satisfy his own feelings of abandonment, and he gave exactly zero fucks about that.

Jackson smiled to think of the Deverauxes. He knew very well what people saw when they looked at his family—a group of dysfunctional, disliked dilettantes. But he saw a stubborn, intelligent, loyal to a fault, hilarious, and above all, resilient family who would never back down. A family that, for some reason, had accepted him. His grandmother had been explicit—she wanted Jackson because she thought he would be able to protect his cousins, and he had taken on the mission wholeheartedly. His cousins had been alternatively resentful, mystified, and then strangely accepting of his arrival in their family. And now things were finally good. His cousins were safe, healthy, and happy. It had taken seven years, but Jackson finally felt that maybe, just maybe, he could relax and try out being just one of the Deverauxes.

The only loose end was J.P. Granger. The spoiled brat of a C.E.O. who couldn't accept being held accountable for his actions. And just when it had looked like J.P. Granger would get the justice he deserved, he had skipped bail. Until Granger was back in custody, Jackson knew he wouldn't sleep soundly.

Jackson looked up from the file and saw his wavery reflection in the plane window. Dark hair where his cousins were blonde, but the same blue eyes and arched nose. Add in a wardrobe that cost more than his old rent, and he knew he *looked* the part of a Deveraux, but in his heart, he still felt like a fraud. Deep down, he knew he was his mother's son. In many ways, Nataliya had been tougher than Jackson knew he could ever be. She had left her religious, ultra-conservative Ukrainian family and stepped outside the only safety net she'd ever known, all so she could be herself. It hadn't worked out exactly. She'd died of a drug overdose, leaving Jackson alone in Chicago. His father might have come to get him, but

Randall Deveraux had been killed in a plane crash, leaving the rest of the Deveraux family in the dark about Jackson's existence.

Jackson sometimes wondered if his mother would consider him a failure. He hadn't been able to make it on his own—he'd jumped at the chance to tie himself to a family—where she had run away from almost everyone. Most people assumed that it was only the Deveraux money that kept Jackson around and, as he had noted on more than one occasion, money was nice, but what he wanted more was a family of his own. The Deverauxes were his family now. And because of that, Jackson couldn't help wondering how he'd sleep if Granger were dead instead of just in custody.

The plane touched down with a gentle bump and taxied to a hanger. Jackson was met by uniformed airport personnel who bowed him into a waiting area with all the deference of welcoming royalty. The airstrip was close enough to Silicon Valley that Pete Schalding, the Deveraux private detective, looked out of place among the expensive furniture of the waiting room. Fiftyish, salt-and-pepper-haired Pete looked presentable, but that was usually as far as anyone ever thought about him. Pete had been in military intelligence, and bland was what Pete liked. He was quickly forgotten, which was one of his most valuable traits. But in a red-carpet world, he looked like a delivery man who'd wandered out front.

"It's definitely him," said Pete, as if they had just been talking moments earlier instead of hours.

"Good," said Jackson.

"He's camped out in the Castro wearing pink and buying copious amounts of blow and H," said Pete. "The hookers he's renting don't really blend in, though."

"Why not?" asked Jackson.

"Wrong gender for the neighborhood."

"Too much titty." Pete gave him a look. "I'm not Eleanor," said Jackson.

"I've noticed that about you," said Pete. "There's a general lack of cardigans and pearls."

Jackson nearly laughed. His grandmother's wardrobe had always been carefully calibrated to be *appropriate*, and Jackson's was almost always calibrated to do his own form of blending in. He was never going to be Pete—the Deverauxes were center stage kind of people—but Jackson had found that if he dressed to meet expectations, people wouldn't notice that he was nearly always wearing a gun, carrying a knife, and was never caught in shoes that he couldn't run in.

"You checked that your license works out here?" asked Pete, jerking his head toward the exit.

"I'm now a fully bonded and licensed bail bond recovery agent in every state that permits such things."

Another perk of being rich was having the time, energy, and paperwork support to make it legal for him to go after his enemies.

"And since he has multiple warrants out for his arrest and a pending million-dollar bond, everything we're about to do is perfectly lawful," Jackson continued.

"Uh-huh," said Pete giving him a stern eye. "But we do it calmly. Rationally. Without a lot of fuss. Or you know… punching. Don't go full Deveraux on me here, kid."

"I'm completely calm," said Jackson. "And I don't know what you mean. The only one of us who goes full Deveraux is Dominique."

"Uh-huh," said Pete again, like he knew Jackson was lying, but shrugged.

Jackson shrugged too. He was only half lying. Dominique

knew her way around a Louisville slugger and wasn't afraid to come in swinging.

"Come on then—car is this way," said Pete.

They drove from the airport into the city, and Jackson watched the high-rises of San Francisco get closer. Watching the neighborhoods change should have been fun, but Jackson barely saw them. Pete drove them without hesitation and barely looked at the map displayed on the dash. The destination arrived all too slowly and all at once. Jackson wasn't sure he was prepared and stared up at the hotel as they approached.

The building had a vintage 1920s exterior with a completely remodeled interior. At twenty-four stories, it had probably been a very tall building at the time it was built. Now it looked quaint. It was lit with a Miami vibe in hot pink neon uplights that made it stand out in the night skyline of San Francisco. Granger had rented the penthouse, which wasn't cheap—even by Deveraux standards. Jackson squinted up to where he could faintly see a balcony railing, glinting pink in the lights and showing the faintest outline of what might have been palm trees.

Pete skipped the front entrance with the valet and drove them down into the parking garage. A quick hand-off of some cash and a waiter let them into the freight elevator and then walked away like he didn't want to remember what they looked like.

The elevator stopped at the penthouse level, and Jackson looked before getting out. No one was around.

"Ready?" Jackson asked.

"As we'll ever be, I guess," said Pete. "It's down there at the end of the hall. I've got the passkey. You want first or second?"

"First," said Jackson, pulling on gloves. Pete shrugged and did the same.

They made their way down to the door at the end of the hall, padding quietly on the thick carpeting. Jackson made a choice and took out his gun. Granger was the kind of person who hired someone to do his dirty work, but Jackson didn't want to be caught by surprise. Pete slid the key into the lock and pulled it out again. The light flashed green, and Jackson opened the door with his free hand.

The suite's interior was a living room and bar area with an accompanying bedroom and bath off to one side. French doors opened out onto an expansive deck, and he could see the lights of San Francisco through drifting sheers. The room *had* been decorated in standard hotel textures of beige and dark wood. Currently, it was decorated in drug-fueled temper tantrum. The couches had been slashed, lamps lay on the floor, and over everything was a fine dusting of white powder as if someone had thrown an entire baggie of coke at the ceiling fan. But aside from the mess, the room appeared empty. If there had been hookers, they were gone now. But Jackson didn't see Granger either.

Jackson advanced a few more steps, maintaining his position as the point person. Pete was behind him and slightly off to the right, maintaining clear sightlines. They picked their way through the debris, scanning for any sign of Granger.

There was the sound of breaking glass and a guttural chuckle, and Jackson froze.

"Whoops," said a male voice, and this time Jackson could hear that it was coming from outside.

Jackson pushed aside the curtains and stepped out onto the balcony. Granger was sitting on the broad balustrade—one leg on each side of the railing. His back was against a potted pam tree, and he was staring at the remains of a crystal tumbler that had shattered on the slate tile of the deck. He had a bottle of Louis XIII cognac in his hand. He picked up his head as Jackson stepped out. Granger had shaved his hair down to the scalp, although a fuzz was starting to grow back. He looked thinner than he had seven months ago.

"Come to gloat?" Granger asked, his words slurring.

"Come to take you home," said Jackson.

"Fuck you," said Granger. "Fuck all of you Deverauxes. What are you, cockroaches? I paid good fucking money. Why can't at least one of you fucking die? It's like people have no pride in their work anymore."

"I know," said Jackson. "It's like, what the hell am I paying a hitman for if he won't even kill one stupid rich kid?"

"Yes," snarled Granger. "Although, I also blame that on you. It's not like I could afford quality hitters. I had to go with the JV team. Fucking Deverauxes." He took a pull from the cognac bottle.

"Well, you could have maybe invested in better hitmen instead of an eight-thousand-dollar bottle of booze," said Jackson. "Just throwing that out there."

Granger drank a little further, then set the bottle back on his leg and belched.

"But then you'd win," he said. "Why should I have to give up one damn thing because of you? I should be at home in bed with someone's wife. And you… You should be in the gutter where you belong."

"Is that where I belong?" asked Jackson, amused.

Granger hurled the bottle at him. Jackson ducked, and it smashed on the tile behind him. Either Granger's throwing skills were weak, or his vision was total shit right now. Pete had come out and was moving to the opposite side, into Granger's blind spot, starting the process of flanking and sheep-dogging the man. The ex-CEO was going with them, one way or another.

"Well, you sure as fuck don't belong here," snarled Granger. There was a loud honk from below, and it distracted him. He looked over the edge, seemingly fascinated. "You know what the funny part is?" asked Granger, his mood shifting again.

"I'm sure you'll tell me," said Jackson folding his arms.

"This was all supposed to go away. I had all the cards. I had the money. I had the people. Eleanor Deveraux and her stupid fucking hearings were supposed to go away. I was never even supposed to have to show up."

Jackson frowned, trying to decipher Granger's ramblings.

"I'm not sure how you thought you were going to avoid a congressional subpoena," said Jackson.

"There wasn't supposed to be one! He was supposed to make her shut her fucking mouth."

Jackson sucked in a sharp breath. "He? He who? Was someone supposed to attack Eleanor?" he demanded.

"Eleanor, pffff," Granger sneered. He reached into the pot at the base of the palm tree and produced a vodka bottle. "He said she would be a push-over. He was supposed to be able to work all the angles. Guess he got outworked. Who knew Eleanor Deveraux had balls that big?"

"Uh, anyone who ever met her?" suggested Jackson. As far as he could tell, his grandmother had a pair made of steel. She probably kept them in a pretty box from Tiffany's, but that didn't mean they didn't clank.

"She's old," complained Granger.

"And mean," said Jackson. "And she doesn't know when to quit."

"Yes!" exclaimed Granger looking outraged.

"It runs in the family," said Jackson. Granger growled at him.

"So who was this fixer?" asked Jackson. He suspected that whatever Granger had thought was going to happen had been a delusion, but on the other hand, he might as well get a lead on whatever other threats were out there.

"Wouldn't you like to know," said Granger. "You think I'm going to hand him over to you all pretty like?"

"Sure," said Jackson, easily. "Why not? Why should you be the only one to go down in flames? Why not flip on this douchebag? He couldn't deliver for you. Why should you cover up for him?"

"Because," said Granger, unscrewing the vodka bottle with a noticeably shaking hand, "I don't want you getting the credit. I want every one of you fuckers to burn. I want you in this same hell that you put me in."

"Going to be hard to do from a jail cell," said Jackson. "But we all have dreams."

"No," said Granger, taking a gulp. "I'm not going to jail. I have one last card to play."

"Yeah, what's that?" asked Jackson skeptically.

"I have all the files. All the emails. All the everything. I got all the proof that my deal with the VA was approved at the highest levels. And when it comes out, everyone will know that I was right and Eleanor was grandstanding and scapegoating me."

"And your partner will go to prison too?" asked Pete, sharing a skeptical look with Jackson. "Why not just do a WikiLeaks dump?"

"Because everything is on paper," said Granger.

Jackson tried not to laugh in the older man's face. "Oh, OK. And they couldn't possibly be scanned. All right, where is your magical paper file full of *allllll* the papery paper-type evidence?"

"I mailed it to a secure location where my representative will release it at the right time," said Granger with dignity.

Jackson shook his head, his black mood lifting. Granger was pathetic. This drunk idiot was going to spend years in jail and learn what it meant to be ignored and forgotten. That was enough of a punishment.

"Uh-huh," said Jackson, reaching into his pocket and pulling out a pair of handcuffs. "I will definitely hold my breath waiting for that. In the meantime, you're going to put those on. Frankly, I wish you'd make my life easier and keel over dead."

"I feel the same about you," said Granger, raising his bottle in a toast. His voice was noticeably getting thicker, and he slurred on the S sound on *same*.

"But since Pete over there disapproves of murder, I'm going to take you back to New York where a very lovely A.D.A. is going to throw your ass in prison."

"I'm not going to prison," said Granger, sounding tired but smug.

"Yeah, you fucking are," said Jackson. "It's not ideal, but seeing you in an orange jumpsuit and knowing you have to squat and cough on command is going to make me laugh every time I think about it. Your only real choice is if you put the cuffs on yourself or if I make you do it."

Jackson suspected that he would have to put them on, but he wasn't looking forward to it because he thought it highly likely that Granger would puke on him or worse.

"I'm not going to prison," said Granger, shaking his head. Then he paused, clearly trying to regain focus on his vision. "Because one of us is going to get their wish."

"What?"

"I called him, and the fucker actually took my call for once. Said I should turn myself in. Said I should just accept it." His voice was getting weaker. "Accept it? I am fucking James Percival Granger, and I don't have to accept anything."

"Granger," said Jackson, taking a step closer. The man's pupils were black pin-points, and his breathing was ragged. "Granger, what did you do?"

"I'm not going to prison," said Granger, with a lopsided grin. "Fuck all you Deverauxes," he said.

"What did you take?" demanded Jackson.

"Oh, I took all the things," said Granger with a laugh.

"Shit," said Pete, taking out his phone.

"You put that away," said Granger, pointing an accusing finger at Pete. "Tell him to put it away," he said, turning back to Jackson.

Pete hesitated, looking at Jackson.

"You're going to take my side on this, aren't you? Just give me what I want, and all this goes away."

Jackson looked at Pete. If he told Pete not to call, there was a chance that Pete would do as he was told—he was that loyal to the family. But if the shit came down, it would land on Pete. It would be Jackson's fault, but it would land on Pete.

"Just call the paramedics," said Jackson, letting out a sigh. "It's the right thing to do."

"I really fucking hate you," said Granger. For once, his voice held some of the old crispness of his former life.

"Great," said Jackson. "You can hate me from the prison hospital."

"No," said Granger, shaking his head. "I go out on my own terms."

Then he pushed away from the palm tree and over the side of the balcony. Jackson dove for him, but it was too late, and a second later, the sickening thump of Granger hitting the pavement echoed up the building side. Jackson stared in disbelief at the twisted body on the pavement below.

"Well," said Pete, after a long moment, "I think I'm going to recommend that we get the hell out of here."

"Yeah," agreed Jackson. "Anything else is going to complicate the fuck out of this. Let's go."

They took the freight elevator back down, and Pete surreptitiously wiped down the buttons and railings where they'd touched them earlier. They didn't speak again until they were in the car.

"That was a lot of hate," said Pete from the driver's seat after he had merged onto the freeway.

"Yeah," said Jackson, trying to muster up some sort of response to that. He thought it probably wasn't right that he didn't feel anything, but Jackson couldn't figure out what he *should* be feeling instead. Probably not relieved.

"Do you think he meant it?" asked Pete. "That there was someone in Congress helping him? And his whole idiotic story about the files?"

"I think he meant every damn word," said Jackson. "Which is unfortunate because now I'm going to have to find the paper printouts of his extra special files."

"With our luck, they'll all just say: *all work and no play makes Jack a dull boy.*"

"Don't curse us," said Jackson.

The city lights were making streaks on the windshield, and Jackson thought he must be tired because the headlights from the opposite lanes were giving him a headache. He'd be glad once he was home and could get some sleep.

Caitlin

The Halloween Party

Caitlin St. Cloud shoved one last forkful of pasta in her mouth and swore to the fashion gods that she would go for a run tomorrow. VAR Events was owned by Vince and Angela Romano, and one of the perks of working for VAR was that Angela always had leftovers for the employees. Unfortunately, the best banquet leftovers were usually carb-loaded fat bombs that weren't the best for her second job as a fit model. On the other hand, before she had pawned her Apple Watch, she'd once clocked seven miles during her shift as a bartender, so it would probably be OK as long as she didn't go back for seconds.

Caitlin's phone rang, and she froze with her fork still in the air. She forced herself to put the utensil down and pick up the phone. She knew who the call would be from before she saw the number. She pushed decline on the bill collector and tried not to feel the hot flush of defeat all over again. It had been three years and five phone numbers, yet they still kept finding her. It had been nearly nine months since the last phone number change. She probably ought to switch it again. Her stomach roiled around the pasta, and Caitlin wished she hadn't eaten at all.

Caitlin looked around the bustling kitchen, breathed in the smell of roasting veggies, and tried to feel soothed by the sound of voices speaking in overlapping Spanglish, with periodic French cooking terms. Vince had turned his brief pro-NFL career into a sprawling old warehouse in the meatpacking district, and he and

Angela had worked hard to turn it into a multi-event space. They had even transformed the back half into an enclosed space for outdoor events. Tonight was busy, with the two main interior spaces hosting parties and the courtyard rented out for some sort of private event—one with purple paper lanterns in the shape of sea animals and the most romantic table for two ever. The paper lanterns had been a bitch to set up, and Caitlin had ended up in the last-minute scramble to help get them in place, but the courtyard was now a sparkling canvas of velvet night and glowing purple squid.

"Oh my God," said Jessica breezing into the kitchen. "Have you seen the courtyard? Who rented that out? Those lanterns are to die for!"

"I don't know," said Caitlin, smiling. "but it's dreamy. You need to see Angela. She'll probably pay you to take some pics for the website." The curvy blonde cocktail waitress was a direct contrast to Caitlin's willowy frame and dark hair, but Caitlin suspected that it was more her sunny outlook on everything that truly made them the opposites that attracted. Caitlin had difficulty wrapping her head around optimism these days, but she loved that Jessica could.

"Ooh!" Jessica squeaked and hurried out of the kitchen. Jessica's dream of being a professional photographer was slowly coming together. She was currently filling in with cocktail waitressing and real estate photography, but something like the setup in the courtyard would look good in her wedding portfolio too.

Caitlin pulled her apron and nametag out of her cubby and headed out to the bar area to set up for her event that would start in another hour. The other half of the building would open to guests momentarily. She was passing the office when Vince stuck his head out.

"Hey, Caitlin."

"Hey, Vince," she said.

He smiled back, but she thought his smile looked tight. He rubbed the bump on his nose—it was from a break during his college football years—a nervous tick that gave away that he was uncomfortable with whatever he was about to say.

"Hey. I was hoping to get a sec to talk to you." He pushed one of his twists behind his ear, and Caitlin felt a flutter of nerves—he was being extra serious. She knew that Vince looked out for her, but nothing good happened anymore when someone wanted to talk to her.

"What's up?" she asked, putting on her most cheerful smile.

"Have you seen the call sheet?"

"No. Why? am I working with Andrew again?" Andrew was nice enough but also the laziest barback in the history of bartending. Vince knew she hated working with him.

"Heh. No. I put Andrew with Sharice. Over on the other side. Um. At the Deveraux party."

Caitlin's heart sank. "The Deveraux party?"

"I swear, you're not going to have to go over there. I just thought you should know."

Caitlin sighed. "It's fine, Vince."

"It's not fine," he said sourly.

"It is what it is," said Caitlin. "Thanks for making sure I don't have to go over there. I appreciate it. And I fully expect you to charge them for every tiny thing."

Vince grinned, his teeth flashing in stark contrast to his to umber face. It was a great smile, and Caitlin could easily see why Angela had fallen for him. "I will nickel and dime the shit out of them," he promised. "OK, um… that was actually the easy stuff."

Caitlin's heart sank. "What now?" she asked, dreading the answer.

"The student loan people called again. They want to garnish your wages."

"Shit," she muttered. "I don't know how they expect me to pay them if they take all my money."

"Do you need an advance?" asked Vince.

"No," said Caitlin, shaking her head vehemently. "No. My paycheck from the agency comes in at the end of the week. I was going to use that to pay them." Which would put her behind on the rent. Again. "I just thought I had a few more days."

"I've been through this before," said Vince. "They can only take money if you clock over a certain amount of hours."

"I can't work less, Vince. I need the money."

"Yeah, I'm saying you have to *clock in* for a certain amount of hours." He gave her a look that said she wasn't getting it. "I could pay out the rest of your hours in cash."

"I'll pay them a bunch, and then we won't have to worry about it," said Caitlin, shaking her head. "I appreciate the offer, though."

Vince smiled sadly. "Whatever you think best, kiddo."

Caitlin shook her head. "I don't even know, Vince. I'm just trying to make it through today."

Caitlin continued out to the main corridor that separated the event spaces. She was lucky to have Vince in her corner. Without him, she would have been homeless on the street. Caitlin pinned on her name tag, her hands going through the familiar motions and feeling the grooves in the metallic-looking plastic. Her fingers rubbed along the *K* in *Katie.* Sometimes she wondered about the girl who had owned the name tag before her, and sometimes, she thought about getting Vince to make her a name tag with *Caitlin* on it, but she never did. These days the name felt like hers.

She had barely entered the corridor and was still tying on her apron when she looked up to find a red-headed man coming toward her with wide eyes.

"Help," he said, grimacing and holding out his lapel. His suit was at least ten grand, and unless she was blind, custom-tailored.

"Of course," said Caitlin. "What can I do?"

"Apparently, I am not qualified for shrimp cocktail. I threw it on my suit, and I can't get into the men's room."

"Shoot," said Caitlin, "the door sticks sometimes. I'll send Vince around in a minute, but come with me."

She led him back to the bar area across the hall from the Deveraux party. She grabbed a clean rag and jammed it between his shirt and the coat.

"Give me a second, and I'll get some seltzer water. Just don't touch it."

His shoulders went down a fraction, but she thought he still seemed freaked. It was a great suit, but he was so tense he was practically vibrating.

"Thank you," he said fervently.

She grabbed another rag and a bottle of seltzer and then went to work on the suit, dabbing cautiously so as not to fuzz the fabric. "I'm going to use a tiny bit of soap," she said. "Just to ensure we get any fish oils out."

He nodded, and she went into her bag under the bar for a hand soap that she kept for this kind of emergency. She worked a bit more and then stood back. She had created a cocktail sauce-free zone, but it was quite wet.

"Give me a sec," she said and returned to her bag. She came back with her flat iron.

"Uh…" he said nervously.

"Don't worry," she said, "I do this all the time. I even know which setting to use for silk."

"VAR Events said they were a full-service event management firm. I did not think they meant this."

Caitlin chuckled as she plugged in her flat iron. "I'm also a fit model."

"Those are the ones that stand around and have clothes pinned on them?" he asked as if dredging up all his model facts from a database. Caitlin laughed as she tested the heat of the iron with her finger.

"Yes, effectively. It means that our proportions are suited to the designer. But bouncing between jobs means living out of a purse sometimes, and that means I now know how to do stain removal, iron a shirt, or in this case, a lapel, and fix a fallen hem. All on the subway, in under five minutes."

"I bow before a true New Yorker," he said, flashing a smile that lit up his face and made him look charming. She pressed his lapel dry and stepped back. He nervously checked the jacket in the mirror behind the bar.

"OK," said the redhead, turning back to her. "I can't see anything. Can you see anything?"

"I can't tell at all," she said honestly.

He breathed out a sigh of relief. "I honestly don't know why I'm panicking. She's not going to care. I could wear my birthday suit, and she wouldn't mind a bit. Well, she might about that. But my point is that she doesn't care about clothes. I'm the one that's freaking out. I just want it to be perfect. And you don't care about this, but I can't stop talking."

Caitlin laughed. "It's a big night?"

"It's our anniversary, and I'm proposing."

"Aw," said Caitlin. "Then truly, even if I could see something, which I can't, you're right, she wouldn't care a bit. Are you doing a big thing over at the party?" she asked, waving toward the Devcraux shindig. Guys in expensive suits always liked to do things in public so everyone would know how cool they were.

"Oh, fuck no," he said vehemently, and Caitlin couldn't keep a surprised laugh from escaping. "No, Olivia would hate that. I'd hate that. Plus, we'd be in costume, and then my cousin would probably want to take like a billion pictures, and then the pictures would all be in costume for the rest of eternity on the family wall."

"You're in costume?" asked Caitlin, looking the suit over in case she was missing something.

"Ah," he said, patting his pockets. He took out a name tag and clipped it to his lapel. "I have horns somewhere too." Caitlin read the tag, let out another surprised giggle, and covered her mouth with her hand.

HELLFIRE INDUSTRIES. HELLO! MY NAME IS: SATAN.

"Well, sure," said Caitlin. "Satan is obviously a ginger."

"Obviously," he agreed, a smile lighting up his face once more. "Of course, that means angels are too. Or at least mine is, anyway."

"So, how are you going to purpose?" she asked, now impressed by his creativity.

"I rented out the courtyard."

"Oh my God, that was you? We've been swooning over that all day. It's gorgeous!"

"Do you think so?" he asked, looking pleased. "She studies squid. I thought maybe the squid lanterns were over the top, though."

"She is going to love it," said Caitlin sincerely. "It's like being under the ocean. You knocked it out of the park."

He grinned. "Thanks for saying that. And thanks for your help."

The unexpected *thank you* made her nervous, and Caitlin tensed for the *we should meet up later to discuss this thing that's going on between us* or whatever line was going to come out of his mouth. There was bound to be a sleazy offer at some point. She had yet to meet a Nice Guy™ in her line of work that didn't make a pass.

"Seriously, I really appreciate you taking time out of your job to help me," he said sincerely.

"You're welcome," said Caitlin, feeling slightly stunned. Of course, this guy was taken. The good ones always got snatched up like a TV on a Black Friday sale.

"OK," he straightened his suit jacket. "Wish me luck."

"As long as you avoid the shrimp cocktail, you won't need it," said Caitlin.

"Good advice," he said with a laugh and headed for the door, just as Jessica was coming in fiddling with her camera.

"Ooh," said Jessica. "Who was that, and can I have him when you're done?"

"That is the very nice man who rented the courtyard so he could propose to his girlfriend in private," said Caitlin.

Jessica blew out a raspberry of disdain. "Losers."

"Marriage is not for losers."

"Ha!" said Jessica. "I will believe it when I see it."

"I mean, I'm not sure I believe in it," said Caitlin. "But I don't think it's a bad idea necessarily."

"Disagree," said Jessica.

Caitlin shrugged. "I can't really argue with you. But this guy looked over the moon about it. Don't rain on his parade."

"Hey," said Jessica, and there was a carefully casual note in her voice that made Caitlin tense, "I got tickets to a concert next week, and I have a spare if you want one."

Caitlin laughed. "I'm eating leftovers here for the rest of the week until my paycheck from the agency comes in. I can't afford to re-up my metro card, let alone a concert ticket. I'm probably going to be hopping turnstiles on the way home."

"Still paying on your mom's medical bills?" asked Jessica, grimacing.

"Probably for the next decade," said Caitlin. She didn't bother to mention her problems with the IRS. Vince was the only one who knew all the reasons for her abrupt tumble from Columbia student to bartender. "I qualified for medical relief, but I have to keep paying until we finalize negotiations on a deal."

Jessica made a face. "That super sucks. Look, the ticket is a spare. Jordan chipped in but can't use it and doesn't want his money back. You could take it. It wouldn't cost you anything."

Caitlin was tempted, but she suspected that Jessica had either bought the ticket for her or was trying to set her up on another blind date.

"What day is it, again?" asked Caitlin.

"Wednesday. It's your regular night off. Come on. It'll be fun."

"Yeah," said Caitlin, thinking that having fun sounded exhausting. "Maybe. I'll think about it."

Jackson
THE HALLOWEEN PARTY

Jackson paused at a stoplight, checked the time on his phone, and saw that he had a missed call from Evan twenty minutes earlier, but at least he would be on time for Dominique's Halloween party. Max had also sent him several urgent texts saying that Dominique was full-on losing her shit because she was worried that no one would dress up or come to her party and reminding him to show up in the most urgent of caps-locked messages.

It was a completely ridiculous and unfounded fear. Dominique Deveraux was beautiful, rich, and had the contact list to guarantee that whatever party she chose to throw would be well attended. But Dominique, like the rest of his cousins, did not want to have what she called, with a disapproving sniff, a Deveraux party. She wanted a party full of people who liked her, and because she was a Deveraux, she sometimes worried that people did *not* like her. That fear, at least, was realistic. The Deveraux family had more than its fair share of enemies. J.P. Granger was just the most extreme example.

His phone plinged with a text, and Jackson saw it was from Ella Zhao, his cousin Aiden's girlfriend.

AIDEN SAYS MAX JUST SHOWED HIM A PICTURE OF A RING. HE CANNOT PROPOSE TONIGHT!! HE'S NOT PROPOSING TONIGHT, RIGHT?

Jackson paused, considering. He was aware that Max had been ring shopping. Max was looking for a vintage ring that would be nothing like anything Dominique's friends would have. The hunt seemed to involve a lot of online scouring and calling of antique dealers. Jackson wasn't aware that a ring had been purchased, but he didn't doubt that if Max had found something he wanted, he would leap on it. However, from what Dominique had said, Jackson thought Max was nervous about popping the question right after quitting his job and starting law school because he knew what that would look like to Dominique's snobby friends. The more urgent question was why Ella was worried about Max asking tonight.

He knew that Aiden and Ella had discussed marriage. He also knew that Ella's family insisted on a prenup because her uncle wanted Ella to take over Zhao Industries after he retired. As lawyers, Aiden and Ella were more than happy to have a prenup and were having, as far as Jackson could tell, ludicrous amounts of fun drafting and negotiating the document, which included clauses on who got to keep pets that they didn't have and whether or not Aiden would pay for dressage lessons for Ella in the event that he lost all their money on horse race gambling. Aiden had never bet on a horse race in his life, but that didn't stop them from negotiating on the topic. It was Jackson's estimation that the wedding was at least two years away because they wouldn't want to give up the fun of the prenup. So Ella's panic couldn't be about any impending proposal on their end. That just left one Deveraux that Ella could be worried about.

He dashed off a quick text.

Pretty sure Max is holding out until the spring. Have you heard from Olivia?

Evan Deveraux was the oldest of the cousins but the most recent to find a partner. Jackson could not have been happier with his redheaded cousin's choice of significant others—Olivia Rose West was an equally redheaded darling who loved Evan as much as Evan loved her. But the pair seemed to be moving on a swifter timeline than either Aiden or Dominique.

I talked to her a couple of weeks ago, and she said she was

ALMOST CERTAIN HE WAS GOING TO ASK SOON AND TONIGHT IS THEIR ANNIVERSARY.

Jackson found himself nodding. As usual, Ella's take on the situation was dead on. He also loved that Aiden had found himself someone brilliant. All of his cousin's partners were solid additions to the family that made him worry less because they each had someone who would protect them, love them, and keep them from going off the deep end in whatever stylish Deveraux way they were inclined to dive.

He put the car in motion and dialed Evan back, waiting to see if it would go to voice mail.

"Hey!" said Evan sounding cheerful.

"Hey! Just saw that I missed a call from you," said Jackson.

"I spilled cocktail sauce on my suit," said Evan. "I was panicking. I've got a half-million-dollar diamond ring in my pocket, and then I blobbed cocktail sauce down my front and had some sort of PTSD flashback to my dad yelling at me for getting dirty, and I panicked."

Jackson tried to pull back a laugh because he wasn't sure that was something it was OK to laugh at, but Evan had sounded so cheerful that it threw Jackson off.

"Are you OK?"

"No, obviously not. That's why I'm in therapy."

"I meant about the suit!" said Jackson as he pulled up at the valet. Evan was clearly in a good mood.

"Oh, it was a tale of trial and tribulation for the ages. Few have suffered more."

"What?"

"I couldn't get into the men's room. So then I called you."

"What was I going to do about the men's room?" Jackson couldn't stop laughing at Evan's glib retelling.

"I was going to have you bring me a new suit. But now you don't have to."

"Ah. I take it you got into the men's room?"

"No, a bartender took pity on me. I'm now freshly laundered, pressed, and back in the game."

"Uh-huh. The marriage game?" asked Jackson, getting out and handing his keys to the valet.

"Caught that?" asked Evan sounding like he was grinning. "I rented out the courtyard. I know she's expecting it, but I still think I've got the jump on her. She won't know where it's going to happen."

"Sneak attack proposal? Nice. I'm almost in. I'll see you in a few."

"See ya."

Evan hung up, and Jackson found himself shaking his head. His family was happy. It had been a long road, but for the first time since Jackson had joined the family, they were all happy. He felt proud of that. Jackson knew it wasn't entirely his doing, but when Eleanor had retrieved him from prison like some bedraggled stuffed animal out of the lost-and-found, he'd had one goal—get himself a happy family. He'd always wanted brothers and sisters and holidays straight off a postcard, and now he had that.

His phone plinged again, and he saw a text from Olivia.

I'M PANICKING. DOMINIQUE SAYS THIS LOOKS GOOD, BUT I THINK I LOOK LIKE A FAT CHERUB ON ROCOCO FRESCO. I WANT EVAN TO LIGHT UP LIKE A DAMN CHRISTMAS TREE WHEN HE SEES ME, NOT WONDER IF I'M PASSING OUT VALENTINES.

The text was accompanied by a photo of Olivia in a flowy white dress and wings. Olivia was, ahem, well-endowed, and he could see why she might be worried about flowy fabric, but as usual, Dominique was right—Olivia looked like a sexy angel.

Always trust Dominique on fashion. You look great. Evan will love it.

I do trust Dominique, but sometimes she's too nice. I need a bro opinion while there's still time to call in a replacement costume. And my own bro is useless and not responding.

Jackson was pretty sure that an angel was exactly how Evan thought of Olivia. He stopped inside the front hallway, trying to pull off to the side to get out of the way of anyone else coming in so he could finish his text.

Bro opinion is thumbs up.

He hit send with a grin. Tonight was going to be perfect for them. He looked up and tried to assess where the hell he was supposed to go. The VAR Events building always seemed to be re-configured into something new. Open double doors to his left showed a bar and banquet tables. He saw a woman standing on a ladder behind the bar reshelving the booze. As he watched, she went up on tip-toe to pull down a bottle of whiskey. Her skirt rode up as one foot lifted. Her ass was a fucking thing of beauty, and her legs were long and slender. He didn't know which party was Dominique's, but he knew which party he wanted to be at. He took a few steps toward the door and was intercepted by a large Black man who seemed to be in charge of security at VAR Events.

"Deveraux party is this way," he said, with a tight smile, pointing across the hall.

"Right," said Jackson, looking over the man's shoulder at the woman on the ladder.

"And if you're carrying, please inform the personnel at the door and show your license," added the man, shifting to block Jackson's view.

"Right," said Jackson, taking the hint. He appreciated the VAR security professionalism, but sometimes it was a real pain in the ass.

He walked across the hall, dutifully showed his concealed weapons permit to the security guard, and went in to find Dominique standing in the middle of the floor, looking like she was about to hyperventilate. His blonde cousin was wearing a cowgirl outfit complete with six-shooters.

"What if no one comes?" she demanded the second she saw him.

"People will come," he said reassuringly. "You're providing free alcohol and food."

"What if they don't dress up? In fact, you're not dressed up." Her eyes narrowed, and she glared accusingly at him.

Jackson looked down at his white jacket, purple shirt, and sleeves pushed up on his forearms. "I'm original Miami Vice. Do I ordinarily wear a white suit?"

"Did you pick a costume you could still carry a gun in?"

"Of course, didn't you?"

"Mine are cap guns!"

"I bet Max's aren't."

"That is correct," said Max, coming onto the floor. He was six-foot-four and looked like a 1950s movie sheriff, complete with a star on his chest and a white cowboy hat. His six-shooters were completely authentic as befitting an ex-US Marshal. "Not loaded, though. I figured the odds were good that some idiot in this crowd would try and grab them."

"Too true," agreed Jackson.

"Hey!" said Evan, coming downstairs, straightening his tie. He had a tiny pair of horns protruding from his red hair and a name tag that said he was Satan. Olivia arrived after him in wings.

"Hey," said Jackson. Olivia looked flushed, and he guessed that the two of them had been making out upstairs. "Where are Aiden and Ella?"

"Getting dressed," said Olivia, coming forward to plant a kiss on his cheek. "There was a lot of giggling coming out of the dressing room, though, so it might be a minute."

"Her costume came with two rolling carts," said Dominique. "I'm not sure what it is, but I must admit that I'm intrigued to find out."

"If it's a two-part horse costume, you know he's the ass," said Evan, and Olivia whacked at his arm.

"I'm going to need you two to stand on either side of me," said Jackson. "And give me advice on everything." Evan, Olivia, and Max laughed, but Dominique was checking her phone.

"OK," said Dominique, "so I said the party started at seven. It's five till, so we have at least a half-hour until anyone shows up."

"Oh, actually," said Olivia. "You said I could invite my work friends."

"Yeah, of course!" said Dominique. Jackson thought she was trying her hardest to be accommodating to Olivia because she knew that Olivia had essentially given up her family to be with Evan.

"Well, we're all nerds, so we arrive on time."

Jackson laughed.

"Yeah, my friends too," said Max. "We're completely not cool. Don and Harris already texted. I'm expecting them any minute."

"Really?" Instead of looking upset at having her timeline thrown off, Dominique looked relieved. "Great! I'll go tell the DJ. We're starting off with mellow mixer music before gearing up for dancing. And I put your names all down for Pin the Tail on the Donkey."

Jackson saw Max cast his eyes heavenward as if praying for strength as Dominique darted away.

"She's really panicking that no one will come?" asked Evan, looking confused.

"Pin the Tail on the Donkey?" Jackson repeated in equal confusion.

"Completely," said Max. "She's freaking out that no one really likes her. And don't ask about the donkey. You don't want to know."

"But everyone likes her," said Olivia, sounding confused. "She's the nicest…" she trailed off and paused to adjust her wings.

"She *is* the nicest Deveraux," finished Evan, chuckling. "Yes, it's true. Way to stop that sentence before it got anywhere."

"I did, didn't I?" agreed Olivia, pleased with the compliment. Evan only smiled and leaned over to kiss her. Max caught Jackson's eye and grinned. Olivia was a teeny bit on the Autism spectrum, and her blunt honesty was well-loved at the Deveraux dinner table.

"Come on," said Jackson to Max, jerking his head toward the bar. "I'll buy you a free drink."

"Count me in," said Max, following Jackson. "Hey, as your friend, I feel compelled to tell you that Dominique is going to try to fix you up with one of her friends tonight. Some girl named Chelsea. But you did not hear that from me."

Jackson groaned. His cousins seemed to think his life was deficient without a significant other and had taken to casually introducing him to women with increasing frequency over the last year.

"I can't date a girl named Chelsea," said Jackson. "Hell, I'm no good at dating anyway, but I extra can't do a Chelsea. Well, I can *do* a Chelsea, but I can't… Oh, whatever, you know what I'm trying to say."

"I do, actually," said Max with a grin. "Why can't you date again?"

"I *can* date. And I do. I just don't do girlfriends. It's not fair to make someone think I will be calling them when I most definitely won't, and I won't be introducing you to my family or showing up to support them in whatever the fuck it is they do. I'm a shitty boyfriend, so I don't bother. Saves everyone time."

"Ah," said Max, nodding. "Right. You have the complete list of people you care about, and you don't need extras." Max's eyes twinkled.

"I don't have *room* for extras, and honestly, that's the way I like it. More people mean more work. I love you, Ella, and Olivia, but sheesh. I can't take having to remember one more person's birthday."

"Yeah, that calendar function is so hard."

"Stop busting my balls," complained Jackson.

"I'm not. I mean, I am on the birthday thing. That's the dumbest reason I have ever heard to not have a relationship. You need to come up with something better to tell your relatives if you want them to stop setting you up."

Jackson laughed. "Thanks for the tip."

"I don't think you can force someone into a relationship, but they seem to think that if they just throw all the fish in the sea at you, you're bound to catch one."

"If I do, I'm tossing it back."

They had reached the bar, and Jackson looked around to make sure they had left Olivia and Evan behind. "Although speaking of reeling one in, Evan's proposing tonight," said Jackson, lowering his voice.

"Yes!" exclaimed Max and then winced and lowered his voice. "Now Dominique will have to commit."

"What does that mean?" asked Jackson. Max did his own look around.

"We've been discussing marriage or at least getting officially engaged for months. Most of a year. But every time I'm like, *let's get serious about this,* she wanders off. Literally, a few weeks ago, she got out of bed, and I found her scrubbing the oven."

"Dominique knows how to scrub an oven?" asked Jackson.

"No," said Max. "Not very well anyway. I have finally found a ring, and I figured once I was in law school and things were settled down, we could, you know… move things along. Instead, she threw a Halloween party."

"Because I have to say that she's been giving the impression that law school is what's slowing the show down and she's upset by it."

"Nuh-huh!" exclaimed Max, clearly so flummoxed that he resorted to childhood rejections.

"That's what I've been getting out of her," said Jackson.

"What. The. Hell?" demanded Max.

"I don't know," said Jackson. "Oh, my God!"

Max turned to see what had caused Jackson's surprise.

Aiden advanced down the stairs in a blue jacket and white pants with a red stripe down the side, looking like Prince Charming straight out of a fairy tale cartoon. Behind him, Ella Zhao floated like Cinderella in an enormous blue poof of a gown that threatened to collect or dislodge the decorations on the stairs.

"God, I love this family," said Max. Jackson began to laugh. "I'm serious. You never go halfway. It's fantastic."

"Well, that's good," said Jackson, laughing. "You're going to end up stuck with us."

"Great," said Max. "I'll never be bored."

Jackson laughed harder than ever. "So true."

"Yay!" exclaimed Dominique, bouncing across the dancefloor and clapping her hands as she caught sight of her brother's costume.

"Occasionally confused, sometimes scared, and periodically

enraged," continued Max, watching Dominique, "but never, ever bored."

Jackson looked around the room at his family and their partners. "That does about sum it up," he agreed.

Caitlin
The Alley

Caitlin filled another gin and tonic and slid it across the bar. The accountant dutifully put a dollar in the tip jar and collected the drink. Caitlin watched the woman walk carefully back to her assigned seat and sit down next to a man who appeared to be unintentionally wearing everything oatmeal colored. Caitlin wracked her brain, trying to think of a party that had been comparably boring. Maybe it was intentional. No party had ever been as dull as this. Maybe oatmeal was their fashion statement. Perhaps they were trying to underline the mediocrity of existence. This event was the party equivalent of that outfit.

"Oh my God," whispered Jessica, approaching the bar. "Please, Katie, please. I'm begging you. Please pour me a shot of something. I'm dying. I think I felt a portion of my brain drip out of my ear a minute ago."

There was a burst of laughter from the Deveraux party across the hall, and Jessica let out a little whimper.

"I want to go to that party," Jessica whined.

Caitlin poured a shot of Jägermeister under the bar and then slid the tiny glass out to Jessica, who palmed it and gulped it down in one go.

"Did you see the Deveraux party?" whispered Jessica. "They have a chocolate fountain. They have costumes. They have a DJ. They have Pin the Tail on the Donkey."

"What? I thought it was an adult party."

"It is. And I swear I'm doing it the next party I hold. Drunken Pin the Tail on the Donkey was hilarious. I was laughing so hard, and then Vince said I had to come back to this absolute graveyard. My soul is dying *right now.*"

Caitlin chuckled. "You? I have been over here all evening! I don't think this accounting firm even realized it was Halloween when they booked the party. I'm not sure they know what Halloween is."

"Why did they book this party? It's horrible."

"I think it's someone's retirement party," said Caitlin, looking around the room. "That guy at the head table seems to be getting some sort of parade of people."

"This is worse than my seventh-grade Sadie Hawkins dance."

"Yes," agreed Caitlin, "it is. And the tips are even worse."

"You should ditch out."

"What?"

"You're coming up on your break. I can cover you for twenty minutes. Pull your apron off and go hit the dance floor over there. I bet no one even notices."

"Oh. Uh… no. I… no. I don't… I don't like the Deverauxes."

"Really? Weren't you on some sort of Progressive minimum wage rant the other day?"

"Yeah, so?"

"Well, that Eleanor Deveraux said the same shit a month ago. Don't you read the Huffington Post? They're always quoting her. She's basically like a grandma version of Bernie Sanders."

"Yeah, come on. Eleanor Deveraux is rich as fuck, and she can spout whatever soundbites she wants. I'm not buying it. Hard to be one with the proletariat when you live in a mansion in Carnegie Hill."

"OK, I have no idea what she's like, really, but it doesn't matter because she's not over there. Her grandkids are, and what I know about them is that they throw banging parties."

"What are they like?" asked Caitlin, unable to stop herself. Why did she care? It was like poking at a scab.

"Blonde? I don't know. I only saw the one dressed like Prince Charming, and he was dancing with a complete Cinderella. I mean, the dress… It was so poofy. If she went somewhere, they'd have to stand her up in the back of a flatbed truck. It was the stuff of my childhood dreams."

Caitlin laughed. "It must be nice to have enough money to make your dreams come true."

"Yeah," said Jessica. "Too bad most rich people are such boring motherfuckers. I swear most of them couldn't come up with something good to do with their money if they tried. Anyway, you should go take your break. Even if you won't go over to the *good* party, at least stop staring at this void of humanity. Are they demons? Maybe this is hell? It is. We've wandered into the fourth circle of hell. Run, Katie, run while you can."

Caitlin tried to think of a reason to object and then shook her head. "Yeah, you know what? You're right. I'll see you in twenty minutes. I'm going to go get a cup of coffee and look at…" she gestured to the tables in front of her, "not this."

"I'll scream if more of my brain goo drips out my ears."

"You do that. I'll send Vince in."

Jessica laughed as Caitlin slid out the bar entrance and into the back hallway.

"*Hola,* Katie!" called Diego as she entered the kitchen.

"*Hola!*" she called back to the chef. He was Angela's second-in-command and head of the kitchen. Mostly everyone loved the round-faced Guatemalan, but he had a temper, and usually Caitlin was glad she worked for Vince. Not that Vince couldn't be a hard ass, but he didn't yell much. Angela ruled over catering, food, and clients, and Vince was in charge of staff and security. It was a system that worked well for them and the rest of the business because they were busy these days. Caitlin was grateful since it meant she could always pick up extra shifts.

She went toward the back corner, where they kept a carafe of coffee for the staff. She poured herself a cup. She wanted someplace quiet, but the kitchen wasn't it. The dinner service for the accountants was about to happen, and the place was buzzing. She pulled her off her apron and *Katie* name tag, and shoved them into her cubby before grabbing her jacket off the hook. She pulled on her coat, rotating her cup carefully from hand to hand, and went to the back alley. It was cold but quiet, and Caitlin leaned against the wall and breathed out a sigh of relief.

It was at times like this that she thought about taking up smoking. Smokers always had something to do and never had to explain breaks—they *needed* a smoke. Caitlin couldn't afford cigarettes and, therefore, always felt like she had to justify breaks. It was the myth of productivity. Busy people were doing and accomplishing. Busy people were good people. And if she stayed active, she wouldn't notice that her life was in the shitter. Quiet moments could be hell, but God, did she crave them.

She was almost to the bottom of her coffee cup when she became aware of someone walking toward her from the far end of the alley. The man was wearing a white suit and seemed to glimmer a little in the ambient glow of street lights.

"Yes," he said, his voice bit at the word as if annoyed. "Yes, I understand, but what I'm telling you is that there is nothing I can do about it right now. Your choices are that I can come talk about this more in person, even though there is literally no action we can take or discuss it in the morning. Considering that I told Nika I'd be back in five minutes, ten minutes ago—"

His stride checked, and she realized that he must have seen

her. He was probably a Deveraux party guest. He paused a distance away, his shoulders turning slightly away as he finished his conversation.

"Yes, all right. Great. I'll see you in the morning. Yes, I will tell Nika that. Yes, bye."

He hung up his phone and took a deep breath. His skin was pale, his hair was dark, and the shadows carved up his face into something wild and hawkish. Caitlin felt a flutter of attraction deep in her belly. The sensation startled her. She hadn't felt anything about anyone for at least a year. He turned back to her, and she felt like he was consciously putting on a polite face.

"It's times like this I miss smoking," he said, unknowingly echoing her thoughts. He hadn't moved from his position ten feet away, and she realized that he was attempting to make himself safe for her. He was staying far away. He spoke directly to her, acknowledging her presence and sticking to a neutral topic. She knew then that he was waiting for her to move so he could pass her and go to the door. She also knew that she didn't want him to. She wanted him to stay here in the dark with her.

"I never started," she said back. "Is it weird that I miss it too?"

He laughed as if she'd surprised him and took a step closer. "Yes, a bit. I don't think you're supposed to miss things you've never had."

"Then I think I've been doing it wrong," she said. She wanted to run her fingers through his hair.

"Doing what wrong? Smoking? Yes, you are if you've never actually done it." He sounded amused and unconsciously shifted his phone from one hand to the other. He had long fingers, and she wondered what it would be like to feel them on her skin.

"Living, maybe," she said, instantly regretting her words, but he took a step closer as if the answer didn't bother him.

"I'm not sure you can do living wrong," he said. There was another step, and his head tilted as if he tried to get a better look at her. A hint of a smile played among the shadows on his face.

"I'm absolutely certain you can," she said and regretted that too. She shook her head. She had forgotten how to flirt. "Sorry. I don't think I'm suitable company anymore."

This time the laughter in his voice came through loud and clear. "Well, that's where *I'm* absolutely certain you're wrong."

"Why?"

"Well, for one thing, you have no idea what I'm suited for." His voice was a deep cocky purr, and Caitlin felt her breath catch a little in her throat. Why was she talking to this man in a dark alley? Why did she want him to come closer?

"For instance, I'm incredibly well suited to—"

His phone lit up in his hand, and he gave an audible grunt of dislike. The backdoor swung open, and Andrew, the bus boy, stumbled out, a very obvious joint in one hand, already starting to light up.

"Seriously, Andrew?" said Caitlin.

"Shit," said Andrew, staring at them, the joint clamped between his lips.

"This is why you get busted. You never even look before you light up," Caitlin said.

"I don't… uh…."

"Whatever," said Caitlin, rolling her eyes. The guy was already walking away to answer his phone. She felt a swell of angry disappointment. She wasn't sure why. It was a conversation in an alley. It hadn't even been decent flirting. It hadn't been anything. Maybe that was the point. She was missing what she wasn't going to get. Caitlin upended her coffee cup into the cement planter that doubled as an ashtray and brushed past Andrew. She had a fourth ring of hell accountant party to get back to.

JACKSON
THE MISSING FILE

"I think we're cursed," said Eleanor.

"We're not cursed, Grandma," said Jackson sensibly, then yawned.

Nika's Halloween party had been an unqualified success, at least for Nika. He'd spent the evening avoiding Chelsea, trying to pin Nika down for a quiet moment to talk about Max and engaging in a vain attempt to find the girl from the alley again. He'd ended up going home alone. Something that had been all too common lately.

"Are you sure?" demanded Eleanor, slapping her laptop closed. "Because I'm starting to think J.P. Granger called down some sort of fiery damnation on us and the only way to get rid of it is to dig him up and hold an exorcism. If his dying wish was that I should come to regret ever having heard his name, then it has certainly come true."

"I'll get in a witch," said Jackson. He was tired enough to start blurting out the random thoughts that sprang to mind, even though he knew Eleanor would disapprove of all of them. "She'll come. She'll do a blessing, some smudging. It'll be good."

"Don't be ridiculous," said Eleanor, giving him a look that said she knew he was being purposely provocative. "How is that supposed to look to my Protestant constituency?"

"I can have her come at night." Jackson didn't think Eleanor believed in witchcraft or Protestants, but he liked to see where she would draw the line.

"Oh, yes, that will be even better. I can see the headline now: Eleanor Deveraux holds midnight Satanic rituals. I'm already on the child molesting cannibal conspiracy Reddit threads. I don't think we need to add witchcraft to the story."

"Not to worry, Mrs. Deveraux," said Theo coming into Eleanor's office to collect the tray of tea things. "I'm fully versed in three forms of household purification. I'll take care of it this weekend."

Eleanor blinked at her usually stoic butler. Jackson did too. The gray-haired sixty-something usually appeared to be the paragon of propriety, except in December when he became a walking advent calendar in a string of hideous Christmas sweaters that brought everyone in the Deveraux family great joy. Christmas without the sweaters would be unthinkable.

"Theo, it disturbs me to no end when you say things like that. I was unaware that you knew about anything remotely related to..." Eleanor hesitated as if looking for the appropriate word. "Spiritualism."

"Well, ma'am, as a butler, I'm in charge of the household, and I have to be familiar with anything that may assist the well-being of those within my house."

"Yes, but you have worked for me since a date that I prefer not to mention. I don't believe I've ever seen you practicing such things. I fail to see how you could have the time to master such skills. Does one send off for instructions?"

"You are quite generous with your vacation benefits, and I like to take continuing education courses."

Theo and Eleanor stared at each other, having come to an impasse. Jackson could never decide in these moments if this was some form of flirting or if Theo and Eleanor were quite serious about the conversation. Neither of them was known for joking, and yet... They couldn't really be serious, could they?

"Well," said Eleanor, making a soft click of her tongue, "I will leave the practice of such things to your discretion. I'm sure it is a relief to know that I have an expert on hand should I need one."

"Of course, Mrs. Deveraux," said Theo leaving the room as if he had scored a victory. It was possible that he had, but Jackson couldn't tell what the game was, let alone the rules.

"I really feel that you have been a terrible influence on him," said Eleanor.

"Me?" Jackson laughed in disbelief.

"He was never this creative before you came to live here."

Jackson chuckled. "I have no regrets."

"No, you never do. It's terribly rude. However, that is as may be. But aside from that, do you have any idea where the hell Grangers' ridiculous paper files are?"

Jackson shook his head, and Eleanor let out a heavy breath of annoyance.

"I suppose the real question to ask is, why haven't the Absolex hearing transcripts been released to the public yet? The Republicans are hinting at impropriety, and I'm tired of it. The entire thing would go away if the transcripts were released, but they haven't. And I want to know why not?"

"I don't know," said Jackson. He disliked giving this answer. He generally kept away from Eleanor's work, but Aboslex was a special case, and the lines were starting to get blurry for both of them.

"It's like Absolex and Granger just won't go away. If his… representative or whatever Granger called this mystery person was going to be publicizing everything, shouldn't they have done it by now?"

"Yes," said Jackson. "Granger's ashes were interred a month ago, and his death was officially declared an accidental overdose. Apparently, he was dead before he hit the ground."

Eleanor frowned at him. "Didn't he leave a suicide note?"

"There was a note. Apparently, it was more an *I hate the Deverauxes* manifesto, and the investigators decided hatred of us was not enough to cause suicidal ideation. Although, I think, more to the point, if it wasn't suicide, it's easier for the creditors to go after his estate."

"Did we influence that? That seems excessive. He's dead. Anything after that is just vindictive."

"We didn't lift a finger in that direction," said Jackson. "Although, it does feel like someone did. Probably just the IRS being the IRS."

Eleanor shrugged. "That seems likely. Honestly, I'm not worried about Granger's files."

"Really? I am."

"Well, since they have not magically appeared by now, it seems unlikely they're real. And even if the files are real, it seems unlikely that they have the power to do whatever it is Granger thought they would do."

Jackson gave a reluctant nod to the second point.

"And I doubt that whatever DC insider he referred to was real either," continued Eleanor.

"That I actually am convinced of."

"What do you mean?"

"The hotel was helpful about handing over his phone call logs, and I managed to get his cell phone records."

"Jackson! That is not legal!"

"It is," said Jackson. "Ish. He's dead with no next of kin. That puts the Right to Privacy in a very gray area."

"Mmm." There was so much disapproval all in one note.

"Unfortunately, the calls to his *special friend* in DC went to a burner phone."

"That doesn't mean whoever he called actually has any influence," said Eleanor, but she sounded less confident.

"Agreed. On the other hand," Jackson said, "if we could find out who it was, we might have a clue as to who is looking into the Absolex hearings."

"Yes, they would, which would just be too convenient for us, and therefore I'm even less inclined to believe in such things."

Jackson laughed. "Your pessimism is at a nearly Ukrainian level."

"I always got along well with Evan's mother," said Eleanor reflectively. "Perhaps that's why."

Jackson knew that the rest of the family had never met his mother, but sometimes it felt like Evan was the only one who remembered that she had also been Ukrainian. It had been their first point of commonality when he'd entered the family. The girl last night in the alley had also had the aura of stand-offish Ukrainian pessimism that Jackson found profoundly familiar and refreshing all at once. Perhaps that was why he'd wanted to find her. Or possibly it was the profoundly desirable ass that had walked away from him.

"Perhaps so," said Jackson. "Do you want me to look into the Congressional stuff?"

"No, I think that's best left to me. Backstabbing senate gossip is the kind of thing my staff lives for."

"All right," said Jackson. "I'll keep digging on the Granger files then."

"Might as well," she said with a shrug. "How are the children doing?"

"Aiden and Ella completed the partnership deal between DevEntier and Zhao Industries. They told me to vote on something. I voted. Apparently, now I have thirty million more dollars."

Eleanor gave him an exasperated look. "The stock value went up two hundred percent overnight."

"That is what Evan said," agreed Jackson.

"You don't care a bit, do you?"

"Nope," said Jackson cheerfully. Eleanor shook her head. He never knew how to explain that too much money was meaningless. He could buy the things he wanted, and after that, it was useless to him.

"How are Evan and Olivia?"

"You mean, besides engaged?"

Eleanor beamed, and Jackson thought he'd rarely seen a happier expression on her face.

"Thank you for all the texts and pictures last night. I don't like to attend such parties, but I like to be included in the news. They looked very happy."

"They were both floating on cloud nine," said Jackson.

"I really wasn't sure she was the one for him," said Eleanor. It was the closest Jackson had ever heard her get to an admission of being wrong.

"I was," said Jackson, knowing his voice sounded too firm.

"I hate that she's Ralph Taggert's granddaughter, but I love how she loves Evan," said Eleanor, meeting his eye, stare for stare.

"I know," said Jackson, relenting. "It's unfortunate that your most hated political rival has any tie to this family, but so far, Olivia's deal with him is holding. She and Ralph don't speak, and he's left all of us out of any of his rhetoric."

"It has been rather refreshing to have him attack me on my record for a change," said Eleanor.

"And Olivia has been enjoying not having anyone undermine her, critique her every decision, or call her a whore," said Jackson. "So, really, it's been winning all around."

Eleanor took a breath and then closed her mouth around whatever hasty words were coming to her mind. "Indeed," she said with a polite smile. One of her many policies was never to say anything bad about her enemies. He was always impressed by her willpower on that one.

"Indeed," he agreed, and her head rocked slightly back in a silent laugh.

"And Dominique and Max?" she asked.

Jackson hesitated. "The party was a smash, and Evan and Olivia got engaged, so Nika's happy about that but upset about Junior League."

"Then she should have said no when I asked her to join."

"There's some sort of old college classmate on the board. Her competitive streak kicked in, but now she's regretting it."

"I'm sure she'll think of something," said Eleanor with a shrug. "As long as she brings in the donations for me, she may burn them to the ground for all I care. They were always an elitist bunch."

"I shall pass that along," said Jackson.

"And how are things with Max? The last time I spoke with her, I got the impression that his admittance to law school was delaying wedding bells for them, and she was upset about it. I was trying not to comment on that since I thought she wanted him to go to law school, and I thought she and his father were of one mind on this topic."

"I thought all three of you were of one mind on the topic," said Jackson dryly.

"Well, of course, *I* prefer it. US Marshal is an admirable profession, but law is a career. Also, it's much, much safer. And he really is such a dear boy. So level-headed and smart. He'll do well." Eleanor paused as if considering. "I wouldn't be surprised if Dominique has her sights set on him being a judge. I imagine she didn't realize getting her way on law school would mean doing things on his timeline. She picked out someone stable and found out she can't push him over."

Jackson laughed. Eleanor was right about Max, even if she hadn't quite figured out Dominque.

"And how is the children's futile attempt at finding you a girlfriend going?" she asked, looking at him with a distinct twinkle in her eye.

"Horribly," said Jackson. "Please tell me you didn't sign off on that."

"I have suggested on more than one occasion that they should not make the effort, but they don't seem to listen."

"Last night was a Chelsea."

Eleanor shook her head. "I cannot have a Chelsea at the dinner table."

"I can't have a Chelsea anywhere," said Jackson. "I think it's mostly Aiden and Dominique, but Evan's put forth a few candidates. His are better, but…." Jackson shook his head.

Not that he was doing so great on his own. He usually had a list of friendly faces that could be counted on for some no-strings mattress time. His main go-to had been the wife of an ambassador who had no interest in leaving her husband. It had been the perfect arrangement until her husband had been reassigned to another country six months ago. And Jackson had to admit that some of the girls his cousins had been flinging at him had been worth someone's time, but it wasn't him. He needed someone who fit his schedule, didn't mind if he disappeared for a few days or weeks at a time, and didn't expect him to show up to be supportive of whatever the fuck they were into. The idea of putting in the work to get to know someone sounded physically and mentally exhausting. He had a full crew of security operatives, his cousins, and his grandmother to look after. Adding one more person was not on his list of things to do.

"I could try talking to them again?" offered Eleanor, but she didn't look like she thought it would work.

"Don't bother," he said. "They won't listen."

She shrugged. "Well, other than their atrocious attempts at playing Cupid. They're well?"

"Basically, everyone is fine except you," said Jackson.

"Which brings me back to cursed," said Eleanor. "I don't understand how it's four years later, and I'm still dealing with this Absolex nonsense."

"I offered you a witch, but you said no."

Eleanor gave him a look, and Jackson grinned. "I'll find the files," he said, standing up.

"I'm sure you will," said Eleanor. "I just hope they'll be worth the effort."

Jackson nodded. He hoped so too, but he couldn't shake the feeling that something was looming on the horizon. Perhaps it was that everything was going too well. Maybe it was just the Ukrainian in him, but whatever it was, he wanted to shore up the family's defenses before whatever storm was coming opened up on them.

Jackson
House of Amery

Jackson followed Dominique into the depths of the House of Amery. He hadn't known what to expect from a fashion designer's studio. Strangely, it reminded him of a chop shop. There were different workstations, dresses lay in pieces, and the workers would glance up, but no one wanted to chat. Headless dress dummies stood at every table and gave him the urge to run shooting target drills in the room.

He had been hoping to get a few minutes alone to talk to Dominique about Max. However, a week after Evan's engagement, she seemed to be avoiding all of her relatives and throwing herself into helping Olivia with wedding planning. The first priority was finding Olivia a wedding dress. Since Olivia hated thinking about clothes, Dominique was taking point on the dress and interviewing multiple designers for the gig. So far, the designers had been uniformly obsequious and excited about the project. Today's designer was Victor Amery, and he was less of a suck-up, more enthusiastic, and definitely had a *vision*. Jackson did not care about the vision. He cared about hurrying Dominique up. They were already late for a meeting with Evan and Eleanor's campaign strategist, and wedging in a heart-to-heart was going to be challenging enough.

He looked around the room and realized that one of the mannequins was an actual person. She was surrounded by three different seamstresses, one of who was minutely stitching something onto the girl's boobs. The model was in fantastic shape. Jackson wouldn't mind getting that up close and personal with her boobs. Unlike most models who seemed gangly and bony, this one had curves in all the right places and long beautiful legs. Not that the seamstress appeared to notice as she stitched with tiny, delicate precision along the breast. It was bizarrely intimate and also impersonal at the same time.

He glanced up at the model and realized that it wasn't just her body that was amazing. Her dark hair was tied up in a messy bun on top of her head, showing off a long slender neck and high-cheek bones. She also was making faces at the sewers, who were oblivious. He began to laugh, and then the model caught his eye and abruptly stopped, going straight-faced.

Her serious expression was what triggered his memory. The model was the girl from the alley, and he felt triumphant. He couldn't believe he'd randomly managed to find her. Of course she was a model with a face and body like that. He should have started his search for her on the nearest catwalk. He wanted to make her laugh again, so he stuck out his tongue at her and watched as she tried to keep a giggle from escaping.

"You're jiggling," complained one of the stitchers near her ass.

"Sorry," said the model and shot a glare at him. He tried to figure out how he was going to talk to her with all the fashion people around. Maybe this time, he could at least get her name.

His phone rang, and he reluctantly walked a few paces further away from both the model and Dominique.

"Jackson," his grandmother said without preamble, "there has been a very unusual occurrence."

"Did Theo make a joke again?" asked Jackson.

"Don't be ridiculous," said Eleanor. "The apocalypse isn't *that* nigh. No, Zoe has just received a call—a direct call—from Ralph Taggert's Chief of Staff."

"Are we sure the apocalypse isn't nigh? Perhaps we should ask Theo."

"Amusing," said Eleanor, not sounding in the least entertained. "OK, what did he want?"

"He wanted to arrange a meeting between myself and Ralph."

"Why?" demanded Jackson. Olivia's grandfather was pompous, conniving, and consistently referred to Senator Deveraux as *Evil Eleanor*. Even with the détente Olivia negotiated, Jackson didn't think Ralph had actually stopped hating any of them. If anything, Jackson thought he probably hated the Deveraux family even more.

"That is unclear, but he offered a suggested date, time, and location and requested no staffers be present. It appears to be serious."

"Do you want to go?" asked Jackson.

"When one's sworn enemy calls up and asks for a meeting for the first time ever, it pays to take it. So yes."

"All right," said Jackson. "Text me the details. I'll get started."

"Started?" repeated Eleanor.

"Well, *one* may wish to take the meeting, but *one* should not take it without scouting the location or assessing the threat risk."

"That seems excessive," said Eleanor, and he could hear the frown in her voice. "I was simply going to have you go with me as you are not a staffer."

"No problem, but I don't go places without scouting the location and assessing the threat risk."

Eleanor sighed gustily.

"Fine. I'll send you a text momentarily. Goodbye."

"Bye," said Jackson, although the line had already clicked off.

He hesitated for a moment and then texted Olivia. Meeting with Ralph Taggert might be only about Eleanor, but he didn't want Olivia to be blindsided, and there was always the possibility that she might have some insight. Moments later, his phone rang, and he saw it was Evan.

"Hey Ev," he said, picking up cautiously, uncertain if Olivia had promptly forwarded the message to Evan.

"Are you and Dominique coming or what? This campaign guy is starting to fidget, and I can't kick him out of my office. And now I'm loitering in the hall because it is my resolution to not be quite so rude to people, but he keeps sniffing."

"Not *quite* so rude?"

"I think we may all need to accept that there is a baseline level of rude that is just part of my personality."

"I do accept that, actually," said Jackson nodding reflectively.

"So should everyone else. Now, where are you?" Jackson checked the wall of mirrors in front of him, scanning the room and sneaking a peak at the model again.

"We stopped at the House of Amery to discuss Olivia's wedding dress."

He quickly glanced at Dominique in the mirrors and caught the designer checking him out.

"Oh God," said Evan. "You're never going to get here."

"What does your brother do again?" asked Victor in what Jackson guessed was supposed to be a whisper. No one could ever keep straight that Aiden and Dominique were the only siblings among the Deverauxes. Jackson didn't mind having his ass admired in general, but Amery seemed callous about it—his attitude was echoed in the way the tailors were treating the model.

"It's fine," said Jackson. "We're almost done."

"Security," said Dominique, without correcting their relationship. Something crisp in her tone told him she also didn't appreciate the designer's vibe.

"Are we sure?" asked Amery. "Because with that build, he could do modeling."

"You say almost done, but…" said Evan.

"I can't think of anything he'd hate more," said Dominique.

"I know, I know," said Jackson. "But we've moved like two entire rooms toward the front door in the last five minutes. I'll pick her up and carry her if I have to."

Evan laughed. "Hey, you're coming over for dinner afterward, right? Olivia's baking, and I can't eat all the cupcakes alone."

"What's wrong?" asked Jackson. Olivia was a stress baker.

"She's stymied at work and presenting at a symposium next month. She's having that school dream where you're naked in front of the class and forgot to study."

Jackson laughed. "I have literally never had that dream."

"I think only people that really cared about school have that dream," said Evan.

"That leaves me out then," said Jackson. He didn't add that GED graduates probably never had that dream.

"Pretty sure Aiden and Olivia have it at least once a year. Considering I was high for most of college, I don't think I'll ever have it." Jackson laughed again. He appreciated Evan's honesty, but he knew that high or not, Evan had still managed to pull down B averages at an Ivy League school. "We'll have to ask Dominique for a true sampling."

"Yeah, we should," he said and looked around for Dominique only to realize that she and Victor had disappeared. "Oh, son of a bitch!"

"What?" asked Evan.

"She got away from me. Now I have to backtrack."

"Time to carry her out," said Evan.

"I'm thinking about it," said Jackson.

"See you in an hour then. Maybe I can shove a Zyrtec up his nose," said Evan and hung up.

Jackson looked up in frustration at the brunette model. She really was gorgeous. It was unfair that he had to leave her standing there, but family came first. The girl subtly lifted a hand and pointed toward the far door.

"Thanks," he said and went after Dominique.

Caitlin
HOUSE OF AMERY

The team had gone down to the back alley for a smoke break and left her standing on the dais still sewn to an entire bolt of fabric. That was par for the course at House of Amery. The employees didn't give two shits about the models. She had thought that when they went on break, they would at least let her sit down, but the lace was wrapped tight around her knees, and they hadn't wanted to disturb the drape of the fabric. They hadn't even had the decency to tell her when they'd be back; they'd just wandered off. The only person who had looked her in the eye today was the hot guy from the alley who'd been with his sister.

She couldn't believe he was here. She supposed if he was the kind of person who would go to a Deveraux party, he was also in the tax bracket of those who could afford to shop at the House of Amery, but it still surprised her.

She remembered the twinkle in his eye as he'd stuck out his tongue and smiled. She wondered if he actually recognized her from the alley. For a moment, she entertained the fantasy of meeting a handsome, wealthy Prince Charming who would sweep her off her feet. Caitlin snorted to herself. That was a pipe dream. When had anything in the last three years gone well for her? It had been one long series of bad breaks ever since her mother's cancer diagnosis. Although, she wasn't sure her father's refusal to help was bad luck. Unless simply having him as a father counted was her unlucky moment, in which case she'd been cursed from the outset, and she was definitely not getting lucky with this guy in any sense of the phrase. She tried to comfort herself with the fact that not only was she *not*

Cinderella material, but she was also dressed in underwear, most of a muslin pattern shift, and about three layers of lace. So basically, she was mostly naked. Having Hot Guy come back now would just lead to some sort of horrifically embarrassing incident.

Caitlin looked around and tried to figure out if she could lean against something without tearing any stitches. She had another two hours of standing here. She needed the paycheck, but her feet were already aching. Her only consolation was that she was scheduled for a break about the time Angela and the VAR catering truck were supposed to arrive for some meeting Victor was holding. Caitlin was sure that Angela would let her scam some lunch, which might make up for the breakfast she'd missed when her train had run late.

There was a resounding screech as the fire alarm began to blare. Caitlin jumped but didn't panic. When was one of these things ever actually a fire? Then smoke began to billow into the room from the doorway down to the basement.

She looked in horror at the smoke and then at the bolt of hand-crafted Italian lace that she was attached to.

There was a quick patter of feet, and the hot guy came running into the room.

"Help!" she gasped.

"Come on," he said, reaching out a hand to help her down.

"I can't! I'm still sewn to the fabric!"

He followed the trail of lace leading from her to the bolt of fabric and grabbed a pair of scissors off the nearest table.

"Don't you dare! That is hand-made Italian lace!" she gasped, pointing to the fabric bolt.

"That is a fire!" He pointed at the smoke in turn.

"If you cut it, I will never get work here again!"

He grabbed the bolt off the rack and wound the lace willy-nilly around it until he reached her, then thrust it into her arms. "Hold that." Then he bent down and grabbed her around the knees, slinging her over his shoulder.

He walked them quickly through the building and out to the parking lot. The rest of the employees were milling about, and when he set her down, there was a cheer, and a press of people surged toward them.

"You saved it!" exclaimed one of the seamstresses. "Billy, get the kit!"

They began to snip her out of the dress form and remove the fabric.

"OK, yes," said Caitlin. "But I need clothes. No," she tried to snatch the last piece of fabric covering her. "No, I need clothes!"

She clutched her hands over her boobs and stared at the hot guy as the team left her standing there in her underwear.

He took off his coat and wrapped it around her.

"Hi," he said as he buttoned the heavy wool coat over her. "I'm Jackson, and I'm suited for talking philosophy in dark alleys, carrying women out of fires in hand-crafted Italian lace, and lending people my coat."

He was tall, about six foot two, with black hair and blue eyes, wearing a sweater, jeans, and peeking out from a holster on his hip, a gun. His sister had said that he worked security, so presumably, that was OK. Staring into his sky-blue eyes, Caitlin felt breathless. She couldn't believe he remembered her.

"Nice to meet you," she said, reaching one hand over the top edge of the coat to touch her fingers to his as they came to the top button. His hands were warm, and his fingers curled around hers.

"I don't know what they are paying you," he said, "but I don't think it's enough."

Caitlin laughed breathlessly. "Is it ever?"

He smiled, and his hand slid upward to hold her whole hand. "Probably not. Your fingers are freezing. Maybe we should—"

"Oh, my God, Katie!"

Caitlin looked over at Angela Ramano as she exited the VAR Catering truck. The sound of fire trucks in the distance probably meant that Victor's meeting was going to be rescheduled.

"Are you OK?" Angela looked at Jackson. She saw Angela take in the gun, the coat, and Katie's naked legs. Angela crossed her arms over her chest, putting a wrinkle in her crisp white chef's jacket, and raised an eyebrow at Jackson. It was the kind of facial expression that gave the sous chef nightmares.

"They took my clothes," said Caitlin, her teeth beginning to chatter.

"What? Why?" Angela lost her angry look at Jackson but still looked perturbed.

"Fashion?" Caitlin couldn't come up with another answer.

"You had better go wait in the truck," commanded Angela. She gestured to Caitlin but kept her eyes on Jackson. Technically, here, at a completely different job, she didn't work for either Vince or Angela, but when Angela spoke, everyone knew better than to argue. Also, Caitlin's toes had now reached the painfully cold stage.

"Thank you," she said, looking up at Jackson. She meant to ask about how to return his coat when she saw his sister waving at them from across the parking lot. "Your sister is over there."

He looked around. "Shit. Thanks."

He walked off immediately. So even mostly naked, she couldn't keep his interest. That seemed about right for her life. Caitlin sighed and went to the catering van.

Dominique
Conversations

Dominique flipped through the campaign finance reports and frowned. The meeting with Eleanor's campaign person had been mercifully quick because there were no problems to discuss. Well, that and because Evan had clearly had it up to his eyebrows with the man. Evan had hustled through the agenda with aggressive speed and then sent the poor fellow all but hurtling out the door with a to-go cup of tea and a box of tissues. Dominique wasn't sure which had frightened the man more Evan's firm goodbye or the box of tissues. She was relieved to be done with it and on her way home, but now she worried that she had missed something.

"Problems?" asked Jackson, fiddling with the radio.

"Everything seems fine," said Dominique.

"There's frowning," he said, finally just flipping the radio off.

"Everything is… fine. I'm not used to it. Since Ralph Taggert stopped being so loudly annoying and Granger took a swan dive, everything is on track. I'm not sure what to do with myself without a mess to clean up."

Jackson let out a short bark of laughter. "I know the feeling. Although there is some shit brewing in the Senate, and Granger's mess isn't entirely cleaned up. But yeah, everything's been quiet."

"Are there really problems?" asked Dominique, worried that he had been holding out on her. "You haven't said anything."

"Because there's nothing to do."

"You'd ask for help if you needed it, though, right?"

Jackson laughed again. "I have lots of help, and the Senate stuff is mostly Eleanor's problem."

"Well, yes, but I'm just saying…"

"And I'm just saying there aren't any emergencies. If there were, I would ask, but there aren't."

Dominique let out a huff of annoyance. "I'm not used to that."

"Neither am I. But I'm heading back to DC with Eleanor tomorrow," said Jackson, as he slowed for the traffic in front of them. "So maybe I can dig one up for you."

"Oh," said Dominque, trying not to sound annoyed. "I wanted you on Sunday. Max is having man-friend withdrawals now that he's not in the Marshals anymore."

"I think we'll be back for Sunday dinner," said Jackson. "And I think Max and Aiden were doing some sort of MMA thing next week too."

"Mmm," said Dominique. She didn't approve of her brother's MMA habit. "He'd better not bring Max home with a black eye or something."

"Dude, your man can handle himself," said Jackson. "Aiden wants to sponge wrestling tips off of him. Stop getting all Eleanor-faced."

"That is mean," she said, but Jackson only chuckled unrepentantly.

"Speaking of your man," said Jackson, and Dominique felt a chill of unease as Jackson looked around her, ostensibly checking the street before turning. "What's up with your oven? Is it desperately in need of cleaning or what?"

"He told you about that?" Dominique felt herself turning pink. Embarrassment and shame flooded up from her stomach, and she felt hot all over.

"He said he'd been trying to put a ring on it, but you seem to be having some sort of oven cleaning, party-planning fetish."

"Why do you have to pry into everything?" she demanded, knowing her voice sounded shrill.

"I don't know. Why did you lie to me?" Jackson replied as he pulled up in front of her building. "You said he hadn't even talked about marriage."

"I don't want to talk about this," she said, fumbling for the door handle and her purse. The meeting papers scattered everywhere, falling into the leg area. She snatched at them as Jackson reached onto the console next to him and clicked a button. She grabbed all her bits and pulled the door handle, but it clunked uselessly in her hand. She flipped the unlock switch and reached for the handle again. There was a second clunk, and Jackson relocked the door.

"Did you just lock me in the car?" she demanded, rounding on her cousin.

"Nika, breathe."

"No, screw you. I'm not doing this!"

"No, I'm serious. You're freaking me out. Please stop and breathe for like ten seconds."

"While you try and talk to me? I don't need you to talk to me!"

"I will stop talking if you start breathing."

Dominique glared at her favorite cousin, and he stared back without saying a word. She loudly inhaled through her nose and then exhaled through her mouth.

"I should have had garlic for lunch," she said, exhaling in his direction. He said nothing and shrugged. She repeated the breaths, and by the third, she felt better. By the fifth, she felt less hot and weird.

"I don't want to talk about it," she said after the sixth. "Can I go now?"

"Are you going to talk to Max about it? What's up? If you want to break up, I think you need to start saying something."

The words stabbed at her heart. Dominique dropped everything to put her hands over her mouth, trying to hold back the tears, but her eyes promptly welled up and spilled over. Dominique gave up and sat in Jackson's car and sobbed.

"Nika, what the…" Jackson reached over and pulled her into a hug.

"I love him so much," she gasped into his shoulder between strangled breaths.

"OK?" He patted her back

"I don't know what's wrong with me!" she wailed.

"OK. Uh… Let's just get the basics out of the way. You love Max?"

"Yuh." She knew the word was muffled by his coat, but she didn't want to move.

"You don't want to break up?"

"Nuh."

"OK. So that's good because Max has recently also said *yuh* about you. So you do want to get married?"

"Nuh. Yuh." She said again, then wailed in frustration.

"You don't want to get married, but you don't want to break up?" Jackson sounded like he was just guessing.

Dominique turned her head to one side and took in a large breath of oxygen. "I had a panic attack."

"When?"

"Last week at work," she said. "Aiden called about something. And then Max called, and we were talking, and we hung up, and I looked at my calendar, and then I thought I was going to die. And one of the nerds at work told me what it was and said he takes anxiety medication, and now he doesn't have them anymore. But I don't want to take medication. I'm totally fine. I am fine."

She pushed away from Jackson and sat up, swiping at her eyes.

"Fine," she said, smiling.

"Uh-huh." Jackson took out his phone and hit one of the favorites in his contact list.

"Hey," said Evan picking up as Jackson put the call on speaker. "Did Nika and Max decide to come with? I need to pull out more wine if they're coming to dinner too."

"No, Nika needs an evening in. And also, I need permission to talk to your therapist."

"Oh, Jesus, what did I do now?"

"Nothing. I need to ask your therapist for a recommendation for Nika or whether or not she'd be comfortable seeing Nika. I can find others, but she's the best one I know."

"I am fine," said Nika. "I don't need a therapist."

"Nika's having panic attacks."

"Nika! Shit. I'm coming over."

"I'm fine!" Dominique slapped her hand up to her face, trying to hide from both of them even though Evan couldn't see her. "I'm not having one now. Does everyone have to know about this?"

"Yes! Of course, we need to know!" said Evan. "How else are we supposed to help?"

"I don't need help. I'm dealing with it. Myself."

Evan's laugh was so perfectly reminiscent of his old derisive self that Dominique groaned.

"Yeah, because that works soooooo well," said Evan.

"I'm not sure sarcasm is the helpful tack to take here," said Jackson.

"It's certainly not something my therapist recommends," agreed Evan. "She recommends way more helpful strategies for dealing with anxiety. And as a result, see how I barely even made fun of Aiden at your party?"

Dominque found herself reluctantly laughing.

"And since you're probably just having some sort of mild issue, she'll actually be able to fix *you*," Evan continued. "So you should talk to her."

"I don't want…." Dominique couldn't figure out what she wanted. But she knew she didn't want to be thinking about this. She wanted everything back to normal.

"Don't want what?" demanded Evan. "People to think you're broken?"

"Hey!" snapped Dominique. "I have never said that. I believe in therapy. I just don't think I need it. I'm sure this will go away."

"No," said Jackson. "It will get worse. Hasn't it gotten worse already? You cleaned an oven, Nika."

"Does she even know how to clean an oven?" asked Evan, sounding confused.

"No," said Dominique. "I don't. That didn't stop me from trying. I just sprayed stuff in there and scrubbed at it. I probably made it worse. I don't know. It seemed like a productive way to deal with things at the time."

"Yeah, I also thought drugs sounded productive," said Evan. "You know what's more productive? Getting help."

"I'll call tomorrow," said Jackson.

"I already texted," said Evan. "She says she can give you a four o'clock appointment if you want to come in and talk about what kind of help you want."

"I…" Dominique looked at her cousin, and Jackson smiled. "You're not going to unlock the car until I agree, are you?"

"I mean, I'm not saying I would hold you prisoner forever, but… I will DoorDash food to the car."

Dominique let out a frustrated breath and swiped at her cheeks again. She probably looked like a disaster.

"Fine. I will go if only to shut the two of you up."

"Works for me," said Jackson.

"Completely fine with that," agreed Evan.

"You're fine with being jerks?" she demanded, even though she knew the answer.

"Yes." Their answer was in unison.

"You won't tell Grandma, will you?"

"Of course not," said Jackson. "Who do you think you're dealing with here?"

"Sorry, I just… I feel like Grandma will put me on injured reserve if she finds out, and I can do all the things. I'm just having one little issue."

"Injured reserve?" repeated Evan.

"Football," said Jackson.

"Well, there's your issue. Stop watching football."

"You're such a dork," she said. "Oh, I meant to ask Olivia if she wanted to look at wedding dress stuff on Sunday?"

"Uh…" said Jackson. "Are we sure that's a good idea?"

"I just said I can do the things!" said Dominique fiercely. "And I am happy for Evan and Olivia." She glared at Jackson.

"Well, Olivia did say she was delighted to have your help," Evan said, but she could hear the new Evan in how he spoke. He was making a measured response, but at least he wasn't flat-out telling her *no*. Dominique took a deep breath, feeling relieved. She didn't think she could stand if the family started tip-toeing around her.

"But we *will* be hiring a wedding planner because neither of us is psychotic, and you know Grandma is going to make it a thing."

"I know several wedding planners that would do wonderfully. I will send you an email. And I have been making progress on the wedding dress. Although, really, I don't think the House of Amery will do. I didn't care for the way he treated his employees."

On Evan's side of the line, a door slammed. "Did Nika talk to Max?" chirped Olivia. "Are they coming to dinner?"

"No, they're staying in," said Evan. "Nika was asking about your wedding dress."

"Is she on the phone?" There was a muffled rustling. "You can't find anything, can you?" Olivia demanded, her voice doubling in volume and worry.

"I've narrowed it down to three designers."

"Really?" Olivia squeaked excitedly.

"I have pictures. I was going to see if you had time to talk on Sunday."

Olivia breathed out a gusty sigh of relief. "I'm so lucky. Ya'll know I cannot be doing this on my own."

"Of course, I'm helping you," promised Dominique. She felt her shoulders drop and took another breath. "We'll look at pictures on Sunday at dinner." Sunday dinner was always good these days. Everything would be fine there.

"Yay! I am handing Evan's phone back to Evan now."

"Thanks," said Evan drily. "Jackson, are you on your way over?"

"Yeah," agreed Jackson. "See you in a few."

He hung up and looked at Dominique. "You don't mind helping them jump the broom, but with Max, you want to clean the oven?"

Dominique looked at him helplessly. "If I could explain it, I wouldn't be going to see Evan's therapist tomorrow."

"I'll send a car for you," he said. "I know you don't usually drive into work."

"You don't have to," she said, knowing he was going to anyway. "I can take a cab."

"Yeah," he agreed. "But it'll be easier if we do it my way."

"I also don't mind helping you manage Aiden, Evan, and Grandma, but I have to say I'm not a fan of it when it's me."

He nodded, but a quicksilver smile flashed over his face—gone almost before she saw it.

"Good thing I don't have to do it very often, then."

"I really am fine."

He nodded again. "Yeah. Deveraux women don't know when to quit."

"Pretty sure that's all of us, not just the women," she said tartly. "Open the door, please."

He flicked the lock button, and she pulled the handle. "Have fun in DC," she said, getting out.

"I think we're going to the Waffle House," he said.

Dominique burst out laughing. "Oh, my God. I'm dying. Grandma at a Waffle House. Like that would ever happen." She got out of the car, still chuckling. "Thanks! I needed a laugh," she said, bending down to look back into the car. She felt stupid for crying on Jackson, but Evan was right. Now that it was out in the open, she felt lighter. "See you Sunday!"

Her family might be weird, but at least they could be counted on to help her. She glanced back at Jackson, still waiting at the curb to make sure she got in the door. It hadn't always been that way. Once upon a time —before Jackson—she would have been alone. But not anymore. She waved again, he waved back, and she went into her building feeling better than she had in a while.

Jackson

The Waffle House

"I don't like this," said Jackson, eyeing Waffle House.

"There's nothing wrong with a Waffle House. They are a bastion of safety and normalcy across the American South," said Eleanor.

"I'm not talking about the Waffle House," said Jackson. "Waffle Houses are fine. Kind of weird, but fine."

"Weird? What is weird about a Waffle House?" demanded Eleanor. "They were fine dining when I was growing up."

"They have their own record label. I don't like my food also making music." Eleanor gave him a look. "What? We don't have Waffle Houses in Chicago. I had to look this shit up, and now I'm uncomfortable with what I've found out. I'm sticking with Denny's."

"Denny's is not comparable in either service or history."

"Like you've ever eaten at a Denny's."

"Admittedly not in at least forty years," said Eleanor. "But I have actually eaten at one. Waffle House is better. Meanwhile, this is not addressing the question or getting us closer to an answer."

"The question of why would Ralph Taggert ask for a meeting at a Waffle House? The solution is simple, I'll just go in and punch him until he answers."

"The question is: why would Ralph Taggert ask for a meeting? The Waffle House is obvious. He likes the Waffle House and thinks I'll hate it."

Jackson had to admit that Eleanor was probably right. "All right," he said with a sigh. "I guess we're doing this."

He got out of the car and then went around to open Eleanor's door. Jackson was dressed casually—very casually by Deveraux standards—but as he looked around the parking lot full of trucks and beat-up cars, he guessed that even in his jeans, he still looked dressed up. He glanced at the front door, where Mateo Garcia was loitering, sitting on the hood of a red Ford Taurus. He was checking his phone. Jackson knew that meant everything was fine. If Mateo had been behind the wheel, Jackson wouldn't have bothered getting out of the car. He hadn't told Eleanor that he'd had three people in place at the Waffle House since this morning. She hated having a security team. She preferred his illusion that she just went places and everything was fine.

Eleanor was dressed in what Jackson thought of as her weekend attire: slacks, flats, and a cotton print top that went well under a jacket or, in this case, a cardigan. Today, she had made zero concessions to the Waffle House dress code. Jackson opened the door for her, and she walked through as if Waffle House's were her usual Saturday brunch spot.

"He's in the main room in the back booth," said Jackson.

"Hello and welcome to the Waffle House!" chirped the hostess. "Can I seat you?"

"No, thank you," said Eleanor, smiling at the young woman. "We're meeting someone, and I believe he's got our seats warmed up for us. Hopefully, he ordered us some hashbrowns already too."

The hostess laughed. "I don't know. My father always says never order for a woman if she hasn't left written instructions and sometimes not even then."

Eleanor laughed. "My father used to say something similar. We'll just have to see what advice Ralph's father gave him."

The hostess beamed. Jackson always marveled at these moments. Eleanor was not an emotive woman, yet she had the knack for making people feel seen. The next group came in, and Eleanor moved away, following Jackson's instructions to find Ralph. Jackson passed Devonte without making eye contact. Eleanor had seen him at least once, but he trusted that she wouldn't say anything even if she recognized him.

Ralph was taking up a large portion of the booth, with his back to the wall. He'd laid out his suit jacket on the bench next to him and was addressing a stack of waffles in front of him.

"Well, hello, Ralph," said Eleanor sitting down and sliding over to make room for Jackson. It made Jackson's neck itch to have his back to the rest of the room, but having his team in place made it moderately acceptable.

"Eleanor," said Ralph, finishing his bite and running his tongue over his teeth. Ralph was a wide-bellied man who wore suspenders and was currently sporting a mustache. Jackson couldn't say he cared for it. It looked small on his face.

"Hi Ralph," said Jackson.

"That's Mr. Taggert to you," said Ralph, pointing his fork at Jackson. "I don't like you."

"Don't be grumpy, Ralph," Eleanor said, placing her purse beside Ralph's jacket. "It starts us out on the wrong note." She raised her hand and waved at the waitress.

"You shouldn't have brought him," said Ralph sourly.

"Well, he's never been to a Waffle House before," said Eleanor. "I have to give him new experiences."

"I would have thought being out of prison would be enough," snapped Ralph.

"I believe freedom as a United States citizen includes the right to waffles."

Ralph stared at Eleanor in consternation while Jackson bit the side of his tongue to stop laughing. Eleanor had sounded precisely like Dominique. It was just that when Eleanor did it, no one could tell if she was joking or not.

"Hey folks," said the waitress, pulling a pad out of her apron without making eye contact. "What can I get you?"

"I'll have a single Pecan waffle with a side of hashbrowns, scattered, smothered, and covered, please," said Eleanor. She hadn't looked at the menu. Jackson assumed that she'd either prepped up for the meeting by looking online or was ordering from childhood memory.

"Sure thing. Anything to drink with that?"

"Just some coffee. Decaf, please."

"No problem. What about you, hon?" the waitress turned to Jackson.

Jackson glanced at the menu in front of him and picked the first thing that jumped out at him. "All-Star Breakfast. Two eggs, over-easy, whole wheat toast, and I guess I'll try the country ham."

"It's an extra buck. That OK?"

"Yes," said Jackson. "Just water to drink."

"You got it," said the waitress and left.

"Didn't think you'd care for this locale," said Ralph, eyeing Eleanor in annoyance.

"What's wrong with a Waffle House?" asked Eleanor, looking around with an expression that was too innocent. Jackson could tell that she was having fun putting Ralph in his place.

"I thought it might be a little too plebian for your tastes."

"No, it's too full of calories, but you can't really say no to the hashbrowns, can you?"

"I never could," said Ralph. Jackson restrained himself from commenting, but it was hard work. "Don't bust a button over there," said Ralph, eyeing Jackson. "You might as well say whatever you're thinking."

"No, sir," said Jackson, who, despite an entire life of evidence stacked against him, knew how to stay out of trouble.

"Uh-huh," said Ralph.

"Ralph, as much as I enjoy the Waffle House," said Eleanor, "I do have to ask why we're here. Instead of, say… at the office. It's enough to make one think you didn't want people to see us speaking."

"Well, you'd be right on that," said Ralph. "I dislike people knowing that we know each other."

"Yes, I imagine so," said Eleanor. "Democrats are so much worse than mistresses when it comes to the press."

"Sarcasm doesn't become you," he said sternly.

"That wasn't sarcasm," said Eleanor.

The two eyed each other, and Jackson had to admit that when it came to confrontations like this, Eleanor was ballsier than he ever would be.

"Although, apparently, that situation is about to become un-avoidable," said Ralph, and Eleanor raised an eyebrow. "How's the wedding planning coming? I heard that our two lovebirds were en-gaged. Hadn't seen it in the paper yet, though."

Jackson turned Ralph's words over in his mind. It was well-known that Olivia and Evan were dating. Eleanor said it had be-come something of a joke on the Senate floor. He wasn't surprised that Ralph knew—Olivia had told her siblings and father, so it was sure to get back to her grandparents at some point. The engagement could not be what had Ralph meeting them in a Waffle House.

"We haven't announced their engagement yet," said Eleanor. "They're still discussing dates, and I thought it might be better to announce after Congress goes on break. It will be nice in my Christmas newsletter."

Jackson frowned at Eleanor. That was far more information than he would have shared with the Senator.

"Meaning that you're still hoping to talk them out of it," said Ralph, slicing into his waffle with vicious strokes.

"Oh, no," said Eleanor. "I love Olivia. She is absolutely the sweetest girl. I cannot imagine anyone making Evan happier. I don't look forward to being related to you, of course, but considering that Olivia is maintaining her policy of not talking to you with a side order of periodically telling you to drop dead… I think I'll manage."

Eleanor ended with a devastatingly sweet smile. Ralph opened his mouth to make a rebuttal, but the waitress returned to pour Eleanor's coffee just then, and Ralph had to stop. Jackson guessed that Eleanor, who had a clear line of sight to the coffee station, had timed it that way on purpose.

"Thank you, dear," said Eleanor, beaming at the waitress. The waitress looked as though it was the first time someone had said *thank you* all day.

"You're welcome," she said with a smile as she left.

"I want that to change," said Ralph, sitting back against the pleather bench, leaving his cutlery on the plate.

"Want what to change?" asked Eleanor, raising an eyebrow.

"Her not talking to us," said Ralph. "Her grandmother is upset."

"Oh, you mean she blames you?" asked Jackson, and Ralph glared at him.

"You need to fix that," he said, ignoring Jackson and turning back to Eleanor.

"Not a chance in hell," said Eleanor, and for the first time,

Jackson heard what he thought of as Iron Eleanor come through in her voice.

"She's my granddaughter," said Ralph. "She needs to pick up the phone."

"She doesn't need to do anything," said Eleanor. "She's perfectly happy as she is."

"Well, I ain't," snapped Ralph. "It's one thing to not get along in private. I don't care if she hates me from here 'till the Resurrection. But I know you. You're going to put on a big shindig for that wedding."

"Yes," agreed Eleanor. "I'm fairly certain I can get at least one past president."

"And how is it going to look if I'm not there?" demanded Ralph.

"Like she hates your guts," said Eleanor, smiling and stirring creamer into her coffee.

"I don't know what happened to that girl. She went to college, and she got all kinds of crazy."

"Yeah, it's almost like she figured out she doesn't have to take your bullshit," said Jackson.

"Shut your pie-hole," said Ralph. "You're not involved in this."

"Yes, I am," said Jackson. "I'm Olivia's appointed representative. She didn't like that you were meeting Eleanor. She thought it was suspicious."

"You told her?" demanded Ralph, looking outraged.

"Yes," said Jackson.

"You got a loose trap."

"Ha!"

Both men looked at Eleanor in surprise. "Sorry," she said. "I just don't think anyone's ever accused Jackson of that. I'm amused. Regardless, I cannot and will not make any efforts to put you on speaking terms with your granddaughter. I'm not a certified family counselor, and I have no wish to involve myself in any of your messes."

The waitress returned and set down plates in front of Eleanor and Jackson. The massive dish of food in front of Jackson had almost certainly been cooked in a vat of oil. It was precisely the kind of food he didn't get at Deveraux House. Theo believed in healthy meals.

"I may have to retract my earlier statement," said Jackson, inspecting the hashbrowns.

"I dislike saying *I told you so*," said Eleanor cutting into her waffle for a tiny bite. "It's unbecoming. But regarding Denny's versus the Waffle House, I will *not* hesitate."

"What? Son, get your head out of your ass. There is no comparison. The Waffle House is by far superior."

"You see now why I had to bring him," said Eleanor, and Jackson watched as Ralph wavered between agreeing with her and still hating Jackson.

"Well, I don't see why you had to do it on my time," complained Ralph.

"As though there were a better time," said Eleanor. "Now, Ralph, I don't wish to be disagreeable, but no, I will not be interceding between you and Olivia. I suggest you try speaking to one of your relatives who like you. If you have those."

Ralph glared at her. "You're going to make sure I get invited to that wedding."

"That seems unlikely," said Eleanor.

"But you're going to do it because I've got something you always want."

"I don't like to underestimate you," said Eleanor, taking a sip of coffee. "But I must admit that you having anything I want, let alone knowing what I want, also seems unlikely."

"Information," said Ralph.

"Ah," said Eleanor. "What kind and from who?"

"Two years ago, homeland security pulled those mercenaries out of testifying against Granger. You ever wonder about that?"

"I must admit that I did," agreed Eleanor.

"And you may have noticed that the release of the Absolex hearing files has suddenly become... slow to materialize."

"I had," agreed Eleanor. She watched Ralph with her coffee cup in one hand and her head slightly tilted to one side with a smile on her face. Anyone watching would have thought she was merely politely listening to an old friend. But Jackson could tell that Ralph had captured her complete focus.

"The wedding," said Ralph. "I can expect an invitation?" Ralph sat back, his chin rising, watching the two of them.

Eleanor looked at Jackson. Jackson nodded. Olivia had been clear on the list of items she was willing to negotiate. Attending the wedding was on the list. He thought it was because she wanted her grandmother there, not for Ralph's sake.

"You may," said Eleanor.

"Just on his say so," asked Ralph, his mustache bristling skeptically.

"He *is* Olivia's representative," said Eleanor, with a shrug. "I assume they have discussed matters."

"I do *not* understand your family," said Ralph, shaking his head.

"Very few people do," said Eleanor. Ralph reached into his jacket and retrieved a piece of paper. He slid it across the table, and Eleanor unfolded it. It was a printout of a photo that Ralph had clearly snapped with his phone.

"This turned up in one of my committee meetings," said Ralph.

"Who submitted it?" asked Eleanor, handing the photo to Jackson. Jackson looked at the memo asking that the Absolex files not be released, per the request of the Ethics Committee.

"The right and honorable Senator Griffeth from New Jersey. Which, coincidentally, is where J.P. Granger voted from, wasn't it?"

"Griffeth also sits on the security committee, doesn't she?" asked Jackson.

"Yes, she does," said Ralph. "You got problems, Eleanor. Someone doesn't want those files released."

"And what do you care about our problems?" asked Jackson.

"J.P. Granger sold medication to the V.A. that resulted in a forty percent increase in suicide," said Ralph, and Jackson saw a spark of righteous wrath behind the fat and mustache. "Suicide is a sin, and pushing our veterans into it, that's the devil's work. Granger is roasting in hell right now, but someone out there is trying to cover up the blood on their hands. I may hate you like a plague of boils, and I may think you're trying to capitalize on this for your own ends, but I'm not going to be a part of that."

"Ralph," said Eleanor, and he tore his eyes off Jackson to look at her, "I don't believe that either of us is confused by our relationship. We don't like each other."

"You're arrogant and elitist," said Ralph.

"And you are hypocritical and intentionally ignorant," replied Eleanor. "And I would go so far as to say that we do not have a sense of shared trust."

"If that's a fancy way of saying I don't trust you further than I can throw a heifer, then yes."

"It is. But," Eleanor leaned forward in her seat, fixing Ralph with a hard stare, "I have never doubted that you thought some things were bigger than politics. The list may be short, but I know you have it. And I also know that those of you clinging to such lists are facing hard times within your party."

"Moderates are gone," complained Ralph. "I used to be considered extreme, but that ain't exactly the case anymore."

"Well, I just want you to know that should this situation blow up on us," said Eleanor, "I will most certainly blame you."

Jackson felt shocked that Eleanor would announce that, and Ralph sat back in his chair, looking stunned.

"Well, thank you, Eleanor. I appreciate that."

Jackson blinked and then realized that he'd misunderstood the conversation. In the event of the situation going tits up, the best protection for Ralph was to have a democrat blame him for everything. It would almost certainly look like Eleanor was grandstanding and trying to scapegoat Ralph. If the left hated him, he would become a hero of the right.

"Our political system was designed for compromise. Without it, we're treading water at best. There should be no complete victories for one side. Everyone should walk out of the room mildly annoyed."

Ralph laughed, his belly bouncing against the edge of the table.

"There must be ways for us to reach across the aisle," she continued. "And if those ways are at the Waffle House, then I, for one," she paused to spear a forkful of hashbrowns, "am willing to suffer through that." She popped the hashbrowns into her mouth and smiled in satisfaction.

Ralph laughed again, and the waitress smiled at them as she passed by.

"I'll keep that in mind," Ralph said, picking up his own fork.

Jackson waited until they were in the car and heading back to the office before asking Eleanor anything.

"You want me to start looking into who's blocking the release of the Absolex files?" he asked.

"No," she said firmly. "It's a political issue. There isn't any point in getting you involved. I'm sure my staff can handle it."

Jackson wasn't so sure, but he switched topics anyway.

"Do you believe what you told Ralph? About our political system being designed for all-around annoyance."

"Yes," said Eleanor. "My basic job is to be a negotiator for my clients—the people of New York. I'm supposed to do everything in my power to achieve what is in their best interests. However, in general, I'm not supposed to get it. Ask any negotiator, and they'll say the same. You're supposed to compromise. But compromise doesn't sell in thirty-second Tik-Tok videos or whatever is popular this week. Although, at the moment, the more important question is whether or not Ralph believes that I believe it, and I think if we can manage to send him an invite to the wedding, he will."

She looked pointedly at Jackson.

"Olivia agreed to it," said Jackson. "She said you would probably think it was optically better for everyone anyway. I think she meant the optics were better. Political jargon still eludes her."

"Politics elude her," said Eleanor. "Never mind the jargon."

"True, but she's figured out a few things. She said she wasn't sure how, but not having Ralph at the wedding would somehow end up looking bad for you and Evan."

"She's right. It will look like I'm punishing my political enemies at the expense of my new daughter-in-law. I'll look like a bitch."

"Then why didn't you say anything?" asked Jackson.

"Because Ralph is abusive and manipulative, and I don't think Olivia should have to deal with him on her wedding day. And besides, my bitch reputation will not be diminished by having him there. It will only remain at its current levels. I didn't think it was worth it."

"She said it would probably make her father more comfortable anyway," added Jackson. "And I think she wants her grandmother there."

"Her father seems like a sweet man with the backbone of a feather boa," said Eleanor. "How fortunate that Olivia inherited Ralph's determination yet none of his mannerisms."

"Uh… Hadn't really thought about it like that," said Jackson, who hadn't considered that any of Olivia was anything like Ralph.

"Abusers have good traits, too," said Eleanor. "That's how they get people to stay with them."

There was a world of experience behind that statement, and had he been talking to any of his cousins, Jackson thought he might have been able to take the conversation further. But it was Eleanor, and getting her even this far was a minor miracle.

Caitlin

Threats

Caitlin opened the door and stood on the doorstep, staring into her bag, trying to assess if she had remembered everything.

"Katie," said Jamal gently, from his usual spot under the overhang. "That's not safe. You gotta stare into your purse inside the house. Don't do it here. Always have your head up out here."

Katie looked at her thirteen-year-old neighbor, intending to assure him that she was fine and there was nothing wrong with looking in her purse, but the words died in her throat. She knew he was right and felt incredibly sad that they both had to know that.

"I left my extra socks upstairs." It was in no way a response to what he'd just said.

"Better go grab them," he said with a smile. Jamal was gangly from a recent growth spurt, and his wrists stuck out of all of his shirts.

She went back inside and up the narrow stairs into her apartment. She liked to change her socks mid-shift. It was a silly thing, but it gave her an excuse for a break and put a little extra life in her feet. She looked in her room and then out in the living room. She had done laundry and then… Where the hell had she put them? If she didn't find them soon, she would miss her train.

She stared in frustration at the oversized sectional couch that she hadn't been able to sell but had been a complete bitch to get up the stairs. She knew it retailed for over four grand, but she also knew that she would probably leave it here if she ever moved out. She couldn't afford to move it. It was like a metaphor for her entire life. She used to be worth something, but now she was just left behind like scraps.

She finally found the socks wedged between the lift-top ottoman where she shoved everything she hated and the couch seat. She barely made eye contact with the ottoman these days. Someday she would have to go with the ever-growing and ever more frightening pile of paperwork inside, but today was not that day. She dropped the socks in her purse and went back down the stairs to her door but didn't open it. Following Jamal's advice, she stared once more into the depths of her bag, checking to see that she had everything.

"Hey! Kid!"

Caitlin froze at the sound of the aggressive male voice right outside her door. Instinctively, she looked at the door. The deadbolt wasn't turned. She'd left it unlocked while she looked for her socks. Another stupid decision.

"I'm looking for someone."

The voice had a Russian accent, although the words were clear. Cautiously, Caitlin tip-toed to the door and peered through the peephole. Distorted by the fish-eye of the lens, Caitlin could see a broad-shouldered, thick-necked man with sandy hair. He walked past the door, going closer to Jamal, and Caitlin fumbled in her bag for her phone. If he laid a finger on Jamal, she would… She didn't know what she would do. Why didn't she have some kind of weapon handy?

"I don't answer questions for free," said Jamal, and Caitlin winced. Jamal was always on the hustle, but she hoped it wouldn't bite him in the ass this time.

"I got cash. You tell me if there is a girl here."

"Lots of girls, but I ain't a pimp. Try two blocks over."

"No, I'm looking for specific girl. Caitlin St. Cloud."

"Huh. Yeah, I don't know anyone named Caitlin," said Jamal.

"You sure? Maybe she uses Katie."

"Sorry," said Jamal. "There's a Michaela two doors up." Caitlin was impressed. Jamal sounded so honest.

"But at this address. Maybe there is some other girl?"

"Nah," said Jamal.

They were just out of view of her peephole. She could only see the Russian's back, and her hand tightened into a fist as he reached into his back pocket. She relaxed when she saw it was cash but then tensed again. Jamal's family was as broke as she was.

The Russian held out the money. "You're sure?"

"I should take your cash," said Jamal, "but honestly, man, there ain't no one living here named Caitlin. There's just old lady Carpetti. Someone was living upstairs, but they just moved out. I don't know who. They worked nights a lot."

The Russian grunted and was about to put the bills away, but then he seemed to reconsider. "If you find anything out about the one who moved. Call me." He wrapped a twenty around a business card and stuffed it into Jamal's shirt.

"What'd this Caitlin chick do anyway?" asked Jamal. "Key your car?"

"Mind your own business," snapped the Russian and walked back across the street to a large black SUV.

Jamal waited until the SUV left and then knocked cautiously on her door. Caitlin opened it with a shaking hand.

"Are you OK?" she asked.

"Yeah, I'm fine," said Jamal. "Are you?"

"People think I owe them a lot of money," said Caitlin. "It wasn't me. I didn't have anything to do with it, but they still think I owe."

Jamal nodded. "He looked like a loan shark. Do you want me to text you if I see him around again?"

Caitlin nodded. "Let me know, but don't… Don't put yourself on the line, Jamal. I'm serious. These are bad people."

"I'm not crazy, but if I see something, I'll text."

"Thanks, Jamal," said Caitlin. "I'm working a wedding today. I'll bring you home some cake."

Jamal grinned. "That's the kind of bribe I like."

Jackson
THE DETECTIVE'S KID

Jackson leaned against the wall and nursed a vodka and soda. The Capitol Hill parties were not parties. They were work events where everyone hoped someone else drank too much and said the wrong thing. They were a competitive sporting event for extroverts. Eleanor, who had spent years training for such events by being married to an abusive husband, was hands down champ of the ring, but Jackson wasn't in fighting shape. He invariably just ended up being rude to someone and walking away. Which at least upheld the Deveraux reputation for assholery but wasn't particularly helpful.

"Found you," said Hannah Nowitsky. She had brown hair and the Capitol Hill intern's uniform of awkward business attire, but at barely twenty, she had a mature presence that Jackson knew many found intimidating. Jackson also knew that she had inherited it and her no-nonsense attitude from her police detective father. Detective Nowitsky had been willing to work with Jackson on a few occasions in return for letters of recommendation from Eleanor to get Hannah into Brown. Hannah wasn't wasting the opportunity. She interned for Eleanor on breaks and was rocking a 3.9 GPA. She was also paying dividends by informing on Eleanor's staff to Jackson.

"There's a lot of red in the room tonight," said Jackson.

"Yeah," said Hannah. "I need to talk to you about that."

"Kay," said Jackson, taking a sip, but neither of them moved. Jackson enjoyed that Hannah had already learned that sudden movement attracted attention. His phone buzzed in his pocket, and he took it out and glanced at the face.

CAN I CALL YOU?

Jackson thumbed a reply to Aiden.

G‌IVE ME A HALF HOUR.

Aiden sent back a thumbs up.

"Who's that guy?" asked Jackson, jerking his chin toward a round-faced man in his thirties. He had been scurrying around the party. "I can't tell who he's with."

Hannah looked around, and Jackson watched her lip curl in silent disgust.

"That guy. That guy is Dennis Houge. He is a *Good Guy*." She put air quotes around *good guy*. "And he'll tell you that if you give him half a chance. When I first got here, he cornered me at one of these parties and spent five minutes warning me off someone while telling me that I was lucky to have bumped into him because he's one of the good ones and how I should have another drink. Like what? I've never been to a frat party? Does he think I haven't heard that shit before? And seriously, am I supposed to fall for it coming out of his face because he's wearing a suit? And I'm not supposed to notice that he's, like, double my age? Fuck that guy. I can find fifty guys who look better in suits and a hundred and ten who look better out of it. He is exactly the guy my dad is scared I'll meet here. You know he tries that shit on every new intern. I bet he even fucking believes his own horseshit and that getting drunk is consent. He's exactly the guy that needs a knuckle sandwich in the teeth and a boot in the fucking taint."

Jackson started to laugh halfway through her rant and continued until tears began to squeeze out of his eyes.

"Sorry," said Hannah stopping and taking a sip from her glass. "I may have strong opinions on douchebags."

"It's fine," said Jackson, still chuckling. "I was just having flashbacks to your dad."

"Yeah, *boot up the taint* is one of his favorites. Anyway, Mr.

Houge currently works for Senator Yamira. They say he's been around since he was an intern, though, with one senator or another. Which I believe because all his lines sound like they haven't changed since then." Hannah paused, scrutinizing the aforementioned douchebag. "Why? What's he doing that's bugging you?"

"He talks to too many people," said Jackson. "He's one of the few that crosses party lines without taking a friend with them. Most people take a buddy with them if they talk to the opposite party. Particularly on the Republican side. I think they want witnesses. He's talking to that Senator whose name I can't remember over there now, but he was talking to one of Eleanor's staffers a minute ago."

"That's Senator Griffeth. Eleanor wanted her invited tonight particularly. Not sure why.

He scrutinized the Senator. It was just like Eleanor to invite a known enemy to her party. But it showed balls from Senator Griffeth to show up.

Hannah looked around the room and then back at Houge as if tallying how many people she'd seen him talking to. "I guess he is kind of weird now that you mention it. He always acts like that, though, so I never noticed."

"If he's been around that long, it might not mean anything. Will the veranda be good enough for us to talk, or should we take a walk?

"Walk," said Hannah. "I'm going to tell someone you're walking me back to the office. For safety."

Jackson looked her over. He knew damn well she was carrying a cute little Walther PPK under her blazer. Jackson had helped her through all the registration at her father's insistence.

"For safety," he repeated. "OK, James Bond."

Hannah chuckled. "Hey, I don't want to have to actually use it. I'd rather just throw you at some mugger."

"Just like your dad," he said, shaking his head and finishing his drink. Hannah shrugged as if she didn't see the point in arguing.

They crossed the room to where Zoe, Eleanor's Chief-of-Staff, was talking animatedly to someone. Jackson always considered Zoe a political tiger and mostly tried to avoid her. Managing one political woman was enough for him. She got the feeling that she mostly avoided him too, but whether it was because she didn't want to deal with anymore Deverauxes or because she didn't think he was worth talking to, he couldn't tell.

"Hey Zoe, Jackson's going to walk me back to the office."

Zoe looked the two of them over sharply. Jackson tried to figure out if Zoe was suspicious politically or if it was the generalized welfare check to ensure he wasn't sleeping with the intern.

"I was going to finish the filing some of the constituent letters and then lock up the office. Do you want me to text you before I leave?"

"Yeah, that would be great," said Zoe relaxing a fraction.

"Tell Eleanor I'll be back after I get Hannah to the office," said Jackson, then shrugged. "If she asks. Which she won't." He knew that Zoe and Eleanor had spent a good half-hour discussing the Ralph Taggert situation after they'd returned from the Waffle House. He didn't think they'd come to any conclusions either.

"She'll wonder," said Zoe smiling. "See you in a bit."

"What's up?" asked Jackson when they were well away from the building. It was a short walk back to the congressional offices, but the wind nipped in hard and biting, and Hannah pulled her blazer tighter around her.

"OK, here's the deal," she said, after a quick look around, "Eleanor is facing some odd pull back from her party. People are distancing themselves publicly. It's not too bad, but it's not a good sign. We traced to an ongoing ethics investigation, except we're not sure what they're investigating or who made the complaint."

"It's the Absolex Hearings," said Jackson. "We're pretty sure that Senator Griffeth is behind it, or at least driving it."

"But she invited Griffeth…" Hannah trailed off. "Your grandma is so smart. If the complaint was legit, Griffeth wouldn't have come. It might taint the investigation or come across as tampering. But if Griffeth doesn't give a shit about the supposed ethics violation and it's just partisan jockeying, then she would come to the party. Griffeth would also have to be confident that she's got the backing to make whatever it is stick against Eleanor. Eleanor just made her show her hand with a party invite."

"Welcome to the world of Eleanor Deveraux," said Jackson.

"That's some next-level chess," said Hannah, shaking her head. They walked a few more steps in silence, and Jackson waited for Hannah to return to Absolex. He didn't doubt that she would—she was smart.

"But why Absolex?" Hannah asked. "I looked over all those files when I first got here. Interns do the filing," she said to Jackson's questioning expression. "They were interesting, but I didn't see anything that looked complaint worthy. If Griffeth is so confident about the complaint, there must be something there, but what?"

"That is my question as well because I'm pretty sure Eleanor followed the book on that one," said Jackson. "She knew everything had to stand up under the strictest scrutiny. Those hearings were under a national spotlight."

Hannah let out a frustrated sigh, started to speak, and then stopped again.

"Whatever it is, just say it," said Jackson.

"Did Dad ever take you to see a guy named Green Potts?"

"No, but with that name, I wish he had."

"Heh. Green Potts is a snitch over on the West Side. And he will tell you so much stuff for the right money, but and, here's the thing, he will *never* volunteer information. You pay him, and he'll squeal, but that is it. But Dad says if Green shows up and starts telling him stuff for free, then Dad pulls out an extra vest and starts putting everything on tape. Trust nothing the guy says because if Green is sharing information, but *you* haven't paid him…"

"Then you need to be asking who has and why?"

"Exactly. So people are telling us stuff, but it's not the right people. And if I'm reading Eleanor's party invite correctly—the complaint and ethics investigation is mostly bogus, then it just adds to my feeling that someone is trying to maneuver Eleanor. It feels like a set-up. And I can't explain it any better than it's got the Green Potts vibe. Which doesn't exactly carry a lot of weight with Eleanor or my co-workers."

"It carries a lot of weight with me," said Jackson.

"And that's why you're walking me back to the office," said Hannah.

"What's the next step?" he asked.

"What do you mean?" she asked, looking up at him puzzled.

"Well, if this was the street, and I started getting some people coming after me on the right, I'd be expecting an offer from the left. Then someone would say, *let's meet – I can help,* and then I'd be alone in a location I didn't pick, and then I'd be dead."

"Oh," said Hannah. She looked like she was trying to graft that onto her mental map of Washington politics.

"So, we're at the threats portion," said Jackson, breaking it down. He needed her to make the leap for him because he didn't know the DC players well enough. "Are we at the asking for a meeting part? Eleanor and I met with Ralph Taggert today, but I don't think that was it. He's got his own oar in the water. His angle makes sense. But who else is out here swimming around?"

"I don't think we're there yet," said Hannah slowly. "No one has approached us, and Eleanor's not desperate enough to take any offers that come at her. She's got a lot of support that isn't apparent from the surface."

"Then they'll come after the family next," said Jackson. "We were involved in the Absolex thing, and they'll want to make her desperate. Everyone thinks they can get to her through us."

"But they can't?" asked Hannah.

"They can, but it's difficult. And people seem to forget that once they involve the rest of us… well, they've involved the rest of us. And while we may not play chess, we do occasionally play hard ball. And we don't care about politics, so there's that."

"Subpoenas," said Hanna, shoving her hands in her pockets. "The ethics committee will probably issue subpoenas for all of you."

"I'll keep that in mind," he said, nodding.

Jackson waited until she had locked the office door before heading back to the party. He was nearly back when his phone buzzed.

"Hey, Aiden," he said, picking up.

"I can call later," said Aiden, "if you're doing a Grandma thing."

"It's a party I hate," said Jackson, "so whatever."

"I talked to Dominique, and she said guys made her go see Evan's therapist."

"We didn't make her. Evan got her an appointment, and I sent a car. She's having panic attacks."

"No, it's great. I had Jenna pull a list of therapists last week, and I was going to talk to her on Sunday."

"You could have mentioned," said Jackson. "I didn't even know she was having problems."

"Uh, well, it wasn't… It was just a couple of weird fucking conversations, and I wasn't even sure what to say. I needed to go away and think about it. And now I'm not sure if I should say something to the therapist or if I should let stuff take its course."

"Well, what kind of weird conversations?" asked Jackson, puzzled.

"Well, after Evan's trip through the ghosts of Christmas past at the stupid storage unit last year, I thought I should probably go through our parent's stuff and make sure I had all the documents, and you know… also that we didn't have any more secret siblings or something."

Jackson laughed.

"What? Apparently, the Deverauxes do that kind of thing. Anyway, I didn't find anything. My parents were marvelous people whom I will forever bless for being boring as fuck. But I found a bunch of stuff like their wedding certificate and that kind of thing, and I called Dominique to see if she wanted to do anything with it. Their anniversary is coming up in January. They would have been married thirty years if they lived, and I thought that was nice. Anyway, I started talking about it, and Nika literally interrupted me in the middle of a sentence, started talking about Grandma, and then hung up on me. And then she did the same thing when I saw her later in the week."

"What were you talking about then? Same thing?"

"I don't know… Yeah. Maybe. I think I said I'd put all the paperwork in my office safe if she ever wanted it. It was just a passing comment, but the next thing I knew, she'd walked off. It was so not like her. And not even like she was mad at me. Just literally like she'd switched channels in her brain. I've never had her do anything like that. Kind of hurt my feelings to tell the truth. Ella's probably tired of hearing me talk about it, but, I mean, it's kind of trippy that we're older now than they were when they died. I'm still trying to wrap my head around it. And I thought Dominique might get that."

Jackson began to laugh.

"It's not funny," said Aiden.

"No, it really not. But yeah, you should tell the therapist. Max has been trying to get engaged and says she's doing the same thing to him. I'm going to go out on a limb and make a very non-professional diagnosis that, yeah, something in that mess with your parents is fucking with her head. Which is good because that will give them something to target in therapy, but I'm not sure that will immediately fix it."

"Oh," said Aiden. "Well, then, I didn't help her at all by bringing it up. Now I feel bad."

"Nah. She's going to have to talk about it in therapy anyway."

"Good point. I wonder if I should talk about it in therapy?"

"Whatever you need," said Jackson.

"Well, I feel like you should have to go if I go."

"What? How do you figure?"

"Well, you'd be the only one not doing it, and all the Deverauxes do stuff together."

Jackson laughed. "This is how we ended up wearing those stupid hats my first Christmas."

"Yes, it was. I still have that picture on my wall. Makes me laugh. Can't believe Evan won."

"We'll get him next Christmas."

"Goddamn right. I don't think I need therapy. I don't feel like I'm avoiding anything. Maybe I'll just go to a meeting and bring it up there."

"I didn't know you still went to those," said Jackson, surprised.

"Oh, sure. About every six months or so. Or whenever I feel like I need a little tune-up. Keeps my feet on the ground. I figure it can't hurt."

"It really can't," said Jackson, reaching the veranda. Inside, he could see that the crowd had thinned out, and the party was winding down. Senator Griffeth and the *good guy* staffer, Dennis Houge, were lingering close to the door and talking to Zoe. "Anyway," Jackson said, pulling the door open, "I'm going to hang up so I can go inside and stop freezing."

Aiden laughed. "Yeah, sure. I'll ask Evan for contact info on the therapist and maybe send off an email or something. Thanks for talking to me."

"Of course. See you when I get home."

"Yeah, uh… hey, how do you feel about meeting this lawyer I know for a drink?"

"This lawyer you know?" Jackson felt puzzled by the idea that he would want to drink with a lawyer other than Aiden.

"OK, that Ella knows. Who I have seen pictures of and can confirm that she is amazingly hot."

Jackson groaned. "No, Aiden."

"Why not?"

"If I say I don't like lawyers are you going to have to go to an extra meeting?"

"No one likes lawyers. We're like plumbers. We both bill by the hour, and if you're talking to us, chances are something has gone wrong, and whatever it is, the solution will never be cheap. But since we're all human and we all like sex, you should consider that you could be having sex with a hot lawyer and as Ella can tell you, that is fun."

A laugh exploded out of Jackson in surprise.

"Or, here's an even crazier thought, you could form a

meaningful relationship with someone and enjoy spending time with them.”

“I don't have time for a meaningful relationship,” said Jackson. “I have all of you.”

“And we appreciate that, but we also feel like maybe you should take some time off. I'm suggesting it be with a hot lawyer.”

“No, Aiden,” said Jackson firmly, and Aiden sighed gustily. “Fine.”

They hung up, and Jackson looked up and realized that Senator Griffeth had now moved closer to him. Or rather, she had moved closer to the door, and he was blocking it.

“Now let's see…” said the Senator smiling at him. She was a brunette fifty-something who, like Eleanor, rode the line of carefully approachable and attractive. Being a woman in politics looked hard. Figuring out what outfit would alienate the fewest people seemed like a calculation that no one should have to make. “You're Jackson Deveraux. The new arrival to the family.” Her head cocked to the right, and she watched him, waiting to see if her words would annoy him.

“You know, I believe that is *exactly* what is on my business card,” said Jackson, wondering when he would stop being the new guy.

“You have business cards?” She looked amused.

“Yes,” said Jackson, “so I can hand them out and remind people who they're dealing with.”

“I don't generally forget,” said the Senator, but her smile had taken on an icy quality.

Jackson nodded. “Good to hear. Have a nice night,” he said and held open the door.

The senator and her entourage of flunkies went through the door, and Jackson laughed as the wind kicked up, and they all shivered. It was hard to look tough when Mother Nature was against you.

"That might not have been wise," said Zoe.

Jackson shrugged. "People should know better than to talk to me."

NOVEMBER 9

Evan

THAT PLACE DOWN THE STREET

"Evan! Jackson is here! So now you can go do something!"

Evan came out of the living room in response to Olivia's unsubtle bellow. In retrospect, he knew where he'd gone wrong, but he wasn't sure he could dig his way out in five minutes or less, so Jackson sounded like a viable alternative. Jackson was standing in the entryway, looking confused. An entirely reasonable reaction.

"I'll get my coat," said Evan.

"Great!" said Olivia forcefully.

"Uh," said Jackson, looking even more concerned.

"He's getting his coat," Olivia said aggressively.

"He's getting his coat," agreed Jackson leaning away from her.

Evan grabbed his coat from the hall closet and scooped up his wallet and keys. He and Jackson could probably find someplace to go for an hour. He jerked his head and Jackson and stepped into the hall.

"Am I interrupting a fight?" asked Jackson once the door was closed behind them. He looked worried.

"Not really. Olivia is trying to concentrate on a work project, but we don't really have the wall space for her to stare properly." Jackson's head cocked to one side, and an eyebrow went up. "She tapes her notes to the wall. Working on a project involves staring at her notes."

"Ah."

Evan pulled on his coat and tucked away his items.

"So I foolishly suggested that maybe we should consider moving to a larger place, and she said that was an egregious discussion of change while she was attempting to concentrate. Which is clearly true. I don't know what I was thinking."

Jackson laughed. "Plenty of wall space at Deveraux House."

"Why are you weird?" asked Evan. As if he would move back into his childhood home.

"Wasn't trying to be weird, but OK. What if you just bought one of the units next door and blew out a wall?"

Evan buttoned his jacket and then opened his front door again.

"Liv, what if we just bought one of the next-door units and blew out a wall?"

Olivia poked her head around the corner of the living room wall.

"Oh! I like that! Let's do that!"

Evan nodded. "OK, we'll do that. Be back later."

"Love you!" Olivia sounded much happier.

"Love you too!" he called back and shut the door. "I'm assuming you didn't just come over to solve my housing issues?"

"No," said Jackson. "Want to walk down and get a beer from that place down the street?"

Evan stared at his cousin blankly. "There's a place down the street?"

"Yeah, it's like two blocks away? It's been there for at least a year. It looks like some sort of posh place that people like you drink at."

Considering that everyone in the neighborhood was someone like him, that was probably accurate, but Evan still had no clue. "We don't really go out much." Jackson was giving him a look.

Evan shrugged, and Jackson shook his head. Evan didn't know how to explain that he'd lost interest in bars the minute he met

Olivia. He'd never liked them particularly. They were just a location that made it socially acceptable to get wasted and hook up with people. But between therapy and Olivia, he no longer needed bars for anything.

"OK, well, can we go there now?" asked Jackson.

"Sure," said Evan, with a shrug.

"I'm just not sure how I'm the weird one," muttered Jackson.

"Well, I'm older," said Evan. It didn't actually explain anything, but a non sequitur was frequently the only way to win an argument with any of his cousins. This one made Jackson laugh.

They had settled into a booth at what did appear to be an up-scale bar with a nice whiskey selection before Jackson returned to the reason for his visit.

"So, I need your advice," Jackson said, stretching his legs across the space under the table, propping his feet up on the bench seat next to Evan. Evan looked from Jackson's feet to Jackson's face. "Oh, my God, that was a total Eleanor."

"You take that back."

"I'm not taking it back. This isn't even your furniture, and you made the face."

"It's rude!"

"I'm not moving them."

Evan scooted over, giving Jackson's feet more space.

"What do *you* need advice on?" asked Evan, picking up his glass.

"Actually, it's about Eleanor."

Evan put down his drink, untasted.

"Nothing bad," said Jackson, waving away Evan's concern. "I'm just not sure what to do, and I think you'll be able to help."

"Mm," said Evan doubtfully. It was his impression that Jackson managed their grandmother better than anyone else. He wasn't sure how he could help. "What's the problem?"

"Well," said Jackson and shifted in his seat. It was a rare display of discomfort from Jackson, who always looked like he was entirely confident no matter what was happening. "I don't think anyone… I'm pretty sure everyone knows that one of the reasons Eleanor got me out of prison was to keep an eye on all of you."

Evan nodded. One of the things he liked best about Jackson was that Jackson actually said the things that the rest of the family tip-toed around and attempted to bury between looks and polite conversation. It meant that then Evan could address those things head-on.

"She never said, but I always assumed that was the reason. I always thought it was a pretty shitty way to treat all of us, but I guess I see why she did it. I'm sorry, for what it's worth."

Jackson blinked and then shook his head. "Why?"

"We should never have been your responsibility," said Evan.

Jackson shrugged. "You're my family. It's fine. It meant she needed me and that you had to keep me around."

Evan inhaled sharply, angry at their grandmother for putting that into Jackson's head.

"You're our family," said Evan. "This isn't a barter system; you don't have to buy your way in."

Jackson cracked a grin. "I've been around. There's always some kind of cost to join up with a gang. I don't mind."

Evan thought about arguing. He thought about telling Jackson that families didn't work like that. But the plain truth was that their family *did* work like that. Or at least it had before Jackson had come along.

"*Brat moya,* the dues have been rendered. Move on."

Jackson grinned again. "I'm trying to, actually. That's why I'm here."

"What do you mean?"

"Eleanor brought me in for *the children,* as she calls all of you." Evan rolled his eyes, and Jackson chuckled. "And she has indulged my whim for involving myself in her security details and opposition research because it gave me a proper job title and made all of you less suspicious. And, also frankly, because I'm just so damn convenient."

It was Evan's turn to laugh. "Something you work hard at."

"Shh, don't tell anyone that. Never let them see you working."

"That sounds like a Grandma-ism."

"Probably. Anyway, my point is that she's facing some opposition in the Senate. I believe I could help, but she keeps waving me off and saying that her staff is handling it. But her staff is *not* handling it. If they were, we'd know where it was coming from by now. And now we've got someone poking into the Absolex hearings."

"Mm," said Evan, taking a drink and leaning back against the tufted velvet back of the booth. "What do you want to do?"

"I want to look into who in the Senate *now* was connected to the hearings back then. There's been an entire election since then and a lot of turnover. I want to figure out who has an ax to grind and why the hearings would matter to them. And…" Jackson shifted again, "we met with Ralph Taggert."

"What?" growled Evan, feeling the hot flush of rage that hit him every time he thought about Olivia's grandfather.

"I discussed it in advance with Olivia," said Jackson.

"What?" demanded Evan.

"He's probably coming to the wedding."

"No."

"Olivia OK'd it."

"No."

"I mean… yeah. She kind of did."

"That man is abusive. He called her a whore. He tried to blackmail us into breaking up, and I don't want him there."

"Olivia says she'll seat him someplace out of your line of sight, and Dominique says that between her people and my people, he won't make a fuss."

"Dominique has people?"

"She said she could recruit some sort of social babysitters. And I figure if he starts saying too much shit, my guys will take over and just chuck his ass out. Don't worry. You won't even have to think about him. It won't be a thing."

"It's already a thing," growled Evan. It was becoming clear to him that his wedding was not going to be *his* wedding but was going to be an Eleanor Deveraux party. Olivia had said as much and declared that she was fine with it, but Evan wasn't sure he was. On the other hand, that wasn't Jackson's fault. But clearly, Evan would have to circle back around with Olivia before going off in anger. "OK, fine. Why did she OK it? Please tell me you got something useful in exchange?"

"We did. Ralph pointed us toward Senator Griffeth from New Jersey. Says that she's been cockblocking Eleanor on releasing the Absolex files to the public."

"OK," said Evan taking a deep breath and trying to let go of his anger, "fine. At least that's progress. As long as he doesn't actually talk to me, then maybe he can come. So what did you find out about the Senator?"

"Nothing," said Jackson. "Because Eleanor keeps telling me not to investigate."

"But," said Evan. He was having trouble picturing a scenario where he wouldn't call Jackson and ask for his help. "But, I mean… this is what you do. I don't understand. Why? I mean, just… what?"

Jackson laughed.

"I'm serious!"

"Yes, thank you. I appreciate that. After wading through her nonsense, I think she has put me in the *looks after the children* box and not the *looks after Eleanor* box."

"Ah," said Evan. "Yes. That makes sense. I had some of that when I got out of school. She kept telling me I was in charge of the finances, but I swear she didn't take my advice for nearly five years."

"Well, it's been at least five years. What the fuck?" demanded Jackson.

Evan nodded. "It's fine. I'm just going to give you some very Jackson advice."

"I can't tell if I'm looking forward to this or not," said Jackson.

"You're not. You're going to be mad," he predicted. "OK, here it is. Do it anyway. At this point, the only person who doesn't believe that you look after Grandma is… Grandma. She's given you the keys to the kingdom. Her staff all know, respect, and listen to you. Pete, maybe, might think to double-check an order with Grandma, but that's only because he's a cautious son of a bitch. Everyone else wouldn't even blink. I know you've end-run her before. Stop hesitating now."

Jackson took a swallow of his drink and gave Evan a very Deveraux look, which made Evan grin. He loved it when Jackson hadn't seen the answer coming.

"You're right. I'm annoyed that your advice is to be more myself. It's the political stuff, and I usually try to stay out of it. She's got all the wheels within wheels. I don't want to mess up her game."

"Agreed. But digging up dirt isn't going to mess up Grandma's stuff, and it sounds like she needs it."

"I don't know…" Jackson shook his head. "Schrodinger's Cat."

"Do I need to call Olivia for an explanation?" asked Evan. It always amused him when his prison-educated cousin got erudite.

"Observation of a thing changes a thing. Even looking for dirt can stir the waters. But yeah, I think I need to do it. I can't shake the feeling that all of this is connected to Granger and Absolex, and nothing good ever came out of that hornet's nest."

"Agreed," said Evan.

"She may not be able to avoid involving us, though," said Jackson, looking thoughtfully at the ceiling. "Not sure I can wait that long." His cousin had devolved into muttering to himself. Evan found it funny that he now recognized Jackson's internal processing from his time with Olivia.

"How are we going to get involved?" asked Evan, and Jackson blinked at him.

"My inside man—girl, teenager, no, she's twenty now, whatever—at Eleanor's office put forth the theory that whoever is pressing Eleanor will try to use us as leverage. She thought the fastest way to that goal would be for the ethics committee to subpoena all of us."

"We're listening to the inside teenager?" asked Evan skeptically.

"She's smart, and her dad's the police detective I was working with on Ella's dad's case."

"Ah," said Evan, finally connecting the dots. "Ms. Nowitsky, who goes to Brown. She made Grandma's newsletter last spring. Does she work for you, or does she work for Grandma?"

"She interns for Eleanor," said Jackson. "But I'm finding it very convenient to have her there. I might need to make the situation permanent once she graduates. Anyway, if the subpoena's come out, my gloves come off. But I'm not sure I can wait that long."

"Start now and then go public if it happens."

"Good call," said Jackson.

"Tell you what. Pull me a list of your top suspects. I'm pretty damn familiar with Granger's finances at this point. Maybe I can find a financial connection."

Jackson's expression perked up. "That would be helpful. And also, if I get busted by Eleanor, I can blame it on you because you're older."

Evan chuckled. "Nice."

Jackson raised his glass, looking pleased, but on the table, his phone rang. Jackson picked it up and then immediately answered. That was a rarity for Jackson, who usually made family time a priority.

"Yeah, I'm with Evan. No, the bar down the street. What? No. I really don't think—"

Jackson pulled the phone away from his ear, looking annoyed. "I swear there is an epidemic of people not listening to me lately." Evan laughed. Jackson looked up at him, clearly conflicted. "OK, so speaking of things that I think you know, but I haven't actually said."

"What now?" asked Evan. The list really could be endless with Jackson.

"Devonte Miller, the guy you got arrested with—"

Evan rolled his eyes. "Yes, the guy who works for you but pretends to do construction while bodyguarding me and stealing all my stock tips. Do you really think I can't tell when Aiden is trying to keep a secret? Or that I wouldn't notice when Devonte's legal troubles magically went away? It was just as though someone had the Deveraux lawyer pulling all the strings." Evan shook his head. "You're crafty, but I'm not that dumb."

"Sorry," said Jackson looking thoroughly not sorry. "But you wouldn't stop riding the train."

Evan shrugged. "It was clearly the right decision. That bullshit on the train with the skinheads would have been a complete disaster without him."

Evan signaled the waitress for another drink, pointing at his glass and holding up one finger. She nodded, and Evan turned back to Jackson.

"Besides, I'm now luring him away with promises of a stable career where no one punches him."

"Yes, I know, and I'm annoyed about it. Devonte is my top guy, and I provide a very good retirement package. I don't understand how you convinced him to change jobs."

"Like I said, lack of punching. Was there anything else, or do you secretly have someone planted at my office."

"Nah, I just call Olivia when I want to know what's up."

"Hey guys," said Devonte, unwinding his scarf as he approached. He was tall like the Deveraux cousins but built on stockier lines and wore his hair in shoulder-length dreads.

"Hey, D," said Jackson. "What's up?"

"Pete's had a brain wave," said Devonte. "I'm rounding up all the loose ends and getting you to sign off on all the things."

Devonte paused and looked at Jackson's feet on the seat. "Were you raised in a barn? What is this?"

"Thank you," said Evan.

Jackson rolled his eyes and moved his feet.

"How am I supposed to sit there now?"

"You want a napkin for your tush?"

"Maybe." Devonte swiped dramatically at the seat with his scarf, and Evan laughed as he scooted around the booth to make more room for the large man. "See, this is why I'm going to come work for you," Devonte said to Evan as he sat down.

"Don't remind me," complained Jackson. "Did you get your Series 7 test thing scheduled yet?"

"Yes, January fourteenth. I'm nervous as fuck."

"You've been studying for a year. You nail every pop quiz," said Jackson. "You're going to ace it."

Evan smiled at his cousin. Jackson's boundless encouragement was not a Deveraux trait, but Evan loved it all the same.

"Well, I hope so, but still, come January fourteenth, say a prayer for me or whatever it is you do."

"Meditation," said Jackson. "Unless I'm about to die, and then it's a lot of prayers. What's Pete's brainwave?"

"OK, so you know how we haven't been able to come up with anyone that would possibly want to help Granger?"

"The man was spectacularly unpopular," said Jackson.

"Understandably so, really," said Evan. The waitress arrived with Devonte's drink, and Devonte looked bemused by its arrival but happy.

"Well, so Pete was over at his in-law's house, and it occurred to him that Granger probably sent his special file to a relative. Because relatives might not like you, but they still feel some form of obligation."

"I'm concerned for Pete's marriage if he had this thought while at his in-laws," said Jackson.

"Agreed," seconded Evan.

"Nah, his husband's solid," said Devonte. "It was probably just one of those word association things that he does."

"Well, we'll hope so," said Jackson. "But maybe I'll remind him to take some of his vacation days anyway."

"I didn't think Granger had any relatives," said Evan.

"He's got a bumper crop of ex-wives," argued Devonte, "and a sister in St. Barts."

"Oh, for fuck's sake," said Jackson. "Please tell me I'm not paying for Pete to go to St. Barts? I know just said vacation days, but please."

Devonte grinned. "If that was the case, you'd be paying for me to go. But no, Pete thinks we can just give her a call or email. He says Aiden can probably put a fancy lawyer touch on it if we have to."

"I'm not sure why she would respond," said Evan. "Unless it was in the hope of resolving some sort of estate issue."

"That was what Pete was hoping to imply—some sort of legal-ese about the hearings or some such. It just has to sound important enough to get her on the phone. But the ex-wives are a different story. They aren't tied to Granger legally, so there's no leverage. But he still thinks they're decent targets. Unfortunately, all of them are sort of off the grid. They all got remarried, and with the additional name changes, it's hard to track them. Pete thinks it would be faster if we fly out to their last knowns and talk to them in person."

"It's not bad," said Jackson. "Where are they at?"

"One in California, one in Vegas, and the third one, we think was in Colorado."

"We might as well try it," said Jackson. "We're all out of other straws to grasp at."

"That's pretty much where I was at," said Devonte. "I mean… we're still totally chasing down leads. Something could pop at any time!"

Jackson snorted. "You are the worst liar. I don't know how you managed to get a P.I. license."

"Charm and good looks," said Devonte.

"Is that what you're licensed to do?" asked Evan. Both of them looked over in surprise. "I mean, you're both actually licensed for something?"

Jackson laughed. "We're both licensed in several somethings. But yes, all of my guys are licensed private investigators."

"Huh," said Evan. "I would have thought there would be more fedoras and trench coats."

"See?" demanded Devonte, glaring at Jackson. "I told you. You should have issued us all trench coats!"

"If I have to give up smoking then I'm sure as hell not buying everyone P.I. cosplay coats."

"I don't think those two are related," said Devonte.

"They're not," said Evan. "He gave up smoking for Aiden, and he's still bitter about it."

"I liked nicotine!" Jackson exclaimed, and Devonte laughed in a big booming chuckle.

Evan watched the two bullshit each other. His coworkers definitely had bullshit, but most of the time, it came down to digs and competition. The idea of a supportive workplace was as unfamiliar to him as a supportive family had been. He hoped that Devonte wouldn't be too disappointed once he switched careers. He got the feeling that having Jackson for a boss was hard to beat.

Caitlin
BILLY BOB

The ginger from the Deveraux Halloween party was in atten-
dance at tonight's event. Which was called something that Caitlin
had already forgotten. It was a banking-related charity. Bank Up,
Bank Over, Bank On… Whatever it was, it had pulled the usual
society crew and a fuck ton of Wall Street Bros and Bankers. Caitlin
glanced at the lanky redhead again, wondering if she should say
something. The day after the Halloween party, Vince had handed
her five-hundred bucks and said it was from the guy who'd rented out the courtyard for saving his suit. Vince had seemed a little
grumpy about it, although Caitlin couldn't tell why. The five-hundred bucks had saved her ass. Thanks to that cash, she'd managed
to keep the student loan creditors and landlord off her back. She
wondered if ginger Satan's angel girlfriend had said yes. In bartending, there were a lot of stories that she never got to see the end of,
but as she glanced at him again, she saw he was clutching a tiny
plastic sword from the container on the bar. He looked like he was
contemplating stabbing it into the neck of the man who was going
on and on in some self-aggrandizing story. He caught her eye and
mouthed the words *help me.*

Caitlin bit back a laugh and nodded. She checked his drink and
saw that it was Scotch. He'd probably been served by Tanja, who
hadn't noticed the topstitching on his Italian hand-tailored suit. She
decided that since Satan had been so nice to her, he deserved a little

extra effort. She reached under the bar and pulled out the good stuff. His eyes widened, and he nodded.

She poured a glass and held up the tongs with a cube of ice in question.

He held up two fingers. Caitlin put two ice cubes in and slid the glass into position at his elbow. He handed her a hundred-dollar bill while nodding as though he were interested in the story. She made change and handed it back, and he dumped it all promptly into the tip jar without looking. She took another look at the guy talking and then moved the box of sword toothpicks further down the bar. She thought the redhead was laughing, but he didn't break.

Jessica flitted by, sparing a look at the red-head, and shook her head. "So cute, so taken," she murmured before heading back out to the floor. The event was busy. Wall Street Bros drank a lot, especially when someone was asking them to donate to charity. Caitlin watched Jessica attract attention as she moved around the floor. Wall Street Bros were something of a specialty of Jessica's. She found them hilarious. Caitlin didn't have the energy to find them anything more than a pain in the ass. The evening progressed and Caitlin thought someone had forgotten the program because cocktail time was going extra-long.

"Hey Katie," said Jessica, bouncing up to the bar, carrying her tray. She yanked some money out of the tip jar and made change, redistributing the cash in her apron before shoving a fistful back in the jar. "This one's going to pick me up after work. His friend thinks you're hot. Want to come along. You know you'll get a free dinner out of it."

"Fuck no," said Caitlin. "They're going to do some E, and then they'll pass out, and I'm going to be unhappy. If I'm just going to make myself happy, I might as well go home where I can take off my make-up. Dinner is *not* worth it." That and she hated being one of the date-to-dine girls. She'd done it a couple of times when she'd been desperate, and she'd ended up feeling like a user.

Jessica snorted. "When was the last time anyone but your dildo made you happy?" she demanded. "Come out with us."

"No thanks," said Caitlin. "I'm telling you, Wall Street bros are like the potato chips of dating. You think you're having a good time, but mostly you just end up feeling unsatisfied and kind of greasy."

Jessica laughed, her breasts bouncing in her low-cut top which caused wistful looks on several customers on the other side of the bar. "I swear to God, I'm going to start cross-stitching some of the shit you say on pillows. I bet I could sell those on Etsy for a mint." Jessica paused, clearly thinking that idea over more seriously, then she shook her head. "But seriously, why aren't you dating? I know you don't approve of my one-hit-wonder lifestyle, but why don't you get yourself some sort of steady guy."

"Oh, hell fucking no," said Caitlin. "I don't have time for a boyfriend. They want shit. They want my time. They want me to be happy and smile on command. They want me to take care of them. I'm not Suzy Homemaker, and I'm not their mother. And if I wanted to get rid of my resting bitch face, I'd look at something other than their dick pics on Tinder."

Jessica was laughing and Caitlin grinned in response, but she didn't add that even if she did meet someone, they probably wouldn't want to date her. Caitlin was pretty sure that anyone who realized the full extent of Caitlin's financial problems from the mountain of debt from her mother's death or the impending IRS shitstorm from her father, they would just run the other way.

"And I don't disapprove of your one-night stands. As long as everyone's safe, knock yourself out. It has just been my experience that one night stand sex seriously sucks. And since I'm not looking for a steady guy or shitty sex that kind of just leaves me with Billy Bob."

"Billy Bob?"

"The previously mentioned vibrator," said Caitlin, and Jessica laughed again.

"I'm knitting you a vibrator cozy with his name on it."

"Thanks," said Caitlin, knowing that Jessica would probably actually do it.

Jessica headed back out to the floor with another laugh and Caitlin made a check of everyone at the bar. The red-head finished his drink and she had a refill ready for him. He tipped the same again. It was going to be a good night.

Jessica came back five minutes later. "So, what I hear you saying is that you need a guy who shows up, fucks you stupid, and then disappears when you're done with him?"

"That guy doesn't exist," said Caitlin.

"What are you talking about? That is, like, everything that guys want."

"That's everything that guys *say* they want. But they lie. And the ones that aren't lying aren't really… equipped to handle the job."

"How do you know?" asked Jessica. "If you don't try."

Caitlin sighed. Her life was a train wreck. Emotionally, mentally, financially. She could not take on one more project. She could barely pay the rent, let alone look for a guy. Sex would be wonderful, but she didn't see how she was supposed to get that without having to deal with a bunch of baggage on the way to an orgasm.

"Tell you what," said Jessica. "Give your number to one guy tonight, and I'll stop bothering you for the rest of the month."

Caitlin turned around and saw Jackson, AKA Hot Guy from the House of Amery, on the other side of the bar. She heard herself sigh. Men should not be allowed to be that good-looking. It wasn't fair to women's higher brain functions. He was looking at his phone and waiting for her to come down to his end of the bar and do her job.

"Done," she said, suddenly making up her mind. Jessica was right. Maybe a quick hook-up was just what she needed, and Jackson was *right there*. Maybe fate was on her side for once. Jessica glanced in Jackson's direction and looked him up and down.

"Nice choice," she said.

Caitlin went to stand in front of Jackson. The chatter from the floor was loud, so Caitlin leaned across the bar to yell at him.

"We're having a fire sale: all the models you can carry!"

His head snapped up, and he immediately grinned. "Hey!"

"Hey!"

"What are you doing here?"

"Two jobs," she said, not bothering to justify her life. What was the point after all? He was either going to be up for this or not, and she wasn't going to try to pretend to be something she wasn't.

"No wonder I couldn't find you," he said. "I was looking in the wrong spot."

Caitlin didn't know what to say to that. He'd been looking for her? She felt her cheeks go a little pink.

"I have your coat." She cringed at herself. Seriously, when had flirting gotten so hard?

"Yes," he agreed nodding, but with a smile. "Also, all the alcohol I want to drink."

"What can I get for you?"

"Bourbon, rocks."

Someone jostled him from behind. The bar area was getting crowded as everyone tried to get a drink before it was time to sit down. He looked around, clearly annoyed at the interruption.

She poured him a bourbon and grabbed a bar napkin, and scrawled her number and a message on it.

"On the house," she said, setting it down in front of him and handing him the napkin. He grabbed the napkin, and he seemed about to say something when the lights flickered, indicating that it was time to move into the main area.

"Never enough time," he said, picking up the napkin and tucking it into his pocket. "See you around, Katie."

The way he said it made it sound like a promise and not a casual statement. Caitlin watched him leave with another sigh. Billy Bob had been going by the name of Jackson lately.

Jackson
Call Me

Jackson looked at the napkin again as he got into his car.

Call for coat.

It was the least sexy pick-up line from the sexiest bartender slash model on the planet. Maybe she knew she didn't have to try to get what she wanted. When he'd carried her out of the House of Amery, he'd been entirely aware of her ass in his hand, the warm curve of it that seemed to fit just right. Then the vultures had descended, stripped her naked, and left her freezing and horrified. He'd been both turned on and horrified on her behalf. Fashion seemed like a hard way to make a living. He'd buttoned her into his coat and found himself staring into a pair of big eyes that were pure amber gold, and just like in the alley, he'd felt like they'd connected. Then that friend of hers had assessed him, correctly, as a threat, and he'd realized he was manhandling a mostly naked girl in a parking lot.

Call for coat.

It was also possible that she hadn't noticed a damn thing and just wanted to return his coat.

He'd tried to swing by the bar area after the show had gotten out, but everything was already broken down, and the staff was buzzing in all directions. He hadn't wanted to detour anyone to find Katie. It felt like a dickhead rich guy thing to do. Evan and Olivia had disappeared earlier, which was fine. They hated public shit anyway—they always turned up their noses at the booze—but Eleanor had declared that some Deveraux had to attend, and it was their turn on the rotation. Although, tonight, at least Evan hadn't complained once and seemed perfectly happy with whatever he was drinking.

Jackson was about to pull out of the parking lot when he saw Katie exit the building. She crossed the parking lot, probably heading toward the metro station a few blocks up. As Katie left the VAR property, a guy got out of his car and went toward her. She said something and detoured around him. He turned and walked after her, reaching out a hand to pull on her arm. She pushed his hand off and kept going.

Jackson reversed the car and pulled up in front of them. The guy was back at it, angling in front of her and blocking her path.

"Get out of my way!" snapped Katie, posturing up as the guy got closer to her.

"I just want to talk," said the guy, his thick Russian accent triggered the memory of Chicago summers and the gritty, dusty feeling of his childhood.

"Hey!" yelled Jackson getting out of the car.

"Piss off," snarled the man, barely glancing over his shoulder at Jackson's approach. Jackson thought he was maybe five-foot-seven, but had clearly been hitting the 'roid cycle. The tattoos on his neck said prison, the off the rack suit that had been tailored and nice haircut said decent money. The accent said Russian mafia, but that was a stereotype. He could just be an off the street asshole.

"*Ebat' mebe,*" snapped Jackson, taking a position comfortably out of reach, but close enough for trouble. The man looked him over more warily this time. *Fuck you* wasn't the same in Ukrainian and Russian, but most Russians knew what it meant.

"This isn't any of your business," said the man, still in English.

"*Ya zroblyu tse svoyim,*" said Jackson, then turned his attention pointedly to Katie. "Ready to go?"

"Yes," she said, looking nervous. She made as it to step around the Russian, but he grabbed her bag. Jackson let out a snarl that surprised even him and took a step forward.

"Call me," said the Russian, shoving a business card into Katie's purse before stalking away angrily toward a black SUV across the street.

Katie let out an angry breath and looked at Jackson as if searching for words.

"Russians," said Jackson, shaking his head. "Am I, right?"

Katie laughed in surprise. He went back to the car and opened the passenger door. She hesitated.

"I don't think he drove any further than the corner," said Jackson and she shivered and got in the car.

"You don't actually have to drive me home," she said as he got behind the wheel. "I think you've reached your quota for rescuing me this week. The metro station is fine." Jackson wasn't about to leave her at a late-night metro station with a stalker watching her every move.

"I don't mind driving you."

"I live in kind of a shitty neighborhood."

"All neighborhoods are shitty," he said. "They're full of people, and people are shitty. Some just tidy up better than others."

"You're a real believer in humanity," she said, sounding amused.

"I believe," he said. "I just believe that we're usually shitty with periodic moments of grace."

He wished he hadn't said that. On the other hand, philosophy in the dark seemed like Katie's thing.

"I can go with that attitude," she said. "I don't know what the car thieves in my neighborhood think, but if you park too long, maybe we can ask."

That made him laugh. He glanced at Katie, illuminated in the flashes of ambient light as they drove. He felt like he should ask about her man situation. But on the other hand, other than the jerk Russian stalker, he didn't really care as long as she didn't.

"You speak Russian?" she asked.

"Ukrainian," he said.

"How do you learn Ukrainian?"

"From your mother," he said.

She laughed. "I learned proper spray tan technique. Somehow I think your mother gave you a more useful skill."

She directed him, and he realized that she did indeed live in a shitty neighborhood. As they parked, he saw a skinny teenager with the screwdriver in his pocket drift into position near the rear of his car. Philosophically, Jackson didn't mind the hustle, but he really didn't feel like taking the train home or having to fill out the insurance claim.

"Let me just run up, and I'll get your coat," she said as he parked.

"I'll come up," he said, getting out. Katie shrugged as if his presence was irrelevant and went to unlock her door. Not exactly, the clearest signal.

"Just a sec," he said and went over to the skinny black kid, who was pretending to hold up the wall and smoking a vape pen.

"Touch my car, and I'll break every bone in your hand," he said, leaning in close but speaking calmly.

"Hey!" barked Katie, hurrying over, ruffling up like a mother hen. "Leave him alone!"

"I don't know what you're talking about," said the kid, looking injured. Jackson reached out and snagged him by the ear, pinching the thin cartilage and twisting a little.

"Tell her what the tool in your pocket is for," he ordered.

"Jamal?" Her eyes went round in confusion.

Jackson twisted a little harder.

"It's for stealing cars," admitted Jamal, trying to pull away from Jackson.

"Oh, Jamal!" Katie looked genuinely disappointed.

"What? I can get five hundred for a crappy Honda Civic."

"You're getting ripped off," said Jackson, letting go. "You should be getting at least seven fifty for a Civic."

"Fuck! I knew I should be getting more. It's because I'm thirteen. Those fucks think they can rip me off."

"Well, if you can keep that crew across the street from jacking my ride then I'll give you some cash."

"Jackson!"

"No," said Jamal. "Two Grants. At least."

Katie and Jamal stared at each other in mutual confusion, and Jackson laughed, which made them stare at him. "He wants two fifties," he said to Katie. "She disapproves and is saying my name—Jackson."

"Ohhh," said Jamal. "What's wrong with his cash?"

"Yeah," seconded Jackson, "what's wrong with my cash? I can't pay him to do a job?"

"Um… Well, when you put it like that, nothing? It just seems like he should be home in bed?"

"Katie…" said Jamal with a sigh.

"What?"

Jackson could see it written all over the kid's face. He couldn't go home. Jackson didn't know the reason, but it didn't matter. He could also see that Jamal didn't want to tell Katie because he liked Katie and wanted Katie to think he was fine.

"Nothing," said Jamal. "A hundred?" he asked, turning to Jackson.

"Yeah," he agreed.

"OK, cool. I mean, if they really want it, I'm not taking a beating for it or anything, but I'll tell them to fuck off."

"If it comes down to it, just yell for me," said Jackson.

"Cool," said Jamal again.

They both looked at Katie, who was frowning with a worried expression. "Be careful," she said. "Do you have a warmer coat?"

"I'm cool, Katie," he said, rolling his eyes.

She looked at Jackson. "He's fine," said Jackson, who knew damn well that Jamal did not have a warmer coat, but that Jamal was not about to admit that.

"OK," said Katie reluctantly.

He wasn't sure what to make of her friendship with Jamal, and he glanced back at the kid, who was settling himself into the overhang of the basement apartment with his vape pen. Most people avoided kids like Jamal. They didn't give a shit if they were home or had warmer clothes or not. No one looked out for kids like Jamal. Or at least, no one had looked out for him when he'd been Jamal's age.

She led the way back to her door and unlocked it. She lived in a narrow row house. The door opened into a cramped space barely large enough to open the door and then launched immediately into a steep stairwell that led up into a converted attic apartment. He followed her up the stairs and popped through into a living area with odd ceiling angles and a skylight that probably leaked, judging from the stain on the drywall. She flipped on a floor lamp by the couch, and he looked around the room. It was crowded with furniture that seemed too good for the apartment. He wondered if she had downsized from someplace nicer.

She took off her coat, dropping it on the kitchen table, and stretched her hands up over her head. Her shape was outlined in stark contrast by the light, and he felt himself get a little hard as she flexed her and isolated her rib cage, shifting her breasts under her shirt and causing her skirt to ride up.

She walked like a dancer—back straight, shoulders back. There was a lot of pride in that posture. He looked around the apartment again. Everything was neatly decorated. She had put effort into it. It was a shitty apartment, and she'd done her best to make it a home. There was a lot of pride in that too. Katie, the bartender slash model, took care of things. In the last five years, he'd become used to women who couldn't figure out how to get to the end of the block without assistance.

She unbuttoned the top few buttons of her shirt and rubbed her neck as she kicked off her shoes and dropped them into a basket at the top of the stairs. Jackson wanted to run his fingers along her throat, over the curve of her collar bone, and down to the swell of her breast. She looked up at him and smiled. Then she walked over to a hat rack and brought his coat back.

He looked at the coat in her hand.

"I didn't really come for the coat," he said.

Her head tilted to just the right angle to be kissed.

"You were thinking of something else?"

"A couple of things," Jackson said and leaned in to kiss her. He gave it a second just in case he had misread the head tilt, but she reached out and pulled him to her.

Their lips met, and a shiver of fire ran down his spine. Katie tasted like something spicy, only he didn't know what. He wanted to grab her and hold her tight to him, to let his hand destroy her carefully pinned hair. He wanted her naked on the damn kitchen table. He tried to slow down. Jackson wanted to make this last as long as possible. She was something sinful and perfect and better than he had any right to, and he wanted to taste every bit of her.

Caitlin
Drive Me Wild

Caitlin felt him push her skirt upward as his mouth pressed into hers and she couldn't stop herself from letting out a little moan. It had been too long since anyone had touched her with any sort of affection and the sensation was heavenly. His hands were just the right amount of rough and smooth. And the smell of him… She leaned into his neck and licked him. He smelled of warm oranges and a hint of bergamot.

He returned the favor, nibbling her ear, and then reached up and freed her hair from its bun. Burying his fingers in her hair, he caught her by the back of the neck and turned her face up to his. She thought she probably should have found the move too aggressive, but instead, she melted against him, giving him exactly what his hands and mouth demanded. His other hand was kneading her ass, and as his tongue slipped between her lips, his hands slid underneath her panties. His palm against her ass, long fingers curling inward, taking a firm handful, was precisely what she wanted.

She tugged at his waist, trying to free his shirt so she could touch his skin and encountered something cold and hard.

"Um, yeah," he said, pulling back. "Just a sec."

"Right," she said, taking a breath. "You have a gun."

"Yes," he agreed. "And the holster is attached to my belt. I can take it off if you want."

He was going to take his pants off. That was great. Was that great? Shit. Did she have any condoms? She was pretty sure she'd optimistically purchased a box at some point. When had that been?

Were they still good? He was looking at her as if waiting for her to say something.

"I don't know how to take it off, so you will have to," she said, hoping that was the right thing.

"Great," Jackson said but instead started with his shoes. He dropped them into the shoe basket at the top of the stairs, hung up his jacket, and then came back towards her as he unbuttoned his shirt.

"Now, where we?"

She reached out and pushed her hand into his shirt, letting her palm slide along the skin of his ribs, feeling the play of muscle as they reacted to her touch. She bit her lip, trying to keep herself from grinning like an idiot. Touching him was luxurious. She was entranced with letting her hands wander over his chest that she missed the fact that he had unzipped her skirt and was pushing it gently over her hips. She didn't miss the feather-light kisses along her neck, though. Those made her heart race and her breath come out in little shallow gasps.

She couldn't believe she was actually doing this. She couldn't believe Jackson had seen her apartment and was still doing this. She tried to shut that thought out. He was here for the same reason she was—they both wanted to feel good. They could do that for each other.

He crooked a finger under her chin and pulled her mouth up to his. The kiss lingered and became deeper. His hands drifted down, cupping her ass again, while her arms slid around his neck. Suddenly he picked her up. She was surprised, but she liked the feeling that he was strong as all that. She wrapped her legs around him and she felt his smile through their kiss.

"Like those legs," he murmured, between kisses before

carrying her into the bedroom. He dropped her on the bed, her feather comforter poofing around her like a cloud.

He finished stripping out of his shirt, revealing a large tattoo along his side, and figured out the gun and belt situation. He plunked the gun and holster down on her bedside table, and Caitlin tried not to have thoughts about that either. He was putting it there, and that was fine. It wasn't going to go anywhere on its own. She pulled off her own t-shirt so that she was down to her underwear and bra.

"Oh, those had better go too," he said gesturing between her remaining clothing items. "I'm not wasting time on the lacey bits."

She laughed. "Lacey bits are half the fun," she said, looping her fingers under the bra straps and running them up and down.

"No," he said firmly. "Lacey bits are just holding up the good stuff."

She was sitting on the bed, and he was slowly unzipping his pants. The tattoo ran from his lower abs down into his pants, and Caitlin wanted a better look, but she wanted a better look at pretty much everything.

"Mmm," she said, sliding the fingers of one hand between her breasts and then down along her stomach. She had his complete attention. "Good stuff. Where do I keep the good stuff? Hmm…." She made purposely confused noise and stopped at the edge of her panties. "I swear I had it here somewhere."

She went up on her knees and peeled her underwear off one hip. Jackson paused, seemingly entranced by her action.

"Keep going," he said, "let's see if you find it."

"Oh, I know where I keep it," she said. "What about you?"

One of his eyebrows went up. Caitlin gestured to his pants and pointed to the floor. So he was hot as fucking bonfire, and he had about melted her panties off her a few seconds ago. That didn't mean she was going to let him run the show.

He dropped his pants. Boxer briefs were his underwear of choice, and the tattoo seemed to go down to his thigh. She peeled her panties off her other hip and wriggled them down so they were halfway off her ass. She was almost showing something, but she waxed regularly for her modeling gigs, so she wasn't down to X-rated, just very, very naughty.

"You know, I don't know… maybe you're right, and I don't need this lacey bit." She put both hands up to her breasts and gently tugged the straps off her shoulders. He made a little woof sound. "Or maybe I do?"

"No."

"You seem very firm in your advice about that. Maybe you're right." She put one finger in the cup and let him get a glimpse of nipple. She looked down at her mostly naked body. Was she over-estimating her current hotness level? She looked up and found that he had crossed the room and was wrapping arms around her. Her bra came off in half a heartbeat and she was on her back on the bed a moment later. His mouth planted on hers. She wrapped her legs around him and wished she'd actually taken her panties off. She wanted to get to the good stuff too.

She shouldn't have worried. Jackson had her panties off in short order, and his fingers and then his tongue located the good stuff. Somewhere around her third orgasm, Caitlin realized that the good stuff just kept coming. His tongue was a blessing from the gods, and his dick might be cursed because she was going to be comparing it to every other one she ever met. He finished with a deep groan that Caitlin couldn't help but agree with and they both collapsed onto the bed. She had lost track of how long they'd been fucking, but it didn't really matter because she was willing to keep going as long as he was. She was just going to need a minute to recover.

He flopped onto his back but wrapped an arm around her, keeping her close. Caitlin rested her head on his chest—his heartbeat was a soothing thump in her ear. The room was dark, with streaks of light shining in from the street lamps outside. She hadn't bothered to shut the blinds. The windows were at head height, and there was a park across the street.

The room was quiet, and even the traffic noise seemed distant. It was as if they were the only two people awake on the block. The heady scent of sex, sweat, and citrus from whatever cologne or aftershave he wore filled her nose. She felt warm and tingly all over, cocooned in the dark and silence, wrapped in his arms, and for once, she couldn't think of anything to worry about. She couldn't remember the last time she'd been quiet with someone. His hand made swooping arcs across her back, petting and rubbing as if he didn't like to stop touching her, and she felt like purring. She kissed his chest. Jackson was amazing, and he made her feel like she was glowing.

"Mmm. More kisses, please," Jackson murmured, his voice gravelly but sweet.

Caitlin gave more kisses, then gave into temptation. She put the tiniest love bite on his chest and then another. She opened her mouth and tasted his skin with her tongue before letting her teeth graze along the surface, closing with the softest nip imaginable. He smelled so good, she didn't want to stop.

"Katie," he growled. "If you're going to keep doing that I'm going to have to go down to the bodega for more condoms."

He didn't have more than one? Wait, he would need more? Shit, they could be doing it again?

"Which I can do. I could do that. I will do that." He sounded like he was working up to putting on clothes and actually making the walk down to the bodega. That was a terrible idea.

"Uh, wait here."

Katie dove into the bathroom and scrambled through the contents of her medicine cabinet. Finally, at the back, she found the dusty box of condoms.

She returned to the bedroom and held up the box triumphantly. The light from the window made high contrast squares of light on the floor and across Jackson's body. He was lying in the middle of her messed-up sheets like he was a goddamn work of art. His tattoo was a dark smear down his hip and leg, and she had every intention of investigating that more closely. But probably only after she'd fucked him again.

"Proud of yourself, aren't you?"

"Yes," she said, prying open the cardboard. "They haven't even expired!"

She could see in his face that he was laughing at her, but he crooked his finger at her and beckoned her back to the bed. She pulled a condom out and dropped the box on the floor. She clenched the edge of the foil wrapper in her teeth and crawled across the bed to him. He looked like he enjoyed that approach.

"Let's see," she said rising up on her knees, "does it go here?" She flopped the little package onto his chest. He was grinning but shook his head. "No? Not there. Maybe here?" She crawled across his chest, dragging her lips and then breasts over his stomach. He let out an animalistic growl. She liked when she made him a little wild, but she wasn't ready to let him have his way yet. She put the condom on his knee. "No, not there." She straddled him, so that she was sitting on his chest backwards. She looked over her shoulder at him. "Wait, I think I see where it goes."

She dipped down and licked his cock. He let out a shocked

breath and his dick stood up straight like she'd given it a jolt of electricity. She lifted her ass in the air and gave him the best possible view while she sucked his cock.

"Jesus, fucking, yes," he groaned, arching his hips up into her mouth. At least she thought that was what he was doing, then he grabbed her hips and pulled her back. She gave a yip of surprise as she felt his mouth on her pussy. She gave it another few minutes, trying to concentrate on his dick and at least provide some payback for the filthy pleasure he was giving her, but it was too difficult to think straight. And finally, she grabbed the condom and used one hand and her mouth to open the wrapper.

"Oh God," she whimpered as he slid his finger along her clit. His tongue fluttered inside her and she ached for more, but he was torturing her on purpose.

Panting, she unrolled the condom onto his dick. Her hand was shaking—she wanted him that bad. She moved away from his mouth, although it took a lot of willpower. She intended to go reverse cowgirl on him, but he grabbed her hips.

"Turn around," he ordered. "I want to see your face."

Caitlin stared down at his dick, trying to absorb his words. He wanted to see her. It was the nicest thing someone had said to her in months. She spun around and posed above him.

"You want to see this?" she said, looking down at him. A wide grin spread over his face.

"Fucking yes, I do."

Caitlin couldn't stop a giggle from escaping. She sank slowly down onto his cock and her head rocked back in ecstasy. He matched her feeling with a groan of his own. How could he possibly feel this good? She started slowly. Rocking against him gently. He was big—she didn't think she could go straight to hard thrusts without hurting herself.

His hands moved up her thighs, caressing her, not pushing her to go any faster, more like he was enjoying the ride just the way it was. His thumb brushed over her breast and she leaned forward, putting her hands on his chest. He cupped her breast more fully, while the other hand went to her waist. He began to give her a little extra thrust as she came down.

"Oh fuck," Caitlin gasped, and he grinned. He began to thrust harder, and then his hands were on her hips, holding her tight. It felt so incredibly right that she couldn't even think. She could only move with him. Caitlin felt drunk as the world seemed to spin, and she pushed on his chest, riding him harder. She couldn't believe he was going to make her come again. This entire evening seemed surreal. He gave her nipple a tiny pinch, and she squeaked and leaned into him. She was so close. So close, but she needed more. His hand slapped down onto her ass, and the suddenness pushed her over the edge. She came, gasping his name, and he pulled her down onto the bed and nailed her like a jackhammer before coming with a groan.

She stared up at the ceiling and tried to remember the last time she'd felt so completely and utterly satisfied by sex. She came up with the answer of never.

"You can keep my coat," he said, picking up his head from the pillows.

"I'm not really here for the coat," she said and he laughed a tired chuckle. He ought to be tired. He had just put in a full night's worth of manual labor on her body.

He pressed his face into her and kissed her temple.

"Katie, you're a goddess."

She thought for a moment about correcting him from Katie to Caitlin, but what was the point? Katie St. Cloud was making it work. Katie was probably a better person anyway. Caitlin Granger didn't exist anymore.

Caitlin

THE NEXT MORNING

They were snuggled together and she was drifting off to sleep when she felt him slide out of bed. She waited for a few minutes, listening to him dress and tried not to feel miffed that he didn't have the decency to say goodbye. He seemed to dress in a hurry and jogged down the stairs. She rolled over and blinked at the clock it was nearly four in the morning.

She rolled back over and tried to assess if her feelings were hurt that he hadn't stayed the night. She had gotten around to just deciding she was too tired to think about it when she heard him come back up the stairs.

"Had to put some money in the Jamal," he said, stripping off his pants and climbing back into bed. She realized that he was only partially dressed his in shirt and pants, socks and underwear were still distributed across the floor.

"Did he go home?" she asked.

"No, he's going to watch the car for the rest of the night. I put him in the backseat."

"His mom must have found someone," she said and then wished she hadn't. That wasn't exactly something that Jamal would want spread around. "She works really hard," Caitlin said. "But sometimes…"

"Rent has to be paid," he said, kissing her shoulder in a gesture that felt genuinely affectionate. "I know."

"Did you take him some food?"

"I took him the coat neither of us are here for and a sleeping bag from the trunk."

"Oh, good." He spooned against her and she tried to decide if his silence was understanding or judgmental. "I never know whether or not to call CPS for him."

"You shouldn't," he said, and she relaxed into him.

Morning came with a bleat of the alarm and she picked up her phone and stared at the time. With a grunt, she stumbled over to the window. Jamal was chatting to one of his loser friends on the stoop below.

"Jamal! Go to school!"

"Goddamn it!" Jamal yelled back. "How are you still yelling at me? Didn't he fuck you hard enough last night?"

"Mind your own business! Go the fuck to school!"

"Can I have food?"

"Yes!"

"OK."

She turned around to find Jackson pulling on his pants. It allowed her to get a better look at the twisting dragon tattoo that wound up his hip and onto his abs. It was hot. He was hot. She wished she didn't have to work.

"I have a modeling gig with Roggario in an hour."

"I'll drive you," he volunteered.

"Thanks. Can you go give Jamal one of the to-go boxes from the fridge? One of the ones on the top shelf."

He nodded and, still shirtless, went into the kitchen while she stumbled into the bathroom. She heard him go downstairs and open the door.

"What do we got?" asked Jamal, his voice echoing slightly up the stairwell.

She eyed her hair while she brushed her teeth. She had third day, no shower, slash sex hair, and it looked fucking fantastic. She decided to leave it.

"Um," said Jackson. "Looks like roast beef with risotto and some sort of vegetable medley."

"Sweet," said Jamal.

"Are you going to actually go to school?" Even with reverb from the hall Jackson sounded skeptical.

"I was gonna go anyway," said Jamal. "But Katie will call the truant officer if I don't."

"Harsh," said Jackson.

"Katie's cool," said Jamal defensively.

"Yes," agreed Jackson and Jamal laughed.

"See you around, man."

The door shut, and Jackson came back upstairs as she spit and rinsed out her mouth.

"Truant officer?" he asked, leaning in the door of the bathroom.

"I only had to do it once," she said. "So he'd know I was serious. Otherwise, he gets into trouble."

He looked amused but didn't say anything. Caitlin applied some make-up and mentally tried to pick an outfit. It didn't matter what she wore to a fit gig. They were only going to strip her down and pin clothes on her anyway, but she wanted to pick something sexy for Jackson. But not so sexy that he would know she was doing it because of him.

She ended up going with her most model-esque look: a black T-shirt, jeans, and a pair of heels. She topped it with a chunky scarf and sunglasses. She thought he liked it because he watched her as he ate leftovers out of one of the white boxes from the fridge. Or maybe he just enjoyed watching her get dressed.

The car was in the same place he'd parked it and Caitlin felt relieved. He'd seemed confident that Jamal would prove an effective guard dog, but she hadn't been so sure.

"Do you always feed Jamal?" he asked as they drove.

"I get a lot of leftovers from work. It's one of the perks of working for Vince and Angela. And I can't eat them all. Not if I want to keep doing fit modeling anyway."

"Who are Vince and Angela?"

"Vince Ramano. He and his wife Angela run VAR Events. She does the food, and he does the security."

"I like their events!"

"You seem overly enthusiastic," said Caitlin, as they stopped at a red light.

"Sorry. I've just noticed that VAR always have their security wired. Their shit's tight. I worry less when it's one of their events."

"That's right. You do security?"

"More or less," he said.

Caitlin pondered that. His knowledge of how much Jamal should get for a Civic said maybe the answer was less. She tried to decide if she cared. Probably not. It was a one-night stand after all.

"Anyway," he said, smiling as if recognizing that his statement was odd, "Vince and Angela? It's a good job?"

"Yeah," she said. She could have said that Vince was the only person who had picked up her call when she'd gone through her contact list begging for a job. He'd also loaned her the deposit for her apartment and helped her move when she was left destitute. But she didn't think it was any of his business. "It's a good job. Vince really looks out for his employees."

"That's rare."

"Tell me about it."

They drove in comfortable silence, while Jackson fiddled with the radio. She thought she probably ought to start some sort of conversation, but other than giving him directions or talking about last night, she couldn't think of anything to say. What was he expecting from her? What was she expecting from him? Was she expecting anything? Giving her a ride was actually exceeding her expectations already.

"It's the building up here on the left," she said as they reached their destination.

He parked and got out to open her door, which she hadn't had anyone do in forever.

"I don't want you to trip and kill yourself in those shoes," he said as she eyed him over her sunglasses.

"You want to feel my ass when I get out of the car," she said accepting his hand and allowing him to help her out.

"I can't have multiple goals?" he asked, sliding his hands around her and putting one distinctly on her ass.

She kissed him and realized that this was her moment. She needed to tell him to call her or keep her mouth shut. He'd been amazing, but amazing turned crappy in a heartbeat. Did she really have room for him in her life? Did he even want the space? Before she could make up her mind, Roggario's assistant ran out the door.

"Oh my God, you're so late. Can you hurry?"

"I'm five minutes early," muttered Caitlin.

"Go get 'em tiger," he said and slapped her on the ass.

She blew him a kiss and went inside.

"Oh my God, so late!" complained the assistant, walking her back to the design area.

"I thought the call time was nine?" She'd worked with Roggario before. He was a petite man who blew through the workshops, marking and giving instructions and then dashing out again. He barely looked at the fit models, but she was the right body type for most of his clothes. They'd been a good client. She didn't want to screw this up.

The assistant gave her a look that said she was an idiot.

"Scarf and glasses off," said a photographer with a polaroid camera.

"Uh, OK." She dropped her accessories and bag on the chair, and he pushed her up against the plain gray wall and snapped her photo.

"I said white T-shirts!" snapped Roggario from the far end of the room, stomping toward her. "Why can't anyone follow directions?" He was wearing designer black and a pair of bright pink sneakers.

The polaroid was promptly taped to a whiteboard with photos of a dozen other girls in white T-shirts.

"I don't think—"

"Sheet?" Roggario demanded, snapping his fingers at her in command.

Caitlin looked around the room at the photographer and assistant and the handsome guy playing on his phone with his feet up on a table covered in model sheets and realized that she'd stumbled into a casting call for the Roggario show.

"I don't have one," she said. "I'm—"

"No one follows directions!" he howled. The guy playing on his phone looked up with an eye roll. He was good-looking in a sexually ambiguous way. Gay, straight, just a fashion model? It was hard to say.

"Fine," said Roggario, "let's just see you walk, and then you can go."

Caitlin stared at him. She had just had the best sex of her life, her hair looked amazing and she was being mistaken for an actual model. Why the fuck not?

"Sure," she said. "Down and back?" She gestured to the open area.

"That is the usual way." His sarcasm was biting.

She did model walks all the time. Usually just to pick up glassware and to amuse Jessica, but it wasn't like she didn't know how. She went down, she came back, and fixed Roggario with her patented *get the fuck away from creep on a train* stare.

"Worked for me," said the guy behind the table.

"Thanks," said Caitlin. "Meanwhile, I'm Kate St. Cloud. I'm the fit model you have scheduled for nine."

"Oh," said Roggario, his face going blank. "You're five minutes early."

"Yes, I am."

"But," protested the assistant, as if her world had shifted on its access, "you were with the hot guy in the car."

"Last time I checked, fit models were still allowed to date."

The guy behind the table began to laugh. "Well, babe," he said standing up and kissing Roggario on the cheek, "I'm going to let you all extract your own feet from your mouths. Miss St. Cloud, it was nice to meet you."

Jackson
Deveraux House

Jackson drove toward Deveraux House and collected at least two tickets from intersections with cameras. He didn't care. Tickets were a line item in his monthly budget. He counted them as a luxury of the rich. Only poor people had to obey speeding laws.

Last night had been a better trip than any drug he'd ever tried. The sex had been mind-blowing, but her personality had been an unexpected revelation. Katie's face when she'd come out of the bathroom with the condoms made him laugh out loud just thinking about it.

"They aren't even expired," he muttered to himself, still laughing. It wasn't often that he'd met someone so undeniably gorgeous, but somehow also the cutest thing on the planet. Who the fuck had she been seeing that they had they had allowed that box to get anywhere close to the expiration date? Katie made the phrase *getting lucky* an absolute truth. On the other hand, he wasn't sure he deserved to get that lucky more than once. Why she hadn't been scooped up by some guy with a fat wallet who would give her fat babies, a diamond ring, and a house to go with it was beyond Jackson. She was clearly forever material. Too bad he wasn't.

Jackson's mood had dipped by the time he got back home, but the sun was still shining so he smiled as Theo opened the front door for him.

"Good morning, Mr. Jackson."

Jackson suspected that Theo had somehow managed to install a camera on the door that allowed him to open it before visitors knocked.

"Morning," said Jackson.

"Mr. Aiden is in the library if you care to join him."

"What's Aiden up to?"

"Couldn't say, Sir," said Theo. "But from the stacks of books accumulating, I believe there was some sort of book hunt going on. Will you be wanting some breakfast?"

"No, I ate already. But some coffee would be good."

"Very good, Sir."

Theo wandered off. Theo was one of the more challenging adjustments for him to make when Jackson had become a Deveraux. Theo resisted all attempts to get to know him. He did not want to be treated as an equal, but he occasionally treated Jackson as if he were a craft project that had gone awry.

Jackson entered the library and found Aiden sitting on a table surrounded by a pile of books.

"Hey!" said Aiden looking up from a four-inch think volume. "Books?"

"Granddad had a book on early New York case law that I want. Only I can't remember what it was called or what it looked like." Aiden paused, his eyes narrowing as they ran over Jackson. "Where have you been? As if I couldn't guess."

"What's that mean?" asked Jackson dropping down onto a couch. He kicked off his shoes and, since he knew Eleanor was in DC, fell over and stretched out full length, putting his feet on the far arm of the sofa.

"You're wearing the same suit as last night," said Aiden, looking amused.

"How would you know?"

"Olivia posted a pic."

"I wish she wouldn't do that."

"Dominique told her to. It's part of her mission to make the Deveraux family more likable."

"Who gives a shit?"

"Grandma's re-election campaign. We all have our jobs, and that's Dominique's. Anyway, was she hot?"

Jackson groaned. "So fucking hot. Like, her ass…" He made a wordless gesture of appreciation. "Her entire fucking body… I can't even…"

"Talk? Yes, I'm getting the picture."

"You don't understand," said Jackson. "Have you ever just… I mean, you get done, and you can't even *think* words?"

Aiden was laughing at him. "Sounds like you still can't think words. Does Miss Mindblowing have a name?"

Jackson sighed. He wasn't going to call Katie. Katie was the kind of girl who cared for stray kids and made sure they went to school. That kind of girl had to be looking for some other do-gooder to pair up with. And that was not him. Not calling her was the right thing to do.

"Yeah," he said, "but it doesn't matter because, as it turns out, she's also a spectacularly nice person."

"What's wrong with that?"

"I don't date nice people," said Jackson.

"I've noticed," said Aiden, putting aside his massive tome and going back to the shelves. "What's with that?"

"I'm an asshole?"

"Try again," said Aiden.

"Nice people want things that I'm not going to give them. Also, I lose interest in about a month into anything."

"Yeah, have you considered that maybe you lose interest because you're dating crappy women?"

"Not always! But I mean, let's face it, my success rate on

monogamy is about sixty percent at best. I'm not interested in getting married. And I don't think kids are a good idea. I mean, maybe I'll change my mind next decade or something, but I don't see it happening any time soon. And that is pretty much the checklist for nice girls. It's not that I don't like nice people. I do. I just like them enough not to date them."

"So what you're saying is that you want a nice girl to fuck you stupid and then kick you out of bed?"

Jackson laughed. "Yeah, pretty much. But I mean, come on, what's the polite thing to say before you leave—call me. And I'm not going to do that. Ergo, or whatever you say all the time, I'm not nice, and nice people should not date me."

"Well, did Miss Mindblowingly Nice say to call her?"

Jackson was silent. Katie hadn't said to call her. She hadn't said anything about future interactions. He hadn't thought anything about it at the time. He had simply been glad to not have any awkward parting conversations.

"Well?" Ever the lawyer, Aiden was prodding.

"No, she didn't," said Jackson.

He looked up at Aiden, who was eyeing him skeptically. "Did she even give you her number?"

"I have her number!"

"Did she say to use it?"

"No," he admitted. Why hadn't Katie asked him to call her? That had been fucking amazing. Wasn't that worth a second try?

"So… you just got exactly what you wanted."

"Yeah?" Jackson suddenly wasn't feeling so certain.

"Too bad what you wanted doesn't get you a second date," said Aiden, and Jackson twisted a little on the sofa cushion. Had Katie not had a good time? He'd thought she'd been enthusiastic about everything. Why wouldn't she want to at least take one more shot at it?

"Hey," said Evan walking into the room, waving a piece of paper, "Well, take your gloves off. The subpoenas have arrived." As usual, his red-headed cousin was dressed impeccably in a navy suit.

"Why is Evan getting a subpoena?" asked Aiden.

"We're all getting them," said Jackson. "Sorry, forgot to call you. Although, we'll see if I can avoid getting served. Not that I mind exactly; I just enjoy the challenge."

"I just got a subpoena!" said Dominique walking into the room. Dominique was also dressed for work, but since she worked under her father's name and avoided having her co-workers know that she was a Deveraux, she currently appeared more low-key than usual with her blonde hair in a bun and a pair of flats under wide-leg slacks. "What the mother fucking hell?"

"Jackson forgot to tell us we were getting them," said Aiden. Aiden held out his hand, and she handed him the paper.

"I told Evan, and I meant to text you," said Jackson. "Sorry."

"But I don't want to go to DC," said Dominique. "It's a stinky little town full of downtrodden masses and a bunch of rich people who ought to know better."

"And that's different from New York, how?" asked Evan.

"Different stink. Also, we *are* New York. Our food is infinitely better, and we have Broadway."

"Fair points, really," said Evan. "I can't argue."

"We're being called to DC to testify about Absolex," said Aiden, comparing the subpoenas. "That can't really be right, can it?"

"Grandma's being investigated by the Ethics Committee for something related to Absolex. Although we don't know what particularly. I'm pretty sure someone is attempting to maneuver her into a corner to get something out of her, but I don't know what because she hasn't been letting me investigate."

"That's dumb," said Dominque, casting herself into an armchair. "You should ignore her."

"That's what I told him," said Evan, taking the opposite armchair. Aiden was still sitting on the table and frowning at the subpoenas.

"I'm going to have to call some people," said Aiden. "These are odd. And I'm not sure we can't just fight them on the grounds of being… bullshit. We were never witnesses in the Absolex hearings. Calling us in smacks of overreach."

"Well, Granger…" began Dominique.

"Yeah, I was there," said Aiden. "J.P. Granger tried to have us killed or whatever to cover up the fact that he'd falsified research and that his drug was killing people. But I'm not sure what the attacks on us have to do with the senate hearings on the drugs themselves. One caused the other, but the attacks are a criminal case that's basically moot now that Granger has offed himself. I don't know why they want us to testify before the Committee. I'm tempted to file to have these blocked just because someone shouldn't get away with practicing such messy law."

"I'd rather you didn't," said Jackson. "Or at least… I want to be in the room. I want to see who turns up to threaten us. I think that will tell me something. But if you think that will expose us to danger, we can do it your way."

"I think it will expose us to being annoyed," said Aiden. "I think they're going to play a giant game of gotcha and try to get us to say something embarrassing. If we just stick to what we've already said in our previous statements, it should be fine, but I'm warning you now we're all going to be pissed off and grumpy. The Deveraux temperament is not suited to answering questions from a bunch of pompous windbags."

Jackson laughed. "I'm sure you're right, but I will buy everyone dinner if you all come and play along."

"Well, when do we have to go?" asked Dominique. "It's not like I can just walk out of work whenever. I've got deadlines and people to manage. Do you know how much graphic designers wanker off if you leave them alone?"

"No clue," said Evan. "But I'm assuming it's a lot."

"Date is unspecified," said Aiden. "Basically, it's whenever they call it. Sorry. But hey, at least we all get to go to DC together. That could be fun."

"He's going to make us go to the spy museum," predicted Dominique gloomily.

Jackson sat up. "They have a spy museum?"

"Yeah! It looks awesome," said Aiden.

"We'll go to the National Gallery of Art," said Evan, turning to Dominique.

"Deal!" agreed Dominique.

"Hey," said Evan, "how's it going with therapy?"

"Uh," said Aiden looking panicked. "Are we… uh…"

Dominique frowned up at him and then looked back at Evan and Jackson. "Why is he being weird?"

"He's Aiden," said Evan. "I thought weird was an inherent part of his genetic makeup."

"I didn't know we were talking about it!" snapped Aiden.

"We talk about mine," said Evan. "Why wouldn't we talk about Dominique's therapy?"

"We don't talk about it," said Aiden firmly.

"Well, I do," said Evan. "I'm not asking for deep dark secrets or anything. I just want to know if she's going to find her own therapist, if it's been helpful, or if she got there and thought it was a waste of time."

"Oh," said Aiden. "Well, I mean, I want to know those things too."

"Um," said Dominique. "I don't… Uh… Helpful, I think. Actually, it's been really nice seeing your therapist because I don't have to explain us to her. Pretty sure she thinks we're peculiar, but, like, in a super not judgmental way."

"I know," said Evan. "Isn't that nice?"

"It really is!" She fell silent again and chewed her lip briefly, which was a sign of nerves for Dominique.

"You don't have to say anything else," said Jackson. "We just want to know if you're OK."

"No," said Dominique. "I'm not. I mean, mostly I'm fine. And Evan was right. She gave me some good immediate strategies for coping with anxiety. And I've only been a few times, but basically, she thinks I'm kind of… off-balance, and I'm being triggered by current events over past stuff. You know, probably because we never talked about anything for our entire lives, and apparently, we bottle stuff up until it's a problem."

"Accurate," said Jackson.

"Well, sorry, but not all of us get to go to prison and talk to a therapist," said Aiden.

"Hey, you could have. You just needed to rob the right liquor store," said Jackson.

"I thought it was industrial espionage in an eighteen-story building," said Evan. "Maybe I read the wrong file."

"Aiden isn't qualified for that. He would have had to start with liquor stores," said Jackson.

"No way," said Aiden. "If I was going to rob anything, it would have been a jewelry store."

"Not as fun as it looks in the heist movies, and they don't

usually have as many loose gems around as you would think," said Jackson.

"I would rob an armored truck," said Dominique. "It looks tricky, but I think I could do it."

"I would not rob anything," said Evan.

"No?" asked Dominique. "How very unsporting of you."

"If you rob things, you get sent to bad prison. If you steal millions of dollars from stupid investors, you get sent to white-collar prison. And I'm sure you get a better quality of prison therapist."

"He's actually right," said Jackson.

"I know," said Dominique, "but I'm weighing the benefits of a better prison therapist against the fun of successfully robbing an armored truck."

"Well, you wouldn't be successful, would you?" objected Aiden. "Otherwise, you wouldn't end up in prison."

Jackson couldn't stop the laughter that rocked his chest from escaping. His cousins were the best.

"This is why your therapist thinks we're peculiar, isn't it?" asked Aiden, shaking his head at Jackson.

"No, actually, but it doesn't help any," said Evan, standing up. "All right, I'm off to work because they expect me to show up eventually. Call me if you need something."

"Thanks, Evan," Jackson called after him. "I'll send you my suspect list by tomorrow!"

Evan waved in reply and headed for the front door.

Caitlin
VAR Events

Caitlin got to work and tied on her apron.

"Your hair looks great," said Jessica, checking the pockets of her apron for pens.

"It's sex hair," said Caitlin.

"No!" Jessica dropped all her pens.

"Yes," said Caitlin.

Jessica scrambled to pick up the pens and stood up, holding them like pointy bouquets in each hand. "That hot guy at the bar?"

"Yeah."

"Oh my God. How was it?"

"Mind-blowing. Seriously, the best sex of my life."

"Fuck yeah!"

"I may have said that, yes."

"Well, who is he? What's his name? What's he do?"

"His name's Jackson, and I think he works some sort of private security."

"That's kind of vague," said Jessica disapprovingly. She began to go through the pens on a bar napkin and discard the non-functional ones into the trash.

"Well, it was a one-night stand. We weren't exchanging resumes."

"You're not going to see him again?" Jessica looked disappointed. "Best sex of your life, and really, you couldn't say *call me?*"

"Well," said Caitlin, feeling less confident than she had a moment ago, "he didn't say to call him, and he didn't even give me his number. So… there you go. Besides, like I keep saying, I don't have time to date."

"Why do you always do this?" demanded Jessica.

"Do what?"

"It's like you're scared to make yourself feel good."

"Uh… I didn't have to because he did a fantastic job of making me feel good all on his own."

"And that was great, but you do know you're allowed to be happy more than one day, night, whatever, in a row, right?"

"No, I don't think so," said Caitlin. "Pretty sure one great night is probably my quota for the decade. Why ask for more?"

"Why not demand more?" asked Jessica.

Caitlin sighed. "Because I'm not going to get it, and I can't take much more defeat. Just let me have this, OK? Just let me be happy about this."

Jessica's face softened, and she flung her arms around Caitlin. "I'm sorry, Katie. Of course, you should be happy."

Jessica went off to help set the tables, and Caitlin began to set up the bar.

"Hey Caitlin," said Vince coming in.

"Hey, Vince!"

"Hey, uh, did you see the news last night?"

"No? Why? Something horrible happen?" She was only half kidding. The last three years of her life had been nothing but horrible things happening.

"Nothing big. I just saw that the Senate was talking about releasing the Absolex Hearing files. I was going to see if that would help you any."

Caitlin flinched, then looked around the bar area. Vince and Angela were the only ones at work who knew about her father and

Absolex. And she intended to keep it that way. The pitying looks from Vince and Angela were bad enough.

"Well, hopefully, that means they will either finish seizing all of Dad's property or unfreeze his remaining assets. It would be nice to be able to sell that shit or stop paying the taxes on it."

"You're paying taxes on it?"

She smiled up at him. "Didn't I tell you?" It was a stupid question. She never told him anything unless he point-blank asked. Thinking about it every thirty seconds of her waking life was bad enough. "Even though the assets are frozen, they're saying I inherited his shit, so there's an estate tax. I owe the IRS like seventy-five thousand."

"Holy fucking shit. You need to get a lawyer and a tax attorney."

"I had a tax attorney, but I have a hard time paying him. The last advice he gave me was to wait until the case wrapped up and then dispute the charges. But that doesn't get all the people that are pissed about their pension funds evaporating off my back."

"Do people actually come looking for you?" he demanded in disbelief.

"They did right after Absolex went under. That's when I switched names. I haven't seen anyone in a while, though. Not since the last time I moved."

She didn't mention the Russian outside her door or how he'd shown up outside of work. She didn't want Vince to think she couldn't handle things.

"I can't fucking believe your dad this to you," said Vince. "Do you even know what he did with the money after cleaning out your college fund?"

"No. Went on some big bender, apparently. The cop I talked to said they found him in San Francisco, where he'd rented out the penthouse suite of some fancy hotel before tossing half a kilo of coke around the place and taking a swan dive off the balcony. The last communication I had from him was some bullshit pile of work papers, and he just rambled on about how everything was the Deveraux's fault, and he was going to get them. Or something. I don't know. Honestly, I only looked at it once and shoved it into the pile. It's not like he was really even talking to me. He just rambled on."

"The Deverauxes have a lot to answer for," Vince growled.

"Do they? I don't even know. I think Dad knew that research was falsified, and I think, at minimum, he put the lives of veterans at risk by selling a defective drug to the VA."

"Eleanor Deveraux targeted him," said Vince. "Never mind the collateral damage."

"Maybe she did," she said with a shrug.

"And I bet that whole fucking family of hers helped tank the stock. One of the kids does investment banking or whatever."

"The market doesn't work that way," she said. "You can't just wave a magic wand and tank a stock. And honestly, I really don't fucking care anymore. It's not like I'm going to meet any of the Deverauxes anytime soon." Vince seemed on the point of saying something. "It doesn't matter," she said, cutting him off. "I'm not getting caught up in Dad's vendetta. I don't' need to be best friends with the Deverauxes or anything, but I just want out from under all his shit."

"No offense, but did he have to off himself? Like he couldn't walk out into traffic and maybe have it look like an accident so you could at least get the life insurance?"

Caitlin laughed, startled by Vince's idea. "Well, J.P. Granger didn't care about anyone, including me, when he was alive, so I don't see why he'd start caring when he committed suicide."

"Such an asshole," said Vince, shaking his head. "I'm really sorry, Katie. I wish there was something I could do."

"You gave me a job, Vince. I called everyone I knew when the school kicked me out. You're the only one who came through, and I really appreciate it."

He smiled ruefully. "Wish I could do more."

Caitlin shrugged. As far as she could tell, no one could help. She just had to put one foot in front of the other, and maybe one day, she wouldn't feel like she was being crushed to death every time she woke up.

Jackson
VAR EVENTS

Jackson leaned on a cocktail table, watched Katie tend bar, and tried not to feel like an idiot. He'd slept with at least five other women in the room. His eyes sought them out. They all looked nice. He had good taste. His eyes flipped back to Katie. She reached above her head to grab a bottle on a high shelf, going up on tip-toe, and he felt himself almost groan out loud as her skirt shifted an inch or two upward. None of them could compete with her tight, round ass, her long legs, her perfect breasts, the elegant curve of her neck, or big eyes.

"Jesus, would you look at that bartender," said a guy at the table in front of him.

"She could be my hostess with the mostess," said his friend, and Jackson found his hand clenched around his drink.

Jackson consciously let go of his drink. He didn't get jealous. He didn't give a shit about women. He hadn't given a shit about women since he started dating. Yeah, there were one or two in the past that he'd gotten twisted about, but even then… it only went so far.

Katie leaned across the bar to listen to a customer's order. The customer was well-dressed in a carefully casual way that had high fashion written all over it and whatever he said made her laugh. Jackson took a breath and reminded himself that Katie hadn't even asked him to call her.

But three days later, he was kicking himself, and when

Dominique had asked him to be her boyfriend stand-in and take her to this event, he'd said yes based on the fact that it was a VAR-catered event, and he thought Katie might be working it.

The guy at the bar leaned in and touched her arm, and not only didn't she pull away, she patted his hand.

Jackson looked over at Dominique chatting with a bevy of society women. She would not miss him if he ducked out, and since this was a VAR event, she didn't really need him for security. Besides, Katie was obviously not thinking about him at all.

Another man approached the bar and slapped the first guy on the ass. He jumped and then turned around and, with a laugh, kissed the ass slapper.

Jackson paused. OK, back to plan A: *accidentally* bump into Katie and see if she'd be interested in round two.

"I'm going to talk to the bartender," said the guy in front of him, finishing his drink in one long swallow. "Bartenders are always poor. A good tip and I bet I can get her on her knees."

Jackson gritted his teeth.

He watched as the guy approached the bar and held up a hundred-dollar bill as he leaned in to talk to Katie. She looked unimpressed. He waved the bill, and she pointed at the tip jar on the bar. The guy's back became tense, and he poked the hundred at her again. She poured a drink, put it in front of him, and pointed at the tip jar again. The asshole at the bar was getting more aggressive and leaning in. Jackson was thinking about going over when the large man who seemed to run security walked behind the bar and stood behind Katie. He didn't say anything, just stood behind her with his arms folded. Jackson guessed that this was Vince Ramano. Jackson liked Vince. He liked the way Vince ran his staff and his security. But, now that Jackson knew who Vince was, it occurred to him that Vince might not like him. He'd been to multiple events where Vince had made him pull out his concealed carry permit. On the other hand, Vince's staff was always courteous, professional, and never put up with shit from anyone. So maybe Vince just didn't like assholes with guns on his premises. That seemed reasonable.

The jerk at the bar with the hundred-dollar bill began to slink away from Katie. Vince picked up the tip jar and held it out. The hundred went into the tip jar, and Katie looked like she was holding in laughter. Jackson certainly was. Vince jerked his thumb toward the back with a smile, and Katie tossed down the bar rag she was holding and grabbed a tray of dirty glassware, hauling it behind some black pipe and drape that disguised the entrance to the kitchen area. Jackson sensed his opportunity and headed in the same direction.

She was coming back out by the time he made it over there. She was fiddling with something in her apron and looked up as he approached, pushing a dark lock of hair out of her face. She smiled, and those amber eyes that reminded him of really good tequila seemed to light up.

"What are you doing here?" she asked.

"Looking for you," Jackson said and kissed her. He hadn't meant to be that aggressive. He'd intended to use more words. Instead, his brain just repeated, mine, mine, mine, like a greedy child, and he'd grabbed her like the last dessert on the tray.

"Oh," she said as they pulled back. She looked dazed. Then she leaned in and kissed him, her body pushing against his.

"Do you have a few minutes?" he asked, kissing the spot just at the point of her jawline. His hand slid up the curve of her rib cage and onto her breast. He wanted her even more now that he knew what was waiting for him under her clothes.

"Katie!" yelled someone from the kitchen.

"Uh, no. I…"

"Katie! Are you bringing that gin?"

She shot a glare of annoyance toward the kitchen. "I'll have a break when the auction starts," she said, turning back to him.

"I'll find you," he said, backing up with a grin.

He waited until the auctioneer had started his patter and then apologized to Dominique with an excuse about needing to use the restroom. He found Katie in the hall outside the ballroom. He pushed her up against the wall, kissing her. She responded with equal heat. Her body was glued to his so tightly he could feel the pen in her apron. Then they both heard the sound of laughter from the bar area and she pulled him into the women's room.

"I should let you get back to work," he said, thinking about at least trying to be a gentleman. "I really just wanted to see about seeing you later."

"You don't want to see me now?" she asked, her hand sliding along his pants.

"No. I mean, yes. Yes, I want that," Jackson said.

They stumbled further into the bathroom and he had her pressed against the sink. He unbuttoned the crisp white button up and pushed his hand inside, lifting her breast from the bra. His lips traveled down her neck and she licked the curve of his ear. He took a step back.

"Need to stop," he said. "Because…"

He was trying to remember what the *because* was.

She pushed away from the sink and went to the condom machine, taking out some change from her apron. She came back with one and handed it to him. "Because why?"

Jackson kissed her again, his hands untying her apron and throwing it on the floor. She fumbled for the buckle on his belt as he hitched up her skirt and pushed down her panties. With the panties around her ankles, he spun her around and unzipped his pants.

He could see her in the mirror as he kissed her neck and pulled her skirt up above her waist.

"We're going to get caught," he said.

"Only if you keep talking," she said and wriggled her ass against his cock. He groaned as it sprang to hard attention. He ripped open the condom with his teeth as he sank the fingers of one hand between her thighs. She moaned and braced herself against the sink as he pushed against her clit. She was wet and her clit was fat under his fingers. He couldn't stop himself from grinning as her eyes closed and her mouth made a little O of pleasure in the mirror. He was going to fuck her and watch her come in the mirror. He pulled the condom on and put his cock right where she wanted. "Yes," she gasped, pushing back against him, but he held her by the hips, denying her.

"Jackson!" She was angry with him, glaring at him in the mirror.

"Do you want me?" he asked her.

"Yes!"

"How do you want me?" he murmured, leaning in to nibble her ear.

"Hard," she said.

He thrust into her and she arched back, gasping in ecstasy. He pushed into her again and again, pinning her against the cold porcelain of the sink. She reached back, pressing her fingers into his ass, moaning his name, the other hand was braced on the mirror. As she got closer she began to bend more at the waist. In their reflection he could see her tits bouncing with each thrust. He reached out and grabbed one, using it to pull her back into him as he pushed forward.

"Fuck yes, Jackson. Like that. Oh God, like that."

He was getting closer too and thrust into her harder and faster.

Her body began to clench around him and her moans got louder. He took the hand off her breast and put it on her mouth. She sucked his fingers in, going down on them like they were his cock. Then her eyes closed, her mouth went wide, her lips trembling and then she came with a hard spasm that clenched around his cock and he came too. He slammed his hand into the mirror to keep from pitching them both into the sink and he stared at her wide eyes in the mirror. They were both breathing hard and he allowed himself a moment to nuzzle her neck. They really were going to get caught if they stood here much longer.

"So what time do you get off?" he asked, lifting his head.

"I thought I just did," she said.

"Work," he said, smacking her on the ass and she giggled breathlessly.

"I won't be done here until two," she said.

"Meet you at your place?" he asked.

"You want to get your coat back again?"

"Yeah," he said. "And possibly two or three more times after that."

Caitlin

Caitlin's Apartment

Caitlin hurried from her train stop to her door. She couldn't believe that she'd fucked Jackson in the women's room of an event she was working. She also couldn't believe how badly she'd wanted to. The second she'd seen him outside the kitchen her entire body had tingled. She spent the better part of the night forgetting drinks while she pictured him fucking her. When she'd seen him in the hallway she decided to take Jessica's advice for once and do something that made herself feel good. And God, had it felt good.

Their night together had been outstanding. Their twenty minutes in the bathroom had been fucking heaven. But both of those were the kind of moments that didn't get repeated. Guys like him were supposed to fuck bartender slash models and leave. Not come over for more.

She had hurried through the entire clean-up routine, and she was a few minutes early as she unlocked the door to her place and jogged up the stairs. Caitlin paused at the landing. There was a post-it note on the banister.

Don't freak out. I'm in your bed.

Jackson

She stared at the note. There were various reasons to freak out about this information, not the least of which was that Jackson didn't have a key.

She took the note and went into the kitchen. She dropped her bag and jacket on the kitchen table and kicked off her shoes before entering the bedroom. She didn't turn on the light; she could see Jackson's outline under the sheets in the light from the kitchen. He was already naked and had clearly been sleeping. He opened his eyes and yawned at her.

"You're in my bed," she said.

"I took the train and I was early and I wasn't going to pull a Jamal," he said.

"You don't have a key."

"Yeah, sorry. But I do have a set of lock-picks. Also, I'm going to buy you a better lock."

Caitlin tried to digest that information. "It's not OK to break into my apartment."

"I agree," he said. "That's why I'm buying you a better lock. It's not really a safe neighborhood."

"It was until you started breaking in!"

"I'm not who you have to worry about. Those two fucking gang-banger rapists in the next building are who you need to worry about."

Caitlin wrinkled her nose. She had also run her address through the pervoid website and had carefully memorized the faces of the two convicted rapists in the next building.

"I do worry about them," she said. "But I also worry about guys who break into my place. How do I know you're not going to go crazy stalker if things go south between us. Then I've got to move or, you know, get a gun, and shoot your dick off. Which would seem like a waste of a good dick."

He laughed out loud, shaking the bed. "I promise, I don't go psycho stalker. But I also don't loiter like a wet cat on anyone's doorstep. Come on," he stretched out his hand for hers, "come to bed. Forget I'm weird. Remember, I'm fun."

"Why do I also think you're trouble?" Her fingers seemed to move to his of their own accord.

"Because I am?" He pulled her down on top of him and began to kiss her.

"Why do you carry lock-picks?" she asked, pushing up and away from him.

"Same reason I carry a gun, a knife and a pocket handkerchief. You never know when they'll come in handy."

"I feel like I should be freaked out by that list."

"I work in security," he said, unbuttoning her blouse and kissing along everything he exposed.

"How often do you use the handkerchief," she asked.

He picked up his head. "A surprising amount. More than the gun or the lock-picks." Then he went back to his exploration of her cleavage. He'd made it through the buttons on her blouse and now he was looking for the zipper on her skirt.

"But not more than the knife?"

"I use that thing every day. Mail, loose threads, back-alley muggings." She tried not to encourage that by laughing, but she couldn't help herself. "If you sat up, I could take off these clothes and you would be naked." She laughed again. He was so direct. She loved that he didn't hedge around about what he wanted. It made things so much simpler.

She sat up and he pushed the shirt off her shoulders and then pulled the skirt up over her head. It was the wrong direction, but she saw his point. Going the other way would have meant a lot less body contact. He popped her bra off with one hand and tipped her back onto the bed to get rid of the underwear. They went flying somewhere into the dark of the bedroom.

Unlike the bathroom, this time he fucked her slowly as if he was enjoying every inch of her body and had all the time in the world to appreciate it. The result was the same though. Soon she was moaning his name and grabbing for his ass. She came, but he continued to fuck her, taking her down and then back up again. A second orgasm, in her experience was harder to achieve, but deeper and richer. He thrust into her harder and she felt the pressure, the need.

"More. Don't stop Jackson, don't stop," she whispered.

He didn't. Jackson was giving her everything she wanted, and Caitlin realized she was holding her breath between each peak. She was so close. She felt her legs widen, inviting him to go deeper and he groaned, pushing harder. She reached up and pushed off the headboard, giving him more resistance.

"Oh fuck, yes," he said. Jackson slid one hand underneath her, wrapping the hand over her shoulder from the back so that he could pull her into his thrust. Caitlin was so close, trembling on the brink in the precarious ecstasy that was the sweetest torture. Then she came with a shout that might have been nothing, but might have been his name. He came almost simultaneously and collapsed onto her.

She groaned as he rolled off of her. She didn't want him to stop touching her. He reached out putting his hand back onto her thigh caressing it possessively. She decided that wasn't good enough and rolled over, flopping onto his chest. He promptly put a hand on her ass and wrapped the other around her in a hug.

"Mm," he murmured into her hair. "You were killing me to-night, Katie. It's a good thing you fucked me in the bathroom, or I was going to have to explain why I had a hard-on during a support the children auction."

Caitlin laughed. "Me? Killing you? No, I don't think so. I think it was the other way around. You were the one that had your hands all over me before dinner. How was I supposed to concen-trate after that?"

"Had I known the bathroom was an option I would have done a lot more than that. Jesus, your ass in that skirt looked like…"

"Like what?"

"I'm not literate enough to have a good simile. Mostly it just looked like I needed my hands on it."

Caitlin laughed, then kissed his chest. She thought about telling him that the idea of unbuttoning his shirt, of unzipping his pants, of reaching inside and touching him, of making him rise, hard and quivering to her touch had caused her to spill two drinks. But he hadn't called her. He had her number. If he hadn't called for three days and then showed up for a second drive-by that meant that she was his booty call, not someone he was interested in. A booty call did not need to know what kind of power he had over her. Although, at the moment, being his booty call felt pretty damn spectacular.

"I probably shouldn't have done that," she said.

"Done what?" He sounded lethargic—not quite sleepy, but like she'd made him lazy and happy.

"Oh, the bathroom. Vince would be pissed. It's hard enough convincing people that cocktail waitresses aren't whores without getting caught in the bathroom with a customer."

"Considering how many actual whores are at those things, it doesn't seem like that big of a deal."

"Yeah, those aren't whores. Those are escorts. As with everything else, money matters." She heard the bitter note in her voice. "Anyway," she said changing the subject and putting on a smile to change her voice, "don't get the idea that bathrooms are on the regular menu."

"Got it," he said. "What is on the regular menu?"

She didn't know how to respond to that. What was she supposed to say? She couldn't have someone around regularly. The idea of having someone investigate the nooks and corners of her life terrified her. She would have to explain Caitlin to him.

"Um… Well, this is great, but, um, I'm not looking for a boyfriend."

He almost laughed. "I'm not really boyfriend material."

"So… We're agreed that we're not dating and this is not a thing?

"Yes?" he sounded suspicious.

"OK, but um, I am free on Wednesday night."

"I could be here Wednesday," he said and she could hear the smile in his voice.

Regular, not to mention fantastic, sex? No strings? Who cared if he seemed slightly on the shady side and maybe had boundary issues?

She could worry about that later.

Aiden

METROPOLITAN CORRECTIONAL CENTER

Aiden leaned against his car and watched as Jackson parked. Jackson was driving a Ferrari this morning. Jackson switched cars the way some people changed jackets. Aiden hadn't quite cracked the code, but he suspected an ex-con rolling up to a prison in a Ferrari LaFerrari made some kind of statement. Personally, Aiden liked to stick with what he knew, and his temperamental vintage Aston-Martin might be a grumpy little bitch on cold mornings, but every piece of her felt familiar, and he knew where the chapstick was and what was in the glove box. Changing cars would throw off the Feng Shui of his life. Ella kept threatening to buy him a new Aston Martin, and he had caved and agreed that if she bought him the One-77, he'd switch cars. He didn't think she'd figured out that there were only seventy-seven of them ever made, so his little James Bond baby was safe for a while longer.

Jackson walked across the street. He was wearing an Ozwald Boateng jacket which had managed the feat of looking tailored and tough. The Saville Row tailor was one of Jackson's favorites, which drove Aiden nuts because it meant he couldn't wear any of his without looking like he was copying Jackson. Jackson glanced upward at the building looming over them, but Aiden wasn't sure what the look meant.

"Are you sure you want to go in there?" asked Aiden as Jackson got closer.

"I'm sure that I don't," said Jackson, staring up at the

monotonous gray brick of the Metropolitan Correctional Center. It was a Federal detention center—the polite term for a prison—in lower Manhattan. It had held many prisoners of note in its time including John Gotti, and Jeffery Epstein. And for a brief period of time, it had held J.P. Granger. And then the Federal charges had been dropped and Granger had wheedled his way into being released on bail. Aiden suspected that Jackson's eight-hundred-dollar coat and two-million-dollar car wouldn't make him any less of a criminal in the eyes of every officer in that building.

"You know they're going to give you a ton of shit, right?"

"Yeah," said Jackson, "but the ex-wife angle is turning up nothing. There's the will angle, but—"

"Will!" exclaimed Aiden, hopefully and then deflated as he realized the problem. "It's not through probate yet, is it?"

"Nope. No estimate on when it will come through either. And I'm officially out of other ideas. But I do have my magic letter." He held up the envelope with the prominent logo from the District Attorney of New York. "And I have you."

"I'm not magic," said Aiden hoping to mitigate expectations.

"I'm out here walking around," said Jackson. "So as far as I'm concerned, you are."

"I keep telling you, there were legitimate legal grounds for getting your case over-turned. That wasn't magic. That was the law."

"OK," agreed Jackson, but by the way he said it, Aiden knew he was being placated and that Jackson was simply choosing not to disagree. It was one of Jackson's more exasperating habits. How was Aiden supposed to win anything if Jackson wouldn't argue?

"You're very annoying," said Aiden, which only made Jackson grin.

"I've been told that before. Frequently by you."

"Well, fortunately, you have other good qualities," said Aiden.

"Can't think of what those would be, but thanks."

"You don't snore," said Aiden. "And you don't make embarrassing faces in family photos."

Jackson's eyebrows went up.

"I'm serious," said Aiden. "I have this client and he showed me his family photo and, while previously I have never thought him to be exceptionally abnormal looking, I took one look at the photo and had to restrain myself from asking if it was a joke. The man is forty years old and still smiles likes he's in that awkward toddler phase where they don't know how to operate their face and can't make a real smile."

"Well," said Jackson, "at least I've got that going for me."

"It's a big relief, let me tell you," said Aiden. "I hadn't even realized that was a possible problem to have."

Jackson chuckled, which had been Aiden's goal.

"Not that you should smile at these idiots. Mostly just do your silent tough guy thing and I will lawyer at them until they get tired and give up."

"It's a system that works," said Jackson.

"It really does," said Aiden. "I've almost gotten over being surprised that it does. I chalk it up to a lack of mental fortitude myself. People have no stamina. Or it could be laziness, I suppose."

"Well, that and I'm annoying."

"I've heard that," said Aiden, straightening his tie, and running a hand over his hair. "Do I look like I make more in an hour than these guys do in a day?" he asked, turning to Jackson.

"You probably do make more in an hour," said Jackson.

"Probably. But that isn't the point. Sometimes how much I make is a moral embarrassment that shouldn't be mentioned. But today the point is to look like I have the time and resources to be more trouble than anyone wants to have in their life."

"Oh. Well, goal achieved. You look like you sleep with super models on gold plated sheets or something."

"Perfect! Let's go get this over with."

Aiden went into the front desk and charmed the front desk clerk until he showed them into the next office and then there was the next office after that. Aiden showed them Jackson's magic letter from the District Attorney's office that asked for cooperation. Aiden was pretty sure Jackson had achieved that through some sort of carnal relations with a very attractive Assistant D.A. but he didn't like to ask because knowing that wouldn't help them should he have to answer any questions on the record. As predicted, none of the people they talked to liked Jackson. Aiden strutted and Jackson growled and the administrators yipped like tiny, but very angry dogs.

And then at some point Jackson disappeared and came back thirty minutes later smelling of cigarettes. By that time, Aiden had gained access to the records and he gave Jackson a look that asked if he was ready to go. Jackson gave an infinitesimal nod and Aiden gave one of his own. They didn't speak until they were out on the side-walk.

"What'd you get?" asked Aiden.

"Who me?" asked Jackson and Aiden shook his head.

"If all you got was a cigarette break, I'm going to be pissed."

Jackson flashed a grin. "You first."

"There was only one visitor who wasn't related to the defense team. She signed in as C. Granger."

Jackson nodded. "That's the third ex-wife – Christina Granger. I talked to some of the guards. They didn't know who came to visit him, but they did tell me that we're not the first ones to come sniffing around. Some guy came around a couple of months ago. Didn't get a name, but he passed out cash to get the same information."

Aiden took a deep breath. "Damn. I don't like being behind someone else."

"Neither do I," said Jackson. "And I don't like not knowing who that person is. I knew we were taking too long. I just didn't think we were on a clock and Eleanor kept pushing back."

Aiden shook his head. "She fucking hates having us mess around with her stuff, but she still needs us."

"Agreed," said Jackson. "Fortunately, we tracked ex-wife number three to Colorado. Devonte headed out there a few days ago."

"Hopefully, he's not just skiing," said Aiden. "Tell him to get a move on."

"Devonte hates snow. And he asked me if there was such a thing as horse repellent."

Aiden laughed. "Does he think they just wander the streets of Colorado?"

"Maybe they do for all I know," said Jackson. "I told him if he saw his horse to flap his arms and look big."

Aiden laughed. "Worst advice ever."

"Yeah," said Jackson, grinning. "But I'm kind of hoping he meets a horse now."

"Got time for lunch?" asked Aiden.

"Nah, I told Eleanor I'd pick up some stuff up while I was down here and then I'm heading back to the office. You guys are coming on Sunday, right?"

"Yeah, Max and I are going to hit the gym first. You should come with. I invited Evan, but he just gave me a look."

Jackson laughed. "Yeah, I'll come. Shoot me a text."

Caitlin
VAR Events

Caitlin felt her phone buzz in her pocket and immediately felt a shot of fear race down her spine. Who would it be this time? Bill collectors, hospital, IRS? No not the IRS. They just sent nasty letters. Reluctantly she looked at the name on the screen.

Jackson Zane.

Caitlin took a deep breath, instantly relieved. But why was he calling instead of texting? She felt a different kind of nerves fluttering in her stomach and picked up, bracing for bad news.

"Hello?"

"Oh, thank God you answered." He sounded as though she her voice was an answer to his prayers and that thought made her smile. "Ok, I'm really sorry to call you in the middle of a work day, but I'm having a fashion emergency."

"I don't know what constitutes an emergency but I will try to help."

"Thank you," he said fervently. "So, I was doing a thing, it's near another thing—long story short, I told my grandmother I'd pick up the clothes she's wearing for tonight's event. Only I got here and something got screwed up because they don't know which outfit she picked. I have tried to call everyone and no one is picking up and the clerk chick will be back any minute and I'm going to have to pick an outfit. Katie. I cannot pick an outfit."

Caitlin laughed. She now understood his emergency.

"Katie, I'm serious! I need help!"

"Yes, sorry. I understand. Are there pictures? What are the choices?"

"Sending now." His voice was clipped and tense, something she wasn't used to from him. He was really upset. The pictures popped through and she looked at them.

"OK, so it looks like option one is black Chanel. Hard to go wrong there. And option two is…ooh, is that vintage Halston?"

"Those sound like words that were said to me, so probably."

"Navy versus black. Hard choice. How fancy is her event?"

"It's business formal with a bunch of judgy people. They may comment on how much she's spending."

"Vintage Halston then," said Caitlin. "It's old, and she can claim to be re-wearing it. Saves money right there. Or at least, have the appearance of saving." And for the rich, appearances were what counted.

Jackson let out a gusty sigh of relief. "Perfect. You're a genius. OK, I'll let you go. I really appreciate you making time for me."

Caitlin wanted to let him be done. He was so stressed about getting this right, but there was one little problem.

"I think you're forgetting about shoes."

"Oh, fucknuts."

Caitlin couldn't help laughing again.

"Uh…" She could hear him moving around. "It looks like we have what I would call tarnished silver, red, and ugly brown. She's not going for the brown. Even I know that."

"Go for the silver then," said Caitlin. "Nothing says *bitch* like a red shoe. So you'll want to avoid that."

"Hmmm…" Jackson sounded like he was actually thinking and not just teasing her.

"Jackson! You can't bring your grandma bitch shoes!"

"You don't know my grandma. She embraces her inner bitch status and sometimes she likes to rub it in people's faces."

"Well, that sounds like the kind of confidence I aspire to, but still… you can't make the bitch decision for her. Take both shoes and let her pick."

"Once again: genius."

Caitlin smiled. "Glad I could help."

"Me too. Hey, if I manage to skip out of this shindig early do you want me to come over and express my gratitude in person?"

"Yes, please," said Caitlin smiling at the idea of having him to look forward to at the end of the day. "But I won't get done tonight until eleven."

"Katie, it's barely noon now. Are you working a twelve-hour day?"

"Fourteen. I picked up a couple of extra shifts. Anyway, I don't get done until eleven and then it'll take me an hour to get home on the train."

"Or I could come get you and save you the trip."

Caitlin's immediate thought was that it would also prevent any run-ins with the creepy Russian bill collector. And then she hated herself for using Jackson that way.

"Oh, no. That's out of your way. I don't want…"

"And I don't want to waste an hour on the train when we could be naked."

"Well, I see your point," said Caitlin.

"So you'll text me, and I'll come get you, and then we'll both be happy."

"Yeah, all right," said Caitlin giving into temptation. He wasn't a boyfriend, but he *was* a friend. If Jessica drove, Caitlin would let Jessica drive her home, so this was practically the same thing. Caitlin hung up and turned around to find Jessica staring at her.

"What?" asked Caitlin.

"I'm sorry, did I just hear the Queen of Does-Not-Wanna-Man make a date?"

"It's not a date," said Caitlin firmly. "It's just sex. It's a hook up."

"But it's like your third hook up with this same guy."

"Uh, yeah, third." Caitlin grabbed her till and tried to head toward the bar station.

"No, no, no. You hang on just a minute, sister. This is that guy, right? The one you gave your number to like a month ago. How many times have you seen him?"

"I don't know. He comes over on my night off."

"It's not your night off tonight."

"OK, maybe some other nights too."

"Does he spend the entire night?"

"We take awhile and we're tired. So… yeah, sometimes." All the time. "It doesn't matter."

Caitlin clutched her till tighter and backed away from Jessica. She didn't want Jessica's congratulations, opinions, or judgement, or whatever it was going to be. She didn't want to talk or think about it. She didn't have the courage or energy to do either and she didn't want to jinx the one nice thing that had happened to her recently.

For a moment, Jessica's face seemed tense and disapproving then abruptly she smiled.

"Well, I think it's great that you found someone flexible with his schedule and who doesn't pressure you." Jessica sounded genuine and Caitlin relaxed her death grip on the till.

"He really doesn't. He always texts if he has to cancel and he drives me to gigs in the morning if I've got one. He makes it really easy."

Caitlin took a deep breath as she realized the truth of her words. She hadn't thought there was room in her life for anyone, but Jackson didn't seem to need things from her the way other people did. He only made things easier. From changing the lock on her door, to driving her places, to whacking her radiator in just the right way to make it shut up, he had made the past month smoother.

"He takes care of you?" asked Jessica.

"No, of course not," said Caitlin impatiently. "I don't need anyone to take care of me. It's just that he's really… respectful, I guess, of my time and boundaries." She felt safer when he was around. And definitely more relaxed after he got done with her. The past few weeks had been like a coming up from underwater and taking a big breath of air.

"And he's picking you up tonight?"

"Yeah," said Caitlin blushing. "It's not a date or anything. He just made the excellent point that we could be naked faster if he drove. And he drives pretty fast, so… I'm here for it."

Jessica laughed. "I think I like this guy."

"Well, that makes two of us." Caitlin felt relieved that Jessica wasn't shoving some sort of *ask for more* nonsense at her.

They were mid-way through the night when Vince stopped by. "I clocked you out," he murmured. "Rest of the night is cash."

"You really don't have to do that," protested Katie, feeling grateful.

"You've hit your hours for the week. You'll get the health care and I'll pay you the time and a half in cash. You need the money and I don't think you need anything else for anyone to seize."

"I really appreciate it," said Katie, with a sigh.

"How's the tip jar?" asked Vince, craning to look at status.

"Good. It's a good crowd. Couple of big tippers."

"The servers say your peach champagne drink thingie is going over great," said Vince. "I keep telling Angela to let you design drinks for all the events, but I'm not in charge of food."

"It's not a big deal," said Caitlin. "I just like coming up with drinks."

"I like it too," said Vince. "Now we just need to figure out how to upcharge for the service of you using your brain powers."

Caitlin laughed. "I'm not sure how to do that, but OK, you let me know if you do."

Vince grinned. "This is business, kid. It's what I do."

Caitlin smiled and went back to the bar. Her signature drink was doing well, but there were still those who wanted something different. A woman approached. She was a flame-bright natural redhead with a set of breasts that defied the standard fashion fit. Considering that she was wearing a pret-a-porter Reem Acra that meant it had been custom tailored for her.

"Hi," she said her voice lilting into extra syllables that only a Southerner could find in a two-letter word.

"Hi," said Katie. "What can I get you?"

"Um, well," she hesitated, "Evan said," she pointed to a lanky redheaded man on the far side of the room. "He said that if I begged for help and promised not to stab anyone with a toothpick, we could get better drinks."

Katie burst out laughing. Evan was her shrimp cocktail wearing, extra good tipper who'd been contemplating toothpick murder. She had now seen him at several events and he'd continued to bribe shamelessly for better drinks. "Scotch two ice cubes for him, right?"

"Yes," said the woman, looking pleased.

"What about you?"

"Oh, I don't know. I don't like any of the wine and I can't drink it straight like he can."

"Do you like whiskey though?" asked Caitlin, rifling through her mental drink index and comparing it with the ingredients she had on hand.

"Well, yes, but it gets awful heavy when it's a whole glass."

Caitlin nodded. "So you and Evan... I was working one of the

Halloween parties that night. We all loved the lanterns." She asked, nodding to the giant sparkling ring on the woman's hand, while she began to mix her drink.

The woman laughed delightedly. "Wasn't that amazing? He spoils me rotten. I do not understand how I got so lucky. Although," she said, looking at the ring, "this still seems a little weird."

"You're going to let him tie you down, huh?"

"Only if he's good," she said, admiring her ring, and then looked up wide-eyed. "I shouldn't have said that."

Caitlin laughed again. Mr. and Mrs. Evan were her new favorite couple. "Bartenders confessional," she said, with a wink. "My lips are sealed."

"Thanks," said the woman. "I'm Olivia, by the way." She reached across the bar to shake hands. None of her customers ever offered to shake her hand like she was a real person.

"Kate," said Caitlin, shaking. She poured out the drink and slid it to Olivia. "Try this."

Olivia took a cautious sip.

"Ooh! That's good. And different. Peaches?"

"I make a peach simple syrup and pour it over the sugar cube. I thought you might like peaches."

Olivia beamed. "Thank you. I do."

Olivia left two hundreds on the bar as she carried the drinks away.

Katie shook her head. She remembered being able to tip like that. It was a different feeling being on the receiving end. On the other hand, at least Mr. and Mrs. Evan tipped like they really liked the service, not like they were trying to buy her.

Caitlin made it through the end of her shift, and out to the parking lot to wait for Jackson, but somehow she wasn't surprised when Jessica magically appeared at the same time as Jackson.

"Oh!" said Jessica, smiling widely. "You must be Jackson." She held out her hand and gave Jackson a firm shake while scrutinizing his face as if looking for evidence of something.

"Yes," agreed Jackson.

"I'm Jessica. I do knitting, needlepoint, photography and shovel art."

"Shovel art?" asked Jackson, looking puzzled.

"When it comes to putting jerks in the ground, I'm an *artiste*," said Jessica, still smiling.

"Oh, my God," said Katie, but Jackson grinned.

"Good," he said. "I'm glad to meet you. I'm more of a shovel craftsman, but next time Katie needs bodies buried, you call me."

"Partners in crime?" asked Jessica, raising her eyebrows, but Caitlin could tell she already liked Jackson.

"Crime? No. I thought we were talking art."

Jessica laughed. "Collaboration. Got it. I'm in." There was a honk from across the parking lot. "That's me. See you guys later." Jessica waved and headed toward her own ride.

"Sorry," said Katie.

"I'm not," said Jackson. "I like her. She's funny."

Caitlin felt her stomach unclench a little. "She's really talented. You should see her photographs."

"Just as long as I don't see her shovel work," he said, grinning.

Caitlin shook her head, but felt relieved that Jessica had liked him.

Jackson
Cheery Bailbonds

Jackson sat at his desk in an ancient office building that still had a sign reading Cheery Bailbonds over the door and flipped through the stack of reports, and frowned. The ex-wives were a bust. Former residences were the same. The sister in St. Bart's had been only semi-cooperative. She hadn't offered anything except that she wasn't involved, and she preferred not to talk or think about her brother because, really, it was just *toooo* much. It was Aiden's opinion that even if Granger had sent her something, she would have burned it. The sister also had a place in the Hamptons, and Jackson had been seriously considering going to check it out, just in case Granger had shipped something there. Except that Pete had called this morning from Hampton's and said it was a bust. That left Devonte, who from the last text had been about to board a plane back home, but gave a frowny face when asked if he'd turned up anything.

Jackson rubbed his head and then dug in his pocket for some gum. Instead, he found a green plastic doo-dad that Katie had given him. He'd complained that he missed smoking because he liked doing something with his hands while thinking, and the next time he'd come over, she'd presented it to him. She'd said the magnetic gizmo that folded into various shapes was a fidget toy.

He put the toy down on his desk and then, after a moment, picked it up and unfolded it. Might as well give it a try. He liked the click and tug of the magnets coming together and then pulling apart.

The stupid toy was actually kind of soothing. He smiled. Leave it to Katie to come up with something good. That girl was way too smart to be stuck bartending. He would have to do something about it if he kept seeing her. Except that he knew that if he offered her money, she'd kick him to the curb faster than he could pull his gun. She *hated* anyone who used others, and she would probably rather starve to death than be one of those people.

The previous week they'd been standing in line at the coffee shop, which was one of Jackson's least favorite activities, but Katie had pre-modeling gig needs. And he also suspected that if he didn't buy her breakfast she wouldn't purchase anything but coffee. Katie was checking her phone, leaving him free to check the exits and sightlines. He didn't see anything suspicious, but he angled himself perpendicular to Katie so that he could keep an eye on the entrance and on the barista.

"I'm serious!" exclaimed the woman in front of them. She was wearing athleisure wear of a brand that he recognized from Dominique's closet, which meant it probably cost more than he considered reasonable. He checked her head and realized she was talking on earbuds, while clutching her iPhone in one hand. "Look, I don't want to be so mercenary, but he has been out of work for six months. He's cut my allowance to five grand a month. What the hell am I even supposed to be able to buy with that? If he can't get it together I'm going to have to file for divorce. I am twenty-eight. I can't allow him to drag me down while I'm still in my best years."

Jackson glanced at Katie, but she didn't seem to have noticed the appalling string of entitlement coming out of the woman's mouth.

"Yes, he's received some job offers, but the highest one was only four-hundred thousand a year. He is one of the top plastic surgeons in New York. He is doing important work. I think I made it clear that he'd better not settle for something like that. I mean, I know we need the money, but that is unacceptable. Hold on—" She rattled off a complex drink order to the barista, ending with a condescending "thanks, sweetie" before moving down to the drink collection area.

"Hi," said the barista. "What can I get you?"

Katie dropped her phone in her pocket and smiled at the girl before ordering her drink. Jackson ordered two breakfast sandwiches and a black coffee with cream and sugar. Katie glared at him when he ignored the cash in her hand and put everything on his card. But then she unexpectedly shrugged and turned back to the barista.

"Thanks, sweetie," she said and shoved all her cash into the tip jar. The barista flashed a wide grin and nodded her acknowledgment. Jackson chuckled.

"Pro-move," he said, wrapping an around her and squeezing. Sometimes he wanted to hug her like she was his own personal stuffie. If Katie got any sweeter she would have been made of sugar.

"Follow me for more tips on how not to be an asshole," Katie murmured. "Honest to God, her husband would be better off if she did divorce him. Maybe he might meet someone who doesn't think he's a walking black card."

Jackson laughed as they moved toward the waiting area. For all her sugar, Katie had a spicy edge that made him more than a little bit hot.

"Oh, my God, Jackson!"

Jackson froze as the entitled bitch came back their direction carrying her drink.

"It's Marissa Shaw! Well, I say Shaw, but I'm about to go back to my maiden name. Marissa Martin."

"Marissa," said Jackson. He had no idea if he actually knew her.

"We met at the Friends of the Trees Fundraiser! You were with Nika! We sure do love her at the Junior League."

"Ah," said Jackson. "Nice to see you again."

"Nice to see you too," she said, playfully patting his arm.

"Excuse me," said Jackson, "I think I see our drinks are up."

"Are you going to the Houston Gala?" Marissa asked brightly, turning to follow them, despite that Jackson had his arm firmly around Katie.

"I really don't know," said Jackson.

"Well, maybe I'll see you there," she said.

"Maybe," said Jackson with a shrug.

"I know. I'll just ask Nika." Jackson gritted his teeth as Marissa used the family nickname again. "I bet she knows your schedule," said Marissa with a laugh.

Jackson didn't respond and stepped forward to get his drink. He handed Katie's to her first.

"Anyway, I'll see you around," said Marissa cheerfully.

"Mm," said Jackson, taking a sip, even though he knew it would be scalding hot.

"Bye!"

Marissa walked off with a cheerful wave.

"You know she will be asking Nika for your complete itinerary, right?" asked Katie.

"Yes, but Nika hates the Junior League and anyone associated with it. She also knows better than to give anyone my schedule. I think I'm safe."

Katie smiled, but shook her head. "I really hate those kind of women. They bring every relationship down to a transactional level and I just… I hate being commoditized like that."

"Some guys like that," said Jackson. "It makes it easier to know where they stand."

"No, it makes it easier to put themselves first. That's all it is on either side. Negotiated and ranked narcissism. It never occurs to them to put someone else first and being kind is considered a weakness."

Jackson had been so surprised that he kissed her instead of saying anything. He wasn't sure he could have said anything, even if he'd known what he wanted to say. It was the kind of statement that came from experience and he was amazed that she was still managing kindness in spite of that experience.

Jackson looked at the fidget toy. Kindness. Katie had more of it than most. He was lucky that she was willing to share her time with him.

The door of Cheery Bailbonds banged open and Devonte struggled through with his bags, scarf wrapped around him up to the eyeballs. The weather had taken an unexpected cold turn. Something else Jackson was going to have to do something about. Katie didn't appear to own a winter coat or decent boots. Maybe he could give them as a Christmas gift? They seemed like shift Christmas gifts, but she really needed them.

"Do you know how much I fucking hate JFK?" Devonte demanded, dropping his bag on the floor and slamming the door behind him.

"Considering the length of a cab ride between there and here and the fact that you're still stewing about it… I'm going with a lot."

"They lost my bag—twice."

Devonte continued to rant while he hung up his coat and went into the kitchen.

"How do you lose a bag twice?" Jackson called after him.

"I don't know but they managed it. I think I walked the entire length of that damn airport about eight times. It's over here. No, it's over there. It went to this terminal while I went to that terminal. At some point I think they just started fucking with me."

Devonte emerged from the kitchen with a cup of coffee and dropped down into the desk chair at the desk next to Jackson's. He took a sip of coffee and let out a deep sigh and slumped, thrusting his feet out.

"Glad to be home?" asked Jackson.

"I'm even happy to be drinking this shit coffee. Also, by the way, that is not what you do for horses."

"No?" asked Jackson innocently.

Devonte gave him a look. "No."

"I grew up in Chicago. What would I know about horses?"

"Why do I feel like you knew that before you said it though."

Jackson shrugged and Devonte laughed.

"OK, you've got your coffee, we've heard about JFK. What'd you find? Please tell me you found something because we're drawing blanks everywhere else."

"Sorry," said Devonte looking genuinely apologetic. "I waded through about eight phone booths of public records, two extra ex-husbands, and made a trip out to a cemetery. I'm sorry, but Christina Granger is dead."

"Wait, what?"

"Yeah, breast cancer," said Devonte, shaking his head. "Three years ago."

"That's impossible," said Jackson.

"I saw the death certificate," said Devonte. "And the headstone."

"Then who the hell signed into the visitor log last year to visit Granger?"

DECEMBER 18

Caitlin
The Russian

The evening's event was lawyers doing lawyer things, although Caitlin wasn't sure what those things were. It seemed like mostly being snooty at each other and handing out awards. At least they tipped well.

"Hello," said a blonde man, looking very serious. Katie looked him over. He was good-looking, stylish, and probably had women falling over themselves, so Katie waited for the inappropriate offer to come falling out of his mouth. "I have been told that if I promise not to stab anyone with toothpicks that Katie, the best bartender ever, will make me a cocktail worth having."

Katie laughed. "Are Evan and Olivia here? I haven't seen them." She scanned the crowd.

"No, but Olivia is almost my sister-in-law and she said if I was coming here you were the bartender to talk to," said the blonde. "Hi, I'm Aiden." He held out his hand, and Katie shook it. What was it with this family and introducing themselves like she was a real human being?

"Well, honestly, I'm not the best bartender in the world," said Katie. "I'll make you whatever drink you want. It's just that we usually only serve well drinks unless someone asks for something specific. Or unless I think Evan may commit homicide with stir sticks."

"Completely reasonable. But, well, here's my specific: can I have something that's like a cocktail without actually having any booze in it? I like feeling like I'm drinking without actually drinking. Unless it's wine that Evan picked out, it's just not worth it."

Katie laughed again. She liked this family. "Strangely, I know what you mean and yes I can do that. We just booked a birthday event for someone who's doing a dry January and I've been trying to come up with good mocktails. How about I make you one or two of my ideas and you can tell me what you think?"

"That'd be awesome," he said grinning broadly.

Katie reached into her cupboards and made him a pomegranate spritzer shrub.

"Do I even want to know what you're drinking?" asked a petite Asian woman scrutinizing Aiden's drink as she approached the bar.

"Yes, because it's delicious," said Aiden. "It has vinegar in it. Which I was not sure about, but Katie has waved her magic wand over it, so it's good. Ella this is Katie, that Evan and Olivia like. Katie this is Ella."

"Hi," said Katie. "I'm flattered, but I'm confused as to why Evan and Olivia are talking about me."

"They usually complain about going to events, but now they say they'll come to VAR events," said Ella. "They're introverts."

"There's nothing wrong with that," said Katie bristling on the red-headed couple's behalf. Then she blushed. Evan and Olivia weren't her friends. She shouldn't have said anything.

"This is true," said Aiden. "But it makes it unusual when they both don't mind going somewhere." He added a smile and Katie could tell that he had noted her defensiveness and embarrassment at the same time.

Katie smiled back. "Sorry. I just get attached when I see my customers being adorable at each other. I worked the night he proposed. He got cocktail sauce on his suit and was freaking out. He wanted everything to be perfect for her."

"Aww," said Ella, visibly melting. "I didn't know that. He didn't say anything." She whacked Aiden's arm. "Why can't you be that cute?"

"*Qīn*," he said using a term of endearment that Katie wasn't familiar with, "I will blob all the cocktail sauce on myself that you want. I did not realize that was turn on."

"No thanks," said Ella with a laugh. She paused and seemed to be thinking it over. "Maybe chocolate syrup."

"Sounds sticky, but I'm in."

Katie laughed. This family was creative. There was an annoying tapping from the main stage mic.

"Attention," droned the MC and Ella and Aiden both groaned.

"OK," said Aiden. "I'll be back. Maybe for one with booze in it if he talks too long."

"I got you," said Katie.

The event dragged on. Katie took her break, and changed her socks as usual then went back out to the bar. Jessica wasn't working tonight, but at least the barback wasn't Andrew. She tried to follow the events on stage, but the MC's voice was so monotone that she tuned out and only came to when there was a sudden movement of bodies on the floor as they hit some sort of intermission.

She could see that Aiden and Ella were heading her direction and Katie grabbed materials for his non-alcoholic drink while she filled her next two drink orders. She thought she was almost through the wave of orders, but she would be glad when the speechifying started again so she could get another break. Jackson had already texted that he would be waiting for her at home. She wanted the evening to be over with so she could be home in bed already. She plopped the drinks down, ran the cards, and collected the receipts before turning to the next customer.

"Caitlin," said a voice and Caitlin looked up into the face of the Russian bill collector.

"This is a private event," she said sharply.

"You no call. Then I show up."

"I don't have to call you," she said.

"You talk to me. You give me what I want. I'm running out of patience."

"Whatever it is you want, I don't have it. Leave now or I will have security throw you out."

"You give me what I want little *сука* or you will regret it."

Caitlin swallowed hard, but shook her head. "Fuck off—" She hadn't finished the words when the man grabbed her by the neck, pulling her toward him across the bar.

"Fuck!" yelled Aiden in surprise and punched the man in the face.

The man let go of Caitlin, clearly stunned, and then lunged at Aiden. Still half-way across the bar, Caitlin reached down and grabbed the first thing that came to hand—a Jack Daniels bottle and swung it at his head. It made a heavy clunk and he staggered backward, but it didn't finish the job. Aiden stepped between her and the man, hands up, clearly ready to make her problems his. The man shook his head and looked around the ever-widening circle of horrified guests. Caitlin could see the security team pushing their way through the crowd. Apparently, so could her attacker because with one final head shake he turned and began to run for the door.

Caitlin slithered off the bar, intending land on her feet, but ended up sitting down on the floor.

"Shit, shit, shit!" Ella was around the bar crouching down to look at her. "Katie, are you OK?"

"Here," said Aiden coming around to join her. "Let's get her into a chair. Maybe in the back?"

"I will handle this," snarled Vince, rounding the bar.

"No, she's hurt," said Aiden.

Vince ignored Aiden, half-picked her up and hustled her into the back hallway. There was a busted down chair there and he plopped her into it.

"What the fuck happened, Katie?" he asked, bending down to look her in the eye.

"Bill collector, I think," she whispered. "I don't really know."

Vince stood up and took half-step away, speaking urgently into his walkie-talkie. Caitlin shook her head, feeling shaky now that everything was over. She saw Aiden and Ella come into the hall and waved weakly.

Vince took a half-step between her and Aiden and Ella as if Caitlin needed protection from them as well. Ella ignored him and went around him to hug her, then pulled Caitlin's collar down with gentle hands to look at Caitlin's throat.

"I'm fine," Caitlin croaked.

"You should get ice," said Ella. "I'll find you ice."

"No," she said smiling at Ella. "No, I'm OK. Thank you."

"Did your guys get him?" asked Aiden, still looking at Caitlin, but half-turning to Vince.

"He had a car waiting," said Vince. "They got the plates. Katie, what do you want to do?"

"Call the cops," said Aiden.

"Maybe she doesn't want to," snapped Vince.

Caitlin looked at the three of them. She knew she should, but the idea of facing one more sour-faced cop made her guts churn. "I can't, Vince. I can't. Please don't make me." She rubbed at her scalp, trying not to dig in with her fingernails. That only led to continuous anxiety ridden scratching.

"Katie," said Aiden, "we'll support you. We saw what he did. We'll make statements. Whatever you need."

She smiled at him. That was incredibly sweet. "It's not tonight," she said. "It's the six months of having to deal with it and then finding out they released him anyway. And that's if they arrest him in the first place. I just... can't."

Aiden was distressed and exchanged a look with Ella, who promptly hugged Katie. "Whatever you want to do," she said.

"There's usually a twenty-four-hour window on these things," said Vince. "If you change your mind tomorrow, we can still call it in."

"OK," said Katie nodding.

"OK," he said. "Go take five. Get some ice. I'll have Steve cover for you."

"Thanks Ella," said Caitlin. "Thanks Aiden."

Aiden shrugged, still looking distressed. "Don't worry about it. Maybe you should—"

"She's fine," growled Vince. "*We* will take care of her."

Aiden backed off a step and glanced at Caitlin. She smiled and shrugged. "OK," said Aiden and held out his hand for Ella. Caitlin watched them walk away.

"They were being nice, Vince," she said, frowning at him. "They tipped really well too."

"Did they?" he asked with a worried frown.

"Yeah, they're really nice people."

"OK," he said, but his expression didn't change. "Just take a break, and we'll put you in a cab tonight to go home."

Jackson
THE UKRAINIAN

Jackson wasn't sure what had happened at work, but Katie had come home angry and now she was staring out the window instead of getting naked.

"What's up?" he called from the bed.

"Oh… Nothing." She was still wearing her shirt, and her pants were in her hand. He liked the way the soft glow of the bedside lamp caressed the curve of her ass. "There's an asshole across the street talking to Rufus."

Rufus was the local drug dealer who worked the park. As far as Jackson could tell, Katie was on a first name basis with literally everyone on the block. Rufus asked if Katie wanted a rock every time she went into to the park and Katie would politely decline with a *no thank you, Rufus* as if that was a normal thing to be asked.

"I imagine there's more than one. Assholes tend to come attached to legs."

Katie snorted. "Yeah, but this particular asshole I had a run in with earlier."

"You need me to go out and explain things to him?" he offered, although he didn't really want to. He was already in bed and didn't want to involve himself in Katie's neighborhood business.

"No," she said shaking her head. "It's my problem. I'll deal with it."

He almost laughed. It was such a Katie answer. "Can you deal with it later, though?" he asked. "Because I'm naked and it's warmer under the covers."

She laughed at him. "Yeah," she said, turning back toward

the bed and stripping off her shirt. She threw it at his face and he laughed. By the time he had cleared it away she had slid out of her underwear and jumped on the bed. He grabbed her and pulled her under the covers with him. They tussled under the comforter, wrestling to see who got to be on top. Finally, she let him win and he pinned her down and kissed her until she stopped giggling.

He moved her hair to kiss her neck and froze. "What's this?"

"What's what?" she asked, looking up at him.

"The fucking fingerprints on your neck."

She stared at him and then felt her neck, she winced as she found the bruises and pressed them.

"Who did that?" he demanded.

"That guy," she said with a sigh, getting up to look in the mirror on the back of the door.

"What fucking guy?"

"That guy outside. He showed up at work again."

"What do you mean *again?*"

"You remember that guy that was waiting for me outside the first night we hooked up? He showed up at work and got all aggro and grabbed my neck."

"What?"

"It's fine. One of the other customers punched him and I hit him with a Jack Daniels bottle."

"Then why isn't he in jail?" demanded Jackson.

"He ran off before Vince's guys could grab him. I don't even know how he got in. Vince was on a rampage about it. They got his license plate, but I told them not to bother calling the cops."

"Why the fuck not? That's assault and battery."

She turned away, rubbing her head in the way she did when she was anxious. "I didn't want to talk to the police. Or follow up.

Or testify. Or deal with that shit. I can't take on anymore projects. I didn't think he'd show up again."

"He's outside your fucking apartment."

She grimaced. "I can't call the cops. He's in the park, which is a public space. I'll go in tomorrow, and Vince and I will report it."

Jackson pulled on his pants and shoes. He didn't bother with his shirt. He wasn't going to need it.

"Where are you going?" She grabbed his button-up and came after him as he went down the stairs, pulling it on as she went. "Jackson!"

He was across the street and into the park before the asshole knew he was coming. Jackson recognized the clipped haircut and stocky build as the Russian from the parking lot. He didn't bother to re-introduce himself. Jackson grabbed him off the park bench where he was laughing with Rufus and some of the regular users, and threw the man down on the ground. The Russian jumped up with a growl. Jackson punched him twice and then began to drag him back to the street. The neighborhood crew just watched.

Katie was on the stoop in his shirt. The man pushed back trying to clear space and start punching. Jackson hit him again and rammed his head into the side of a car.

"*Komu vona nalezhyt?*" Jackson demanded in Ukrainian and punched him again. He pulled him into the street and kicked him. "*Komu vona nalezhyt?*" Jackson yelled again, grabbing him by the hair. Blood was dripping from the man's face. Jackson punched again and shoved him toward the car. The man fumbled at his waistband for his gun, and Jackson took it away from him and pistol-whipped him with it.

"*Komu vona nalezhyt?*" he asked standing over the man.

"You!" the man yelled.

Jackson cocked the gun.

"She belongs to you!" the man screamed putting up his hands.

Jackson looked up and realized that he was in front of an audience that included most of the street dealers and a group of kids that included Jamal.

"Come back again, and no one will find your body."

The man staggered to his feet and then stumbled to his car. The tires squealed as he left the neighborhood.

"Jamal, it's a fucking school night, go home," said Jackson as he went back across the street. Katie didn't say anything. She just turned around and went inside. He locked the door and followed her up the stairs. He could see her ass under his shirt as she climbed the stairs in front of him. It made him hard.

"Go to the bed," he said when they reached the apartment. He knew the sentence was off, but was having to work hard not to say it in Ukrainian. He tossed the gun down on the table and went into the kitchen.

"Are you coming?"

"I don't want to touch you until I've washed my hands."

She was naked on the bed when he came in. The lights were off, but he could see her in the glow of the street lights. He stripped off his pants and pulled on a condom.

He kissed his way up her legs and body. It was perfunctory. They both knew it. He moved her leg, holding her by the hip, but she locked her legs, squeezing him tightly, preventing him from entering her.

"I don't belong to you," she said.

He stared down at her. Yes, she did. She was his. No one else was allowed to touch her. He pushed against her leg, but she refused to move.

"Say it," she said, her eyes were dark and glittering in the shadows.

He hesitated. He didn't want to say it, but the muscles under his hand were unyielding.

"You don't belong to me."

Her legs relaxed and he thrust into her, claiming her anyway. He felt it like a chant in his head with each thrust, mine, mine, mine. Her arms were around him, pulling him into her and she put her legs around him as well, digging into his ass with her heels. She was silent as he fucked her, the only noise in the room was the ragged sound of their breathing and the creak of the bedframe.

She came with a gasp and he came a moment later, collapsing down onto her.

Caitlin
The Morning

Caitlin woke up to the bright light of morning. Jackson's arms were wrapped around her, spooning to her tightly. She stared at herself in the mirror on the back of the door. Her throat was sore this morning and although she couldn't see them, she suspected the bruises would be more pronounced.

In the mirror she could see the black shock of Jackson's hair behind her shoulder. She closed her eyes and saw his face from the night before. Harsh, unforgiving, and cold. She had no trouble believing that he would have killed that man if there hadn't been witnesses. Was that what Jackson was?

And then he had come inside and fucked her. Not just fucked her—claimed, taken, owned. He'd fucked her like it was his right. He'd said the words, but it hadn't mattered. It had been in every single thrust and touch. She belonged to him.

Did she?

She didn't feel owned. She didn't feel like he kept her on a leash. Jackson had never once crossed her boundary lines. He'd never taken or demanded anything that she wouldn't give.

Caitlin turned over, wriggling in his arms, and with a sigh he relaxed and let go, but didn't wake up. She stared into his face. It was nothing like his expression from the night before. In sleep, he was sweet.

Which was the real Jackson?

She kissed him softly, and he opened his eyes with a confused and sleepy smile. She kissed him again, and his smile got wider. His hands sought her body, caressing her. His hand gently pushed her legs apart, and he stroked her.

"Go down on me," she said. She didn't make it a question, and he didn't argue, disappearing beneath the covers.

His tongue circled her clit with barely any pressure, and she moaned his name. His tongue pressed harder, and she found her body throbbing with each pass. His fingers stroked lower, gently tapping just inside her, as his tongue continued to circle. She gasped and clutched at the sheets as she hit a new peak. He pushed harder and went faster, and she began to writhe as she felt the need, the pressing pleasure that was almost torture. She came, clutching at his hair under the covers.

He kissed along her thigh and sat up, flinging off the covers and leaving her exposed.

"My turn," he said with a cocky smile.

She laughed. That was Jackson. She turned over to grab him a condom from the bedside table and he grabbed her by the hips and pulled her back to him as soon as it was in her hand. He took her from behind, fucking her into another orgasm and they ended up in the same position she'd woken up in. This time he nuzzled her ear, tickling her and making her laugh.

His phone went off and he reached up to grab it from the bedside table.

"Oh, fucknuts," he said, scrolling through a message.

"Problems?"

He grunted. "Sort of. I have to go."

He pushed himself out of bed and began to get dressed. She watched Jackson put his clothes back on, realizing how familiar his movements had become. That was what he did every time. He wasn't her boyfriend. He didn't bring clothes. He didn't have a drawer. He didn't even keep a toothbrush here.

If she belonged to him, then it was an unequal ownership—Jackson did not belong to her.

He finished dressing and leaned down to kiss her. Then he lifted the covers to look at her naked body.

"Killing me," he said, shaking his head, and let the duvet fall down again, and she laughed. "Call me when you're free," he said, kissing her again.

"OK," she agreed. It was their standard exchange. Jackson texted sometimes, but mostly she was the one that sent for him. He jogged down the stairs and was out the door before she could decide if that was fair or not.

Jackson
Deveraux House

Jackson returned to Deveraux House, and Theo opened the door with a frown. Frowns from Theo meant anything from broken dishware to Jackson mangling some social nicety, but in December, frowns were hard to take seriously from Theo. Today's Christmas sweater had reindeer with fuzzy things for noses and tails.

"Everyone is in the drawing room, and I believe Mr. Ames is upset."

"Max is mad?" asked Jackson. Max was usually laid back. Jackson couldn't imagine what they were arguing about. He also hadn't expected Max to be at the house.

"Mr. Deveraux and Miss Dominique are with them, but I think perhaps it would not do to dally."

Mr. Deveraux, in Theo-speak, was Evan. Dominique had once forced Jackson to watch *Pride and Prejudice,* and Jackson had realized that the eldest sibling got the family name treatment and everyone else was a Mister and Miss with their first names. Jackson also realized that not dallying was Theo-speak for *hurry your ass up* and put a little extra speed on, hurrying past the tree in the front hall.

When he entered the drawing room, he saw Aiden and Max unexpectedly squaring off. Dominique pushed Max backward while Evan was herding Aiden back toward the couch.

"You don't get to tell her what to do!" barked Aiden.

"He's not!" Dominique yelled back.

"OK," said Jackson, "what'd I miss?"

"He's trying to boss my sister around!"

"He is not!" Dominique yelled back. "I want to take the train!"

"You've never taken the train in your life!"

Jackson stared at his cousins and Max's frustrated expression. Whatever this was about, it wasn't about the train. "Evan, why don't you take Aiden out for a walk around the garden?"

"Yes," said Evan, pulling Aiden by the arm.

"What? Why am I being sent outside? You saw that, right? You saw what he did."

"I validate your feelings while suggesting you go the fuck outside," said Evan.

"That's not how feeling validation works," said Aiden while allowing himself to be pushed out of the room.

The cousins left, and Dominique and Max stared at him mutely.

"OK, so," said Jackson. "Train?"

"I'm taking the train to DC," said Dominique. "They called in our subpoenas. We have to be there tomorrow. I don't want to fly with the rest of you. I want to take the train. Max said we were taking the train because he knew you wouldn't want me riding by myself, and Aiden flipped out."

"Did I miss some sort of Max and Aiden are fighting memo?" asked Jackson. "I thought everything was fine last whenever it was that we went to the gym."

"It is," said Max, tiredly. "It was. I just said I wanted Dominique to take the train, and Aiden went ballistic. I'm not sure what I did."

"I want to take the train," said Dominique.

Jackson scrutinized the pair and tried to weigh what he knew about both of them and their current miserable expressions.

"Then, I think you should take the train," said Jackson. Dominique's shoulders sagged as if in defeat, but Jackson thought Max looked relieved. "Oh." It was right there on her face.

"Oh?" Dominique looked confused.

"It's OK. It's fine. We'll do the plane thing next time," said Jackson trying to mentally reshuffle his travel plans. Now both Dominique and Max both looked confused. "Max, can I go on the train instead of you?"

Max looked at Dominique uncertainly. "I mean, I'm fine with that. I didn't want to miss my class, but…"

"But you'd do it for me," said Dominique, squishing herself into Max, who automatically put his arms around her.

"What if I make Aiden go instead? We'll buy him a conductor's hat, and he'll get over it."

Dominique laughed. "What?"

"It doesn't matter," said Jackson. "Wait here. I'll go get Aiden to stop being weird. Be right back."

Evan was sprawled across one of the reclining lawn chairs while Aiden took giant steps over the paving stones surrounding the gazebo. He was making an endless loop of funny walks.

"She wants to go on the plane," said Aiden, pointing at Jackson angrily. "Don't tell me she doesn't."

"Yes, I think she does," said Jackson. Aiden stopped abruptly and came back in his regular stride.

"Then why is he making her go on the train? I don't understand. I've never seen him do anything like that before."

"He's not."

"It was written all over her face," snapped Aiden. "She was disappointed. And sad. My sister is not supposed to be sad!" His voice rose angrily as he talked.

"Slow down," said Evan. "Dominique is allowed to be all of those things."

"I'm not saying she can't," snapped Aiden. "I'm saying she

could go on the plane if she wanted, and there is no good reason not to except for Max telling her not to."

"Max is taking the rap because she doesn't want to tell you she's freaking out about going on the plane. And I think she's also disappointed in herself that she's scared."

"Oh, shit," said Evan. "I didn't even think about that."

Aiden looked between the two of them and made a confused noise.

"The last time all the Deverauxes were on a plane, it didn't end well," said Jackson. "You know, what with the crashing and the dying."

"Well, shit," said Aiden. "Now I want to go on the train."

"You can," said Jackson. "Max doesn't really want to go on the train. He just doesn't want Dominique to be by herself."

There was silence in the garden while Aiden seemed to take stock of things. "I think I may have overreacted," said Aiden.

"Mm," said Evan. "She looked like your mom, didn't she?"

Aiden looked at Evan, clearly frustrated. "Mom never wanted to do things, but she never said no. It was always right there on her face, and everyone just walked all over her."

"That is not Max," said Jackson. "And it really isn't Dominique."

"I don't want to apologize to Max," said Aiden sullenly.

"I didn't say you had to," said Jackson.

"I mean, as someone who has had to own up to saying lots of horrible things, I would recommend it, but…" murmured Evan.

Aiden barked out another expletive and stomped off toward the house.

"She's not great about admitting vulnerability," said Jackson, as Aiden slammed the door.

"None of us are," said Evan. "But I kind of thought we were at a place that we could tell each other."

"She's embarrassed, and I think she's surprised. She's always said the plane crash was something for you and Aiden to deal with because she was too young to remember."

"She was ten," said Evan, looking puzzled. "That isn't *that* young, and Aiden is only two years older. What… Hm. She's the one that's fine?"

"She's the one that's fine," said Jackson.

"For the life of me, I do not know why Grandma didn't get us therapy at the time."

"She says that wasn't something people did back then. I have actually heard her express regret about that one."

Evan's eyebrows went up. "Maybe it was something that Deverauxes didn't do, but I'm pretty sure that therapists were in existence at the time. Well, this will sound weird, but it makes sense to me that Dominique's having issues now."

"What do you mean?" asked Jackson.

"Life is going pretty good right now. She and Max are solid. We're all doing well. Grandma is playing nicely. This is when the gremlins start being like, *hey, remember that thing we've been holding down because you didn't have space before? Well, look at all the space you have now!*"

Jackson laughed. "That's not cool. Someone should tell the gremlins to get back down."

"Yeah, they don't listen," said Evan bitterly. "OK, so… they're taking the train. Are we taking the train? It seems like if we all take the train, we're just replicating the problem but in a less fun mode of transportation."

"That was my thought," said Jackson. "And now that I've successfully passed off train duties to Aiden, I think you and I should stick with flying."

"*Brat moya.* This is exactly why I always wanted a brother

when I was a kid." Evan looked so satisfied that Jackson couldn't help laughing. "Come on, let's go see if Aiden has managed to patch things up yet."

He had. It was one of Aiden's better traits that when he apologized, he meant it, and when he forgave, he meant that too. Dominique and Aiden had now moved on to discussing how much seating they could rent out without being total douchebags. Max just looked tired.

"How are you holding up?" asked Evan.

"What do you mean?" asked Max.

"Caretakers have a hard job, too," said Evan. "Dominique's dealing with some shit, and you're trying to hold down law school and keep her from losing it. So, how are you doing?"

"Well, I didn't punch Aiden, so I've got that going for me," said Max ruefully. "And I'm now able to say the word *marriage* without Dominique leaving the room. So, we're making progress. I just… I want to be able to fix things for her, and I can't. I knew she was a high-performance kind of person, but I think I underestimated how much pressure she puts on herself."

"I doubt she knew she was doing it," said Evan. "After a while, you think that much pressure is normal. I'm glad she has you, but let us know if we can help."

Max looked like he genuinely appreciated the comment, but Jackson frowned. How much pressure could one person take before they snapped? He didn't think he'd been under pressure. Katie was the one who seemed like she was holding the weight of the world, but he was the one who had lost his cool. He hadn't lost it like that in a long time. Katie had every right to want him out of the house, but he thought things had been all right this morning. Everything had been normal except for having to drop the Russian's gun off at the office. Maybe? He probably ought to check in with Katie.

"Jackson?" Max was looking at him as if expecting a response, but Jackson had no idea what the last comment had been.

"Sorry," said Jackson. "I need to go pack. I'll be back down in a bit. Evan, can you call about the plane?"

"Yeah, no problem," said Evan. Jackson smiled reassuringly in response to Evan's questioning expression and headed upstairs.

Dominique
The Drawing Room

Dominique waited until she was sure that Jackson was upstairs before interrupting everyone.

"OK, show of hands: who thinks Jackson is seeing someone?"

Max's hand shot up. "I was trying to bite my tongue. I know he's anti-girlfriend, but come onnnnnn. I'm not even a Deveraux, and I know that was an evening outfit, not an *I got up early* outfit."

"But that doesn't have to mean anything," said Aiden. "I love the guy, but he's kind of a man-ho."

"I wouldn't go that far," said Evan. "It's not like he doesn't have standards. I believe he simply prefers his sex to be relationship-free and generally keeps his partners on a rotation so that no one feels used or like they mean more than they do."

"He said he didn't want to learn someone else's birthday," said Max.

Evan snorted out a laugh of surprise.

"I don't understand," said Aiden. "Don't you just put the birthdays on your calendar? Or, failing that, get an assistant."

"Either of those would work," said Max. "But he literally said no to birthdays. I told him to get a better excuse."

"OK, yes, but regardless of the birthday situation," said Dominique. "This is at least the third time I've caught him coming back to the house in the morning. And I would have to say that I agree with Evan's assessment on his usual system, and I have also noted that his usual system does *not* include sleeping over."

"She's right," said Aiden. "Sleeping over is relationship-y. Sleeping over means, I don't mind your cold feet on my leg."

"Basic signifier of a relationship, right there," agreed Max.

"My feet get cold," said Dominique.

"And I don't mind that you put your ice cubes on my leg," said Max. "Because I love you."

"I just turn up the heat," said Evan.

"Yes, well, Tuesdays are a thing at your house," said Dominique. "Investing in in-floor heating was clearly a prescient decision on your part."

"That's true," agreed Evan.

"We tried Naked Wednesday at our house," said Aiden. "We did not care for it."

Evan looked surprised. "Well, maybe Wednesday is an off day."

"No, I believe we are fundamentally unsuited for nudity in non-bedroom situations. We have decided not to go that route. We did decide to invest in more lingerie and food delivery options, though, so don't feel like we're sad."

"You bought yourself more lingerie?" asked Dominique, thrown off.

"That depends on what you mean by *myself* and who you think lingerie is really for."

"Focus, people," said Max, snapping his fingers. "Jackson. Girlfriend. What do we think?"

"I'm not convinced," said Aiden. "I'm not saying there isn't evidence in that direction, but it may not mean what we think it means."

"He's made it pretty clear that he's not interested in anyone we've picked out," Evan said.

"Wait," said Dominique. "I know." She went to the door and stuck her head out. "Theo!" She tried to whisper and yell simultaneously, and it came out as a hoarse croak. But Theo prompt-ly poked his head out of the kitchen hall.

"Yes?"

She waved her hand frantically. Theo came into the drawing room with a cautious expression that was at odds with his festive green Christmas sweater with fuzzy pom-poms. She eased the door shut behind him and pushed him into the room.

"Is there a problem?" asked Theo, looking the boys over.

"I believe Dominique is trying to covertly discover if Jackson has been seeing anyone," said Evan.

"Well," said Theo, "I believe we all know that he would never bring anyone back here."

"He wouldn't?" asked Evan.

"I believe that he feels Sunday dinners are sacred, Mr. De-veraux," said Theo, "and I believe he would never like to give any-one the impression that they have a chance of attending when they don't."

"That makes sense," said Evan.

"Only if you're a Deveraux," said Max. "But OK. So he hasn't been bringing anyone home?"

"Yes, but," Theo leaned in and lowered his voice, "I would say that, on average, he has only been spending three to four nights at home per week for over a month."

"Half his time," said Aiden. "That's… I mean…"

"That's a relationship," said Max.

"OK, but who is she?" asked Evan.

"Over a month?" demanded Aiden, looking thoughtful. "That's got to be Miss Mindblowingly Nice."

Dominique turned to look at her brother. "Who?"

"The day you and Evan got your subpoenas, Jackson came

home from a night out. He said she was mind-blowing, but he wasn't going to see her again because she was too nice for him.

"Why is our cousin an idiot?" demanded Dominique. "Although, this does make sense. I thought Marissa was just being a wench."

"It may make sense to you, but we're going to need more than *Marissa is a wench,*" said Evan.

"Marissa Shaw from Junior League," said Dominique. "She asked about Jackson a few weeks ago. Said she bumped into him at a coffee shop, which sounded like bullshit. And then she had the gall to ask about his schedule. She said she didn't think he was serious about the model-girl he had his arm around, which sounded like a heaping pile of elephant-sized dung to me because— in order of objections—Marissa is married, Jackson doesn't like models, and he never puts his arm around anyone except us."

"Yes," said Theo, sadly. "I believe that, like Mrs. Deveraux, he is a very affectionate person who has been trained not to show it in public."

Dominique froze as she considered this. Her grandmother was distinctly not a hugger. What did Theo know that she didn't?

"Well, that makes me sad for both of them," said Max.

"Yes," agreed Theo.

Dominique looked frantically at Evan and Aiden. They also looked immobilized.

"Well, we can't go around hugging people in public," said Dominique. "Then people would know that we had feelings."

"OK," said Max. "And now I'm just generally sad."

"That's because you have feelings," said Aiden.

Dominique reached out and grabbed Max's hand, and he squeezed it back. "OK, but basically, what we're saying is that he's seeing someone? A model-type someone who likes coffee, but who is nice?"

"Yes," agreed Theo.

"That's what I'm hearing," said Evan.

"Well," said Dominique, "I guess I could like someone who likes coffee. I drink coffee-based drinks sometimes."

"Pretty sure that's not her only personality trait," said Evan.

"Well, I'm trying," said Dominique, "but *nice* doesn't really sound very fun."

"Well, how are we supposed to find out who she is?" demanded Aiden.

"I'm going to go out on a limb," said Max, "and suggest asking him."

Dominique could see that Aiden and Evan were trying not to outright tell Max what a ludicrous suggestion that was.

"I mean, I could even go upstairs and ask him right now," said Max and then looked at the trio of Deveraux faces. "But obviously, you're going to run some top secret mission on him while you're in DC, and I wouldn't want to ruin your fun."

Dominique laughed and kissed his cheek. "It's not going to be fun. It's serious. What if he's in love?"

"It's only been a month," said Aiden reasonably. "Jackson is like Mister-Plan-It-Out. We don't really think that could happen, do we?"

Max started laughing.

"Mm," said Evan. "And how long did it take you?"

"Right," said Aiden. "I mean, that sounded stupid coming out of my mouth, and I don't know why I even said it."

Caitlin
Out of Town

Caitlin stared at her phone.

I'M GOING TO BE OUT OF TOWN FOR A FEW DAYS.

What did that mean? What was she supposed to say to that?

THANKS FOR LETTING ME KNOW.

She hit send. And stared at the message again.

"Hey!" said Jessica, going by with a tray of glassware. She was back again a few minutes later. "What's with the face?"

"Jackson said he would be out of town for a few days. I think he's breaking up with me."

"Breaking up with you?"

"Or whatever you call it when you stop fucking someone," said Caitlin angrily. She was tired of Jessica's jokes that she and Jackson were dating.

Jessica made take-it-easy gestures. "I meant, why does going out of town mean breaking up?"

"He goes out of town all the time for work. He doesn't usually tell me unless it's a Wednesday."

"Right, because he's what you do on your night off," said Jessica with a grin, and then she saw Caitlin's expression. "I'm teasing. OK, but again, I'm not seeing it. So he politely let you know that he would be unavailable. Why does that mean something bad?"

Caitlin opened her mouth. Jessica waited, eyebrows raised. "Things got kind of… weird last night."

"In what way?"

"That guy who grabbed me last night? He was at my place last night."

"I thought Vince gave you a ride?"

"He did, but I think he followed us. I didn't notice him until Vince had pulled away. Anyway, I went upstairs, and Jackson and I were fooling around, and then he saw the marks on my neck and…"

"And what?"

"He lost his shit and went out to the park and beat the guy up."

"Seriously?" demanded Jessica grinning.

"Yeah. Pretty sure he broke the guy's nose." She hesitated, remembering the gun but uncertain what to say. It hadn't seemed important at the time. Jackson hadn't treated it like it was.

"Cool."

"I guess," said Caitlin. Jackson dropped the gun on her kitchen table in utter contempt. It was a microcosm of the way he'd treated the owner. He thought nothing of that man. The gun had been gone this morning.

"Then what?"

"Well, then sex was a little… off." She didn't want to go into detail on that part. She wasn't sure she could put it into words for herself, let alone Jessica. "But this morning, I thought everything was fine again. Only now, he's saying he's out of town. Maybe he… maybe he had time to think about it and decided he didn't need my bullshit."

"Your kind of bullshit? It's not your kind of bullshit! It's some random stalker asshole. And it sounds like he took care of him. How is that your fault?"

"I don't know," said Katie. "It feels like my fault."

"This isn't a fault situation. There's no fault. Some guy threatened you. Jackson beat him up. And now he's going out of town. It's not a crisis. It's not necessarily even linked."

Caitlin nodded. "It might even be good," she said. "I mean, it got weird there for a minute. Maybe this will just be a nice reset and we can get back to normal."

"Back to fucking each other's brains out, you mean? Yeah. God, I want your normal."

Jackson
Packing

Jackson tossed his shirt into the suitcase. And looked at his phone on the bed.

Thanks for letting me know.

That wasn't what he'd wanted her to say. He didn't know what he'd expected, but whatever it had been, he hadn't wanted that. He'd meant the text to be more of a conversation starter, only he realized that they didn't have any practice at conversations like that, and her response left him no openings.

The bruises on her throat had hit him like a punch from a prizefighter. His first thought was that they looked like the bruises on his mother's throat. And then all he could think was that they were from someone else, someone that she had asked to do that to her. The fact that she hadn't was a relief. His anger was easy to transfer to someone who deserved it.

Thanks for letting me know.

But the impersonal message had brought the anger back, and with it came the startling realization that she could very well be sleeping with someone else. And the idea of someone else touching her…

He looked up and saw himself in the mirror and was startled to see his mother looking back at him. It was in the hard, angry set of his mouth. He looked away, annoyed. This had his mother all over it. It was like tripping over something he thought he'd put away. He didn't get possessive like she did. He didn't get jealous or dictate sex and pain, doling out either as rewards or punishments. He kept himself free and unencumbered on purpose.

But the idea of someone else kissing Katie, some other man putting his hands on her body, of her saying else's name as she came, was like burr in his shirt that poked him no matter which way he turned.

He'd tied himself to his cousins on purpose; they were the only ones with any claim on him. But that was the problem, wasn't it? Katie didn't want to claim him.

Yes, he had fucked her, but she had made him say the words. She didn't belong to him.

Thanks for letting me know.

He took a deep breath. Katie had been perfectly clear. He loved that she never mixed signals. He was never confused about where she'd drawn the lines. It was just the bruises. It was too much like his mother. It had tripped him up. This feeling would pass. It was probably good that he was going away for a few days. He could get back to normal. And then he could come back, and he and Katie could return to normal. Weren't they happy the way they were? Why was he trying to fuck up a good thing with his baggage?

Jackson
The Hotel

Jackson staggered to the door of his hotel room and opened it. Evan was on the other side, wearing jeans and a Gen-Tech T-shirt.

"What time is it?" he asked, blinking at Evan.

"Six forty-five. No one is up, and I'm bored."

"So you thought you'd inflict yourself on me?"

"Yes," said Evan with a grin. "I want to watch cartoons and eat breakfast."

Jackson shrugged and walked back to the bed. He climbed in, and Evan flopped down next to him.

Eleanor owned a two-bedroom apartment for when she was in DC, but with all of the cousins in town, Jackson had elected to stay with them at the hotel. At the moment, he regretted that decision.

Evan called for breakfast on the hotel phone and then turned on the TV to the cartoon network. Jackson ignored him, burrowed deeper under the covers, and wished he had Katie to wrap himself around. He was in the drifting place of almost sleep when his phone rang. He grabbed it and saw Dominique's picture. He grunted, unlocked the phone, and shoved it at Evan.

"Hey, Nika," said Evan, taking the phone. "No, I'm in Jackson's room watching cartoons." There was a pause as Dominique spoke. "Yeah, of course. I'll order more breakfast."

"They're coming up?" asked Jackson.

"Yeah," said Evan, handing the phone back.

Jackson grunted again and burrowed deeper. The next time he

poked his nose out, his cousins were occupying the other bed and eating cereal.

"But why is he green?" asked Dominique, in a hushed voice, her eyes glued to the TV.

"Nika, I don't know why he's green," said Aiden. "He's just green."

Jackson moved the covers and stared at the strange cartoon on the TV. Dominique noticed he was awake. "How do you ever sleep through us?"

"You're quieter than prison, and I trust you're not going to try and kill me."

"I'm not sure why, but I find that deeply touching," said Aiden, pointing at Jackson with his spoon.

"Lack of murdering each other is a building block of family love," said Evan from behind his newspaper, and Dominique laughed. "Also, Beast Boy is green because he received an infusion of an experimental serum from his parents to cure a rare disease. The serum turned him green and gave him the power to transform into any animal."

"The more you know," said Jackson, getting up. He was halfway to the bathroom when his phone rang. He turned back, but Evan waved him off and punched in Jackson's passcode before picking up the phone. Jackson realized he'd underestimated Evan's memory for numbers. He was going to have to switch back to the thumbprint for security.

"Hi, Grandma," Evan said. "No, we're all in Jackson's room eating breakfast." Jackson waited. "Because we all like cartoons, and you would make us eat something healthy. Aiden wanted Count Chocula. Yes, I'm aware we're not twelve." There was a pause, and Jackson decided that there would not be an immediate need for him and continued to the bathroom. "Well, I expect we'll be over after

Teen Titans Go. No, you don't want to know what *Teen Titans Go* is. I can only explain Beast Boy so many times in a day, and we don't have time to cover Starfire and Robin. Also, Jackson still needs to eat. So probably an hour. Yes, see you in a bit."

When he returned, the TV volume had been turned down, and Aiden and Dominique's bed had been covered in papers Aiden and Evan were making stacks of the documents while Dominique was noting something on a tablet.

"Phone," said Evan, waving it at him and then placing it on the table.

"Thanks," said Jackson, pulling on his sweats and t-shirt. He was about to ask what they were doing when there was a knock on his door.

"That's your breakfast," said Aiden. "So don't shoot them."

"Hey, I haven't nearly shot room service since Utah," Jackson called as he went to the door.

"What?" asked Evan, looking up. "When we're you in Utah?"

"As your lawyer, I advise you not to answer that," said Aiden.

Jackson opened the door and saw that the bellhop had clearly been able to hear him through the door.

"We're joking," said Jackson.

"This is DC, man," said the bell hop who looked all of about twenty. He reminded Jackson of Jamal. He was skinny and a little too tall for his pants.

"Point taken," said Jackson. "But don't worry, I was sent up for armed robbery, not murder."

"Ha. Ha."

Jackson took the tray and handed the kid a fifty.

"On the other hand, who am I to judge?"

Jackson grinned. "Thanks."

The kid waved and took off. Jackson went back inside and set down his food tray.

"What are we doing?" he asked, putting the shmear on his bagel.

"Dominique and I pulled all the members of the ethics committee, and we're comparing them to the list you gave Evan of all the members of the Senate who were there during the Absolex hearings," said Aiden.

"The problem is," said Evan, "that Absolex was a publicly traded company, and when I tanked the stock—"

"We," corrected Jackson. "It was a group effort to set up that run on the stock."

Evan shrugged. "Whatever. Point is that holding Absolex stock wasn't illegal, and most members of Congress divested when the hearings were in full swing. No one wanted to be called out for supporting a company that killed veterans. So now we're an entire election and 4 years away from the hearings, and it's a little hard to see who would have a vested interest in Absolex. I'm not seeing any names that match up with investors that I knew about."

"I don't think it is an interest in Absolex," said Jackson. "I think it's a vested interest in revenge, and I think possibly someone doesn't want those hearings transcripts to go public."

"But most of the hearings were broadcast," objected Dominique. "I don't see the point in blocking them."

"Not everything was broadcast," said Aiden thoughtfully. "The Absolex lawyers successfully argued that some of their testimony could be in the realm of intellectual property. Before it became clear that Absolex was acting in extreme bad faith, some of the early testimony was behind closed doors. Meaning that something could have been said behind closed doors that would still be a threat to this person."

"I think," said Jackson, "that Granger said something that could incriminate his would be partner. At least, that's what I'm hoping. I can't find Granger's files, but if I can figure out who is behind this maybe I can get him another way."

"You keep saying him," said Dominique, "but right now, Griffeth is my top contender. You said Taggert implicated her as the motivator behind blocking the file release."

"I keep saying him, because Granger said *him*," said Jackson. "Right now, Griffeth is screwing up my perfectly good theory and it's annoying me. So if you could find a way for my theory to still be true, I'd appreciate it."

Aiden laughed. "I hate it when the evidence won't cooperate."

"Me too," said Jackson.

"I don't see how she's not involved," said Dominique. "Particularly with Ralph Taggert pointing the finger at her."

"She could just hate Grandma," suggested Evan. "It might not have anything to do with Granger or Absolex."

"That's sort of what I'm thinking," said Jackson, with a shrug. "I'm hoping to get something out of this hearing today, although I'm not looking forward to it. Aiden, any pro-tips on how to do this properly?"

"Keep your answers short and to the point," said Aiden. "They're going to be annoying and they're going to bluster and grandstand even though there won't be anybody to show off for really. There may be some that are actually doing their job, but there are going to be a few that are just trying to score points."

"OK," said Jackson nodding. "I never did actually get my subpoena. Do I actually have to show up?"

"How'd you manage that?" demanded Evan.

"I'm sneaky," said Jackson. "And I rotated my schedule."

"Are you telling me that you intentionally started spending

time other places?" demanded Dominique, giving him a look that was surprisingly disapproving.

"No," said Jackson. Although spending nights at Katie's hadn't hurt anything. "I don't think it's playing fair if I don't go to all my usual stuff. I went to all of my appointments. I just did not use the usual entrances or exits, and I changed some of my appointments at the last minute. It's not my fault they use shit process servers."

"You still have to go," said Aiden, shaking his head. "They talked to your lawyer who has advised you to show up."

"I was going to anyway. I just wanted to know how the game is played," said Jackson, grinning at Aiden's annoyance. "How'd they get you?"

"Coming out of court," said Aiden, with a sigh. "A week ago."

Jackson grinned. "Can't avoid court."

"No, and the judge wouldn't put off the date. I knew that was how they'd do it, but I couldn't get out fast enough. Stop looking smug."

Jackson grinned. "I can't help it. I told Pete you'd make it past the fifteenth. He didn't think you'd make it past the fifth."

"What?" demanded Dominique, looking offended. "Why wasn't I in on this pool?"

"It wasn't a pool," said Jackson. "There wasn't any money on it. We just had a conversation. I thought for sure Aiden would make it well into December. He's crafty."

"Well, hopefully he's crafty enough to get us all through this hearing," said Evan. "And frankly, I'm a little more than pissed that they called it right before Christmas."

"That's on purpose," said Aiden. "This is my point. Christmas thieves are the kind of people we're dealing with."

Aiden

After the Hearing

Aiden exited the hearing and did a little Bruno Mars spin.

"That was awesome," he declared and then got a full look at the expressions on the faces of his relatives. They clearly did not share his enthusiasm.

"That was a bunch of fucking bullshit," said Evan.

"What he said," agreed Dominique.

"Well, completely. I would even go so far as to rate it up there with a pile of rhino dung in order of magnitude, but I looked good, so… you know."

Jackson was the only one who laughed.

"I did like the part where you corrected Senator Griffeth on the actual rules of procedure," said Evan.

"Studying does pay off," said Aiden, feeling smug.

"I liked it when he emailed all of them the correct documents while she was still trying to sputter out a complete sentence," said Dominique.

"Well, that was Jackson having prepared me with the email list ahead of time," said Aiden. "I can't take full credit for that."

Aiden's phone dinged, and he pulled it out. He'd texted Ella, and the others live time updates during the proceedings. Looking like he was goofing around on his phone had annoyed multiple senators, which had been the point.

Are you done now?

Ella had switched to a private thread.

Just got out. I kicked ass. Even Evan said so.

You are so hot. I will be sending you nudes later. Way to rock that. XoX

Aiden couldn't stop the grin that was spreading across his face. "Ella says hi."

"Uh-huh," said Dominique. She looked like she would have other things to say, but her own phone made an alert noise, and her face softened when she checked the messages. Evan was checking his texts at the same time. Aiden glanced at Jackson, who wore a wistful expression as he watched Evan and Dominique get messages.

Their morning's covert inspection of Jackson's phone while he'd been in the bathroom had been a dead end. Aside from Pete, his most frequent non-family member was someone labeled Kati-eSC. KatieSC was a very dull text partner. She invited him over and said when she was busy, but her texts were neither sexy or even particularly friendly. If that was who Jackson was in love with, Aiden wasn't sure it was mutual. Which was annoying because Jackson was a goddamn wonderful human being who deserved someone awesome.

"Olivia baked her way through the morning," said Evan. "She appreciated Aiden's group text updates and audio clips."

"So did Max," reported Dominique. "But he wants to know how to get Olivia to stop baking."

"Yeah, he can't," said Evan. "Just tell him he'll have to go to the gym extra this week."

Dominique shrugged and went back to her phone.

"Olivia wants to know if Dominique can teach her how to say *what an interesting question* like she does," said Evan, continuing his scroll

Jackson laughed again. "I also enjoyed that part."

"Did I say that?" asked Dominique looking puzzled.

"Yeah, to his face," said Jackson. "It was brutal."

"It was kind of Grandma level," agreed Aiden. "The best part was when you stared at him with your eyebrows raised and just let him twist before responding."

"I learned that from Evan. It makes people terribly uncomfortable. And then, when they open their mouth like they're about to say something else, you talk. It throws them off."

"Timing is everything," said Evan with a shrug. "But asking you about a brutal physical assault with the implication that you had in some way caused it was beyond sexist. He earned every second of that discomfort. Not that he learned anything from it."

"It's generally very unlikely," said Dominique. "Can we get lunch? I'm starved. Turns out sugar cereal is not a real breakfast. How did we ever eat that crap?"

"We didn't," said Aiden. "Theo made us have like squirrel food or eggs."

"I forgot about the squirrel food," said Evan, with half a laugh.

"Is that the trail mix stuff he makes?" asked Jackson. "I swear he toasts that shit with brown sugar or something. Makes the whole house smell like the sugar fairies have blessed it."

"Sadly, I asked him for the recipe and now make my own. The toasted almonds are such a good source of protein, and Max loves it."

"Why is that sad?" asked Jackson looking puzzled.

"We always swore we were going to grow up and eat whatever we wanted," said Evan. "Theo and his food pyramid!" Evan shook his fist in mock rage.

"How dare he try to keep us healthy," said Aiden.

"Well, we're here at least for lunch," said Jackson. "Come on, we can go eat something ridiculous. There's some fancy place a couple of blocks over that does a Monte Cristo sandwich with crème fraiche that makes me drool."

"He speaks my language," said Aiden. "Let's go."

"Whatever," said Evan. "You're going to eat some sort of lean protein and a salad."

"I… might not," said Aiden. "OK, probably I will. I have a fight in a couple of weeks. But I will enjoy watching you eat bad things."

"You are the worst at being bad," said Dominique shaking her head.

"Jacks, are they allowed to gang up on me?" demanded Aiden, glaring at his sister.

"Yes, but it's OK. I have the car keys. We'll just ditch them."

"And that's why you're my favorite relative," said Aiden.

"I believe his favorite rankings are based on bribes," said Evan.

"Completely," agreed Dominique, "but he forgets that Christmas is coming."

"No," said Aiden. "*You* forget that Christmas is coming and this year… This year is going to be epic. I have plans."

That made Dominique laugh again and Evan grinned. Their bad moods from the hearing were already dissipating. Before Jackson had arrived Aiden had never realized how much fun Christmas could be, but now it was by far his favorite family holiday.

Jackson's phone finally pinged and Jackson took it out with a frown, as if he hadn't been expecting anything.

"Well, son of a bitch," said Jackson.

"What now?" asked Dominique. "Why do I feel like it's bad news? It's going to be bad news, isn't it?" she asked turning to Aiden anxiously.

"No, actually it isn't," said Jacksons. "We've been haunting the New York Public Records site for weeks and it finally paid off."

"Why?" asked Evan.

"Granger had a will. It might have been years out of date, but you don't get to be a Fortune 500 CEO without some lawyer making you do one."

"It's a reasonable, adult thing to do," said Aiden, feeling the sting of *some lawyer.* "You didn't even have to do any work. All you had to do was tell me who you wanted to have stuff and then sign it."

"He made me do it when I was still in college," said Dominique, rolling her eyes.

"After I bought my apartment," said Evan.

"It's the responsible thing to do," reiterated Aiden.

"I wasn't actually complaining," said Jackson. "Just saying that it's something that lawyers make you do. My point was that we know the IRS has been going after his assets. We had been assuming that they were simply fighting his creditors for them, but if there's a will then..."

"The will would point you at someone who Granger might send files to," said Aiden.

"And it hit public records this morning," said Jackson.

"Well, what did it say?" demanded Dominique. "Don't keep us in suspense."

"It said that Granger had a daughter," said Jackson. "To whom he left the bulk of his estate. A Caitlin Granger."

"C. Granger!" exclaimed Aiden. "Not Christina. Caitlin."

"Right," agreed Jackson. "And if she came to see him in prison, then she might like him well enough to hold his papers."

"Not well enough to do anything with them, apparently," said Evan.

"Who knows why she hasn't come forward," said Jackson. "Maybe she's looking for the best place to sell them. Maybe she's waiting for the perfect moment." He shrugged. "We will have to find her and ask. Come on, let's get lunch."

They had only made it a few steps out into the main foyer when Jackson paused, his expression sharpening. Aiden watched as Jackson made eye contact with a non-descript person on the far side of the space. Aiden couldn't even say if it was a man or woman—just someone in a drab sport coat with short hair.

"Who is Griffeth talking to?" hissed Dominique.

"Keep walking," said Jackson, heading for the exit with a casual stride.

"He looks like a douchebag," said Dominique, but did as instructed, following Jackson toward the front doors.

"Well," said a smooth voice, as they neared the exit, "if it isn't the Deveraux family. My, my." They all turned to see Ralph Taggert coming out of a side door. Beside him, Aiden felt Evan stiffen. "What? No Eleanor to hold your hands through this ordeal?"

Aiden looked over the assembled GOP group that was well within earshot. His lawyer's instinct was to tell all of his cousin to shut the hell up and keep walking, but Jackson had already stopped and Dominique had done the same, standing shoulder to shoulder with Jackson as if they were blocking for Evan.

"Mr. Taggert," said Dominique, looking the big man up and down and enunciating with clarity. "I dislike you."

Aiden could practically see ears getting bigger as everyone leaned in to hear the exchange. It was like some sort of schoolyard fight scene, except for some reason they had elected Dominique to square off with the big kid.

"Well, my dear, the feeling is mutual," Ralph said with great relish.

"I assumed as much. So, for future public interactions, since there will be no private interactions—because we hate you," Dominique added as if trying to further clarify matters. Aiden tried not to embarrass the family by letting out a laugh. "I'm informing you that you will be seated as far from Evan as possible while still being within what can be considered family seating. Any attempts to change seats will be grounds for removal. Also, Olivia says that her grandmother *may* call her, but use of the words *harlot* or Bible quotes will be cause for immediate hanging up."

"I can't control the Bible thing," said Ralph. "Wish I could, but ya'll get what ya get on that one."

Dominique wrinkled her nose. "She thought that might be the case," she said. "Fine."

"See you at the church," said Ralph, grinning at Evan.

"It's not going to be in a church," said Evan and turned on his heel and walked out.

Aiden followed his cousins, trying not grin.

"Was it loud enough?" asked Dominique when they were outside.

"Perfect," said Jackson. "Pretty sure they heard you in the hall. Nice job. I wasn't going to be able to pull that off."

"Pull what off?" demanded Evan, glaring at Jackson and Dominique.

"We have to normalize relations with the Taggerts," said Dominique.

"Why? I don't want to," said Evan.

"Yes, but Olivia wants to talk to her grandmother and it will make things a teeny bit less awkward with her father." Evan frowned as if he knew Dominique was speaking the truth but didn't want to admit it. "And you and Olivia getting married puts Ralph in an awkward position politically. He's already getting push back from his party. Being related to us could look bad and his upcoming challengers are straight QAnon wingnuts. Grandma says he's the devil we know, so she wanted to help shore up his position. And that means we have to make it clear that we hate him. Jackson didn't think he could do it without sounding threatening and obviously it can't be you. Aiden could totally do it, but I thought it would be easier if I did it. Plus, I really enjoyed it. It's not every day that Grandma lets me tell someone I hate them."

Aiden laughed. Dominique was beaming.

"It's times like this that I remember you're Aiden's sister," said Evan.

"What did we do?" asked Dominique looking at him, mystified.

"I thought it was brilliant," said Aiden with a shrug.

"You have a very warped sense of fun," complained Evan.

Dominique laughed whole-heartedly and Aiden grinned.

Jackson
The Restaurant

Jackson thought that all things considered the hearing had gone well and Dominique's *I hate you* speech had gone over perfectly, although Evan was still stewing about it. Jackson checked his phone for the tenth time, and pulled Katie's fidget toy out of his pocket.

"I feel like I'm being managed," said Evan. Dominique and Aiden were laughing about something on the other side of the table.

"No," said Jackson. "We're managing parts of your life for you."

"I dislike that," growled Evan.

"Yeah, but you don't actually want to be in charge of managing Ralph Taggert, do you?"

"I don't want Ralph Taggert to exist," snapped Evan.

"Well, unfortunately for you and everyone else, he does," said Jackson. "What we're trying to do is make sure he doesn't cause friction for you or Olivia and minimize his friction for Grandma."

"I dislike that Olivia is talking to you about it instead of me."

Jackson flipped the toy around, trying to reframe that into something that wouldn't piss Evan off more.

"That isn't your fault," said Evan, tossing his napkin on the table. "That's on me."

"This is my job," said Jackson. "I'm supposed to manage the Ralph Taggert's and Olivia being Olivia accepts that at face value."

Evan gave him a look. "And I have made it clear that I don't want to talk about it, which means that Olivia is out in the cold if she wants to process anything to do with her family. I need to do better."

"Olivia has never said that," said Jackson.

"Thanks," said Evan. "But next time let me know when you're managing Ralph Taggert. I would like to be kept in the loop."

"OK," said Jackson, he was surprised enough that he stopped fidgeting with his toy and Evan took it out of his hand.

"Better than cigarettes?" he asked, a smile quirking up one side of his mouth.

"Surprisingly, yes," said Jackson. "I had forgotten that when I was fourteen, before I started smoking, I had a butterfly knife. I used to play with it all the time."

"And then you found nicotine?"

"Yes. But, strangely, this little doodad reminds me of the knife, but you know, way more socially acceptable than either the knife or the smokes."

Evan chuckled and handed it back to him. "Where'd you get it?"

"Oh," said Jackson, "uh… a friend of mine gave it to me."

Evan's head tilted like he knew Jackson was being evasive, but fortunately Jackson's phone lit up with a series of pictures of Dennis Houge talking to various people.

"That's half the ethics committee," said Evan, looking over his shoulder. "Who's the douchebag?"

"That's Dennis Houge, professional Nice Guy TM and Senate Staffer."

"He's also coming this way," said Evan, looking over Jackson's shoulder.

Jackson opened an app, locked his phone down and dropped it on the table. "We're about to get an offer," said Jackson, trying to keep his voice low. "Whatever it is, agree to consider it."

Dennis Houge was wearing a gray suit and had his sandy hair combed to just the right degree of carelessness so that he seemed approachable without being messy. He seemed about to pass the table without stopping, but then he pulled up. He scanned the table and focused in on Jackson.

"Jackson Deveraux, right?"

"Yes," said Jackson.

"We haven't met, but well, we've seen each other a couple of times."

"Um, yeah," said Jackson. "You were at Eleanor's cocktail thing the other night, weren't you? You were talking to Zoe?"

"Yeah, that's right. I'm Dennis Houge. Look, I shouldn't really be talking to you. To any of you." He paused to include the rest of the table in an awe-shucks kind of smile. "But well, I've been in the Senate a long time."

"I thought you were with… Yamira? Isn't he first term?" Jackson feigned puzzlement.

"Yeah, he is, but he's my fourth senator. Like I said, I probably shouldn't be talking to you, but honestly, none of my Senators are as red as they look on paper if you take my drift and I've always liked Eleanor."

"That's nice of you to say," said Dominique, smiling up at Dennis. "We always feel a little bit like she doesn't have any friends."

"Well, she's got one at least in me," said Dennis smiling back. It was an open, friendly, genuine smile, and Dominique's head cocked to one side as if she believed it and liked it. "And well, I feel like I should say something."

"About what?" asked Aiden, slouching down in his chair and spinning the salad fork around on the table. It was a move that read as vacant and ditzy.

"The ethics committee. I know all of you were in there this morning, but I think it's going to get worse."

"In what way?" asked Evan. He spread an arm out along the back of Jackson's chair, taking up space and watching Dennis through hooded eyes.

"I don't know what they're after Eleanor for specifically, some sort of violation in procedure, but I think… well, I think if they can't get to her directly, they might target all of you."

Aiden opened his mouth and Jackson could see his bullshit-o-meter going off like a claxon, but then Aiden shut his mouth and shrugged. "What can we do about it?"

Dennis looked around and then leaned in. "I might be able to help." He took a business card out of his pocket and held it out to Jackson. Jackson didn't move as Evan took the card and looked at.

"Forgive me, Mr Houge, but I'm not entirely clear on what *you* can do for *us*." Evan's expression was condescendingly skeptical.

"The Senate works in public and in private," said Dennis. "I can help behind the scenes. Like I've said, I've been here a long time and I know a lot of people. I might be able to convince some of the committee to let the matter drop, particularly if Eleanor could offer them some concessions in return. You only need a couple of votes to turn the tide. And as a neutral third party I can broker that kind of deal."

Evan dropped the card on the table in front of Jackson.

"That's your department. Can you wrangle Grandma?"

Jackson shrugged. "I have before."

"Give him your card," said Evan, jerking his chin at Jackson.

Jackson fished in his suit jacket pocket for his wallet and handed over a business card.

"Call Jackson when you have something," said Evan, holding

up a hand to signal the maître d'. "Don't bother calling if you can't do what you say you can do."

Jackson saw the flare of anger in Dennis's face.

"Ignore Evan," said Dominique, with a giggle. "He rubs everyone the wrong way. It's practically what we keep him around for."

"It's my job to make deals," said Houge. "I assure you I can deliver."

"Sounds like you work too hard for my taste," said Aiden.

"That's because you pay people to pick your fights for you," said Evan, brutally and Aiden's eye twitched, but Dominique couldn't hold it in and let out a surprised giggle.

"That's funny because it's true," she told Dennis, "but don't listen to either of them. I appreciate your efforts." She beamed at Dennis in a hundred-watt smile and Dennis smiled back clearly impressed. Jackson watched as he lifted a hand to check his hair and then his tie. Then he seemed to notice Jackson's gaze and he straightened up.

"I'll be in touch," said Dennis, directly to Jackson. Jackson nodded and they all watched Dennis walk toward one of the private dining rooms.

"I pay people to pick my fights?" demanded Aiden.

"Perhaps I should have specified pick *out* your fights. Kind of changes the meaning a bit though," said Evan, faux innocence dripping off of him.

Aiden threw a crouton at him and Evan batted it away grinning broadly.

"Meanwhile, this wasn't a threat against Grandma," said Aiden. "It was us. The hearing was supposed to scare us. He thought he could intimidate us into flipping on Grandma."

"I'm sorry," Jackson said, looking around the table apologetically. "I hadn't even considered that possibility."

Dominique laughed. "You look so embarrassed," she crowed. "Oh, my God, this is hilarious."

Jackson felt himself blushing. "I'm sorry, but it didn't occur to me that having to go talk to people would be considered a threat."

"Trust me it is," said Evan, as the server slid the bill onto their table. "People are scary as fuck. Fortunately, they were just Senators, and those barely even qualify as humans."

Dominique laughed harder and Aiden looked like he was trying not to join her, but he was only partially succeeding.

"No, let me get this," said Aiden, grabbing for the check as Evan picked it up. "I want to spend cash."

"Who the hell carries cash?" demanded Evan.

"Aiden does," said Dominique. "He gets his prize money in cash and he has to spend it somewhere. You know from all the fights other people pick out for him."

"Josh, his name is Josh, not *other people*. And he's my manager."

Evan rolled his eyes and passed the check over. Aiden produced a drug dealer amount of bills and put it into the folder.

"Well, at least you've got a target now," said Evan to Jackson. "That's something."

"It's something," agreed Jackson.

Jackson let his cousins get in front of him on the way to the car. Evan was right, he had a target now, but the next steps were still vague. Pete could start digging into Dennis Houge's life, but would that get the Absolex files released? Or shut down the ethics committee investigation into Eleanor?

"You're frowning," said Aiden. "Why? Today has gone exactly according to your plan."

"Not exactly," said Jackson, still feeling embarrassed. "We've got a suspect," said Jackson. "That means new problems, and I'm not sure how to get him all tied up in a bow. Whatever offer he makes, I can record him and turn him down, but I'm not sure that gets me anywhere."

"Well, you recorded his offer at lunch, didn't you?"

"Caught that?"

"Of course. But if he makes a second offer, that's enough to be considered selling influence. We can take it to the FBI."

"That's the slow road to nowhere. We've been down it before with Granger. I need more. I need something airtight that shows he was working with Granger."

"You need Granger's files," said Aiden understandingly.

"Right."

"Well, you've got Caitlin Granger now. You can't tell me Pete and the crew haven't spent all day hunting her down. I bet by the time we get home they'll have a location."

Jackson took a breath. "Yeah. At least, I hope so."

"You'll get him," said Aiden confidently. "But, all that aside." Aiden lowered his voice, and Jackson tried to imagine what could make Aiden look so severe. "Are you dating someone?"

Jackson was caught off guard. "What? Uh, no. I mean… no."

Aiden was giving him a lawyer look that said he didn't believe Jackson in the least.

"You saw Miss Mindblowingly Nice again, didn't you? The girl who gave you her number but didn't say to use it."

"Well, yeah. But. It's not."

"Not what?" asked Aiden, obviously waiting for a complete sentence.

"It's not dating."

"But you keep seeing her?"

"She doesn't want a boyfriend and I don't want anything either, so… it's just hooking up."

It sounded so lame when he said it out loud. It sounded belittling to Katie. She was important. Hooking up sounded like they were teenagers and she didn't mean anything.

"Oh," said Aiden. "Kay."

Evan and Dominique had stopped and were waiting for them by the trunk of the car.

Jackson let out an angry snort. "You're annoying," he said trying to fit the last word in before they reached the others.

"I've heard that," said Aiden. "Mostly from you, but still…"

"I'm certain I say it too," said Evan.

"I'm pretty sure I say it as well," said Dominique, smiling wickedly.

"I'm not feeling very loved," complained Aiden.

Dominique dashed the few steps back to Aiden and hugged him. "Love you, big brother."

"What did we say about Deverauxes and hugging?" demanded Evan.

"We said we were going to do more of it?" asked Dominique, sounding puzzled.

"Oh, right," said Evan. "I forgot."

Jackson laughed, as Evan put an arm over his shoulders. "You're all ridiculous."

"And that is why you like us," said Aiden confidently.

"True," agreed Jackson.

Jackson
The Plane

Jackson waited in the hotel lobby for his cousins. Dominique arrived first. She bucked gender stereotypes by being the most organized packer of the bunch.

"OK," said Jackson, "I've got a car coming to take you and Aiden to the train station. Aiden said you had the tickets—"

"Jackson," said Dominique, interrupting him. He looked up and saw that she was looking unhappy, "I want to go on the plane."

"We want you on the plane," said Jackson.

There was silence as she seemed to be working up to something.

"I'm scared of dying."

"Well, we get that. I mean, it's hard to say planes are the safest mode of transportation with our family history."

She nodded. "It's also the same reason I'm scared to get married."

Jackson tried to twist his head around the pretzel of that logic.

"I can kind of understand the plane, but you've lost me on marriage," said Jackson honestly.

"It's what happens. You find somebody, you fall in love, you have two kids and then you die and I don't want to do that to my kids."

"Your parents didn't *do* that to you. Pretty sure they had no intention of dying. Also, you don't have any kids."

"Yes, all of that has been pointed out," said Dominique nodding. "And honestly, I didn't even know that those two things were connected in my head, but after some time spent with Evan's therapist—who, frankly, is worth every damn penny—it's quite clear that they are. And it's also quite clear that I've been avoiding some stuff for years. It's just that having Max talk about marriage made me… you know…"

"Freak the fuck out?"

"Yeah," she said, looking glum.

"OK, but," said Jackson, "maybe this is weird, but if I was going to die then going down in a plane crash with all of you really wouldn't be the worst way to go. It'd be over fast and then at least we could all hang out and be ghosts afterwards."

"I'm sorry, what did I just walk into?" demanded Evan, coming around the corner.

"Jackson was trying to cheer me up," said Dominique.

"That is not… How was any of that helpful?"

"It kind of was actually," said Dominique. "I hadn't really thought about it like that. I do like all of you. And if I died then at least I'd take all of you with me."

"I'm not sure that's what I said," said Jackson.

"That's what I heard," said Dominique. "Evan, on a scale of one to ten how scary is it to face something you're really anxious about?"

"Everyone's scale is different. I find honesty really helps and taking someone I trust with me helps even more."

"So, getting on a plane should be…" Dominique's voice petered out, then she straightened up and squared her shoulders. "I will have all of you, and I will be fine."

"But you don't have to be," said Evan. "It is OK to not be fine. You can spend the entire flight hiding under the chair and crying and it would still be fine."

"Ew. No."

"Yes," said Evan.

"I don't want that to be me," said Dominique, sounding pissed that he would even suggest it.

"Well, honestly, I have a hard time picturing that being you," said Evan. "But what I'm saying is that you don't have to be fine. Aiden and I are doing all right. There is room for you to be sad or freak out or even be happy. You don't have to hold the space for us anymore."

Jackson watched Dominique's eyes well up with tears. "I don't…" Jackson put his arm around her and she leaned into him for a moment. Then she lunged forward and hugged Evan fiercely. Evan closed his eyes and hugged her back.

Aiden came around the corner and stared at them. "I feel like I should be a part of this, but I don't know how."

"We can hug if you want," said Jackson.

"Feels awkward," said Aiden. "I kind of want one, but now it doesn't feel spontaneous." Dominique gave a watery giggle and then turned to hug Aiden. "This is nice. See, spontaneity is key."

"Where's mine?" asked Jackson, when she stepped back. He got a hug too and then Dominique smiled at them and wiped her cheeks.

"I'm going to go on the plane and I will not crawl under the chair."

"I don't know why you would," said Aiden, "but thank you for not doing that? I really am going to have to stop missing out on these conversations. I end up completely lost. But yay, plane?"

"Yay plane," said Dominique.

Jackson could tell Dominique was nervous boarding the plane, but Aiden cracked jokes, and Evan offered tips on breathing and basic statements of safety, and she made it into her seat and through take-off without panicking.

"Evan's right," she said when he took the seat next to her for check-in. "It's a lot easier to face something when I have people I trust with me. Do you know how much that would have killed me to say when I was twelve? God, I hated when Evan was right. I just plain hated him, actually. Now I can't imagine him not being here. It scares me—how close we came to losing him."

"He's come through all right," said Jackson, although he understood her fear.

"Yes, he did. We all have. Our family has changed so much, Jackson."

"Well, I'm here for one thing," he joked.

"Yes," she said, but her expression was serious. "That's what changed everything. You're a goddamn miracle."

Jackson laughed. "Not a miracle, just Pete's sleuthing skills and Grandma being stubborn about collecting the full set of kids."

Dominique nodded. "If you say so. But still, thanks for sticking with us. I love that you are part of our family now."

Jackson knew he blushed. He didn't know what to say.

"And I love being part of the family," he said at last.

"Good. Now, go away. I'm going to take a nap."

Jackson laughed. "Yes, Nika."

He returned to his own seat and tried to settle in for the remainder of the flight. He checked his phone again, knowing that there wasn't any point. Katie hadn't called the day before and she wasn't going to call today either.

"Miss Nice still hasn't called?" asked Aiden without looking up from the tablet he was looking at.

"What?" asked Jackson, even though he knew exactly what Aiden meant.

"You've checked your phone three times in the last half-hour without an alert. You talked to Pete an hour ago and agreed that he would call if there were news. So, it can't be Pete. That means it's someone you would like to call, but that someone has not called."

"Stop prying," said Jackson.

"Not so fun when it's you, is it?" Aiden finally looked up, his eyes dancing. He was enjoying this far too much.

"Shut up."

"What are we talking about?" asked Evan dropping into the seat on the plane across from Aiden.

"The girl that Jackson is dating."

Jackson glared at Aiden. Did he have to blab everything to everyone? Evan was going to think is sounded even worse than Aiden did.

"We're not dating!"

"Ask him why they're not dating," whispered Aiden.

"Why aren't you dating?" Evan whispered at Jackson. They both stared at him, waiting.

"She doesn't want a boyfriend," Jackson repeated, twisting awkwardly in his seat. It was a private plane. How were the seats still uncomfortable?

Aiden snickered and Evan frowned. "I'm confused. How long have you been seeing this girl?"

"We're not seeing each other!" Evan gave him a skeptical look. "I don't know. A month or two, maybe." Had it really only been two months? Halloween. They'd met on Halloween. "We're not seeing each other," he reiterated.

"They're just having sex," said Dominique from where she was laying down in the chair across the aisle with a sleep mask on.

"You are napping," snapped Jackson, irritably. "And it's god-damn fucking fantastic sex."

"Got it," said Evan. "OK, but why doesn't she want a boyfriend?"

"Probably for the same reason I don't want a girlfriend." Evan raised inquiring eyebrows. "Because she doesn't want to deal with all the boyfriend shit. Holidays, families, where are we going, having to check in before planning anything. It's bullshit. She doesn't want it and neither do I."

He didn't add that Katie St. Cloud was a broke college dropout who probably had some problems with the IRS. He'd come over one night to find her crying over a crumpled fist full of mail that had an IRS logo on it. The second he'd asked about was the second she'd kicked him out. The message was clear. She didn't want his help, she didn't want his money, and she didn't really want him involved in her life. It was Jackson's guess that she didn't want boyfriend shit because she had enough shit of her own to deal with. And he was fine with that. Mostly. It bugged him that she had to deal with so much on her own. He'd thought about digging into her life and arranging things for her the way he sometimes did for his cousins, but they were family. They had to accept his help. He had the feeling that if Katie caught even a whiff of interference from him that it would be a deal breaker.

"You just still wish she'd call while you're out of town," said Aiden.

"Shut up," said Jackson.

"I think," said Evan, then paused. They waited. "Never mind. It's none of my business."

"Thank you," said Jackson, glaring at Aiden, who chuckled in unrepentant glee. "You think it's weird though, don't you?" he asked, turning back to Evan.

"No. Not really. It's just... OK, sex aside. Relationship status aside. Do you like her? As a person?"

"Yeah, of course."

"Well, not *of course*," said Evan. "You've had lots of hook ups with women you wouldn't actually spend time with if you had to talk to them."

"Well, yeah, but I mean, she's..."

Jackson hesitated. Katie was creative. One of his favorite post hook-up rituals was trying out one of her cocktail experiments. And funny. Her dead pan sarcastic commentary kept him in stitches. And beautiful. That went without saying. But most of all she fucking genuinely cared about people. Jessica, Jamal, annoying Mrs. Carpetti downstairs, Vince and Angela, even damn Rufus the drug dealer out in the park, she really worried about them and tried her best to look out for them. It frequently made him wonder who was looking out for her.

"She's a really good person," said Jackson, knowing it sounded lame.

"OK," said Evan, with a shrug. "So, I mean, if this is where the two of you are at, then fine. But if you're at a place where you would like to be able to, I don't know, call her when you're out of town, then you should just tell her that. You don't have to put a ring on it to want to be able to talk to someone. If spending twenty minutes talking to you is too much effort, then maybe you're not in the same place or maybe she's not the person you think she is."

Jackson and Aiden were both silent.

"Well, fuck Evan," said Aiden. "You need to go back to drugs or something. I'm not sure I can handle you being insightful. It freaks me out."

"Deal with it," said Dominique. "It's working for me."

Caitlin

CAITLIN'S APARTMENT

Caitlin passed by the window, then frowned and went back. The blue sedan was back. As she watched, a guy in khakis got out. They weren't even good khaki's—they had pleated fronts. As she watched, he walked along the sidewalk toward Mrs. Carpetti's stoop. The same location she'd seen him in earlier in the day.

Caitlin felt her jaw clench. Mrs. Carpetti had a lot of nice and antiques, everyone in the neighborhood knew it and no one fucked with her because, in some ways, she *was* the neighborhood. Who did this guy think he was? He didn't get to come in to her neighborhood and mess with people. She marched out to the living room and grabbed the golf club out of the shoe basket and went down the stairs. Someone was getting a five iron up-side the head.

"That is it!" She yanked open the door and raised the golf club. Jackson paused with his hand raised to knock. He looked surprised. "Ah!" She dropped the club and flung her arms around him.

She was most of the way through the hug when she realized that she had planned to be reserved with him and clear up any boundary issues by reinforcing all the boundaries. Instead, she had jumped on him. So much for reserved.

"Hi," he said, hugging her back. "Am I getting beat with a golf club?"

"I thought you were a weird white dude."

"Not any more than last week," he said.

"No! There was a guy. Earlier. I thought he was casing Mrs. Carpetti's place."

Jackson looked around, checking the street. "Looks empty."

"I don't know. There was some guy. It doesn't matter."

He took the opportunity to kiss her and her arms went back around him, as the kiss became deeper.

"Did I miss a text? Did I know you were coming?" she asked pulling back. This was her moment to switch to cool and reserved if it was going to happen. Jackson tucked her golf club into the corner by the door, which was probably a good place for it.

"No," he said, looking a little embarrassed. "I was…" He shook his head. "I thought I'd take a chance and see if you were home. I should have called."

She didn't know what to make of his sheepish look. Other than it was adorable. She felt a flutter of frustration. How was she supposed to reinforce boundaries if he was going to be charming? She wanted to hug him again.

"Well, I'm home," she said, giving up. So they'd had a weird moment due to heightened emotions and violence, so what? All of her fretting while he'd been gone seemed silly now that he was here. "Come inside." She tugged him by the collar. She made room for him in the tiny foyer. He came in and she shut and locked the door. He jogged up the stairs ahead of her, pulling off his coat. He dropped it on the coat rack and ditched his shoes into the basket, while she went back to the kitchen.

"Drink tests?" Jackson asked hopefully, looking at the mess on the table.

"Yes! Go sit down and I'll bring you a tester."

"You need to start writing these down, so I remember which ones to ask for," he said dropping onto the couch and putting his feet up. She loved the way his long legs looked stretched out on her couch.

"I do write them down," she admitted, blushing. "Sometimes think it would be fun to write a cocktail recipe book. But you have to be famous to sell one of those. It would never work," she added in case Jackson thought she was silly enough to believe she could do something like that.

She used the ice pick on the lump of ice in the ice bucket and he laughed. "Remind me not to argue with you when you've got the ice pick handy."

"Eeee. Eeee. Eeee!" She mimed *Psycho* stabbing motions and he laughed again. "How was your trip?" She selected a wide bowled glass that she'd picked up at the second-hand store and poured in a careful measure of her infused bourbon.

He took a deep breath. "Fine."

She looked up. "That seemed like there was going to be more than fine?"

He shrugged. "I like my family the more time I spend with them."

She laughed. "I really thought that was going to go a different direction."

"I sometimes feel like…" He ran his hand through his hair, making it stand up in spots. "They are really smart. Educated. The best at what they do. And sometimes I feel like the shaggy kid they let follow them around."

"Do they say that?" Her hand curled a little tighter around the icepick. From his occasional comments he'd made, she knew Jackson had grown up poor and come into money much later. She admired the way he was navigating the transition and she thought it was impressive the amount of research he put in to learning his new life. He genuinely cared about making his stupid family look good, and she could tell that he cared about their opinions. The idea that they might treat him badly made her angry.

"No. That's just it. They never do. They are ridiculously loyal. And they treat me like I… well, they treat me like I can keep up. But damn, it's a stretch sometimes."

Caitlin looked down at the table. "All I have is booze," she said.

"What?"

"I can't fix that. All I have is booze."

"You don't have to fix that. This is just me bitching about my cousins being hyper-successful bastards. There's nothing to fix."

"Oh," she said.

"I'll still take the booze though."

"Not quite yet." She tossed the ice cubes into the glass.

"How was your week?" he asked, as she went to the cupboard for the Frangelico.

"Good!" Better now that he was back. "Really good! Jessica got five of her photos in a gallery, which is really big! She's over the moon. They even took that one of me on the beer kegs."

"Beer kegs?" he repeated, smiling but confused.

"We were waiting for a venue to open up, but we still needed to unload, so I was taking a wee little nap on top of the pony kegs and while the van went back for a second load and she took a picture. Which sounds ridiculous, but because it's Jessica it looks amazing. I can't wait until they're hanging so I can go see them."

"Which gallery is it?"

"The Three Bridges. And they charge an arm and a leg for everything there. Hopefully they sell. They might ask her for more if they do."

"We'll have to go see them," he said smiling. "What else happened this week? What's the occasion for the drink?"

"Oh! Angela wants me to come up with the signature event for an event they're doing. Which, I'm kind of proud of because I've only ever slid it in under the radar. This is the first time she's actually asked me to come up with one and present it to the client. And they're charging the client for it, which I think is kind of crazy, but Vince said it was a specialized service and none of the other catering companies were offering it. How about that? I bet you didn't know I was special."

Jackson chuckled. "I did actually." She smiled at him because she knew even though she'd been joking, he was serious.

"But the biggest news, you'll never guess."

She paused to concentrate on floating the Frangelico across the top of the bourbon.

"Guess, what?"

She put the drink on a tray so she wouldn't warm the glass with her fingers and brought it over to him. "I booked the Roggario New Year's show."

"What?"

"The *runway* show. I've been doing all their fittings and they've been dithering over the last slot and finally Roggario was like, *I'm not having any more of this shit, they all suck*! And then Chase, his boyfriend, was like *make Kate do it, you know the dresses will fit*. So now I'm doing it."

"No way!" He was beaming.

"Yeah! I mean, it's a little like being picked for teams because I was the only one left, but I'll take it!"

"I'm going to sit in the front row."

"Can you really?"

"Yeah, Nika tries to get me to go to this shit all the time. You just call up and tell them you want to sit in the front."

She blinked at him. That was really not how it worked. Unless you had shit tons of money. Did he really have shit tons of money? She knew he had money. But she was assuming it was some sort of Russian mob money. She didn't think it was tons of money. Tons of money people wouldn't be with her. Well, maybe his cousins or sister had the tons? She had been at the House of Amery, so that was probably the case.

"OK, well, don't stare directly at me if you do. If I make eye contact I'll probably trip."

"Got it," he said reaching for his drink, with a wide smile.

"OK," she said, sitting on the ottoman to watch him drink it and biting a nail. "Tell me what you think. Be really honest."

He took a sip and closed his eyes. "Fuck me."

"You like it?"

"God, yes. What did you do to make bourbon better? Bourbon can't get better."

"I told the guys at work about it and they didn't think it was a good idea."

"Fuck them," he said, taking another sip. "Seriously, what is it?"

"It's brown butter infused bourbon with a hazel nut liquor over the top."

"Brown butter? How do you do that?"

"Carefully." Switching the drink to his left hand, he pulled her off the ottoman and into his lap. "Do you really like it?"

"Yes," he said, kissing her neck. She shivered. His lips were cool from the drink. His hand around her waist slipped under her T-shirt.

"I'm glad you're back," she said, leaning into his lips.

"You should have called to tell me about the show," he said. "I would have brought other celebratory booze."

"I thought about it, but I didn't know..."

"Didn't know what?" Jackson was looking up at her with those blue eyes of his that made her lose all common sense. This was how she ended up fucking him in bathrooms. He smiled at her, and her brain went south for the winter.

"I didn't think I should bother you."

"You don't bother me," he said. He set the drink down on the ottoman and began to work her T-shirt off. Caitlin was pulling off his shirt when he reached for her shorts. "What the hell are you wearing on your feet?" He had finally noticed her custom leg-wear.

"Jessica made them for me. They're thigh-high slippers."

He looked in bemusement at the cable knit gray wool legging slippers that ended at her thighs with a pair of pom-pom tassels. "I am *so* fucking you with those on."

"Well, my feet will be warm then."

He laughed and pulled her shorts off. As usual, he had her naked before she'd even gotten halfway through his attire. He pushed her onto the couch and kissed along her thighs, biting at the pom-poms until she giggled. He paused to take a drink and swallowed enough to capture one of the ice chips in his mouth. Then he went back to her thighs. She gasped as he began to drag the chip along her skin, leaving a cold trail. Her heart was pounding as he pressed the ice chip to her center. He circled her clit lightly with it, and she shivered involuntarily. The chip was melting and bringing his lips ever closer to her, and she felt his hot breath as he circled again. His lips brushed over her with the lightest of touches, and she moaned. When the chip was nearly gone, he let it slither down as he opened his mouth and licked her. She let out a small squeak of shock and clutched at his hair as the temperature difference catapulted her into a near orgasm. Her body began to rock with the rhythm he set, and she moaned his name. How could he always get her to this spot so fast?

"Oh God," she gasped. "Oh, God. Jackson. Jesus, I'm going to come. Harder. Oh, God." He pushed his tongue into her, and she let out another wordless exclamation, pulling his hair, pulling him into her. Then she came, and she arched back in release.

He sat up, and stripped out of his shirt, laughing at her.

"What's so funny?" she demanded, breathing heavily.

"Nothing," he said, dropping his pants on the floor. "It just makes me happy when you make that noise."

"That noise is your fault."

"I know. That's why it makes me happy."

"Well, let's see what kind of noises I can make you make," she said, sitting up.

"OK."

"You're not supposed to agree!" She rose to kneel on the couch and laughed up at him as she rolled his underwear down. She ran her hand over his cock and felt it quiver as she touched it. She kissed along the dragon on his hip while she continued to lightly run her fingers up and down the shaft. It got harder with each pass of her hand.

"Mm," he groaned and slid his hands into her hair. She had to admit that she did like that noise. The dragon ended around his navel, and she continued upward, letting her breasts brush over his cock. She couldn't quite reach his mouth while kneeling, so she pulled his neck, making him bend toward her. She let her lips part, inviting him in. She could taste herself on his lips still. She supposed that ought to be gross, but it was a turn-on. She pulled back, letting her teeth sink just a little into his bottom lip. She opened her eyes and smiled at him. He was staring at her as if she had rocked his world. She smiled wider. Good. Let him feel the earth shift for once.

"Katie," he murmured, kissing her again, more urgently. He

was hard between them, and she knew what he wanted. He abruptly pulled away and went to rummage in his jacket pocket on the hat rack.

"We need to start stashing these around the house," he said, coming back with a condom. "We should just stick a box in the ottoman."

"No! That's where all the horrible things live." She laughed, realizing that she'd sounded sharper than she meant to. "I just… It's stuff I don't want to look at." She stumbled, looking for words to explain. "I don't want to put good things next to the bad things."

"Yeah," he said, nodding. "I have a box that I put in the attic." She relaxed at his tone. "And we put all the portraits of my grandfather down in the wine cellar, but to be honest, that makes me a little worried about the wine."

Caitlin laughed. She should have known he'd understand. She started to sit back down.

"No," he said, the word coming out as a half groan. "Please. Those things, you, on your knees. That is…"

She turned, grabbed a seat cushion and looked over her shoulder at him.

"This position?" She tried to sound innocent but wasn't sure she made it. She arched, and he really did make a noise. "This is working for you?"

He growled and ripped open the condom. Caitlin laughed as he fumbled to get it on quickly but stopped laughing as he thrust inside her. His hands traveled her body as he fucked her, roaming her breasts, stroking her clit, neck, and hair. She was half in his lap, half-supporting herself on the back of the couch, and she watched the pom-poms on each thigh bounce with his thrusts. His skin was warm against hers, and she arched, leaning back into his hands, letting him take her weight.

"Right there, Katie, right there."

She made a noise that she hoped he understood as agreement. His fingers were on her clit, and he swept her hair back with the other so he could kiss her neck. His kisses made her moan. She wanted this. She loved it. She wanted him. She wanted him to do this to her always. She loved him.

Her eyes flew open, and she stared at the wall. Seconds later, she gasped as he pushed her into a peak of pleasure. She bit her lip and moaned. She was trembling as she drew closer. She thought about shoving his hand away and kicking him out. She couldn't do this. She couldn't have him here.

She reached for his hand but couldn't make herself do it.

"Oh God, Jackson, Jackson, please don't stop."

He began to thrust more urgently, and she gasped. He was going to make her come. And she wanted him to. She jerked forward, clutching the couch. She wanted him here with her more than anything because she belonged to him. She came then, breathlessly groaning his name.

When he was done, she burrowed against his chest and tried not to let him see her face. She wanted to cry. She was ruining everything. She loved him, and there was no going back. But if she told him, he would leave. He had been clear that he wasn't looking for a girlfriend and didn't want a commitment. And even if she could persuade him to want her, there was still the fact that if he found out who she was and didn't hate everything her father had done and what mobster could afford to have a girlfriend who was being investigated by the IRS?

Jackson
NEXT MOVES

Jackson held Katie in his arms and tried to figure out his next move. They were snuggled under her down comforter that enveloped them like a marshmallow cloud. Like most of her furniture, it was expensive but several years old. This was where they spent all their nights together. In some ways, it was more comfortable to him than Deveraux House. The occasional gunshots and two o'clock bar rotation down the street, the creak of the building, the freezing mornings when the heat had quit, and the drip of the broken faucet all reminded him of his childhood. Deveraux House, in its staid neighborhood with a fully functional heating system, was too quiet and too comfortable. He suddenly realized what his first mistake had been—spending the night. If he had truly wanted just sex, he should never have spent the night. But it was too late. He wanted more.

He'd taken Evan's suggestion. It might not have been a direct, declarative sentence, but it felt pretty clear that casual phone calls were now on the approved list. And she hadn't objected to his dropping by. He could stop. He had what he'd said he'd wanted. He had his *more*. But then she'd kissed him and looked up at him with those amber eyes, and he'd realized how far beyond phone calls he was.

He tried to go back in time and visualize not spending the night. No cuddles. No morning sex. No arguments with Jamal out the window. He could do without Jamal's commentary on their sex life, but otherwise, he loved mornings with Katie. He loved nights with Katie. He loved Katie.

Aiden was going to laugh at him. Probably a lot.

He adjusted his position and kissed her neck. He loved the soft, concave spot just below her jaw. She squished tighter against him, pushing her face into his chest, and inhaled deeply—her night-time ritual—done when she was only half-awake. It was the tiniest gesture, and it absolutely wrecked him. He realized that he had no idea what to do next. How was he supposed to tell a girl he'd been sleeping with for months that he loved her? Particularly when she wasn't going to want to hear it. He hugged her tighter and said nothing, letting himself relax into her warmth. He could deal with it tomorrow.

He woke up in the dark to the sound of Katie crying. It hit his nervous system like a jolt from a crash cart, and he grabbed for his gun on the bed stand.

"Katie?"

He put the gun down and reached for her, but she didn't respond, only flailed an arm at him. He found himself entangled and half on top of her as he tried to grab her hand. He realized then that she wasn't awake. "Katie!" He put his hands up to her face. *"Sérdeńko!"* He wasn't sure why he picked that endearment, but heart seemed to work. She opened her eyes, blinking at him, a strangled sob catching in her throat.

"Katie, you're dreaming," he said, stroking her face.

"He's not… They're not here."

"No one's here." He wiped her tears away.

"My father," she said, her voice thick with sleep and confusion. "He was yelling at me. He said I was useless." Her body was tense underneath him, and her hand struck out, flailing against the comforter. "Like always."

"No *sérdeńko,*" he said, pushing his anger at her absent family away. "No, I wouldn't let that happen. It was just a dream." He kissed her damp cheeks and then her mouth, and, as if his kiss had been the key, her body relaxed, her arms curving around him.

"Just a dream?" she asked.

"Yes," he said, kissing her again. "Nothing bad can happen to you. I'm here."

She laughed a sleepy chuckle. "Don't ever leave me then."

"*Ya ne mozhu zalyshyty vas. Ya tebe lyublyu.*" He kissed along her neck, telling her his secrets.

"*Ya tebe lyublyu,*" she repeated the words slowly as if testing them out in her mouth. He kissed her again, reveling in the sound of *I love you*, even if she didn't know it or mean it.

She kissed him back this time, her body lifting to his. He grew hard as their kisses grew more passionate. Her legs parted, accepting him. He pushed inside her feeling her rise to meet his thrust. The room was quiet except for the sound of their breathing. She pulled his head down to kiss him. He complied, tasting her lips, feeling her tongue against his. She broke away with a sigh of pleasure.

"Katie," he said. "We didn't get a condom. I should…"

"No," she moaned. "Keep going. I want you."

He wanted it to, but he could count on the fingers of one hand the number of times he'd failed to glove up. Her hands pulled on his sides, urging him on. He knew she was on birth control. This should be fine. It was just that he had never lost control like this before. Jackson groaned as her legs locked around him. He thrust harder and deeper as she moaned his name again.

"*Sérce moje,*" he groaned as her body pushed him to a new high.

"God, yes, Jackson. Yes, I want you. I need you."

Her desire for him pushed him forward. She came, gasping his name, and he came inside her with a final jerk of ecstasy. He lay between her thighs, feeling exhausted and content but not quite satisfied—he had wanted her to say she loved him. He began to pull away from her, and she groaned, holding him tight to her. That made him smile.

"*Sérdeńko,* you're going to have to let me go at some point."

"No."

He laughed and kissed her until she reluctantly released him. He rolled away from her and flopped onto his back. With a groan, she got up and went to the bathroom. When she returned, he held the covers up for her and she climbed in. He settled her in next to him, with her head on his chest.

"There," he said, hugging her tight. "This is where you belong."

"Yes," she said with a sigh. "Right here."

Caitlin

CAITLIN'S APARTMENT

His phone rang, waking both of them up.

"*Shcho?*" he demanded, grabbing the phone, sounding angry.

The man on the other end of the phone responded in Ukrainian and Jackson grunted in response. Caitlin turned into him, trying to shut out the daylight and the fact that he was going to leave.

"*Dobre.*"

The man spoke again, still in Ukrainian.

"I'm not grumpy in Ukrainian. I'm grumpy when you wake me up." The man on the other end of the phone laughed and said something else. "Yeah," said Jackson, his voice relaxing, "I'll meet you at the house in an hour."

He hung up the phone and collapsed back into the bed, pulling the comforter up around them. Katie didn't object and snuggled against him, tucking her head under his chin and hiding from the light.

"I have to go," he said. Caitlin could hear his voice and feel it in his chest.

"Yes, I heard."

"Are you working tonight?"

"Yes, it's a dinner event."

Did he want to come over? He usually didn't ask. He usually waited for her to suggest.

"Let's go out to dinner after," he said. "I'm tired of take-out. I want something nice where we can sit down."

Caitlin wasn't sure how to respond. He'd never taken her to a sit-down restaurant before.

"I won't be done until nine," she said.

"That's fine. I'll pick you up."

Caitlin blinked into his chest and didn't dare look up at him. "Um, OK."

Jackson pushed the comforter off and held up his hand to block the sunlight streaming in the window. "Fucking mornings. Who invented this shit?"

She laughed and turned over to burrow back under the covers as he got dressed.

"You'll text me tonight?" he said, leaning over to kiss her.

"Yes," she said, smiling shyly up at him. He kissed her again and smiled his cocky grin.

"See you tonight."

He left her with one final kiss and jogged down the stairs. She stared at the cracked ceiling and tried to figure out what the hell she was feeling. Last night, she had gone to bed feeling like she could never tell him how she felt, determined to keep her mouth shut and take whatever he was willing to give her. But somewhere in the middle of her nightmare, he had whispered words to her that felt like *I love you*. She didn't know if they were or not, and she didn't have the courage to ask, but this morning had felt like he had actually wanted her. And that was... terrifying? Euphoric? No, terrifying. No, euphoric.

Caitlin swung back and forth on the teeter-totter of her own emotions. By the time she made it to work, her stomach was a nervous knot of butterflies.

"Katie? Katie!"

Caitlin looked up at Jessica as she snapped her fingers. "What?"

"Earth to Katie. Are you with us? I said your name like five times."

"Sorry," said Katie, rubbing her scalp. "I was just thinking about something else."

"I could see that. What's going on with you?"

"Um… Jackson came over last night."

"So he's back in town? Did it get weird again?"

"No. Yes? I mean, he didn't get weird. I think maybe I got weird."

"What happened?"

Caitlin hesitated. How was she supposed to explain what had happened? "I had a bad dream, a nightmare, last night. And uh… I don't know… he…"

Jessica was staring at her, waiting.

"He what?"

"Um."

"You've got to give me something to work with here," said Jessica. "He screamed at you? He beat you? What?"

"No! He talked to me in Ukrainian, and then we had sex."

"OK, I'm not seeing a problem with this. Sounds like a great cure for a nightmare."

"We didn't use a condom," said Caitlin and Jessica grimaced.

"Is there any chances of anything…"

"No, I'm fully covered on the birth control front and I'm not sleeping with anyone else, so, that's not a problem."

"But you don't know if he is?"

"No," said Caitlin. "He hasn't mentioned anyone."

"Well, he wouldn't would he? Why didn't you tell him to grab a condom?"

"I actually told him not to."

"Katie!"

"I know. I just didn't want him to stop. And I think maybe…" She blinked back tears, feeling unexpectedly emotional. "I think maybe… I… really…"

"You're kind of in love with him?" suggested Jessica.

Caitlin blinked away tears and nodded.

Jessica hugged her. "I know, baby, and it's going to be OK."

"Is it?" asked Caitlin. "Because I'm really scared."

Jessica sighed and hugged her tighter. "Do you think maybe, just maybe, he likes you back?"

"He asked me to go to dinner tonight," whispered Caitlin.

Jessica shrieked and jerked back to look in her face. "You couldn't lead with that? That's a date. He's taking you on a date."

"Is it? He didn't say it was a date. He said he was tired of take-out and he'd pick me up after I'm done here."

Jessica gave her a look. "It's a date, sweetie. He's taking you out in public. For non-sex related activities."

"Oh. I hope there's sex later," said Caitlin. "I like the sex."

Jessica rolled her eyes. "Considering the way you two fornicate like bunnies, I'm positive there will be sex. I'm just saying, this is a very relationship-y step."

"Yay?"

"Stop looking terrified. You're going to love it."

"Am I?"

"Yes. You'll see him more, and you'll go out together during the day. It's going to be very exciting."

"He did say we should go look at your photos at the gallery," said Caitlin.

"Really? That was nice. And see? Daytime activity, right there. Relax. You got this."

"What if he breaks up with me?"

"What if you break up with him?"

"Why would I do that? He's perfect!"

Jessica laughed. "Katie, sweetie, deep breaths. Seriously, you're freaking out."

"Yes! That's what I'm telling you!"

"It's going to be OK," said Jessica. "You'll see. Besides, it's just dinner? What could go wrong with dinner?"

Jackson
VAR Events

Jackson entered Cheery Bailbonds and looked in dismay at the blizzard of papers that had been spread out across three desks. Devonte had retreated to a corner with a laptop and Pete was standing over the disaster with Kim Kerschel. Kerschel was their resident tech expert and Jackson couldn't believe that she was happy with the paper snowstorm. Pete was wearing reading spectacles and had at least three different collections of papers in his hands, separated by his fingers.

"This is…" Kerschel tucked a short lock of hair behind her ear. Her black clothes, shaved hair style, and piercings stood in stark contrast with Pete's chinos and sweatshirt. She looked up and saw Jackson. "I am not responsible for this."

"Yes, this looks like a Pete special," agreed Jackson.

"Devonte keeps printing out more," she said, clearly offended.

"But I'm not happy about it," said Devonte.

"This is the system," said Pete. "Don't like it, go elsewhere."

"How can you get anything out of this?" demanded Kerschel. "I sent you three perfectly clear spreadsheets."

"You can't absorb the information off of spreadsheets."

She looked up at Jackson in disbelief.

"Take a break," said Jackson. "Go get dinner. Come back in an hour and he'll have something."

"I'm torn," she said. "This is torturing me, but I kind of want to see how he does it."

"Up to you," said Jackson, struggling not laugh.

"Dinner, for me," said Devonte, slapping the laptop shut and putting it on a nearby desk.

"You talked me into it," said Kerschel. "Let me get my jacket."

Jackson got a cup of coffee and wandered around the office, but he waited until Kerschel and Devonte were out the door before trying to talk to Pete again. He had some time to kill before he went to pick up Caitlin and he liked watching Pete solve problems.

"You have a spreadsheet too, don't you?" he asked, sitting in his usual desk chair after moving one of the stacks to the floor.

Pete looked up, a smile flashing across his face. "Of course. I based it on hers. But I can't picture the data on the screen. Or I can, but I need like eight more screens."

"Should we do a multi-media room? We've got that unused space back there. We could convert it."

"Sounds great, but that doesn't help me tonight. Where are you going? You look like you're dressed up as yourself for a change, and you usually only do that if you have to be Jackson Deveraux."

"I have a date," said Jackson trying the words out on Pete before he had to admit it to his cousins.

"New girl or the same girl you been fooling around with since November?" asked Pete, giving him a frown over his reading glasses.

"Have you been tracking my phone or something?"

"No, you just been in a good mood since November, which is weird considering this shit that we're dealing with. Do we need to run a background check on her?"

Jackson sighed.

"You would do it for your cousins."

"Yeah," said Jackson. "I know. I also know that she's dealing with a financial shitstorm of some kind, and she doesn't want help, opinions, or people looking into her shit. If she finds out I ran her, she'll be pissed and embarrassed."

Pete looked pained. "Isn't that exactly the kind of thing you would describe as a red flag for your cousins?"

"It would be except that literally she gets grumpy face when I buy her coffee. She wants my time, not my money. Which, to be honest, is frustrating as hell."

Pete laughed. "You finally found someone who doesn't treat you like a meal ticket and look where it gets you—a girl with standards who likes you for you. It's a goddamn tragedy."

Jackson laughed. "It's a tragedy I'm willing to endure."

"Look, you know your business, but I do think we should just run a basic on her."

"Yeah," agreed Jackson, with a sigh. "Tomorrow. Where are we at on Caitlin Granger?"

"She was at Columbia when the shit hit the fan with her father, but she was already struggling because her mom was sick back in Colorado."

"That sucks," said Jackson, feeling a pang of sympathy.

"It does. Then her mom dies, and they do the funeral. Then she comes back to New York and tries to go back to school, but then Granger stops paying her tuition and living expenses," said Pete.

"Jesus, what a prick."

"Yeah, no shit, because that's about when her mom's estate winds up and it turns out she was in debt up to her eyeballs. Pretty sure they are all going after Caitlin now. They are actually one of my stronger leads. I've got some calls in. If you want to find someone talk to their collections agency." Jackson shook his head in disbelief. "We know, thanks to you and Aiden that she goes to see Granger in prison at that point. Not that he did anything to help her."

"It's like he went out of his way to be an asshole," said Jackson. "His assets weren't frozen at that point. He could have helped her. He just didn't. What kind of dad does that? I can't imagine why she would do anything to help him. No wonder she hasn't come forward. We'll be lucky if she hasn't run everything through a shredder. Where'd she go next?"

"We lose her after that. She leaves slash gets kicked out of Columbia. She changes phone number and I think she goes up to the Hamptons to her aunt's house for a bit. I can't prove it yet, but I'm closing in."

"We know that she didn't stay there though. You were just there."

"Yeah," agreed Pete nodding. "But you can't skip ahead. You have to follow the trail. That's the system."

"Well, work the system," said Jackson. "I'm going to go out to dinner."

"That does sound like a way better system," said Pete.

Jackson took out his phone and placed an order for Pete's favorite Chinese place. Then he texted Pete's husband, who gave an eye roll emoji about Pete being heads-down in a project but said he'd be there for dinner. Jackson washed his mug and stared at the empty space they'd been using as a storage slash workout area. They could go full multi-media bat cave up in there, but he'd miss the workout equipment. Maybe they could go small bat cave and keep the gym. He went back to the front. Pete had tidied some papers and made some new piles.

"Food will be her in thirty minutes," Jackson said, as he buttoned his coat.

"What?" asked Pete, looking up from the pile of papers.

"Your food," said Jackson.

"I haven't ordered any. I should order some." Pete patted his pockets and looked around for his phone, which was undoubtedly somewhere under the piles of papers.

"I already did. It's on the way."

"Right," said Pete, squinting at the clock. "I should call John."

"Also, John said he'd come over and eat dinner with you after he finished grading papers."

"Oh," said Pete. "Thanks!"

Jackson shook his head and headed for the car. He liked his crew. They were all weirdly obsessive in ways that he enjoyed.

He was looking forward to a restaurant with Caitlin. He'd found someplace perfect. The food was delicious, but the venue was small, so it didn't *feel* expensive, and she wouldn't get mad at him when he paid. He'd tried to pinpoint why this dinner mattered. They weren't going to be doing anything they didn't always do, but it felt important. Maybe it was the going public factor. The idea that she would have to publicly admit that she was with him gave him a thrill. He parked in the VAR lot and knocked on the side door as instructed.

"Hey Jessica," said Jackson as she opened the door.

"Hey!" she said, cheerful as always. "She'll be out in a minute. She's changing." She eyeballed him. "Date, huh?"

"Yeah," he said. Then looked at her barely concealed smug expression. "Just say it. Your head's going to explode otherwise."

Jessica giggled, and her face split into a grin. "I'm not saying anything! Except... called it. Three weeks ago."

"You couldn't have told me?" he complained.

"Are you kidding? I couldn't even tell *her*," Jessica said, lowering her voice. "She is freaking out about being serious. You'd better treat her right or I will go shovel art on your ass."

"It's just dinner," he said. "And I intend to."

Jessica went back to grinning like a fiend.

"Whatever," said Jackson, shaking his head but relieved to see that at least he had the best friend seal of approval.

Jessica laughed again. Vince came around the corner and stopped in his tracks.

"What's he doing here?"

Jackson turned to face Vince. He'd never officially met the big, ex-football player.

"He's here to pick Katie," said Jessica. She glanced at Jackson nervously—he wasn't the only one who had caught Vince's tone.

"Fuck no, he's not. Get out."

"What?" Jackson had no idea how he was supposed to respond and he smiled awkwardly.

"You think this shit is funny? You can't mess with Caitlin like this. Get out."

"Hey, has anyone seen my coat?" asked Katie coming into the room. Jackson smiled. She had put her hair down and was actually wearing lipstick. She always looked gorgeous, but lipstick told him she was making an effort for him, and he reveled in that. "Oh! Hey! You're here." She smiled at Jackson. "Vince, have you met Jackson? Jackson Zane, this is Vince Ramano."

"Zane?" repeated Vince, pivoting to look at Katie. "He told you his name was Zane?"

"It's the name that comes up on my phone," said Kate with a laugh, as she spotted her coat on a chair and came toward him.

"Yeah," said Jackson awkwardly, realizing that he'd never actually covered that with her. It hadn't seemed important and he kind of assumed that everyone knew who his family was. "I got the phone number before the name change went through and now no matter what I do they can't seem to correct it on the caller ID."

"Name change?" repeated Kate, frowning at him. "You changed your last name?"

"To my family's name." Jackson had the feeling of shifting sand under his feet—like the ground was eroding out from underneath him as he stood.

"Tell her," ordered Vince.

"What?"

"Tell her your name!" barked Vince.

He suddenly didn't want to say it. He didn't know what was wrong with his name, but he didn't want to. He looked at Katie, who was waiting with a worried frown. "It's Deveraux," he said, with a shrug.

Her face went white. Her mouth opened and closed. "Why would you…" Her voice was a whisper. He reached out for her, and she stumbled backward, eyes wide. "Don't touch me. Why would you do this?"

"Katie?" He reached out again, and she flinched away, turned, and ran from the room.

Jackson took a step after her, but Vince put out a hand and slammed him backward. Jessica looked at both of them and then ran after Katie. A decade ago, Jackson would have started punching, but now he tried to use his brain.

"What did you do?" demanded Jackson.

"Me? Me, no I didn't do anything," said Vince. "I'm not the one who put Absolex in the national spotlight. The Deverauxes did that. The Deverauxes tanked the stock. The Deverauxes left her family destitute. And when her dad cleaned out her college fund and committed suicide, well, the way I figure it, the Deverauxes did that too. I didn't do anything but pick up the pieces. This is on you."

Jackson felt the pieces click. "No," he said, not wanting it to be true. "She's not… She's not Caitlin Granger. Her name is St. Cloud."

"Her mom's third ex-husband's name. She's been using it to avoid all the creditor's still trying to collect on her parent's debts."

Jackson looked at the empty doorway where Katie… Caitlin had gone. Katie wasn't coming back.

"Get out," said Vince.

Jackson took a deep breath. Nothing he had to say was going to make this situation better. He turned around and left.

DECEMBER 23

Evan
The Condo

"Dominique," snapped Evan, annoyed that his cousin was on the phone again.

"Sorry," she said, putting her phone down on the coffee table. It was the first time that Evan had the entire family over to his condo at one time. Evan was finding it very strange, but they couldn't use Deveraux House.

"I'm letting Tami Tang know—as a friend—that Marissa Shaw has been putting the moves on her husband."

"Is that necessary to do now?" demanded Evan. He couldn't believe the family was being ignored in favor of Tami Tang and Marissa Shaw.

"Well, yes. I'm in the final stages of torching the Junior League," said Dominique. "There's a Board Meeting tonight, and if I can make sure there isn't a quorum, the chapter will be forced to dissolve. And right now, Tami Tang is the Treasurer, and if she doesn't show up because Marissa Shaw is a predatory skeezbag, then that's the nail in the coffin."

"You were serious about that?" asked Ella. "I thought you were being metaphorical about raining destruction on their League of Evil." She glanced at Aiden, who made an *mmmmm* noise and shook his head. "Which apparently I should not have assumed. I just thought that Junior League was something that couldn't be stopped like athlete's foot."

"Yes," said Evan, "we all hate the Junior League. They are

pretentious, socially cruel, and generally unhelpful to whatever charity they attach themselves to for woke street cred. Dominique is doing the Lord's work, but can we move on?"

"Yes," agreed Max. "We need to figure out what the hell happened to Jackson. He no showed at the gym this morning and when I found him at the house he looked like he'd been run over. And then Theo gave me a look."

"Yes, but which look was it?" asked Aiden. "Was it the *why are you here* look?"

"The royal *we do not approve*?" asked Dominique.

"It was the *I have three empty vodka bottles in the recycling and I'm really worried* look," said Max.

"That one must be new," said Aiden.

"Well, so is Jackson's drinking," said Max.

"Max is right. He doesn't drink like that," said Dominique.

"She must have broken up with him," said Olivia, sounding distressed. "I tried drinking when Evan broke up with me."

"I also tried drinking when I broke up with you," said Evan.

"I couldn't make it through the entire bottle of wine though," said Olivia.

Evan glanced at his cousins. Aiden was openly grinning, and Dominique was giving a very strained neutral face.

"I baked several cakes instead," said Olivia. "And a pie."

"Good effort," said Aiden, encouragingly. "But back to Jackson. I don't think it's just breaking up. After he tried to give Max the brush off at the house, I called him."

"You called him?" asked Dominique.

"Yes, it's what you do when your material witness tries to give you the slip and doesn't think you're going to follow up. It's also a thing I do when Max says Jackson looks like he hasn't slept in twenty-four hours and probably hasn't been home except to drink and pass out. The surprise full frontal assault worked on him in DC. I thought I'd give it another try."

"What did he say?" asked Evan.

"He said they were trying to deal with the Caitlin Granger situation and that everything was fine and we'd talk later, then he hung up on me," said Aiden. "More or less."

"That's about what I got," said Evan, "when I tried to talk to him last night. After I talked to you this morning, I called Devonte, which is… tricky. I don't like to put him in a position where he has to choose between us."

"Did you get anything out of him?" asked Dominique hopefully.

"He said…" Evan hesitated thinking over the conversation. "There was a lot he didn't say actually. But I think they have found Caitlin Granger and she doesn't want to talk to them and now they're looking for alternate ways to deal with it. His crew are also aware of the break up and are trying to help, but reading between the lines…"

"What?" asked Aiden.

"It seemed pretty clear that they thought the break up was understandable? Like they thought Jackson had fucked up and weren't surprised with the reaction."

"I can't really picture that," said Max. "He's a stand-up guy. Half of his weird relationship issues are because he wants to be honest. I don't see what he could have done."

There was a chorus of agreement around the room.

"Well, did it sound like Devonte and the guys were actually doing anything?" asked Aiden.

"Yes, but I wouldn't have described his tone as hopeful," said Evan

"Well, that sucks," said Max.

"I feel so bad," said Ella. "Is there something… He's going to hate it if we do something, isn't he?"

"Yes, but do we think that should stop us?" asked Evan.

"Not particularly," said Aiden.

"One hundred percent," said Dominique and held up her hand for a fist bump from Aiden.

"Yes, but what are we actually going to do?" asked Ella.

"Well," said Olivia, "I thought maybe Dominique could go and talk to her."

The assembled family members turned to look at Olivia. She was sitting cross-legged on the couch and had her hair up in a bun. She was also wearing her favorite Star Wars t-shirt. She made Evan smile just by existing, but currently she was frowning as she looked at the puzzled expressions around the room.

"What? When Evan tried to do our stupid break-up Jackson came over and we figured out what the problem was and then I ended up threatening my grandfather. I've lost the thread on that sentence, but the point is that we solved the problem. So why can't we do the same thing for Jackson and this girl? I feel like sending one of the boys over to a strange woman's house might seem sort of intimidating. But I thought Dominique might have a better chance. If Jackson really did screw up somehow then maybe we can figure out how to fix it for him."

"I think she's right," said Dominique. "And I'm happy to do it."

"Well, I did get her address when we looked at his phone," said Evan. "So… is that the plan?"

He looked around the room.

"I haven't got anything better," said Max.

"I might if you gave me a week and let me use the Zhao security team," said Ella.

"Pretty sure he'd hate that even more than this plan," said Aiden and Ella nodded her agreement.

"All right," said Dominique. "Well, the mission is clear. I go, I meet Miss Mindblowingly Nice, the model who likes coffee, and I see what could have possessed her to break up with Jackson."

"And then you get her to issue a retraction," said Aiden.

"I don't think that's how break ups work," said Ella.

"I don't see why not. When a statement gets issued in error, you… retract it."

Dominique laughed. "OK, well, I'll give that a whirl and see how far I get. And if nothing else, then I'll be able to get a feel for her and what the issue is. I don't want him to be heartbroken, but if some relationships are meant to be, then so are some break-ups."

"Use your best judgement," said Evan. "But let's see if we can't pull this out for him. We owe him."

Caitlin
Work Day

Caitlin made her way down the stairs to answer the door. She felt a hundred years old. She'd stopped crying awhile ago, mostly because she was dehydrated and didn't have any more tears. Jackson had stopped calling before she'd stopped crying. She knew she looked a red-eyed mess, but she no longer cared.

Caitlin opened the door and eyed the blonde in the doorway.

"Hi?" asked Caitlin suspiciously. The woman was wearing low-key designer everything. The outfit was probably more than Caitlin's rent, but she had managed the feat of looking gorgeous, but only a *little* expensive.

"Whatever he did, he will apologize for it," said the blonde.

"What?" She looked familiar and Caitlin tried to remember where they had met.

"Whatever made you break up with Jackson, he'll apologize for and then you will make up. Hi. I'm Jackson's cousin, Dominique."

"Dominique Deveraux," said Caitlin, finally putting the full name together. "He calls you Nika."

If only he'd said her full name, Caitlin might have put everything together earlier. Before he broke her into a million pieces.

"Yes," agreed Dominique. "And we were hoping that you could take it back."

"Take what back?"

"The break up. Just… retract it."

"Do you know who I am?"

"You're listed as Katie S.C. in his address book."

"You looked at his phone?" Caitlin was shocked.

"Yes. Jacks thinks he's very clever, but he can't really handle all of us."

"All of us?" Caitlin felt like the entire conversation was surreal. Dominique Deveraux could not be standing in her doorway telling her to un-break up with Jackson.

"Aiden and Evan and I. We're his family."

"I'm aware of the Deveraux family," snapped Caitlin. Dominique's eyebrows raised. "Why are you here?"

"Well, I have been designated to address the problem," said Dominique.

"The problem of our break up?" Caitlin found herself wheezing out a shocked chuckle.

"Yes. It's a problem. But we think we can fix it."

"No," said Caitlin and swung the door shut.

Dominique put her foot into the door way, blocking the swing.

"He'll apologize. Whatever he did, he'll undo it. He'll fix it. Just stop being stubborn."

"My dad's dead," said Caitlin. "I don't really think he can fix that." Dominique was silent, which Caitlin guessed was a rare event. "Didn't really talk to him about this before you came over, did you? Maybe next time you'll mind your own fucking business."

She went to swing the door shut again, but Dominique blocked it with her hand.

"He killed your dad?"

Caitlin stared at Dominique. She couldn't believe that hadn't been the end of the conversation.

"I don't really think Jackson or your lawyers would want you to be here," said Caitlin. "You should leave."

"My lawyer is my brother, so whatever. Answer the question. What the fuck happened? We can't fix it if you don't talk to me."

Caitlin burst out laughing. "You're going to fix it? You'll just wave your magic wand and make everything better? Is that what Deverauxes do?"

"Well, usually we fuck things up first."

"Yeah, like my life. Go away."

"He loves you," said Dominique, still pushing on the door.

"No, he doesn't," said Caitlin. "At best, he liked fucking Katie St. Cloud. Dating Caitlin Granger was not on his agenda and if it was, then fuck him."

Dominique blinked and stepped back in shock. Caitlin took the opportunity to slam the door shut and lock it.

Caitlin leaned against the wall breathing hard. After a moment she heard Dominique's retreating footsteps outside. She climbed the stairs and stopped at the top, staring at Jackson's goddamn navy blue peacoat still hanging on coat rack.

Caitlin ignored it and went over to the couch and collapsed face first on to the cushions. There had been several points during the last few years where she couldn't believe that this was her life now. But somehow this seemed like a new low even for her. She curled into a ball and pulled the blankets over her head. She didn't even bother to pretend that she was going to watch TV or something normal. Instead, she stayed in her cocoon until she heard her phone beep with an alert from her room.

It was time to go get ready for work. Another stupid workplace Chirotmas party where Debbie from Accounting would get drunk and the managers would feel like it was OK to hit on the interns. Given her pick, she would have stayed home, but VAR was closed for most of the week between Christmas and New Year's and Caitlin would lose hours. She needed to cram in all she could. The upcoming Roggario show would help a bit, but it wouldn't be enough. Of course, there was really no such thing as enough. She was always in debt and one missed payment away from someone calling her about something.

Caitlin struggled off the couch and went toward her room, but her eye was once again drawn to Jackson's coat on the rack. It was the only thing he'd ever left at her place. She picked it up and carried it into her room. She ought to burn it. Or donate it. She doubted she would do either of those. She would probably pay too much money to have Task Rabbit person take it back to wherever he lived. Something he'd never told her. Once again, if he'd had told her anything about his life, she might have figured it out earlier. Not that she'd asked him anything. She hadn't wanted to know.

She pulled off her sweats and put on her work bra. Wide straps, good support, practical. That was what she needed out of life. She didn't need a handsome bad-boy prince who crept into her bed and wrapped her up in dreams of everything working out alright. She looked at the coat again. Reluctantly she picked it up and held the collar to her nose. It still held traces of bergamot and citrus, and she found tears prickling the inside of her eyelids. Why had he done this to her? Did he hate the Granger family so much? She pulled the coat on, trying to pretend that the sleeves were his arms.

There was a sharp crack and Caitlin's eyes flew open. Then a splintering sound and she heard her front door slam against the wall of the hall.

Caitlin ran out into the main room and saw two men charging up the stairs. She had barely a second to recognize the Russian who had been stalking her, his face still bruised where Jackson had hit him, before he grabbed her by the arm and threw her across the kitchen table. He grabbed her by the back of the head and held her against the rough wooden boards. On the far side of the table the ice bucket bounced and fell over, the ice pick inside jangling with a harsh clang.

"OK," said the second man, leaning down to look her in the eye. He had sandy brown hair, that was carefully tousled but was wearing a bandana over his face. "Hi Caitlin. So, you've been avoiding my guy Baranov here and you don't call us back. And then you have your piece of shit Ukrainian thug boyfriend get all aggro on him. That's not cool. We don't like that." His voice was warm and friendly, but his gray eyes were cold.

"What do you want?" Caitlin gasped. The pressure on the back of her head increased.

The man laughed, the bandana puffing slightly at his exhalation. "Caitlin. Please. Stop pretending. We know that you got all your father's things. You're the only person he could possibly have sent anything to. We know you have the file."

"What file?" Caitlin managed to get out. The only thing she had was a pile of bullshit paperwork that had arrived a week after her father's death.

"Really, Caitlin, this is stupid. I would have paid you for it. You obviously could use the money. Or maybe not. I don't know what your Ukrainian pays you. But now we have to do it the hard way. Now you're going to give me what I want or Baranov is going to break a few things. Probably that you're attached to. Or that are attached to you. I hear you've been doing some modeling. That's going to be a little hard once he breaks your nose."

"Sounds fun," said Baranov, his voice a harsh grumble.

"See? This is why I pay him. He enjoys these kinds of things. I don't. I just want results. Give me the file Caitlin. Give me the file and we go away."

It was in the ottoman. All the papers that gave Caitlin a headache and made her sweat were inside the ottoman where she could lift the lid, throw them in, and never look at them again. It was her own personal portal to hell. That's why she never looked inside it if she could help it, and she certainly never did more than glance at her father's pile of shit.

"I don't have anything," said Caitlin.

"Fine," said the guy in the bandana, he grabbed a chair and swung it at the floor, shattering the old wood and paint. Caitlin line flinched and let out a little scream, which made Baranov laugh. Next the man, grabbed her tiny refrigerator and pulled it over, dumping the contents onto the floor. Left over boxes spilled out, their contents splattering.

"Next we're going to start on you," he said. The Russian's hand on the back of her head moved down to the back of her neck and he picked her up, keeping one hand on her arm.

"Tell him where the papers are," Baranov growled and shook her like a rag doll. Then he leaned in close, so that his breath tickled her ear. "After he leaves you and I are going to have some fun."

"I can call him off," said the bandana guy. "I can. Or not. I don't really give a shit. What I want are my papers. Your father sent you papers, right?"

"Yes," gasped Caitlin. "But they were garbage. They were just junk from Absolex."

"Finally getting somewhere!"

Baranov let go of her arm and she felt his hand slide down to her thigh and then up to her ass, but the hand on the back of her neck was as firm as ever.

"That's fine. They probably were. Your father was batshit insane toward the end. Just tell me where they are."

Baranov gave her a shake and Caitlin stumbled forward, her hand coming to rest on the ice bucket.

"You are going to pay for what your boyfriend did," Baranov grumbled.

Caitlin swallowed hard and flipped the lid off the ice bucket. The ice pick came tumbling out effortlessly into her hand.

"Where are my papers?" the man yelled, screaming it into her face.

With one hand, she shoved him backward. Then she yanked herself free of Baranov's grasp and, whirling around, stabbed out and upward with the icepick, driving it into his neck. She pulled back and blood fountained from the wound. Baranov made a hoarse yell and grabbed for his throat. Caitlin didn't stay to look at what happened next. She sprinted down the stairs and out the ruined door.

Dominique
What We Do

Dominique was still standing on the top step of Deveraux House when Theo opened the door.

"Is Miss contemplating the door knob or actually planning on coming in?" asked Theo.

"Theo, Jackson is in trouble, but I don't know what to do about it."

"Call the boys, circle the wagons, and set fire to your enemies," said Theo promptly. "I believe that is the usual method."

Dominique laughed. "It is, but I think maybe... We already did that and now there's collateral damage?"

"Do you need to come in and have a cup of tea?" asked Theo. "Mr. Jackson still isn't home."

"He's been dating Caitlin Granger," said Dominique.

"Oh, dear," said Theo. "Well, that explains the drinking."

"Yes, but I don't think he meant to. And I don't think she meant to. And now they're both miserable. You should have seen her—she got so mad and she *still* looked heartbroken. And she lives in the worst neighborhood. I just called Pete and asked him about Caitlin Granger. I figured he'd at least answer some basics if he thought it was a general inquiry. He said she owes the IRS on all of the frozen assets that she inherited from Granger. She can't sell them but they're still demanding money. And then he said her mom died three years ago and left a ton of debt too. She doesn't have anyone, Theo. Just one horrible aunt that clearly isn't helping a bit. Theo, I'm just... I think maybe we ruined her life when we set out to destroy Granger."

"Mmmm…" said Theo. "I believe that Mr. Granger made his own choices."

"OK, but we helped."

"Perhaps so. Don't you think Mr. Jackson will sort it out?"

"Maybe. I mean, I'm sure Jackson will fix whatever needs fixing for the family, but you know he won't try and get back together with her. He'll just stay heartbroken because he'll think it's the right thing to do."

"That does sound like him. So, what are you going to do?"

"That's what I've been standing here trying to figure out. I mean… She's Caitlin Granger. I pictured him falling for a lot of people, but I have to admit, that is one person that didn't pop up on *any* of my lists."

"If Mr. Jackson loves her than does her last name matter? Asked Theo, practically.

"No," said Dominique. "But it's a lot. I mean, a lot *a lot*. And I'm sort of floundering here, Theo. I'm not sure what to think, let alone what to do. Except that she looked *so* hurt."

Dominique felt her eyes fill with tears. Jackson couldn't have known who she was, because otherwise it was just cruel.

"Miss Dominique, do you know why I have worked for your family for all these years?"

"Grandma has excellent retirement benefits?"

"Yes, but also because your family, even in your darkest moments, have never stopped trying to make things better for each other. You take action and I like that. I like being around people who help and don't take no for an answer. When I was a boy, we did not have any indoor plumbing and we only had three forks. Six people, three forks. It sounds like a joke and certainly there were people treated my family like one, but that was how poor we were for a time. But being born poor is not a sin, and being born rich is not a virtue. And when I needed help, and I looked around for a hand, I only found one person reaching back for me—Eleanor Deveraux. If you think there is someone who needs your help, then I suggest you remember that you are a Deveraux and you go do what you do best."

"Don't take no for an answer, and help someone even if they don't want it?"

"Damn straight," said Theo with a nod.

Dominique thought that over. "You know what? You're right. That *is* what we do. Weird habit, but we're good at it, so I will embrace it. OK, Max and Evan were meeting me here, but give me some car keys. I'm going back there and I'm going to talk to her. If we hurt her, then we can fix it. And then I will figure out how to get them back together because Jackson fixed this family and I cannot let him be miserable for us."

"Good," said Theo. He disappeared back into the hall and came back with keys. "I believe the Mercedes has a full tank. I will inform Mr. Deveraux and Mr. Ames of your progress."

"Excellent," said Dominique. She grabbed the keys and headed toward the garage. She wasn't entirely sure what she'd say to Caitlin, but there had to be something. By the time she made it over the bridge and cautiously parked on Caitlin's street, she had a rudimentary speech worked out, but it rather depended on Caitlin talking to her.

She was approaching Caitlin's apartment when the door flew open with a sharp bang and Caitlin came out into the street wearing only a bra, underwear and a coat. Dominique watched in shock as Caitlin sprinted toward the corner and then moments later a man came out after her. He wore a very prosaic set of khakis and a polo shirt, but around his face he'd tied a bandana like he was an old-time train robber. He stumbled through the door knocking over a golf club, and leaving bits of wood from the door strewn on the sidewalk before running after Caitlin.

Caitlin reached the corner and didn't stop as she ran out into the street. A taxi rounded the corner just as Caitlin entered the road, and she bounced off the hood with a sharp smack that Dominique could hear even half a block away.

Dominique grabbed the golf club off the pavement and ran after Caitlin. Ahead of her, the man in the khakis and mask seized Caitlin by the coat lapels as she lay on the pavement and thumped her back onto the ground again, banging her head off the pavement.

"Where is it, you dumb bitch?" the man screamed.

Dominique came in swinging hard. He turned at the last second and put up an arm, half blocking the swing. The golf club bent and he went sprawling onto the pavement. He rolled and came up, awkwardly pulling a gun out of his waistband with the arm she hadn't hit.

"I'm calling the cops," yelled a skinny Black kid running out into the street, waving a cell phone. "I'm calling the cops right now. They are on the way!" He stopped mid-way out onto the road as the man pointed the gun in the kid's direction. The taxi driver looked at the scene and then pulled away with a screech of tires.

The man in the khakis looked between Dominique and the kid, clearly trying to weigh his options.

"Don't fucking do it," said a man's voice. Dominique looked around and saw another guy in jeans and a puffer coat with a gun come out of the park. He was holding it sideways, like they did in the movies, but it was pointed at the guy in khakis. Dominique took a firmer grip on the golf club, standing over Caitlin's prone body.

Slowly, the man in khaki's put up his gun and backed away. They watched as he jogged back down the block and got into a blue sedan. Moments later, the car disappeared around the corner.

"Oh, fuck," said the kid, putting his hand on his knees and inhaling. "Fuck. Rufus, shit, man, thanks."

"Jamal, you dumb shit, you don't run up on someone like that," snapped the man.

"I didn't know he had a gun. He looked like he worked at an Apple store!"

"Is Katie OK?" asked Rufus, stopping a few feet away.

Dominique looked down at Caitlin. She had bruises and there was blood on the pavement, but she was breathing and nothing appeared obviously broken. "I don't know. She's unconscious. Did you call the cops? Tell them to send an ambulance."

"I was lying," said Jamal. "My phone's dead. I was on my way to Katie's to see if I could charge it up for a bit."

"OK. Uh…" Dominique shook her head, trying to focus. "I have a phone. I will call for an ambulance. I am doing that."

"We should call Jackson," said Jamal.

"He's going to be pissed," said Rufus, looking over Jamal's shoulder at Katie.

"Pissed is *not* going to begin to cover it," agreed Dominique, dialing. "But ambulance first. Take care of Katie, and then I'll call Jackson."

"You know Jackson?" asked Jamal.

"He's my cousin."

"Oh," said Jamal. He and Rufus both nodded as if she had explained everything.

Jackson
St. Anne's Hospital

Jackson felt his heart race as he saw Katie's number on the phone.

"Hello?" He picked up cautiously, not really sure what to expect.

"Jesus, thank God," said Jamal. "Jackson, you've got to get down here. I don't know what to do."

"Down where? Jamal, where are you? Where's Katie?"

"We're at the hospital. You've got to get down here. She got hit by a cab. And I think that guy."

"Which hospital?"

"The big one with… St. Anne's. It's St. Anne's. And you cousin is trying, but the hospital bitch is being a dick. You've got to get here before they call the cops and kick us out." Jamal's voice dropped on the last words as if he was trying to say it without being overheard.

"Jamal, what the happened? Which cousin? What the fuck is going on?"

"I'll explain when you get here. Go to the emergency room."

The emergency room was a hive of activity, and Jackson felt his temper rising as he sorted his way through the levels of people who didn't give a shit until he was finally directed to the correct desk.

"Oh, Caitlin St. Cloud," said the nurse frowning as she typed. "Right. The sex worker and her *friend.*"

"Excuse me? Did you just call her a sex worker?"

"She was brought in in her underwear and a coat," said the

nurse without looking up. "Do you happen to have her insurance information? The blonde woman didn't. She gave up after I explained things to her." The nurse looked up with a smug smile.

Jackson pulled out a business card. "Send all of her billing to this address," he said.

"Jackson!"

Jackson turned to see Dominique and Jamal heading toward him trailed by someone who he assumed was a hospital administrator from his panicked expression and swinging name badge.

"Sir, it's going to be very expensive," said the nurse without taking the card in Jackson's outstretched hand. "If she doesn't have insurance, you'd be better to let social services and the police—"

"I don't believe I asked for your advice," said Jackson. "Send the billing to that address and take me to my fucking girlfriend."

"I can't take non-relatives back to patients."

"Jackson!" Dominique rushed forward and hugged him. "Oh, thank goodness, you're here. This Nurse Rachtett wannabe—"

"Excuse me?" snapped the nurse.

"Won't let me through to see Caitlin. My friend was the victim of a vicious assault and I swear to God if you imply that she was a hooker one more time I will personally see to it that you get fired."

Dominique seldom made that kind of threat and Jackson was shocked. The hospital administrator gave a high-pitched nervous laugh.

"No, no, no, no, she did not say that. She is showing you and your brother through to your friend."

"I can't take non-relatives through," said the nurse. The administrator snatched the business card out of Jackson's hand and shoved it into the nurse's face.

"Do you see the name on that card?" he hissed.

She looked at the card. "Jackson Deveraux," she read out loud, sounding unimpressed.

"And the name on that donor plaque on the wall, what does that say?" the man demanded, pointing. She turned slowly and read the name on the sign behind her.

"Deveraux Foundation," said the nurse, suddenly looking nervous.

"So we are taking our multi-million dollar donors through to their friend, aren't we?"

The nurse nodded mutely.

They were ushered down bustling hallways and Jackson felt like his heart was going to jack-hammer out of his chest. He needed to talk to Dominique, but he wanted privacy.

"Thank you," said Dominique firmly, turning to the administrator when they were finally escorted to someplace. Jackson couldn't tell where they were. He was having a hard time focusing on the things people were saying. The noise washed out of their mouths and through his ears. The only one he could really seem to absorb was Dominique. "You can go. Just send us Caitlin's doctor."

The man nodded and left them. Dominique promptly yanked open the door they were standing in front of and hurried in.

"Dominique, wait. What—"

Katie was unconscious in the bed. She looked dirty, and Jackson would swear that her right hand had blood caked under her nails.

"What the fuck happened?" demanded Jackson looking between Dominique and Jamal.

"Katie was attacked," said Jamal.

"I was going to talk to her," said Dominique. "But she came running out of her apartment with this man chasing her. She was just wearing underwear and a coat. I think it was your coat, actually. Um. Then I hit the guy with a golf club, but he had a gun."

"A gun," Jackson turned back to look at Dominique. "Are you alright?"

"Rufus pulled his piece," said Jamal. "The guy ran off. Dominique hit him hard! She bent the golf club."

"She's a heavy hitter," said Jackson numbly.

Jackson flipped on the light by Katie's bed to get a better look and saw the very clear bruises imprints where someone had grabbed her upper arm. He felt himself flush and then grow cold. He wanted to punch something. He looked up at Dominique and found that he couldn't even form words.

"Who did this?" he demanded, but Dominique hesitated. "What did he look like? Give me something."

"Jackson, this isn't… He had a bandana tied across his face, but between you and me… I'm pretty sure it was Dennis Houge."

"Houge?"

"It was the hair," said Dominique. "It was the same. But I'm not sure that would stand up in court."

"It doesn't have to," said Jackson.

"Ms. Deveraux?" asked a tired-looking doctor peering into the room.

"Yes," said Dominique. "Can you tell us how Caitlin is?"

"Concussion," said the doctor. "Some other bruising and contusions. And um…" He glanced at Jamal and Jackson. "Due to her state of… state of her clothing…"

"Just say it," snarled Jackson.

"We ran a rape kit," said the doctor. "It came back negative, but that doesn't mean, um."

"Yes, thank you," said Jackson.

"But the concussion is the worst of it."

"The man hit her head on the pavement," said Dominique. "And she might have hit it on the cab. I don't know."

"She should remain in the hospital for at least the next day or two," said the doctor. "We'll run an MRI tomorrow when she wakes up."

"That's fine," said Jackson. "I'm going to be bringing in some security personnel and have them in the room. Jamal will also be staying here."

"I'm not really sure…" said the doctor looking warily at Jamal.

"He saw the man who attacked her. I need him to be able to identify him if he comes here."

"Oh," said the doctor. "Um… shouldn't the police…"

"I will involve the police at the correct juncture," said Jackson. "In the meantime, please let your staff know that they must have their ID in place and may have to identify themselves."

"Of course," said the doctor.

"Thank you. You can go," said Jackson.

"OK," said the doctor and backed from the room.

Jamal was eyeing him with awe. "You're badass."

"If I were badass she wouldn't be here," said Jackson, dialing his phone. "Devonte, it's Jackson."

"What's up?"

"I need you over at St. Anne's."

"On my way."

"Room 325," said Jackson, hanging up.

"I already talked to the cops," said Dominique. "They said they would send someone to take my statement, but they didn't exactly sound in hurry and I was trying to get around that stupid nurse. She was a total cockblocker. I had to rustle up someone who knows me so I could throw my weight around. I had Jamal call you when I thought I was going to have to have some sort of crazed woman fit just to get Katie proper care. I called Aiden after I talked to the cops and he's on his way, but I didn't know how much police involvement you wanted."

"Sic Aiden on them," said Jackson. "It doesn't matter. It will take them too long to get moving."

"What are you going to do?"

"I'm going to go to Katie's. I'm going to find out what the fuck happened, and then I'll find the guy who did this."

Jamal nodded and then looked nervously between him and Dominique. "I saw Katie yesterday, and she'd been crying. Did you and Katie break up?"

"Yes," said Jackson.

"Why?"

He looked at Dominique. How the hell was he supposed to answer that?

"Because her dad tried to kill us, so our family fucked up her dad's life and then he committed suicide, which fucked her life," said Dominique.

Jamal looked shocked. "That's hard to come back from."

"Yes, it is," said Jackson.

Jackson
Caitlin's Apartment

Jackson climbed the stairs to Katie's… Caitlin's apartment. The door had been kicked in as Jamal said. The new lock he'd gotten her had held up all right, but the hinges had given way and the ancient, cheap door had splintered. He pulled his gun and nosed his way into the living area.

The place had been trashed. A chair had been violently broken, and the refrigerator was lying on its side, the contents spilling onto the floor. But the real problem was the dead white guy sprawled across the collapsed kitchen table with an ice pick sticking out of his neck. Jackson squatted down and stared into the man's face. He recognized the pistol whip mark and tattoo on his neck. It was the Russian who had been stalking Katie.

Holstering his gun, Jackson reached into his jacket pocket and pulled out a pair of gloves. Once he had gloved up, he gingerly lifted the Russian enough to rifle through the pockets on his jacket. He extracted the Russian's wallet and flipped it open.

Stepan Baranov was based out of Jersey and had a business card that listed him as a Vice-President of Quickie Payday Advance. The next card in Baranov's wallet gave Jackson pause. Dennis Houge's card, complete with the congressional logo and DC address, looked out of place in the snakeskin wallet. He snapped a picture of both cards and the ID before returning them to the wallet and pushing it back into the jacket pocket. He tried to match the placement, but everything was sticky with blood. He guessed that Baranov had died within minutes, but it wasn't a good way to go. Blood was everywhere, even dripping from the ceiling. Jackson stripped off one of the gloves, turning it inside out to contain contamination. Then he sent the photos of Baranov's wallet to Pete. His phone rang almost instantly.

"I talked to Devonte," said Pete, without preamble. "What the fuck happened? Who is this guy?"

"Baranov. I think he's some kind of loan shark. I had a run-in with him last week. I thought he was a stalker. I thought I'd scared him off, but apparently, the message didn't take. Pretty sure Houge and this asshole broke into Katie's apartment and attacked her. Probably looking for Granger's papers. And she appears to have stabbed Baranov with an ice pick."

"Is he dead?"

"Oh, yeah. All the way dead."

"Shit. That's a different kind of trouble. What do you want to do?"

"I want to find Houge and rip his fucking head off," said Jackson, trying to keep his anger from bleeding through into his voice.

"Do we know if he got Granger's papers?" asked Pete. Always sensible.

"I don't know. I don't think so. Dominique and Jamal didn't mention that he was carrying anything. I'll look around here, but I want to leave before the cops show up. Find me Houge. Call in everyone. Get it done. I don't care what favors you have to burn or cash you have to put out. Find him. Dominique said he was driving a blue sedan. She's not great with cars, but she knows four doors when she sees them. She also ID'd Houge from his hair."

"Good as a fingerprint for me," said Pete without irony. "I'll call you when I have something."

The line went dead, and Jackson dropped the phone into his pocket. Slowly, he surveyed the room. Despite the mess, not much had actually been disturbed. Houge hadn't done much searching.

Most of the furniture was in its usual place. Katie—Caitlin—kept the place tidy. She didn't like a mess. She said it made her anxious. So where would she put a bunch of papers from her father? A tiny desk was next to the computer with orderly rows of envelopes. He knew Katie didn't like the desk—he got the feeling that she managed the finances from there—but nothing looked like Granger's mysterious paper files. He went for a moment to stare into the bedroom and found himself closing his eyes against the physical sensation of pain.

This place had been a haven. Someplace sweet and safe that made him happy. A sanctuary that had been violated. He didn't think Katie would stash anything from her father in the bedroom, and he did an about-face and inhaled sharply through his nose, trying to clear his head.

Katie didn't keep secrets. Not really. She just wanted to handle everything herself. Because there was no one else. But he'd been able to see how worn down she got from dealing with it. She was good at tucking things out of sight, and maybe when she'd been with him, she'd been able to hide from it herself, but it had been crushing her.

She tucked things out of sight.

Jackson moved toward the couch, stepping gingerly around the body and blood spatters. He had one hand on the ottoman when he heard the soft clunk of the remains of the door hitting the wall.

"Katie?"

Jackson recognized Vince Romano's voice.

"Up here," Jackson called. He didn't wait and flipped the lid off the ottoman. Inside was a mess of papers. Bills and letters from the IRS were layered on top, but underneath he could see the corner of a yellow mailing envelope.

Vince came up the stairs with his gun drawn. He took in the

scene at Jackson. "Where the fuck is Katie?" he asked, not putting his pistol away or taking it off Jackson.

"Hospital," said Jackson. "I've got a guy with her. What are you doing here?"

Vince dropped the gun and looked around again. "She picked up an extra shift tonight and then didn't show. She never does that. Then she didn't answer her phone. I thought I'd swing by."

"Good idea," said Jackson. He bent down and extracted the envelope with his gloved hand. The postmark was from San Francisco.

"Who did this?" demanded Vince, pointing at the body.

"Pretty sure that was Katie."

"Fuck. We need to call the cops."

"Not yet," said Jackson.

"What do you mean, not yet?"

"Well, once the cops get here, they'll seal the scene, which means all of Katie's clothes will be stuck here. I want to pack her a bag."

"Pack a bag? Who gives a shit about a bag? We need to figure out what the hell happened and get the cops up here."

"I know what happened. Her father's partner in the senate sent that asshole after her, looking for these papers. But after I beat the shit out of him last week, they came back when I wasn't around."

"You're taking this pretty damn calmly," growled Vince. Jackson finally looked him in the eye.

Jackson was aware that he was going full Deveraux, but he couldn't stop the sheer rage that was churning in his gut.

"It's Wednesday, Vince," he said quietly. "She never works Wednesday nights because she's *supposed* to be with me."

"Well, how was I supposed to know you were actually into her?"

"You could have tried asking either of us," snapped Jackson.

"She has been in hell because of you and her dad. Since when do the Deverauxes ever give a shit about anyone? Everyone knows you're all assholes."

"That is true," said Jackson, taking out his phone again. "We really are."

I HAVE THE PAPERS. I'LL BRING THEM TO THE OFFICE. FIND ME HOUGE.

Jackson went into her room, brushing by Vince. Her work clothes were still on a hanger on the bedroom doorknob. He left most of the clothes, just taking what he thought were her favorite items. He would get her more clothes if they were needed. Then he packed a toothbrush and all the random necessities of phone chargers, hair brush, and bras and dumped everything into a gym bag he found in the closet.

"You're not going to call the cops, are you?" asked Vince when he came out again.

"Someone will," said Jackson with a shrug.

"You're going to go after the other guy."

"Yeah," said Jackson, "I am."

Vince looked like he was running some calculations in his head. "All right, I'll go with you."

"If you wanted to be helpful, you could take this bag to Katie at the hospital. I could use my guy back, and she could use someone she trusts to watch her back. That's not me anymore."

Vince took the bag. "You gotta twist the knife, don't you?"

"Didn't I just say we were assholes?"

Jackson brushed past Vince and headed down the stairs. He hadn't slept properly in twenty-four hours, and he knew he probably was at his best, but right now, all he wanted to do was punch something. The only problem was that his preferred target was nowhere to be found, and all he had to show for it was a pile of papers.

Evan
CHEERY BAILBONDS

Evan arrived at Cheery Bailbonds at nearly the same time as Aiden.

"I didn't think you knew where this place was," said Aiden.

"I helped with the purchase paperwork. I just pretend not to. Why doesn't he get new signs?"

"I think he likes it this way," said Aiden, looking up at the faded sign on the building. "I think comfortably downtrodden is the look he's going for."

"Meanwhile, what the fuck?" asked Evan. "I have three messages from Nika, and none of them are good."

"She leaves the worst messages," said Aiden, shaking his head.

"No, they were perfectly clear. I mean, they were all bad news. Jackson's mystery girlfriend is Caitlin Granger? Only she's been assaulted by Dennis Houge? She's at the hospital? I can't even… What the fuck?"

"Oh. I guess her messages were clear for you. I had to call her back."

Garcia opened the door and looked at both of them. Garcia had been Aiden's assigned minder before Zhao security had pretty much co-opted the job due to Aiden's proximity to Ella. "Are you two coming inside, or did you just want to loiter and make people suspicious?"

"Um… suspicious?" offered Aiden.

"I was coming in," said Evan. "I just stopped to talk to Mr. Suspiciously Loitering With Intent."

"Cool," said Garcia. Evan suspected that Jackson had hired

the dark-haired ex-cop due to his unflappable nature. It helped when dealing with Aiden.

"So," said Aiden, as they filed into the building. "Jackson was dating Caitlin Granger. Didn't he run a background check or anything? I mean, seriously, how much shit did he flip us about that kind of thing?"

"I think he was in denial about dating," said Kerschel from her spot and a desk.

"Ditto to that," said Garcia.

"He feels like an idiot," said Pete, looking at the Deverauxes over his reading glasses. "However, having just run a background check, I'm not sure it would have helped. She's been using her mother's third ex-husband's last name. She worked a lot of cash gigs and changed phones and addresses multiple times. She pops up with terrible credit, but legitimately as Caitlin St. Cloud. We might have got a head start if we'd known her name was Caitlin, but there wasn't any reason to connect the two."

"Are we sure it wasn't some sort of con?" asked Aiden.

"No," said Garcia, shaking his head. "If that had been the case, there would have been an ask for funding, and she wouldn't have told him to fuck off so hard. She does *not* want to see him."

"I wanted it to be a con," said Aiden sadly. "Then we could hate her."

Kerschel looked up from her computer, clearly startled. "No, bruh. I'm pretty sure Granger wiped out her college fund to hire the guys who tried to kill Evan and then used whatever was leftover to pay for his run from the law."

"Son of a bitch," said Aiden. "That's like a two for one asshole maneuver. How do you even get to be that much a dick?"

"By being a complete narcissist," said Evan with a shrug. "OK, so where does Dennis Houge come into this?"

"Unclear," said Pete. "But Dominique ID'd him at the scene. Said he attacked Caitlin, and then she and some kid and possibly a drug dealer had to run him off. I'm still working that one out. Cops are on the scene now, so maybe we'll learn more, but probably not. Jackson said Dominique hit Houge with a golf club."

"Classic Nika," said Aiden, nodding. "Although, I wish she wouldn't. Once is an accident. Twice… It's the kind of thing that looks like it's becoming a habit."

"Oh. Are we caring what people think? I thought we weren't doing that."

"Not in general, but legally," said Aiden. "I dislike establishing a pattern. I did offer to take her to do some training with Ella and me, but she said that she likes her kickboxing class doing batting practice with Max on date night."

"She's always had very good aim," said Evan. "Remember the time she pegged you in the forehead with the suction cup arrow."

"That would have been funny if she hadn't tipped it in ink first," said Aiden.

"No," said Evan, "it was still funny."

"It's moments like this that give me insight into your family," said Pete. "Although, frequently, they are insights I didn't want. Meanwhile, I'm now about to go chase down a lead on a guy with a broken arm. When Jackson gets here, tell him to call me. Garcia, you're with me. Kerschel, call me when you've got something on Baranov."

"I have it already," said Kerschel getting up and following Pete and Garcia as they put on their jackets. "Stepan Baranov. Legal non-citizen. Ties to the Russian mafia, but who the fuck doesn't? I called Houge's office in my cheerful lady voice and asked where Baranov could send his invoice, and she got annoyed and said to send it to the same place as last month and gave me an email address. I'm hacking that. I'll have financial ties between him and Houge by the time you get back."

"OK," said Pete, "but don't leave any fingerprints. The police have to be able to find all this on their own and it has to be clean. We can't look like we were doing anything more than hitting people with golf clubs."

"I believe you mean protecting the innocent from assault," Aiden called after him.

"What he said," said Pete. The old-fashioned bell bounced and jangled as the two men left, and Aiden turned to Evan.

"I don't like doing nothing. Jackson had better get back soon, or I shall be forced to come up with something."

"Like what?" asked Evan. His cousin was creative, but he was unsure which direction that would go in the current situation.

"Honestly, I'm thinking about calling Zoe, Grandma's Chief-of-Staff and start doing a little digging on Houge from that direction."

"Grandma might not appreciate that," said Evan, thoughtfully, trying to weight the pros and cons.

"Didn't you just say we weren't caring what people think?" asked Aiden.

"Grandma isn't people," said Evan drily.

"Jackson needs help."

"Start with Hannah Nowitsky," said Kerschel. "She's Jackson's inside man."

"Thanks," said Aiden, flashing her a smile. "Now is there an office I can use somewhere?"

"There's the kitchen, the supply closet, the locker room, or the storage room with the gym equipment."

"Gym equipment!" said Aiden, perking up.

"Down the hall, last door on the left," said Kerschel, pointing.

Aiden went, but Evan decided not to go with him. He looked around and eventually located the desk with the green fidget toy on top and sat down. He opened a drawer found Jackson's pack of gum and then put it back. "Hubba-Bubba," he said shaking his head.

"He ran out of regular gum a couple of days ago, and we keep forgetting to put in the supply order," said Kerschel. "We're down to eggs, a box of staples, and one pack of post-it notes. Everyone keeps complaining because there aren't any more microwave breakfast burritos, but no one will just make eggs."

Evan nodded.

"You know what? I'm going to put the order in now. He should have gum." She switched tabs on her screen, and a few minutes later, he heard her make an affirmative noise. "It won't make any difference," she said with a sigh. "But it will be here by tomorrow."

"Thanks," said Evan. "Keeping him off cigarettes is a group effort."

Kerschel laughed. "Yeah, it kind of is." She hesitated and then blurted out the words all in a rush. "When my girlfriend broke up with me last year, he ate dinner with me every day for a week. He really pulled me through that initial stage where all you want to do is drink and cry."

"He's there for his friends and he's always there for his family," said Evan. "That's why this is so…"

"I want to fix it for him," said Kerschel.

"If we can," said Evan. "Yes."

"This girl better be worth it, because he is fucked up over this."

"I haven't seen him and he's sent three of my calls to voicemail," said Evan.

Kerschel grimaced. "Oh, that's not good. He always talks to you. OK, when he comes in, I'm going to pretend I have to talk to

Aiden, and maybe you guys can talk. Bro to bro or whatever dudes do."

"I have no idea," said Evan. "I think I'm fundamentally un-dude."

Kerschel laughed. "Well, you're more naturally equipped for the job than I am."

Evan shrugged just as the bell jangled over the door and Jackson came in. He looked pale and was definitely working more stubble than usual. But it was the hard set of his jaw that worried Evan. It carried the echo of their fathers and grandfather. It was the hard-driven look of the Deverauxes that caused misery for everyone around them.

"I have Granger's files," said Jackson.

"Good," said Evan. "Kerschel—I'm sorry, Jackson calls you Kerschel, but would you rather I called you Kim?" She barked out a surprised laugh.

"That would make me very uncomfortable," she said.

"Kerschel it is. Did you say there were eggs in the kitchen?" She nodded. "Great. Can you let Aiden know that the files are here and I'm making eggs?"

"Yes, great idea," she said and hurried out of the room.

"We don't have time for eggs," said Jackson.

"We do," said Evan. "Because I'm hungry, and I won't be able to concentrate on papers on an empty stomach. And you know Aiden won't do anything without food."

"Aiden's here too?"

"He was making calls and discovered that you have gym equipment."

Jackson let out a frustrated breath and ran his hand through his hair. "I appreciate the support, but we can handle it."

"Not really. Garcia and Pete went to chase down a lead on

Houge. Devonte's at the hospital with Caitlin and Dominique, and Kerschel's working on the links between Houge and Baranov. You need Aiden and me to go through those files."

"Pete found something on Houge?"

"Maybe. He said to call him when you came in."

Jackson thrust the manila envelope he was carrying at Evan, and turned away already dialing his phone. With a sigh, Evan set the papers down on the desk and went into the kitchen.

The kitchen was a disaster. It was clean, but Evan felt reasonably certain that every appliance was from 1984 or earlier. And why was everything goldenrod yellow? He took off his jacket and tucked his tie into his shirt.

Evan had located the pan and eggs by the time Jackson came to hover in the doorway.

"I have severe doubts about this stove."

"It's kind of temperamental," Jackson admitted.

Evan nodded and carried on with the cooking.

"Pete says there's no point in meeting him. It would take too long to catch up and there's nothing I can do. I can't—" Jackson cut off and Evan looked at him. Jackson looked miserable.

"You could be at the hospital with Caitlin."

Jackson reared back a step as if Evan had hit him. "I can't. Evan, I can't. She doesn't want me there and it's even worse than here. I feel helpless."

"Did she say she didn't want you there?"

"She would have to be conscious for that. But the last phone call was pretty specific and clear. How could I let this happen?"

"You met someone, and you didn't exchange entire life histories. Believe me, it happens. You said she was nice?"

"She *is* nice! She cares about everybody. She cares so fucking much and nobody cares for her and it is killing me."

Evan stopped cooking to hug his cousin. Jackson gave a growl of frustration and finally hugged him back. After a moment, Jackson stepped back and wiped his nose.

"Your eggs are going to burn."

"I believe the burner would have to heat for that," said Evan, returning to the stove. "OK, so Aiden and I are here. We will go through the files. We will find whatever it is that Granger thought he had—"

Jackson's phone rang and they both jumped at the sudden sound. Jackson answered it, with a frown.

"Hey Nowitsky," he said, sounding tired. Evan couldn't hear the other side of the conversation, but Jackson rolled his eyes. "That is not *my* dead body. OK, yes, I know Dominique hit someone again. Twice is not a habit."

"Hm," said Evan. "Aiden was right. How annoying."

He slid Jackson's eggs onto a plate and put them on the table, giving Jackson a little shove. As Evan predicted, Jackson couldn't focus on being stubborn at Evan and Nowitsky simultaneously and started eating. Evan started on the next round of eggs for Aiden.

"Well, if you talked to Dominique, I don't know why you're talking to me. I'm at the office. No, Nowitsky, I'm really at the office. I don't know why you're so suspicious."

"I do," said Aiden. "I heard there were eggs. Is that Nowitsky?"

"Yes," said Jackson grumpily, handing the phone over. "Here. You talk to him."

"Hello, detective," said Aiden cheerfully. "No, we're at the office. Well, now he's eating eggs. Well, I don't know. Probably because he's hungry, and Evan made him eggs. That's why I'm going to be eating eggs in a minute."

"More than a minute," muttered Evan.

"Yes, I believe we're aware that he's a loan shark with ties to the Russian mafia. I'm sure I couldn't speculate as to why he was attacking Caitlin Granger."

There was a long pause while Nowitsky said something loudly and angrily.

"Well, I'm not aware of what name is on the lease, but I assure you that *is* her name. As I said, I couldn't speculate…"

There was some more angry chatter on the other end.

"Yes, Dominique and Jackson said her injuries were very worrisome. I don't know who the other attacker was. I wasn't there. Would you like us to send our research on Baranov over to you? Perhaps that could tell you something. No? Are you sure? We're happy to. I'll just have Kerschel email you in a minute. Yes, I'm sure we'll be available for conversations whenever you like. Hm. OK. Well, whatever you think best. The Deveraux family always likes to cooperate with the NYPD."

Evan put the eggs on a plate as Aiden handed Jackson his phone back.

"He told me to go fuck myself and hung up on me. I think I'm offended. I wasn't lying. We do always *like* to cooperate."

"We just don't always do it," said Evan.

"Thanks for the food, Ev," said Aiden tucking in, and Jackson made an agreeing grunt with his mouth full.

Evan poured himself a cup of coffee and watched his relatives eat.

"Didn't you say you were hungry?" demanded Jackson as he scraped the last of the eggs off his plate.

"I lied," said Evan. "Unlike other people, I had a healthy breakfast."

"I had a healthy breakfast," said Aiden. "This is just usually when I get my protein shake. He's the one that didn't eat."

"I was too hung over." Jackson looked at them both. "I haven't looked at the papers yet. They might be complete shit."

"Doesn't matter if they are," said Aiden. "I mean, I hope they aren't. But at this point all we have to do is prove that Houge and Baranov attacked Caitlin and it's going to cast doubt on everyone he's ever talked to. And you have photos of him talking to half the ethics committee. He's going down one way or another. What we need is for Nowtisky to put the pieces together on his own. Which we will help do."

As Aiden shoveled eggs into his face and talked between bites, Evan watched the tension in Jackson's shoulders ease fraction by fraction.

"It takes too long," complained Jackson.

"But it *will* happen," said Aiden. "He overstepped when he went to her place. If he'd let Baranov handle it then he might have been able to pretend there wasn't a connection, but from what Kerschel says even that would have been a stretch. We will get him."

Jackson rolled his head around on his neck, popping a vertebrae with an audible clunk. Aiden grimaced at the noise.

"Do you need a chiropractor?"

"I need to find Houge," said Jackson.

"And a chiropractor," said Aiden with a nod and a shrug.

"How do you like the coffee?" asked Jackson, glancing up at Evan. Evan was encouraged by the twinkle of humor in his eyes.

"It's total shit," said Evan. "What is it? Folgers with an old gym sock for a filter?"

"Pete makes it. He says he uses real beans, but they could be pinto beans, for all we know. We don't understand how it turns out like that. The weird part is that we can't stop drinking it."

Evan took a sip. "It can't be any worse than the time we found out one of the traders on the Australian desk had been sprinkling coke in the collective coffee pot for about three months. Can we look at papers now?"

"Clear," said Aiden dropping his fork onto his empty plate. "Let's do this. And yes, I'm ignoring that comment about the coke."

"We switched to the coffee pods after that. I feel bad about killing the environment, but a lot less jittery."

"Still ignoring you," said Aiden, dropping his plate in the sink, before going back out to the main room.

"I don't think that is a good place for you to work," said Jackson.

"Topic for another day," said Evan. "Come on."

Aiden passed out stacks of papers from the manila envelope but was soon making grumpy noises. Granger's stacks of precious documents were not sorted by any discernable method. Although, every so often, they found random sheets scrawled in blocky handwriting directing Caitlin to do this or call someone.

"This is ghastly," said Aiden, lifting one of the notes. "He basically just shipped her a mess and a to-do list. There isn't even any note of goodbye or I love you or… just anything. It's all about him and what he wants her to do."

"That's probably why she shoved it in the ottoman," said Jackson. "She said that was where all the horrible things lived."

"This definitely qualifies," agreed Evan.

Jackson shook his head took a step back. "I don't even know what I'm looking at. I'm going to go talk to Kerschel."

"OK, but I'm pretty sure she's hiding from us in the gym slash storage room."

"I'm the boss. I get to bug whoever I want," he said with a shrug and walked off toward the back room.

"Good call on the food," said Aiden when they heard the door shut down the hall.

"Nothing ever gets better on an empty stomach."

"I think he perked up there for a bit, but this pile of bullshit is not helping. I think it just reminds him of how fucked up her life has been. Although I have to say, in looking at this shit-pile and the financial background that Kerschel has been putting together, it was not all our fault. Which I was worried about. It was like Granger went out of his way to screw her over too. Who does that to their kid? Even our asshole relatives didn't do that. You were properly in your dad's will. And I really do think Randall was planning on going to get Jackson."

"Dad loved me. He was an abusive trauma survivor with anger management issues and deep feelings of shame about his sexuality which made him a terrible parent and human being, but he still loved me."

"See? That's nice."

"No, it's not."

"I mean, it's nice that you know that about him. The rest of it isn't great, but Uncle Owen wasn't…" Aiden gestured at the pile of papers in front of him.

"That's true." Evan thought it was one of the first and only times that Aiden had admitted to anything positive about Owen. They lapsed into silence. Evan sorted through the papers, stopping each time his eye caught an interesting word. Granger's top secret file appeared to be a morass of transcribed phone calls, emails, and Absolex memos. It was probably all interesting if he'd been immersed in the Absolex case, but he didn't see a smoking gun.

The door to the back room crashed open and Jackson ran by. He didn't stop to speak to either of them. Evan felt his stomach drop as he recognized the expression on Jackson's face.

"Do we think it's a good thing that he just ran out of here?" asked Aiden.

Evan felt a familiar churning in his gut. "No."

"Like that was a very Uncle Randall look?" asked Aiden, giving voice to Evan's fears.

"Mm," said Evan.

"Do we think he's going to kill Houge?" asked Aiden bluntly.

Evan found himself tapping his teeth together, his jaw clenching and unclenching.

"I don't want to think that," he blurted out.

"Part of my job is to think about all the unthinkables," said Aiden. "And then I help all of you prepare and I make you laugh so you don't have to think about them anymore."

Evan felt his shoulders slump. "I know you do that. I appreciate it. You don't have to make us laugh. You aren't the family jester."

"I'm also just a very silly person," said Aiden. "It's not really a stretch."

"You're a brilliant and also very funny lawyer," said Evan. "It's a weird combination and it makes a lot of people confused and uncomfortable."

"So you *do* think I'm funny?"

"I think you're fucking hilarious," said Evan. "I also think we should go get Jackson."

Aiden looked down at the pile of papers in front of him and then slowly reached out a hand and extracted one. "I think *you* should go get Jackson," he said, holding up the paper. "I have to call the Justice department and be brilliant."

"What did you find?"

"What Houge is afraid we'll find. It's an email assuring the VA that Zanilex has been approved. It hadn't. It also assures them that they have the full support of Senator Harrison. It's signed by Dennis Houge. No wonder Granger thought he'd skate. He should have been able to whip this out, and Senator Harrison would start throwing up roadblocks to the hearings because he wouldn't want to be implicated."

"I remember that guy. He had a heart attack and retired…" Evan thought about it. "He retired and there went Houge and Granger's leverage."

"Exactly," said Aiden.

"Call Nowitsky first. We need a reason not to let Houge leave New York," said Evan.

"Shit," said Aiden and grabbed for his own. "What am I telling him? Not everything."

"Tell him Caitlin gave Jackson her father's papers. And we just started looking at them."

"Got it," said Aiden. "Go. I got this."

On the way out to the car, he dialed Pete and got him on the first ring.

"Jackson just left," said Evan as he headed for his car. "Where is he going?"

"Are you going to talk him down?" asked Pete.

"That is my general goal."

"Good because I think you'll get there faster than me. He's going to the Hilton by JFK."

"On my way," said Evan and hung up.

Evan realized multiple things all at once and felt the familiar panic churning in his gut. Aiden was better at fighting than he was, but they needed him here. Dominique was better at talking, but she was still at the hospital with Caitlin. Evan hoped he was enough because he was the only one left.

Jackson

The Hilton

Jackson was driving seventy-five on a side street before he realized that maybe he should have stopped to talk to Evan and Aiden. Having them show up had been a relief. They made everything seem manageable in a way that it hadn't only moments before, but one call from Pete and it was though everything was on fire all over again.

He tried to talk himself through the plan. Was there a plan?

Go. Get Houge. Put him in the ground.

Pete's tip had been accurate, but Houge was ahead of them. He'd driven out to Jersey for a shady veterinarian to get his arm splinted. Which left Pete and Garcia in Jersey and Houge within an easy cab ride to the airport.

Jackson knew that Houge could be on a plane already. But if Houge thought he would be able to leave this behind, he was delusional. And Jackson wanted to stop him now. He'd had enough. This had to be done.

The front desk staff took four hundred dollars to compromise their principles and tell him what room Houge was in. Fifth floor, room 513.

Jackson took the stairs and arrived on the landing just as Houge entered the hall, his arm in a sling under his suit jacket and wheeling his suitcase with the free hand. When he saw Jackson, he dropped the suitcase handle and drew his gun.

Jackson stared at him, waiting for fear to arrive in some form, but it didn't. Houge licked his lips and took a step toward the elevators, bumping the button with his elbow.

"Something I can help you with, Jackson?" asked Houge. He looked a little pale.

"You can turn yourself into the cops," suggested Jackson.

"Why would I do that?"

"I don't know. Maybe the assault on Caitlin Granger? Maybe the massive attempt at covering your tracks for supporting Absolex? I'm not sure what the penalty is for using the Senate Ethics Committee to cover up your crimes, but I'm pretty sure they will be pissed off."

"I don't know what you're talking about," said Houge. "I don't have anything to do with the Ethics Committee. I just offered to help your family."

"Yeah, I have that on tape. You do know that selling influence is also a crime, right?"

Houge licked his lips again, his eyes narrowing.

"Do you think you're getting out of this somehow?" asked Jackson taking a step closer.

Houge's hand shifted on the gun. It was a basic nine milimeter. Probably a Ruger, although Jackson couldn't tell from just looking down the barrel.

"I think I am leaving New York, and you can't stop me," Houge said evenly. "You're not the cops, and I'm not on the run. You lay a finger on me, and that's assault. You'll be the one that gets locked up. I don't know about anything that you're talking about. I didn't even know Granger had a daughter."

"Really? How'd you hurt your arm?" asked Jackson, jerking his head toward the sling.

"Golfing injury," snarled Houge.

"Yeah, I've met that golf pro. You're lucky. The last guy that went up against her still walks with a limp."

"Shut up," snapped Houge. "And get out of my way."

"I'm not going anywhere, and neither are you," said Jackson, edging another step closer. Houge growled in frustration.

"Why are you even upset? You hated Granger. What do you care what happens to his kid? She's a fucking waitress or some shit now. She's not even smart enough to do anything with her father's papers. She fundamentally doesn't matter. People like her aren't worth thinking about."

Jackson had been worried. He'd faced a couple of guns before, and he didn't like doing it. There was always a chance for things to go badly. But it was as if Houge's words solidified something inside him. His fingertips felt cold, but he could feel a trickle of sweat run down his spine. He wanted to crush Houge's skull.

There was a sharp ding, and the elevator opened. A bellhop with a luggage trolley trundled out into the hall, startling Houge, who swung the gun toward the young woman in the red Hilton vest.

"Holy shit!" yelped the bellhop and jumped back in the elevator but managed to shove the cart at Houge. Jackson crashed into Houge just as the gun went off. The sound was deafening in the enclosed space of the hallway. Houge staggered backward, managing to keep his feet under him. Jackson clamped his hand over the top of the gun and felt the slide rack back and pinch into his hand as Houge pulled the trigger for a second time. That would hurt later.

Jackson slammed Houge's hand against the trolley and wrenched the gun away. Houge yelled angrily and punched at him. Jackson shook off the punch, grabbed Houge by the throat, and headbutted him. Houge's nose fractured and began to gush blood. Jackson punched Houge with his free hand even though it still held the gun. That would just add extra weight to the hit.

Houge staggered and went down on one knee. Jackson hit him again, watching in satisfaction as the skin split at the eye bone.

He grabbed Houge by his artfully tousled hair and punched him. Houge's head rocked back. Jackson didn't think he was conscious, but there was something left, and he planned on taking everything.

"She matters more than you," hissed Jackson and raised his hand again.

"Jackson!" Evan's voice was crisp, loud, and carried the authoritative weight of someone who was used to being obeyed.

Jackson looked up in surprise. The bellhop was huddled in the elevator, frantically pushing buttons, but Evan had come up the stairs.

"That's enough," said Evan. That was it. No fancy speeches. Just *that's enough*.

Jackson looked back down at Houge and let go of his hair.

Houge collapsed onto the ground, and Jackson lashed out with a final kick to the man's ribs.

"Now it's enough," said Jackson.

"Holy shit," said the bellhop again, and then the elevator door finally closed.

Evan ran a hand through his hair and looked around.

"We've really got to get better at not scaring the shit out of hotel personnel."

"I think you meant to say *I* need to," said Jackson.

"I was trying not to. Nowitsky is on his way. Apparently, Houge's office called Baranov's phone when they couldn't get ahold of him. And then they confirmed that the two were together at the time of the assault, so…"

Jackson laughed and found his hand unconsciously echoing the gesture Evan had just made, his fingers ruffling through his hair, trying to push it back out of his eyes.

"I wasn't going to kill him."

"I didn't think you were," said Evan. Jackson thought that was probably a lie, but Jackson still appreciated it.

"I mean, I wanted to. A little bit. A lot."

Evan shrugged. "We just need to keep things tidy for Nowitsky. No sense in making a mess."

"No," said Jackson laughing and leaning into Evan for a hug. "No, Grandma hates messes."

"She already called," said Evan.

"I turned off my phone."

"That's why she called. I think she's having a panic attack. I told her to call Dominique."

Jackson sighed and straightened up. "I really did make a mess of this."

"Nah," said Evan grinning. "Not by Deveraux standards anyway. We'll come through OK. I promise."

Caitlin

St. Anne's Hospital

Caitlin opened her eyes and tried to focus. There was an annoying beeping somewhere. She finally focused on Jamal lying on a bed across the room and reading a *Sports Illustrated.* It looked like a hospital bed. That meant she was probably in a hospital? That was probably good. She felt like she should be. What had happened? She had been getting ready for work…

Caitlin felt her heart rate pick up as the memories came flooding back. She looked around the room again.

There was a big dreadlocked guy in a chair by the door who was looking at his phone. He looked like one of Vince's people, although she didn't recognize him. She looked back at Jamal—he was staring at the centerfold.

If Jamal wasn't worried, she could probably just go back to sleep. She looked back at the dreadlocked guy again. He had noticed that she was awake. He was wearing a shoulder holster and a gun. He smiled at her. She gave a weak smile and felt her heart rate dip down again. Sure. Giant dude with a gun in her room. What did it say about her life that this made her feel like everything was totally fine? She closed her eyes. She couldn't deal with that right now.

The next time she woke up, the dreadlock guy was talking to Vince, and Jamal was bouncing up and down like an excited puppy.

"Vince," she said, then said it again because no sound came out. "Vince."

"Hey Katie," he said, coming over and leaning down.

"Vince, there were some guys."

"Yeah, we know. Don't worry about it."

"I may have…"

"Stabbed one of them in the neck with an ice pick? Yeah, we noticed. The cops are going to come and talk to you about it." She gulped. "Don't sweat it, though. It'll be fine."

"They wanted something of my dad's."

"Yeah, that's fine. Don't sweat it."

"It's in the ottoman."

"What?"

"The ottoman lifts open and it's in there. I shoved all of his paperwork in there under a blanket so I wouldn't have to look at it."

"Don't' worry about it. I think the cops have it now."

"There were two guys," she said. She kind of thought that the guy she'd stabbed with the ice pick might be dead. There had been a lot of blood. But there had been another one. The one calling the shots.

"Katie, stop worrying. Jackson took care of it. Everything is fine."

She blinked up at him in confusion.

"You get some sleep," he said, tucking in her blanket. "We're going to go now. I'm going to take Jamal home and Angela will be by in the morning with some real food. Don't worry about anything. Everything's fine."

"OK," she said feeling slow and stupid and tired. He couldn't have said that Jackson took care of it. Why would Jackson take care of it?

The next time she woke up, dawn light was creeping in around the curtains and Jackson was in the second bed that had been previously occupied by Jamal. He was asleep, but she could see a bandage wrapped around one hand.

She scratched at her hand with the IV in it. She felt better, but still foggy.

Jackson moved and she turned to him. He rolled to face her more directly.

"Hi," he said. He looked tired.

"Hi," she said.

"I didn't want you to be alone in the hospital. But I can leave if you want."

She thought about that. She didn't want to be alone at the hospital either. "No."

He nodded. After a moment, he rolled back onto his back and stared at the ceiling. Caitlin stared at his profile in the twilight of the room. She had thought she'd never look at it again. Did her father's obsession count for anything? Did it matter? What if he was right? Did any of it matter compared to late-night whispered conversations with Jackson's arms wrapped around her and his laugh and the way he closed his eyes when he really liked one of her drinks or the way he touched her or the way he made her feel?

"Jackson?" Her voice was barely above a whisper.

"Yes?"

"Did you really like me at all?"

"No *sérdeńko,*" he said. "I love you."

A tear leaked out of her eye without asking permission. "Jackson?"

"Yes?"

"Can you come over to this bed?"

"I don't think the nurses will approve in cohabitation," said Jackson getting up.

"I don't care about nurses," said Caitlin.

He settled gingerly against her, and she attempted to scoot over enough to give him room, but her muscles weren't cooperating, so they ended up wedged together in a lump. She didn't mind. Caitlin turned her face into his shoulder and inhaled, breathing in the reassuring scent of him. Then she fell asleep again.

Jackson

Deveraux House

Jackson peered into the library. He had arrived at Deveraux House with Caitlin in the afternoon, but it had taken longer to get everything sorted out than he had thought, and he kept having to run off and talk to someone. Not that Caitlin had noticed. She kept falling asleep. Eleanor had been home and seemed to have taken charge of keeping an eye on her, which surprised him, but he was grateful for it. Eleanor was at a desk signing thank you cards while Caitlin was asleep on the couch. Eleanor beckoned to him. He came in, and she handed him her teacup. He held the tea cup while she picked up her pile of thank you notes. Then she led the way through the house to her office.

"This is my fault," she said, thumping the cards down on her desk. Jackson raised an eyebrow but didn't speak.

"It never even occurred to me that Granger would be able to do something like this. Where the hell are her relatives? Why aren't they taking care of Caitlin?"

"I believe that when she asked Granger's sister for help, she said she did not wish to be involved," said Jackson. "Her mother's family is apparently, not around. I don't know."

Eleanor threw her pen down violently on the desk.

"I cannot believe…" She took a deep breath. "She is a child and they just abandoned her. You don't do that."

"No, *you* don't do that. Apparently, other people have no problems doing that."

"I told her I would have our attorneys review the frozen assets. It was all I could get her to agree to."

"That's better than I did," said Jackson. "She doesn't like charity."

"It's not charity when we're the ones that did it to her!"

"Yes, but I couldn't exactly state that without implicating Evan or the rest of us in a massive insider trading conspiracy. Also, I didn't want to tell her that her dad used her college fund to hire mercenaries to go after Evan."

Eleanor grimaced. "I went ahead and told her that."

"How did she take it?"

"She was upset. Understandably. It was how I got her to agree to the lawyers. It made her feel like she should make it up to me and that was what I wanted in exchange."

"That makes no sense."

"She has a concussion. It doesn't have to make sense. It just has to feel right." Eleanor dropped into her desk chair. "What are you going to do?"

"I already paid off the remaining medical bills from her mother. Evan and Aiden are looking into the other items."

"Even though she didn't agree?"

"By the time I tell her, I'm hoping it will be conveniently resolved and she can be mad all she likes."

"She might break up with you," said Eleanor.

"We're not exactly on the firmest of footing right now," said Jackson. "She may break up with me anyway. At least this way I know she'll be OK."

Eleanor nodded. "We should have taken Dominique's suggestion and just had Granger whacked."

Jackson laughed. "Well, maybe next time. What's it like on the Senate side of things?"

Eleanor let out a wicked chuckle. "Oh, the sun is shining and we are making hay. The Absolex Hearing transcripts are being released early next week. The Ethics Committee has abruptly declared their investigation into me closed." Eleanor looked guilty and leaned in as if telling a secret. "I told Aiden to go ahead file his complaint anyway. Those subpoenas were really unacceptable and he seemed to be excited about it." Jackson grinned. "Senator Griffeth, having successfully managed to embarrass herself and her party, is having to step down from the Ethics Committee and Ralph Taggert will be taking that position. Something that I shall probably regret, but it looks good since Dominique told everyone how much we hate him."

"We do hate him," said Jackson.

"Yes, but now he owes us," said Eleanor, with the cheerful smile of a mob boss. "Anyway, they are even planning on revisiting the Homeland Security decision to pull those mercenaries as witnesses against Granger. If they can prove Houge tampered with that case as well… He's already going to prison, but that would be Federal time. In short, matters in the Senate are going well, and if we can make sure that poor Caitlin is taken care of, then we will have successfully and finally put an end to this matter."

"I'm doing my best," said Jackson.

"Jackson," said Eleanor, "do you think I don't know that? Your bad days are better than most people's good days. You will succeed. And if she still rejects you then it will because she is a fool not because of anything you did. You are a good boy," she said firmly. "And I'm always so happy that Pete found you in that horrible prison. And I know the others are too. I'm sorry we didn't find you earlier."

"Grandma," Jackson stuttered, blushing.

"What? It's true. Now why don't you go get a soda from Theo and let me get on with my paperwork?"

"Yes, Grandma," said Jackson, shaking his head. He was going to have to tell Evan about this one, but later after he'd taken care of Caitlin.

Back in the library, Caitlin was still sleeping. She looked pale and still dirty from the assault. He thought the hospital had swabbed down her injuries but that she hadn't ever gotten a proper bath.

"Caitlin," he shook her shoulder gently, and her eyes opened, and she smiled at him. "Do you want to go upstairs and go to bed in an actual bed?"

"I want to go home," she said.

"No, sorry. The police still have it taped off. You can't go back yet." Or ever, if he had anything to say about it.

She sighed and rubbed her head. "I'm not really tired."

"You just keep dropping off to sleep because you're so full of energy?"

"I think my schedule is all screwed up. My body is confused because I haven't been to work."

He smiled. "Dinner will be in a little bit. Why don't you come upstairs and take a shower and wash the hospital off. We'll get you settled and then you can come down and show us how awake you are."

She sat up, took a deep breath, and looked around the room. She had severe bedhead, but she looked more awake than the rest of the day. "That sounds good," she said. "A shower would be nice."

She seemed to take in the Christmas decorations for the first time. "It's Christmas, isn't it? I've ruined your Christmas."

"No, it's fine," said Jackson. "We'll have a do-over day like last year when my cousin… was… gone." Jackson tried to abort that sentence but only managed a half correction.

"You mean when my father tried to have him killed in Tokyo?"

"Um… Well, yeah, OK. Yes."

Caitlin's eyes filled up with tears.

"No, *sérdeńko*, don't do that! Ev's fine. We're all fine."

"I don't understand why he hated you," she said with a sniff.

"And I don't understand why he didn't love you better," he replied. "I don't understand how he could do half the things he did."

"He was the most selfish person I ever met," she said, wiping her cheek with the back of her hand. "He smiled so much when he was giving things, but he was always taking at the same time. I saw it when I was a kid. Mom had to make me do my weekends with him, and I was so relieved when she met… I don't remember his name. Whoever, and we moved to Colorado. I liked it there. But mostly, I liked not having to see my dad."

"I'm sorry," said Jackson, and she shook her head. "Come on," he said, lifting her to her feet. "Let's get you cleaned up."

He led her upstairs and into his suite. He wasn't sure that was the right decision, but it felt weird for her to have her own room. He figured he could sleep on the couch if she didn't like it.

"It's like you have your own apartment inside a house," she said, looking around.

"Yeah, pretty much," he agreed.

"Weird."

"Yeah," he agreed. "Bathroom's through here."

She went into his room and sat down on his bed. "It doesn't seem like you." She looked around again. "Some of it does, I guess. This comforter does not."

"Yeah, I keep thinking I want one of those down comforters like you have, but I'm not actually sure how to get one. Do I buy it? Is that allowed? I don't know."

"You tell Theo, and he arranges it."

"Is that how it's done?"

"Yes, he's in charge of the household. It'll come out of the household budget."

"Oh. Cool. Thanks."

"Jackson, is my apartment really taped off?"

"Yeah," he said apologetically, "and even if it wasn't, the door is still broken and only fixed with a piece of plywood. It wouldn't be safe to stay there."

"Oh." She looked around again, then down at her hands, and grimaced. "I do need a shower. I'm icky."

"Honestly, I wasn't sure about living here when I first moved in, but this bathroom is what sold me," he said. "Come on, I'll show you the shower."

"Oh my God," she said when she saw his walk-in multi-shower head personal spa.

"You can even have steam and make it a sauna. And it never runs out of hot water, which I know because I've stayed in for, like, an hour before."

She laughed, which was the first time she had since the hospital. "I may try that out myself."

"Feel free," he said, pulling a pile of fluffy towels out of the cupboard and hanging two on the towel warmer.

A few minutes after the water had started, he heard her call his name.

"Yeah?" he asked, poking his head around the edge of the shower.

"Um, can you tell me if I'm bleeding or just rinsing out? It seems like a lot of… red coming out of my hair."

She turned her back to him, and he gently parted her hair. "I think you're OK," he said, squinting. "You know what? Hold on."

He went back, stripped off his clothes, and then came into

the shower with her. He moved her under the overhead light and inspected the back of her head again.

"I think you're OK," he repeated, kissing the back of her neck. Then he put his arms around her waist, and she rested her arms on his, leaning back against him and breathing out.

"I feel like I should be worried about something," she said.

"No," he said, "there's nothing to worry about."

"There's always something," she said tiredly. "It's just that usually, I can only focus on the pot that's boiling over right this second. If I'm not worried about something, then I must be forgetting something."

"Nothing is boiling," he said. "Everything is currently at a controlled simmer."

She laughed and turned around in his arms, tucking her face into his neck.

"This is nice," she murmured.

"Mm-hm," he agreed, closing his eyes and enjoying the warmth of the water, the smoothness of her skin, and the feeling of her body pressed against his. After a few minutes, she leaned back and looked at him with a worried expression.

"Once I get out of the shower, do I have any clothes?"

He grinned. "Yes, I had Claude send some over. He's the family's personal shopper. He was ecstatic."

"You have a personal shopper?"

"He dresses the entire family," said Jackson with a shrug. "I thought it was weird when I first came here, but I have to say, we use his services all the flipping time. Money well spent."

"Why was he happy to find me clothes?"

"Well, I sent him your modeling sheet, which meant that he had actual measurements to work with and photos for color choices. And then I told him you were working with Roggario, which apparently means he knows what will look good on you? I don't know. I wasn't following, really."

"Jackson, did you just buy me a lot of clothes?"

"Not a lot. Just some. Because as much as I like you naked, I thought others would disapprove, and I only grabbed you like three T-shirts out of your apartment before the police came."

"But—"

He kissed her.

"You can't kiss me every time you buy me something and expect to get away with it," she said sternly.

He kissed her again. This time, she gave in, kissing him back, her arms pulling him tighter to her. He slid a hand down her back, cupping her ass. Her body softened, even as his became harder.

"We should… Bedroom," she said, pulling back. "Softer surfaces."

Jackson nodded but pulled him back to her. Finally, he reached out a fumbling hand and flipped off the water. They stumbled into the bedroom and onto the bed. His hands explored her body, trying to find every curve that he had been missing. Her fingers were buried in his hair, and she found a way to recapture his mouth with hers every time he pulled away. He gave up and kissed her while he reached one hand between her thighs, running one gentle finger across her sex, then up and down, stroking and teasing. She moaned, breaking away from his kiss and arching underneath him. Her eyes closed as she submitted to his touch, opening herself to him.

"Do you want me?" he asked, whispering as he nibbled her earlobe.

"Yes," she moaned. "God, yes. I missed you so much."

He moved on top of her, pressing his cock against the entrance. She opened her eyes and smiled at him, then her legs wrapped around him and pulled him into her. They both groaned at the sensation of him inside her. He moved gently. He didn't know how battered she was, but it became clear that gentle was not what she wanted.

He pushed harder, and she moaned his name at each thrust, arching back with her eyes closed. "Yes, Jackson, yes, Jackson, yes. Fuck me more. Oh God, more."

He thrust harder still, and her hand smacked down onto his ass like it always did when he was getting it just right.

"Of fuck, Jackson," she gasped, opening her eyes. "Don't ever stop. Just fuck me forever. Please baby, please. Forever."

It was the first time she'd ever used a pet name.

"Nazuvzhdy," he promised.

She came, gasping his name and clinging to him, and he finished moments later. She wrapped her arms and legs around him like she had the night she'd woken up crying as if she was never planning on letting go.

"Sérdeńko," he groaned and scooped an arm under her so he could shift them to one side.

"Sérdeńko," she repeated, mashing the pronunciation.

He repeated it for her, and she repeated it back, almost making it sound right.

"What does it mean?" she asked.

"Mmm… heart? But cute. Like a diminutive of *sérce moje.* Which means *my heart.*"

She smiled, looking pleased. "But I can't think of anything to call you that's romantic like that."

"Well, I expect you to work hard at it," he said, giving her tiny kisses between each word. "Bae, boo, baby. We'll have to invest in a thesaurus."

She giggled, turning her head away, and wriggling in his arms as he left kisses all over her face. This was better. This felt like them. He stopped kissing, and she immediately snuggled against him.

"The unfortunate part about this," she said from her place on his chest, "is that I'm going to have to get up at some point and finish my shower."

He laughed but tightened his hug. "But that's whole minutes away. Possibly hours."

She laughed but then became quiet, and he reveled in the feeling of her heart beating against his chest.

"Jackson," she said, "I really do wish I had some romantic way of saying it."

"What's wrong with Jackson?" he asked.

"No," she said, looking up at him. "A romantic way of saying *I love you.*"

"What's wrong with *I love you?*"

"It doesn't really cover it."

"Mm," he said, "I see. Well, say it Ukrainian. Maybe it will sound bigger."

"How do I say that?"

"*Ya tebe lyublyu,*" he said.

She stared at him. "OK," she said slowly, a smile curving up the edges of her mouth. "I'll say it *again. Ya tebe lyublyu.*"

"It does sound better when you know what you're saying," he said with a grin.

"Shut up and kiss me," she said, and he complied.

Caitlin
Deveraux House

Caitlin waited nervously on the couch in the library. "I feel like I should be doing that," she said, looking at Jackson pouring the drinks at the bar.

"No, I like doing it," said Jackson with a smile.

She smoothed her dress and tried to take deep breaths. "So," she said, standing up, feeling like movement might help. "All your family is coming?"

"You'll like them, I swear," he said.

"OK," said Caitlin. She tried to decide if feeling like she wanted to puke was nerves or the concussion. She was halfway across the room when the door opened, and Olivia came in.

"Well, how would I know, sugar?" she said over her shoulder and then turned to see Caitlin. "Oh! It's Katie! Evan, it's Katie that we like! Did we know you were going to be here? Oh, wait, we did, if you're Caitlin Granger. You're Caitlin, aren't you?"

"Yes," said Caitlin, and then found herself being hugged as Evan came in the door behind Olivia carrying a load of Christmas presents.

"Oh, goddamn it, Jackson, no! That's our Katie. You can't have her."

"I beg your pardon?"

Caitlin heard an unexpectedly frosty note in Jackson's voice.

"She's the only thing that makes those events bearable!"

"I'm going back to work next week," Caitlin said. "I'll still pour you drinks."

"You say that," Evan said, transferring his boxes to one arm, so he could give her a half-hug, "but then he'll decide it's not safe or something. Like he keeps telling me about the subway."

"Her work is the only place I think she is safe," complained Jackson.

And Olivia beamed at her. "I'm so glad you're you!"

"It is a relief," said Evan. "I was trying to work up the enthusiasm for a new person, and now I don't have to!"

Caitlin looked at Jackson, trying to determine if Olivia and Evan were being serious.

"Well, it would get weird if she wasn't her," agreed Jackson.

"I think he just means we're glad you're not dating someone objectionable," said Olivia.

"What do I have to do to be objectionable?" asked Caitlin, now fascinated. She couldn't imagine what could be in her favor other than Evan and Olivia liking her cocktails.

"Sasha Beckstale," muttered Evan going behind the bar.

"I never dated her," laughed Jackson.

"Much to her chagrin," said Evan. "I'm just saying she would be extremely objectionable."

"I don't know what a Sasha Beckstale is," said Olivia. "But it sounds horrible."

"She really is," agreed Jackson.

"Yes, but…" said Caitlin, now feeling entirely uncertain, "Really? You don't mind about my father?"

Evan blinked at her as if trying to wrap his head around the concept.

"Well, I'm the granddaughter of Eleanor's main political enemy," said Olivia.

"And Aiden's dating a girl who tried to run a hostile take-over on a business or grandfather founded," said Evan. "So, you know…"

"Oh," said Caitlin. "I'm not even cracking the top ten of objectionable, am I?"

Evan laughed. "Not even top twenty."

"Hey, guys!" chirped Dominique coming in, followed by a handsome guy who was tall even by Deveraux standards.

"Hey Nika, Max," said Evan. "Drink?"

"Yes, please," said Max, but Dominique headed straight for Caitlin.

"Oh my God, Katie, are you OK? Should you be standing up? I saw that MRI. I think you should sit down."

Katie found herself being hugged by the blonde. "I was sitting down," she said around the hug.

Dominique pulled back and stared at her with big eyes. "And oh, my God, your apartment. The pictures made it look like World War III."

"I wouldn't know. Jackson won't let me go home."

"That sounds like him," said Dominique shaking her head.

"It's taped off by the police!" objected Jackson.

"But you're doing all right?" Dominque was still staring at her as if looking for signs of distress.

"Bump on the head," said Caitlin.

"Massive concussion," said Jackson.

"I'm fine."

"She's pretty beat up. Don't hug her too hard," corrected Jackson.

Dominique laughed. "I'm glad you're OK. This is Max," she said, gesturing to her partner, and then her chin came up a little. "My fiancé."

Olivia made a little shriek of delight, and Caitlin saw Evan and Jackson's faces light up.

"Hi, I'm Max," said the man, stepping forward to shake her hand.

"Caitlin," said Caitlin. "Or Katie. Whichever. Um… Congratulations."

"Thanks," said Max, with a smile that revealed how happy he was.

"And look at this ring!" Dominique exclaimed as if she couldn't hold it in any longer and held out her hand to Olivia.

"Yay!" said Olivia and grabbed Dominique's hand to look at the ring.

"Oh, wow!" said Caitlin without forcing the sentiment. The ring was platinum, and the center diamond was at least three karats, but the setting itself was gorgeous, even without the sparkle of additional diamonds and aquamarines. "It's beautiful. Is it vintage? It looks deco. That is so unusual. Where did you find it?"

"Kansas," said Max. "At an Antique Auction that was held at a Grange and Feed Lot."

"They usually have good stuff at the ones where I'm from," said Olivia. "My dad got an apple press last year. But how did she not get suspicious when you said you were going to Kansas?"

"I had to tell her I was going to California to visit my mom," said Max, glancing at Dominique sheepishly.

"And I totally fell for it," said Dominique. "Of course, it helped that his mom was totally in on it and posted pics on social media." She let out a disgusted breath.

"I went the next day," he said, laughing. "Most of those were real!"

Dominique laughed but turned as they heard the sound of the door in the hall.

"Ella," called someone from the hall, "I don't think…" The door opened, and a petite Asian woman came in carrying a massive stack of presents. Aiden came through directly behind her, carrying one box. "Can you wait? I want to put them under the tree."

"The tree? I want to show them off, so people spend all of dinner wondering what's in them."

Ella dropped the boxes on the sofa and turned to the room.

"Katie!" she and Aiden exclaimed at the same time.

"Oh, thank goodness," said Ella, coming forward to hug her. "We've been worrying about you."

"I was going to have Jackson…" Aiden looked around the room and nodded as if his sentence had been either finished or responded to. "Ah. You're Caitlin. Well, damn. You are having a rough month. I'm sorry. Are you doing OK? Is Jackson taking care of you?"

"Does everyone here already know my girlfriend?" asked Jackson, sounding annoyed. "And what were you going to have me do?"

"There was a guy at Katie's work," said Ella. "He attacked her. I know you didn't want to press charges, Katie, but I also thought that maybe Jackson could look into it. It was *not* OK."

"Um. Jackson took care of it," said Katie.

"I did?"

"Yup," said Katie, giving him the eye.

"Oh. That guy. Well, I mean, technically you…" Caitlin glared at him. She did not want to talk about ice picks or dead bodies in front of the entire Deveraux family. "OK, well, let's just say it's taken care of and we will leave it at that."

Caitlin looked around the room. "You're all Deverauxes?" she asked realizing how often she'd met them previously.

"Well, just us," said Dominique. "And technically, just those two," she said, pointing at Evan and Jackson.

"Yes, but…" Caitlin wasn't sure what to think. "You're all…" Then she laughed and looked at Jackson. She was at a loss to explain how much she owed his family.

"We're all what?" asked Jackson.

"Annoying?" suggested Aiden.

"Charming and wonderful?" suggested Dominique.

"Strange and in desperate need of help?" offered Evan.

"Thoughtful and kind," said Caitlin.

"Mmm, no," said Aiden. "That doesn't sound like us at all."

"I told you she needs to sit down," said Dominique. "Head injury."

Caitlin looked in frustration at Jackson. "But they are."

"Yes," he agreed, smiling at her, and it was the softest smile.

"But don't tell them that," said Max. "They get confused."

"That's true," agreed Olivia. "I've tried, but they just wander off."

"That's when I hug them," said Ella. "It completely short-circuits their brains."

"Ha!" exclaimed Max.

"Are they allowed to gang up on us like that?" asked Aiden.

"Yes," said Jackson. "They are."

The door opened, and Theo looked in. Caitlin liked Theo. He seemed so incredibly reassuring and stable.

"Dinner is served," said Theo.

"Thank you, Theo," said Jackson, holding out his arm to her as if they were in a period drama. Caitlin took his arm and they paraded across the hall to the dining room. She couldn't believe the acres of food on the table. There was a genuine Christmas goose and she felt like she'd wandered into some sort of fairy tale as the table seemed to spring to life with food and laughter. She wondered when she'd wake up.

But by the end of the meal she hadn't woken up and everything had taken on a warm glow, tinted rosy by a glass of wine. Caitlin looked around the table. The couples had all started out sitting together, but then the coffee cups had come out and as if that was the signal everyone had rearranged to make conversations easier. Eleanor and Caitlin were the only ones who hadn't relocated. Eleanor was at the head of the table, sipping tea, and picking at a serving of the blueberry tart. Jackson was arguing with Evan about something, both of them falling in and out of Ukrainian. He was also trying to steal the last of the mashed potatoes from Aiden. Max and Aiden were talking law and also negotiating the mashed potato issue. Dominique was on the other side of Caitlin with her elbows on the table to discuss the potential impact of a new law on the tech industry with Ella across the table. Caitlin looked at Olivia who was on her left and looked up from her phone with a smile. She and Olivia had been talking earlier, but there had been some sort of work email that had required a response. Caitlin hadn't minded. She was happy for the break. Olivia hit send and leaned over to speak to Caitlin without being overheard by the rest of the table.

"Feeling overwhelmed?"

"A little bit," said Caitlin. "This is a lot of people for me. I usually just eat by myself in front of the TV."

Olivia smiled. "I like being here, but Evan and I usually go home and collapse on the couch."

"Oh, good. It's not just me."

"If you wait long enough, they'll all go find couches to nap on and then it gets quieter. I mean, not quite all the way quiet because I don't think Aiden can do that, but quieter." Caitlin laughed. "What I like, though, is Eleanor."

Caitlin glanced at the head of the table where Eleanor sat with a smile on her face. She thought Eleanor looked incredibly pleased.

"She looks happy?"

"Every Sunday dinner. I think this is her happy place."

"Sunday dinner?"

"We usually eat dinners here on Sundays," said Olivia. "And I think we're her happily ever after."

"It must feel weird that I'm here then."

"No, you're included," said Olivia. "Jackson has to be happy too."

"I'm not sure I believe in happily ever afters," said Caitlin.

"Neither does she. That's why I like seeing her have one," said Olivia.

"Olivia…" Caitlin trailed off, not sure of what to say. Olivia smiled at her inquiringly. "Happily ever after scares me," Caitlin blurted out.

Olivia reached out and grabbed her hand. "I know what you mean, but I just hang on to mine real tight and ignore him when he says he wants to breathe." Caitlin giggled, but suddenly found Dominique grabbing her other hand.

"You never know when people will disappear from your life," Dominique said, leaning close. "You have to love them all you can when you have them. Don't let anyone or anything scare you away because you'll regret it later."

Caitlin took a deep breath and found the butterflies in her stomach settling. "Thanks," she said. She looked over at Jackson and he gave her a wave with his fork that lost him the mashed potatoes to Max. Caitlin smiled. They were such a strange family, but she couldn't imagine finding a better one.

Eleanor
The Deveraux Legacy

Eleanor Deveraux looked around the ballroom and took a deep breath. The wedding had gone off without a single hitch. The children were having a lovely time. Evan and Olivia looked radiant. Ralph looked surly, but everyone was ignoring him. Which was probably why he was disgruntled. Caitlin was checking in with the catering staff for the hundredth time. She was a very dear girl. Eleanor found that she was quite pleased with Jackson's choice in partner. Caitlin had an endearing sweetness; of course, the way she so obviously loved Jackson was enough to make her welcome. But having spent several months with her, Eleanor found that Caitlin was also quite intelligent and much more interested in making changes in the world than any of the other children. Eleanor thought it might be wise to shift some of Dominique's charity work to Caitlin. Perhaps Caitlin could rebuild the Junior League into something useful. That might be a bit much to ask—Dominique had rather sewn the earth with salt there—but it was a thought.

"Well, Mrs. Deveraux," said Hannah Nowitsky handing her a small plate with a piece of cake on it. "Is this what's called a social triumph? Because I have to say, it kind of feels…"

"We had press, presidents, movie stars, and a national poet," said Eleanor, allowing herself a bite of cake. "It's a *colossal* social triumph."

"Zoe says it got a mention on the national news and Entertainment Tonight."

"I'm sure she's elated about that," said Eleanor, taking a deep breath to quell the flutter of nerves in her stomach. She didn't like having the children in the spotlight so much, particularly Evan, but it was unavoidable for this event.

"She was," agreed Hannah.

"Young lady," said Eleanor, scrutinizing her young intern. "Has Jackson spoken to you about more permanent employment once you graduate?"

Hannah froze, a bite of cake halfway to her mouth.

"I don't wish to discuss it again, but it would be nice if you agreed to it. It will make things easier for him."

"Yes, ma'am," said Hannah.

"Good," said Eleanor feeling relieved. When Jackson was content, he didn't pry into things. It had been a near thing the previous year when Evan had started poking into the plane crash documents. She didn't need Jackson, who was more level-headed than Evan, prying into why she had real estate investments in Florida. Eleanor looked around again. "They all look so very happy."

"I think they *are* happy," said Hannah, following her gaze around the room.

"Yes," said Eleanor, taking another bite of cake, enjoying the warm fizz of the orange-flavored sugar on her tongue. "That's the real triumph, of course. Everyone else can go jump in a lake."

Hannah laughed. "My father says that you know if you're a success as a parent if you turn out a fully functional human being."

"Your father is a smart man and a good parent," said Eleanor.

"I think Senator Yamira is about to come over and pretend not to suck up to you," said Hannah.

"You are quite correct," said Eleanor. "That is exactly what is about to happen. Give him two minutes and then come over and say I have to attend to something."

"No problem," said Hannah, moving away.

Jackson's talent for picking out quality human beings was unmatched. Hannah was a bright girl who would go very far. Eleanor smiled and talked and talked and smiled. It was the same merry-go-round of chatter that kept the world spinning. None of it meant very much. Or it meant everything, depending on one's point of view. She stepped into the hall and found that there wasn't anyone around for once.

"Glass of wine?" asked Theo, and Eleanor breathed a sigh of relief.

"Yes, please," she said, taking the offered glass. "But pour one for yourself. We need to celebrate."

Theo did as instructed and held up his glass. Eleanor clinked it and felt a smile settle onto her face.

"Do you know," said Eleanor looking up at the family portrait over the fireplace. She was holding Genevieve on her lap, with Owen and Randall on either side of her. Henry loomed over all of them. It was the only remaining photo of her husband still hanging on the walls. Eleanor tried to remember what it felt like to be that young and couldn't. "The first day I came here, I said it would be a beautiful place for a wedding, but I think this is the first one that has ever been held here."

"You made it happen," said Theo.

"No, Jackson made it happen. I just got out of the way." She looked around again. "Henry hit me for the first time right over there at the foot of the stairs. I was so surprised."

"An unfortunate memory," said Theo.

"They layer, you know. Like leaves. The good ones over the bad ones. But sometimes the bad ones just make their way to the top of the pile."

"Yes," said Theo. "I know what you mean. It's one of the

reasons I don't like going home. Nothing but piles of bad memories there."

"It's one of the reasons I stayed here," said Eleanor. "Henry was so insistent on doing things the Deveraux way. He was so high and mighty, and he used to spit on how poor I was. He said I would never really belong here. But," Eleanor looked around the hall, "now this is *my* place, and those are *my* children. I took *everything* from him."

"You *are* Mrs. Deveraux," said Theo, a smile crossing his face. She knew he understood.

"And he doesn't own one damn part of us anymore," she said, holding out her glass, and he tapped his against it once more.

"No, he does not."

"I may not have gotten everything right," said Eleanor. "But the Deveraux legacy is mine now."

"No," said Theo, shaking his head, "it's theirs."

Eleanor laughed. "Yes. As usual, you're correct. And that is far better than I could have hoped for."

Find out more at:

www.BethanyMaines.com

ABOUT THE AUTHOR

Bethany Maines is the award-winning author of action adventure and fantasy tales that focus on women who know when to apply lipstick and when to apply a foot to someone's hind end. When she's not traveling to exotic lands, or kicking some serious butt with her black belt in karate, she can be found chasing after her daughter, or glued to the computer working on her next novel.

OTHER WORKS BY BETHANY MAINES

CARRIE MAE MYSTERIES

Bulletproof Mascara (#1)
Compact With The Devil (#2)
High-Caliber Concealer (#3)
Glossed Cause (#4)

THE DEVERAUX LEGACY

The Lost Heir (#0)
The Second Shot (#1)
The Cinderella Secret (#2)
The Hardest Hit (#3)
The Fallen Man (#4)

Galactic Dreams

When Stars Take Flight (Vol.1)
The Seventh Swan (Vol. 2)
The Beast of Arsu (Vol. 3)

Tales from the City of Destiny
Short Story Collection

San Juan Islands Murder Mysteries

An Unseen Current (#1)
Against the Undertow (#2)
An Unfamiliar Sea (#3)

Shark Santoyo Crime Series

Shark's Instinct (#1)
Shark's Bite (#2)
Shark's Hunt (#3)
Shark's Fin (#4)
Peregrine's Flight (#5)
Shark's Blood (#6)

The Supernaturals

A Little Red (#1)
A Deeper Blue (#2)
A Brighter Yellow (#3)
Maverick
Wild Waters

BLUE ZEPHYR PRESS

Enjoy other books from Blue Zephyr Press!

THE FAARIAN CHRONICLES: EXILE
by Karen Harris Tully

Fifteen-year-old Sunny Price dreams of being an Olympic gymnast, but thanks to the worst custody agreement in the universe, she finds out she's half-alien and is exiled to her absentee-mother's home planet. She has to give up her friends and elite gymnastics career to live with a mother who only wants to give orders? This. Sucks.

THE CHRISTMAS SPIRIT
by J.M. Phillippe

In this award-winning dark comedy inspired by Charles Dickens A Christmas Carol, Charlene Dickenson's untimely death in a Christmas-related accident means she must do whatever it takes to become a Ghost of Christmas Past, Present, or Future or spend her after-life in chains. Can she learn to embrace the Christmas Spirit?